And Eternity

Books by Piers Anthony

INCARNATIONS OF IMMORTALITY

And
Eternity

PIERS ANTHONY

WILLIAM MORROW AND COMPANY, INC.

NEW YORK

Library of Congress Cataloging-in-Publication Data

Anthony, Piers.
   And eternity / Piers Anthony.
     p. cm.—(Incarnations of immortality : bk. 7)
   ISBN 0-688-08688-8
   I. Title. II. Series: Anthony, Piers. Incarnations of
immortality : bk. 7.
PS3551.N73A8   1990
813'.54—dc20   89-3418
                                              CIP

Printed in the United States of America

First Edition

1 2 3 4 5 6 7 8 9 10

BOOK DESIGN BY PATRICE FODERO

Contents

And
Eternity

CHAPTER ONE

Orlene

JOLIE WAS IN FRANCE WHEN SHE FELT THE PAIN. Someone close to her was dying!

She was conducting a routine observation, animating a servant girl in the house of the man she was studying. She had to extricate herself in a hurry—but not in such a way as to alienate her host.

Please, Marie—something pressing has come up. May I leave you for a time?

The girl was startled. "You will return?" she asked in French. She enjoyed their association, because she was dull and Jolie was bright. When Jolie animated her, she carried herself with greater flair and was more alert, and her employer liked that. There was nothing untoward in this, and the employer had no designs on Marie; he merely liked to think that his relatively egalitarian household was good for her.

When I can, Jolie reassured her, communicating mind to mind because she did not want the girl to seem to be muttering. *I fear a friend is in trouble.*

9

"Of course you must go to her!" Marie agreed.

She had spoken too loudly, and the employer looked up from his book. "What was that?" he inquired, also in French.

Jolie took over. "I beg your pardon, sir. My mind garbled, and I misspoke myself."

He smiled indulgently. "It happens to the best of us, and to me also. But if someone needs you, you may have time off, of course."

He was a good and generous man—which was why Jolie was observing him. "Thank you, sir. But the need is not pressing. I will finish here."

He nodded, and returned to his book. He was a portly married man, and Marie was young and shapely and not bright, but he treated her with perfect courtesy, much as he would a visitor. That, too, counted in his favor.

Jolie returned control to the maid, and reverted to her home immediately. This was a drop of blood on the wrist of Gaea, the Incarnation of Nature. Gaea was at the moment making an observation of her own: the pattern of weather in the mid-Pacific ocean, which might require delicate modification to weaken an untimely storm. She felt the return, and lifted her wrist. "Back so soon, Jolie?"

"Gaea, I felt the dying of one I love. I must go to her!"

"Go!" Gaea agreed. She was another ideal employer and friend; she did not inquire into Jolie's private business, either overtly or covertly, but allowed free rein. This was the type of generosity afforded by one with such enormous power that she could, if she chose, destroy the world. Any of the seven major Incarnations could—but their thrust was not to harm the world, but to preserve it.

Jolie oriented on the pain she felt. In a moment she was there.

"Oh, Orlene!" she exclaimed, horrified. For there, slumped at her treasured piano, was the lovely young woman Jolie had known for fifteen years. She was dying, and Jolie knew that it was already too late. Stunned, she could only hover, unable at first to grasp the enormity of this event. How could this have happened?

Then the body expired and the soul floated out diaphanously. It resembled a translucent film marked with a patina of shadow. The light color predominated, indicating a positive balance; this soul was destined for Heaven.

But the soul twisted as if still in pain, and a part of it clung to the dead body. Jolie understood that phenomenon; often it took time for a person to grasp the reality of death, and the soul hesitated to leave the comfort of the familiar body. More darkness was manifesting; there was a surprising amount of evil on this soul, though Jolie knew it was good.

"Orlene, let go!" she cried. "You will float directly to Heaven!"

The soul writhed, drawing itself clumsily down. "No—no," it said blurrily. "I must not go!"

"Orlene, it is Jolie! Your dream-friend! I would not guide you falsely! You are good; you have nothing to fear from the Afterlife! Let go your body, and you will soon be in Heaven!" Though not as soon as one with less evil. How could the balance be so close?

"I must not!" Orlene replied, still clinging.

A skeletal figure appeared. It was Thanatos, the collector of the balanced souls of the dead. He saw Jolie and paused, surprised. "You know this client?"

"She is my friend, my cherished—almost my child," Jolie said. "She has died, and I don't know why."

Thanatos glanced at the struggling soul. "She is bound for Heaven; I can see that without testing, though she could not afford very much more evil. Let me facilitate her passage." He reached out with a bonefingered hand.

The soul cringed away. "No! No!"

"Orlene, it's all right!" Jolie cried. "This is the Incarnation of Death, come to assist you on your way to Heaven. Your pain of the body is over!"

"No, I must not go! I must find my baby!"

Thanatos nodded. "Ah, the baby; I remember now. Her son died ten days ago; he was in balance, and I came for him and talked with the father. A terrible irony, but destined. Gaea's error."

Jolie was astonished. "Gaea? I know nothing of this!"

Thanatos made a gesture, and the soul froze in place.

11

Time was still, except for the two of them. "This was the bride in a ghost marriage; the ghost could not impregnate her, so she had a living companion, a man of sensitivity. She conceived by him, the child to be the legal heir of the ghost."

"That much I know," Jolie said. "She married Gawain, the ghost of a dragon slayer who was killed by an allosaur, who needed an heir. Then she found Norton, who was just right for her. I had other business, so I did not check on her once I knew she was fulfilled and happy. Evidently I should have! How could she have lost her baby, and died, when it was going so well?"

"The ghost prevailed on Gaea to modify the genetic pattern of the baby to match that of the ghost, so that there would be true continuity. Gaea did it as a favor without researching, and so incorporated a negative aspect of the ghost's heritage. The baby developed a recessive malady that killed it, no fault of either of the biological parents. That was the point at which her fate was sealed; she could not endure without her baby, and was destined for suicide as soon as she put her affairs in order. It is of course an unfortunate waste, but was fixed from the moment of Gaea's error."

"Her baby!" Jolie exclaimed. "That's why she is resisting her passage to Heaven! Where did the baby go?"

"It was in balance, by definition, and could travel neither to Heaven nor to Hell. It remains in Purgatory."

"And she wants to be with her son! If he's not in Heaven, she doesn't want to go there herself!"

"But there is no point—"

"Please, Thanatos, I'm her friend. Let me try to help her. Does she have to go to Heaven right away?"

The cloaked figure shrugged. "She does not. Her balance is actually fairly close, because she was born illegitimate, had an affair outside her marriage, and committed suicide. Those three sins would have been enough to send her to Hell were she not otherwise of virtually complete goodness. If she exerts her will, she may remain indefinitely in the mortal realm, as a ghost like you. I came only because it seemed she was having difficulty extricating herself from her body. I leave it in your hands."

"Thank you, Thanatos. I will take care of her until she accepts her situation." Then, as an afterthought: "How can so much sin attach to her soul for being of illegitimate birth, when she was not at fault for that? Or for having an affair, when the conditions of her marriage required it to enable her to have a baby for her ghost husband? Or for seeking to help her baby, even in the Afterlife?"

The skull seemed to grimace. "God made those definitions, not I. Were I to have authority, I would change them, and allow only evil motive to stain a soul. But it is not my place. I must operate within the set guidelines."

Jolie sighed. She had known it; her question had been mostly rhetorical, borne of the pain of this unexpected death. "I agree. But I am no person to attempt to criticize the Incarnation of Good."

Thanatos nodded, then turned and walked through the wall. As he did so, the scene reanimated. The struggles of the soul resumed.

Jolie put out a hand and caught the hand region of the soul. "Peace, Orlene, Thanatos is gone! You do not have to go anywhere you don't want to!"

The struggles diminished. The soul began to assume a better semblance. "My baby—"

"Your baby is in Purgatory. I will take you there, if you wish. I am Jolie, your friend of dreams; do you recognize me now?"

Slowly the recognition came. "My friend of dreams? I begin to remember, but . . ."

Jolie knew how hard it was to get organized after death; she had been through the process herself and had seen it many times in others. Normally a newly separated soul drifted either Heavenward or Hellward on its own, its direction determined by the balance of good and evil burdening it, and remained unconscious until arrival. In Heaven it assumed the form of its lost body and seemed like a living person in a new setting, and angels came to guide it to its appropriate level. In Hell it also returned to seeming life, but had a harsher welcome. Thus, to the individual, it seemed as if there were little or no transition between the last breath of life and appearance in the designated realm of the Afterlife.

But some few were unable to travel directly to a realm, either because of an almost perfect balance of good and evil or because their business among mortals was unfinished. Thanatos came to assist the former, while the latter often wandered for some time as ghosts. This had been the case with Jolie—and now with Orlene.

"Yes, I am a ghost," she said. "I could not approach you in your waking state for several reasons, but when you slept and dreamed, I was your friend. You perhaps thought me a mere creature of your imagination, but this was not the case. I was sent by a friend of your mother to watch over you, and that I did, until I saw you secure and happy. Now I regret I did not follow you further, for your life seems to have been destroyed during my brief absence."

"Jolie, my friend of dreams," the soul repeated. "Yes, now it returns. How glad I am to see you! Will you help me find my baby? I must have him with me!"

"I will help you," Jolie agreed. "But we must talk, to give you time to acclimatize, to learn the ways of the ghostly existence, so that you may operate with competence and confidence. Let me guide you to a better setting."

Orlene looked down at her body, to which she still clung. It remained slumped, one hand on the piano keyboard, looking gaunt and uncomfortable in death. "Are you sure I dare let go? I won't be launched to Heaven?"

"I will hold your hand and keep you from Heaven," Jolie said. "Trust me; I love you in a way you hardly know."

Nervously, Orlene clutched her hand and let go of the body. She did not float away. But she was not reassured. "Oh, I wish I hadn't killed myself! Yet if I hadn't—"

"Come, I know a house where we can relax," Jolie said, drawing her toward the wall.

Then the door opened, and there was Orlene's lover, Norton. He stared at the body. "Oh, Orlene!" he breathed with horror, instantly knowing. "Oh, my love!"

"Oh, my love!" Orlene echoed, appalled. "Oh, why did I

14

do this to you!" She floated toward him, arms outstretched.

"He cannot see you," Jolie said, sharing the pain of the situation. "Few mortals know how to see the supernatural, and few spirits can manifest visibly or audibly to mortals. I can teach you—but it will take time. Let him go, Orlene; that aspect of your existence is over."

"I know," the soul said sadly. "I just can hardly accept it. I wish I had loved him as he loved me; then I would not have done this awful thing! But my baby—"

"Leave him; it is all you can do now. Come with me."

Reluctantly, tearfully, Orlene acquiesced. They left Norton staring at the body, and Jolie guided her through the wall and away.

But as they moved, Jolie thought of her own death, the memory triggered by the recent scene. She had died early in the thirteenth century, in southern France, victim of a crusader who was trying to rape her. Her husband had tried to save her, but the agony of her wound was too great, and she had begged him to let her die. He had done so, then fled the crusaders, his life irrevocably altered by that experience. In retrospect she believed that she should have tried harder to live, so as not to leave her husband desolate, but at the time the physical pain had been overwhelming. She had been selfish, thinking more of her immediate pain than of his long-term pain.

She brought Orlene to the Treehouse in Purgatory, a place that was guaranteed private from all except its mistress. It was in the form of a phenomenal living tree whose trunk was hollow and whose branches twisted around to form upper chambers. Here the two of them assumed full human shape and substance. Had either been mortal, there would have been a severe complication, for Purgatory time was different for mortals. But Incarnations and ghosts were immune to that effect. Jolie bade her guest take one of the comfortable vine-woven chairs.

"But how can I be alive again?" Orlene asked, bewildered, feeling her solid flesh.

"You are not, and neither am I. This is Purgatory, where

15

souls assume their living forms, just as they do in Heaven and in Hell. I brought you here because it will be easier for you to adjust in your normal semblance."

"But this is a house!" Orlene exclaimed. "A strange house, with leaves sprouting from the walls and soil for the floor! How can this be the realm of spirits?"

Jolie realized that it was best to focus first on the basics. Soon enough they would get to the specifics of the woman's situation, when she was ready for them.

"All the Incarnations have homes in Purgatory," she explained. "They each have servants and staff to assist them in their formidable duties. But the Incarnation of Nature prefers to run her household alone, so that none may know her comings and goings, and indeed it can be quite difficult to visit. That is why I am certain of our privacy."

"This—is the home of Nature?" Orlene asked, amazed.

"Yes. That is why it is alive. All living things, and most dead ones, are her business. She is perhaps the most powerful of the Incarnations, aside from Good and Evil."

"But how can we be here?"

Jolie smiled. "I am a friend of the Incarnation. Indeed, I am her closest companion and confidante, for all that I am merely a ghost like you. That is why I was able to bring you here."

"I thought you were just a dream figment—a companion I invented in my sleep! You never said anything about Incarnations!"

"Not that you may remember at the moment," Jolie said. "It was not relevant. I am part of a complex skein, and am not free to discuss much of it, but this much you may accept: I came to you by design, not chance, and I have loved you as I would my own child."

Now Orlene remembered something. "You said you were a friend of my mother! But my parents never said anything about the supernatural!"

They were about to get into the woman's history. That was good, because the more time and thought that separated her from the concept of her recent death, the better. "You were adopted. I referred to your natural mother, who had to give you up when you were just a few weeks old."

"A blind Gypsy," Orlene agreed. "There was never any secrecy about my origin. My parents were always good to me, and I am thankful to have come to them. I had hoped to be as good for my own baby as they were for me." Then, abruptly, she clouded up, remembering the tragedy.

"A Gypsy woman gave you to your family," Jolie agreed. "But she was not your mother. She was a friend of your mother, before I was. Your mother conceived you out of wedlock, and your father was unexpectedly prevented from marrying her, and she had other business, so had to give you up. The Gypsy would have kept you, but fate denied her; it was her charge to give you to a suitable American family, and that she did. Your mother could have followed you, but elected not to interfere; by her own design, she let you go so that you could be a complete part of your new family. Except that—"

"She sent you!" Orlene exclaimed.

"Not exactly," Jolie said. "It was another who did that. He told her nothing except that you were well and happy. I came to you in your dreams and helped you to learn things you could not otherwise have learned, so that some day you might better understand the situation of your mother. In the course of that I soon came to love you myself, and now I regard you as mine too."

"But you are no older than I am!"

"My dear, physically I am not. But I died in the year 1208. I have been a ghost ever since."

Orlene stared at her. "But that's almost eight hundred years ago!"

"Almost," Jolie agreed. "I was seventeen, divinely married, and learning sorcery in southern France. But there was a crusade against the Albigensians, because they were resisting taxation, and the first thing the Church went after was opposing sorcerers. I died, and my husband fled—but he prevailed on Thanatos to let him carry me with him in a drop of my blood on his wrist. I could not quite depart the mortal

17

realm, you see, because of an abiding evil in my situation, so I remained. When my husband was confined in Hell, Gaea took my drop of blood, and I became her companion instead of his. I am omitting considerable detail, but that is the essence. I remain in appearance as I was when I died: younger than you."

"So you are seventeen—and eight hundred years old!" Orlene exclaimed. "And you knew my genetic mother!"

"And know her still. I can introduce you to her, if you wish."

Orlene considered. "No, I think I would rather not know. I would not see her as my mother, and it could be awkward, especially since I am a ghost."

"Perhaps that is best. She knows that I have been in touch with you, but does not know your identity or that you have died, and I will not tell her if you prefer."

"Do not tell her," Orlene agreed. "I have sown enough pain already! But do tell me—if you are the companion of the Incarnation of Nature, how is it that you had occasion to interact with others, such as my mother or myself?"

"I am bound to Gaea by my drop of blood, the sole remaining vestige of my mortal body. But she is busy with many things which are hardly my concern, and gives me leave to go where I wish and do what I wish. I always return to her when she needs me, but most of the time I am on my own, and so I meet many folk, living and dead. At the moment I am engaged in a project to locate suitable candidates to become Incarnations, and this is a most challenging enterprise."

"Incarnations! They are looking for replacements?"

"Not precisely. They merely want to have a pool of excellent candidates to draw from when the need arises. The candidates in the pool are not notified, they are merely observed, and then when the occasion should come, one of them may be tapped. It is better than allowing it to continue at random. I was observing a man in France, not far from my mortal residence, when I felt your dying. The observation is long-term and can wait, while your death was immediate, so I came right away."

"I would not want to keep you from your job! Once I am reunited with my baby, I have little care for what happens to me. I would rather be in Hell with him than in Heaven without him." She was evidently sincere.

"I will help you find him; my time is not pressed." Jolie looked at the ghost. "But, if I may, let me get you into better shape."

"Shape?"

"You look exactly as you were when you died. This is not kind. It might be better to restore you to your aspect of health."

"I can have no joy until I find my son, Gaw."

"Who?"

Orlene smiled. "He was named after his legal ghost father, Gawain. Gaw for short, or Gaw-Two."

"Gaw," Jolie agreed, understanding. "Come, here is a mirror." She stood, beckoning Orlene to a full-length mirror set in the living wall. It was formed of level water, tilted vertically; Gaea preferred natural things, with some leavening of magic.

The woman looked, and was appalled. "I look awful!"

"Your grief caused you to waste away. You might have died in due course even if you hadn't taken poison. But as a ghost you may assume any appearance, and it would be pointless to remain gaunt."

"But I have sinned by killing myself, and should pay the penalty."

"By the existing standard, yes, you have sinned. But your appearance can neither aggravate nor atone for that. If you are to recover your baby, it may be best to assume an appearance that does not advertise your grief. We may have to query many folk."

Orlene, gazing at herself, seemed inclined to agree. Like most lovely women, she was conscious of appearances. "How can I—?"

"As you become experienced in your present condition, you will gain proficiency in form changing. But for now, why don't you just lie down and rest or sleep, while I investigate

19

the location of your baby? Think of the form you wish to assume, and your body will gradually approach it."

"But I must search Gaw out myself!" Orlene protested.

"And so you shall! But there are queries I can make most readily by myself, such as with the Purgatory Computer, which is in a public region. Let me do this while you rest; I promise that you will be the first to know anything I learn."

Orlene wavered. "Can the dead sleep?"

Jolie laughed. "The dead can do what they choose! I slept for centuries when my husband associated with Hell. I did not truly come awake until Gaea took me. I had much to catch up on then! Part of it I learned while being your friend, in your dreams, for you were a girl of the modern world."

"My friend," Orlene echoed. "Those dreams—I forgot them by day, but they were wonderful by night! We did so much together!"

"So much," Jolie agreed. "It was almost like being alive again."

"And now I am dead," Orlene said sadly. "Already I regret my foolishness. I wish I had had your advice, before I . . ."

"I wish I had been watching!" Jolie said. "It is my fault as much as yours." Indeed, she felt the guilt! To allow this woman, of all those alive, to die so pointlessly—Jolie felt she had been criminally neglectful. She dreaded the revelation she would at some time have to make.

"I think I will lie down," Orlene said. "So much has happened! I never expected the Afterlife to be like this. It will take time to adjust."

Jolie led her to a guest chamber in the residence. There was a bed of roses, literally, fragrant and soft. "Rest, here, and I will return shortly," she said. "Remember, you are absolutely safe here; no one, mortal or immortal, will intrude. Only Gaea and I can enter without challenge—or those we bring."

Orlene lay in the bed. The bright petals rose up around her like the decoration on a fluffy quilt. She closed her eyes and in a moment was asleep.

Already she was looking better. The deep lines on her

face were easing, and her gaunt body seemed to be filling out. She had been beautiful, very like her mother, and soon would be again.

Satisfied, Jolie faded out of the scene.

She went first to Gaea. This was easy to do; she merely relaxed, and her home drop of blood hauled her in elastically. In an instant she was there.

It was a biological laboratory. Gaea had assumed the form of a gallon of air, making her effectively invisible. Jolie didn't have to bother; as a ghost she was naturally invisible, unless she made an effort to manifest optically or sonically. Only another ghost or an Incarnation could perceive her now.

"Business settled?" Gaea inquired, spying Jolie.

"Only begun, it seems," Jolie replied. "My friend died because she lost her baby, and she wishes to find him. I told her I would help."

"By all means. You mean to check the Computer?"

"Yes, by your leave."

"Granted. As it happens, I have a spot of research myself. Perhaps you could check that at the same time."

Gaea was always polite about her requests. The truth was that she had complete power over Jolie, who was now one of her staff members, but she never abused it. Quite the opposite! It was possible that she did have research to do—but as likely that this was merely a way of legitimizing Jolie's mission. "Certainly. What do you need?"

"This is a genetic laboratory. The gene splicing is routine, but the project isn't. They have, they think, perfected a variety of fruit fly that will consume residual oil pollution, and they are breeding it in sufficient number to colonize the Gulf coastline where the spill of 'ninety-five still festers. My concern is that a random mutation could direct those flies elsewhere. Here is the key aspect of the pattern; have the Computer run a check for possible mutations within my specified tolerance." She held out a ghostly pebble.

Jolie took the pebble, knowing that the pattern was imbued; the Purgatory Computer would know what to do with it. "I shall be back shortly, Gaea."

"And perhaps, thereafter, we shall make a visit," Gaea murmured. "If you feel inclined."

"Always." They never spoke directly of this particular matter; it was an understanding of long duration.

The Purgatory Computer had not been changed in twenty years. At this point, the equipment of the mortals was far more sophisticated. But the Purgatory Computer had magic and personality, and it did the job, so there was no push to replace it. Jolie had come to know it well, in the course of her errands for Gaea; they got along just fine.

A GREETING, BRIDE OF SATAN, the screen printed as she entered its main chamber.

"And half a greeting to you, obsolescent machine," she responded cheerily. "Got a pain in your nuts and bolts?"

NOT UNTIL THIS MOMENT, GHOST GIRL.

"Watch yourself, or I'll kick you in your data base."

YOU CAN'T. IT WOULD BE ANACHRONISTIC FOR A THIRTEENTH-CENTURY PEASANT TO KNOW THAT TERM.

"I learn quickly, you overachieving word processor."

ENOUGH OF THIS FOOLISH BANTER, EVIL EMISSARY. WHAT IS YOUR WILL?

"Two items, you arrogant device. Run this sample through your files and see what it matches." She fed the pebble into a little hopper.

The computer blinked. THERE IS A 15% PROBABILITY THAT THIS WILL MUTATE INTO A FUEL-EATING SPECIES WITHIN FIFTY YEARS. THE GREEN MOTHER WILL NOT LIKE THAT.

"She certainly won't! How much damage would occur if that happens?"

DEPENDS ON THE FUEL. BY THAT TIME THERE MAY NOT BE A LOT OF CRUDE OIL LEFT, BUT IF THE FLY GOES FOR SYNTHETIC OIL, THERE COULD BE A MAJOR DISRUPTION. IT CAN BE EXTREMELY DIFFICULT TO REVERSE SUCH A COURSE, ONCE ESTABLISHED.

"In other words, the mortals are playing roulette again?"

AGREED, SORCERESS.

Jolie sighed. The mortal realm could be a real pain in the buttock on occasion. But that was Gaea's problem; she might elect to force a prior problem that would wipe out the fly before it could mutate. The mortals would curse their misfortune, not understanding that they were being protected from worse.

"Second item: the present location of the infant Gawain Junior, otherwise known as Gaw-Two, who died ten mortal days ago."

NOX.

"What?"

THAT INFANT WAS TAKEN BY NOX, THE INCARNATION OF NIGHT.

"Oh, my!" Jolie breathed. She had not anticipated that. Usually babies were left to the Purgatory Playpen, because it took some time for them to achieve independent function. In the Playpen they could mature slowly; elsewhere they did not. "What does Nox want with a baby?"

NOX DID NOT VOUCHSAFE THAT INFORMATION TO THIS MACHINE.

Of course not! Nox allowed few to know her business. She knew all of the secrets of the world, and kept most of them. "Have you any conjecture?"

CONJECTURE: THAT BABY IS THE GRANDCHILD OF A PERSON SATAN LOVES, THEREFORE OF PROBABLE INTEREST TO HIM. NOX MAY HAVE SECURED THE BABY AS A LEVER.

"But Nox needs no lever! She can have her will of Satan—or any male Incarnation—anytime she chooses. I know, for I love Satan."

ADMITTED. IT IS AN INSECURE CONJECTURE. THE MOTIVE OF NOX IS UNFATHOMABLE TO A MERE MACHINE.

"Or a mere ghost," Jolie said. "How may Nox be approached?"

THROUGH THE REALM OF DREAMS—IF IT IS FEASIBLE AT ALL.

That was what she had feared. This simple quest had abruptly become a complicated one! Orlene was going to have real trouble recovering her baby—unless the Incarnation of Night chose to give him up.

She returned to Gaea, who was now back at the Treehouse. "Oops, I forgot to tell you about—"

"I saw her," Gaea said. "Your new ghost? I did not pry."

"My new ghost," Jolie agreed. "She suicided over bereavement for her lost baby. I have known her for years, and want

23

to help her, so I asked her to sleep and resume a more healthy form, knowing that she was completely protected here."

"There is something you are not telling me," Gaea said.

"Yes. If I may, I prefer to handle this myself, though it may be complicated."

"Can it wait a few more hours?"

"Yes. It is better that she sleep until her recovery is complete. And—" Jolie hesitated.

"And there is more you need to ascertain before she wakes," Gaea said.

"Yes. In fact, I think my husband . . ." She did not finish, as was their convention. Jolie's husband was the current Incarnation of Evil, and all the other active Incarnations opposed him. Her marriage had been dissolved when she died, and he had later remarried, so she had no legal claim, but they chose to maintain an honorary designation. The truth was that there were private understandings—and Gaea was Satan's current spouse. This was a technicality, and the marriage had never been formally consummated, but the two were indeed in love, and had been for the better part of twenty years.

Thus Jolie was free to go to Satan, but because she was not evil, she was unable to manifest in his presence or in Hell. Gaea, with the powers of an Incarnation, could go to him, but did not because it would seem to be a conflict of interests. Both loved him, and he loved both, but they were unable separately to fulfill their desires. This was the origin of the unspoken compromise.

"When it is done, ask him, and I will tune out," Gaea said.

"Thank you, Orb," Jolie said gratefully. She used Gaea's private mortal name only when especially moved. What she could not say was that by her generosity and understanding, Gaea was also sparing herself pain, for Orlene was her natural daughter. She had been conceived before Orb became the Incarnation, and as an Incarnation she had deliberately neglected to keep track of her child, so that she would not be unduly influenced by purely personal considerations. She had not asked Jolie to do so, but Satan had, and that was what had brought Jolie to the child. Jolie had developed many other associations, as well as her program of observations of candidates for future Offices, so it was by no means obvious that it was Orb's daughter who had died. If Gaea had any suspicion, as she might when seeing the sleeping woman so like herself in outline, she kept it to herself. Jolie would tell her when the time was right.

But if Gaea had reservations about knowing the identity of her daughter, Satan had none. Orlene was the child of the woman Satan loved, and therefore he had an interest. If advice or action was needed, Satan would not hesitate to provide it. That was an advantage to being unbound by ethical considerations.

"I have appointments four hours hence," Gaea said.

"I will see that you return in time," Jolie agreed.

Then Jolie moved to Gaea and into her, superimposing her ghostly essence on Gaea's solid one and animating Gaea's body. She could do this only with the permission of the living person and only with the active cooperation of an Incarnation. She had it. Gaea became a resident soul, and Jolie became alive in her stead.

She walked to the mirror. Her features shifted slightly, so that her semblance became her own instead of that of the host. Her clothing also changed, becoming that of her ancient mortal state: a long peasant skirt and rough blouse, unattractive in themselves, but becoming lovely because of the excellent proportions of her body. Jolie lived again, seventeen years old.

She drew on one of Gaea's powers of travel: she reached up, grasped the invisible corner of a page of reality, and turned it. Suddenly she was in the following page, which was Hell itself. The body of the host was proof against it; there was nowhere in the cosmos where Gaea could not go if she chose.

She stood before a massive desk, and a somber male figure sat at that desk. "Hello, Ozymandias," she said.

"Hello, Jolie," the ancient king replied. "Go to the bower; He will be with you in a moment."

She nodded. They knew her in Hell, and knew her

25

business; no one here would bother her, and not just because they were aware of whose body she animated. She was Satan's lover, under his protection; woe betide the demon who molested her! She was also the only good soul they were likely to see here, and as such she was a considerable curiosity.

Jolie had deeply regretted dying young, and had in a fashion died again when Parry (as she had known him in life) was seduced by the demoness Lilah, for Jolie had been rendered unconscious by the presence of evil. But now, protected by Gaea, she was able to enter this dread realm freely, and she saw that it really was not evil in the way she had imagined. Hell was a place of punishment for evil, which was a different matter. The end purpose of Satan's work was the clarification and purification of imperfect souls, making them fit for Heaven, and in that fundamental sense it was not evil. Thus it was that her former husband, certainly a good man, was able to serve as the Incarnation of Evil, and she was able to love him still.

She walked to the bower. She could have conjured herself there, but she preferred to take her time and see the sights. There were no tortures in this region of Hell, perhaps by design; it was very like a giant hall, with curtains in the likeness of towering flames, and executive demons hurrying to and from the central command post. Ozymandias had been installed by Satan decades or centuries before—she had never inquired about the details—and had fashioned it to resemble an infernal palace. It was actually rather grand.

The bower was a modern apartment, replete with conveniences. Once the door closed, it was impossible for an occupant to distinguish this retreat from one in the mortal realm. Both Jolie and Orb preferred it this way. She entered and sat on the plush bed.

Why was it, she asked herself, that to a man a liaison was always sexual? She would have been glad to come and chat with him about old times and new, requiring nothing more than time in his presence and maybe a kiss or two. But she knew from experience and observation that this was not the way of a man. He would not be good for much dialogue until he had completed intimacy. Well, thanks in part to the power of the Incarnation and in part to experience and in part to the sheer abandon of love, she was able to accommodate him readily enough. Her imperatives might differ from his, but she did enjoy these visits.

He appeared. He seemed to be about twenty-five years old and more handsome than she had known him in life. This was because he had chosen that age when he assumed the Office; he had been only eighteen when she died. He had developed confidence and aplomb in the ensuing centuries, and garnered a great deal of experience. She hated to admit it, but the demoness Lilah had been good for him, fashioning him into a very fine figure of a man in both appearance and action.

"Ah, Jolie!" he said, and the manner of the utterance sent a thrill through her, as it always did. He sat beside her, and put his arm around her, and drew her in for a kiss, and her heart went out to him, as it always did.

The man has magic, Orb thought, sharing the feeling. Their pretense remained, outwardly, but the inner truth was that both of them loved this man, and both thrilled to his touch. They forgot their disinterest in the purely sexual aspect, and soon were taken by the joy of the experience, thrilling to his penetration and culmination with much the same verve he expressed. There was indeed joy in sex, when it was right.

"I have only one regret now," he said as they lay cooling. "We can never have children."

That reminded her. "I have something to ask you, Parry," she said. As she spoke she felt Orb fading out, granting her the privacy she had requested. She could speak freely now, and her host would not overhear.

"Anything, my love," he replied, kissing her hand.

"Orlene is dead, and I must help her. She—"

"*Orlene?*" he demanded, recognizing the name.

Then Jolie was weeping. She had held it back, needing first to help the newly dead soul, then to run her errands, then to mask her emotion from her host. Parry held her close, but his body was shaking; he was affected much as she was.

Haltingly, she described the events leading up to Orlene's suicide, and her determination to help the new ghost. It helped her grief to be able to express it to one she knew understood. For Parry loved Orlene too—because she was his stepdaughter. Jolie had not reported to Gaea, but had reported to Satan, and for no evil purpose.

"So Gaw-Two was taken by Nox," she concluded. "I must find out how to approach the Incarnation of Night."

"I have had contact with Nox," he said. "She alone could have taken me from the demoness at the height of my passion. I dare not approach her, lest she take me from you." He spoke without the inflection of godhead, preferring to be Parry for this private tryst. "But I can give you some advice. Look for her in the region of chaos, where Clotho goes for new thread, but turn to the side before chaos is complete. If you get lost, call for help; there is one who will answer."

"But suppose we can't find Nox?"

"You will find her if she chooses to be found. If she chooses otherwise, you are helpless. But I suspect she will let you approach."

"The Purgatory Computer conjectured that she means to use the baby as a lever against you."

"Nox needs no lever against me! I am a major Incarnation, but I exist by the sufferance of Nox, as do we all. She predates us, and can foil our powers whenever she chooses."

"But she has no power by day! She is only of the night!"

"She can influence us in devious ways. She has chosen not to, but there is night in all of us. She understands us far better than we understand her."

This was not reassuring. "Can it be coincidence that she took this particular baby?"

"Hardly. She has a purpose—and perhaps she will tell you, if you go to her. She may have taken the baby for that reason: to bring you to her."

"So maybe we'll find her—but not be happy when we do," Jolie concluded.

"That is my fear. But you will have to ask."

"We will have to ask," Jolie agreed.

"Have you told Orb?"

"No."

"That is best, for now," he agreed. "If Nox's purpose is not malign—and she has no need for malignancy—then it may be better to talk with her first."

"I hope so. Oh, Parry, I never knew the baby, but I hurt for Orlene! I wish I had been watching when—"

"Only Fate could have known—and I think she was not watching, either."

Lachesis, the middle Aspect of Fate, was also Orb's mother, and Orlene's grandmother. She did her job in the way she saw fit, but certainly she would not carelessly sacrifice her grandchild. If it had become necessary for her to do that, she would have consulted with other Incarnations, seeking some better way through. No, this seemed to be a thing only Nox was involved in.

"I must go," she said. "Gaea has appointments, and I—"

"You want to follow up on this," he finished. "Do so, and keep me posted. I hope this is not more than it seems."

Jolie hoped so, too, but her fear was growing that it was only the beginning. She kissed him again, dressed, and turned the page back to the Tree.

She separated from Gaea, and Gaea woke. "Your affairs are in order?" the Incarnation inquired with a partial smile.

"Something complicated may be afoot," Jolie said seriously. "May I take longer leave of you for a special mission?"

"As you wish. Is there anything I should know, in case your return is delayed?"

Jolie considered. She could not afford to say too much, but it was only right to let Gaea know where she would be. "I think we have to visit Nox."

Gaea gazed at her. Then, without comment, she turned a page elsewhere, leaving Jolie alone with the sleeping ghost.

Jolie went to the bedroom. Orlene looked much improved; the restoration had proceeded nicely as she slept. It had, of course, been enhanced by the Tree; all the things of Nature were strongest here. Soon the woman would be ready for the journey—as ready as it was possible for anyone to be.

Jolie took a chair and allowed herself to fade out. She would wake when Orlene did. Then there would be more explaining, and a challenge of uncertain nature. Already the mystery of it disturbed her; nothing like this had happened since she had joined Gaea.

Could this be an aspect of the great contest between God and Satan for dominance of the mortal realm? She loved Parry, but knew that in his guise as Satan he fully intended to take power if he could do so. Yet even that did not seem to make sense, for Nox had never before participated in this eternal struggle. No, it seemed to be some incidental ploy, of interest only to the Incarnation of Night, and secret from all but herself. With luck, it would prove to be a harmless diversion, something Nox was doing merely for amusement. Who could comprehend what might amuse such a creature?

Jolie had little confidence in such luck. She slept without truly relaxing. Her ghostly state made sleep unnecessary, physically, but she certainly could use something of the sort emotionally!

CHAPTER TWO

Nox

"AND SO WE SHALL HAVE TO BRAVE THE VOID TO locate Nox," Jolie concluded. "That seems to be the only way to reach your baby."

"Then I shall go there!" Orlene exclaimed, brightening. She was now as lovely as she had been at the height of her mortality, though her grief and worry detracted somewhat from it. "I thank you, Jolie, for your support and research; you have given me genuine hope."

"*We* shall go there," Jolie corrected her. "I would not send you alone to such a treacherous region."

"You have already done too much, my friend. You must return to your interrupted task."

"My observations are ongoing and not immediately pressing; this is more urgent."

"For me, yes, but it is not your concern. I would not—"

"Orlene, it is my concern," Jolie said firmly. "I was watching over you, and I neglected that, and you died."

"I took my own life!"

"Because your baby sickened and died—because his genetic pattern had been changed, because your ghost husband sought a favor from Gaea without reckoning its consequence. I am Gaea's companion; had I been watching, I could have warned her, and Gaw-Two would have been spared. That is my guilt." That was only part of it; she had let this happen to Gaea's mortal daughter! How could she ever make up for that? She dreaded the inevitable time when she would have to tell Gaea.

Orlene gazed at her and did not speak.

They left the Tree together. Gaea was off on another mission; they did not see her.

There was an access to the Void at the edge of Purgatory, the one used by Clotho when she went to fetch more thread. They followed the road, and then the path, through a dense forest. The trees become so large and close that they shaded the path, making it seem to be dusk. Their gnarled trunks seemed to assume grotesque faces, the sinister recesses staring out at the trespassers. Even Jolie, who had become familiar with Purgatory and other aspects of the Afterlife, found herself becoming apprehensive. How was it affecting Orlene?

The great trees encroached further, their roots clutching at the path like twisted talons. A trunk blocked the path ahead; they had to squeeze around it, only to encounter another in the way. Soon they were lost in the maze of dark columns, unable to see far in any direction or to discern a coherent path. Jolie was not at all sure she could find her way out naturally; fortunately she could always revert to her home drop of blood, heedless of the route between. If that became necessary, she would clasp Orlene by the hand and bring her along.

The trees became gradually different. It wasn't just a matter of species, but of realm; their trunks were assuming surfaces and colors not seen in nature, such as tinted glass or bluish steel. Their foliage became geometrical, each leaf fashioned as if by compass and straightedge into circle, oval, hexagon or square. Light came through, reflecting from mirror surfaces and refracting through transparencies. This was now a fairyland forest, with bright rays splaying out from many nexuses, splendid in an unsettling way.

The path became clear again—but it diverged. One fork progressed into a region of disintegrating trees, some even floating upside down, their colors inverted, too, with green roots and brown leaves. The other fork wound toward some kind of mountain. Perhaps both paths went there, for both were devious, but would they rejoin?

The two women looked at each other. "I'm afraid my expertise was left at the edge of the forest," Jolie said. "I have never been into this region before. I have no idea how to proceed."

"I see that one path is better used than the other," Orlene said. "Would that be significant?"

Jolie hadn't noticed. The new ghost was recovering her mental acuity! "Clotho, the youngest Aspect of Fate, comes here monthly to renew her supply of Thread, as I understand it. She must use one path, and that one has become worn."

"Does Clotho go to see Nox?"

"I don't think so."

"Then maybe the other one is ours."

Jolie shrugged. She had no better logic.

They took the path less traveled. It made its way toward the mountain, which rose up monstrously as they approached. The peak was lost in cloud, and the base seemed to delve down below the ground, as if it were no natural configuration, but an alien object set within the scene.

"There is something strange about this landscape," Orlene remarked.

Jolie laughed. "You are just noticing? This is the fringe of the Void, where the laws of reality start breaking down!"

"Apart from that," Orlene said. "So far we have seen odd trees, but now—I don't know."

Jolie had to agree. The oddness was shifting from quantitative to qualitative, as it were; the trees were obvious, but now there was something subtle. "It seems to relate to the mountain."

When they reached the base of the mountain they had another clue: it was indeed set into the terrain. There was a gap a handsbreadth wide between the land and the slope of the mountain, and this was maintained below. The gap extended as far and deep as they could see. It was as though the mountain were a jewel set in the land and had contracted slightly, leaving a space. If nothing were done, in time the jewel would fall out of its setting and be lost. Meanwhile it remained, and it seemed it was theirs to climb. The path went up to the edge and on up the slope, neatly ignoring the gap.

"Nox is there?" Orlene inquired, glancing up.

Jolie considered. "When Gaea is busy, or wishes to make a point, she makes it difficult for others to approach her residence," she said. "Even other Incarnations lack power to approach her in her domain, unless she accedes. Nox is by all accounts the most seclusive of Incarnations, so perhaps this is her challenge that keeps away intruders. If so, then it means we are on the right path."

Orlene grimaced. Even in that expression she looked better than she had been when grieving for her baby. The challenge was taking her mind from her personal problem, and that was good. "Then we had better get moving."

They stepped over the gap and stood on the mountain. The oddness abruptly magnified; this was definitely an unearthly structure! There was a vibrance about it, an animation not as of life but as of an awakening machine with sophisticated circuits. Suddenly Jolie was uncertain of the security of her ghostly state; whatever was here seemed competent to capture her spiritual aspect as readily as it might have her physical aspect.

Orlene, too, hesitated. "Something about this," she said. "I feel a power I don't trust."

"The power of an Incarnation, perhaps," Jolie agreed. "Sometimes Gaea manifests physically in the mortal realm, and when a mortal becomes aware of her, he is awed by her mere presence. This feels somewhat like that. An Incarnation is to ordinary folk what a mountain is to a molehill. They have powers we hardly dare dream of. If this mountain is of Nox, she is aware of us, and we are in her power."

"She wants us to desist?"

"I think if she wanted that, she would have removed the

mountain entirely, or made the path impenetrable. No, I suspect this is merely her warning: we are in her territory now, and must obey her rules. She will let us proceed if she chooses."

Orlene gazed up the slope. "You say she is the Incarnation of Night, yet this is light."

"I confess I don't understand this aspect, but surely we shall be in darkness before we reach her."

"Let's hope it is only physical."

Then Orlene noticed something in the path. It looked like a stick, jammed in so as to stand vertically. But it wasn't natural; the upper end was shaped into a handle.

Jolie reached down to take it, but her hand passed through it. "An illusion!" she said, hardly amused. In a sense, everything here was illusory, including themselves, but so far it had all been in a common framework, interacting as if physical. She didn't want the confusion of layered illusions.

"You mean it isn't real?" Orlene inquired, reaching for it herself. This sort of thing evidently remained a novelty to her.

"It's real, just not on the same plane—the same level of being," Jolie explained. "There are an infinite number of planes of being, and the Incarnations can craft them to their needs. We, as ghosts, are on one plane, and seem solid here, but not on Earth. It depends. This must be Nox's doing."

Orlene's hand touched the stick. "But it's real!" she exclaimed. Her fingers closed about the handle and she drew it out of the ground. "A wand!"

"A magic wand!" Jolie agreed, trying to touch it and failing again. "One only you can wield!"

"But what can I do with it? I know nothing about this!"

"It must have been left for you. This may be Nox's invitation for you to proceed. The wand may be the key to progress when some barrier appears."

"You mean I wave it and magic happens?" Orlene waved it experimentally. Nothing happened.

"You may have to invoke it," Jolie offered. "But it's best not to play with unknown magic. Keep it with you, and invoke it only at need."

Orlene nodded. "I have magic, but it doesn't focus on inanimate things. I can't tell whether this wand is good or evil or neutral, but I suppose I would be foolish to set it aside until I discover its purpose."

"I think so," Jolie said. "Nox evidently has something in mind for you." She was reassured by this evidence, but not completely; if Nox was watching them and wanted them to proceed, why the mystery?

They moved on up the path. In this region they seemed solid and alive, for this was at the fringe of Purgatory, but they did not get hungry or tire in the way a mortal might. They made good progress, following the path in what they hoped was a spiraling ascent. It might have been more direct to go straight up the side, but there were loose rocks and steep faces and prickly briars that seemed worth avoiding. They were both dressed in light blouses and skirts and comfortable slippers, having no way to anticipate what they might encounter in their approach to Nox. So far, this was good enough. Jolie had expected to conjure whatever outfits they required, for the magic she had learned in life remained with her in death, and indeed had grown with experience. But when she had tried to conjure sturdier walking shoes, it hadn't taken; it seemed that Nox banned magic other than her own here.

Orlene paused, listening. "What is that sound?"

Jolie concentrated. There was a faint humming or buzzing in the distance, getting louder. "Bees?"

"Do bees swarm in the Afterlife?"

"I never heard of it. Bees and most other creatures seem to have their own Afterlife, which only rarely intersects ours. This could be one of those intersections, though."

"If we remain perfectly still, they should pass without molesting us. Norton was a man of the wilderness; he educated me on the beauties of nature."

Norton was her lover, in life—the one who had sired her baby. He had arrived just as Jolie guided Orlene away from her dead body. Jolie kept silent, so as not to encourage saddening memories.

The noise increased, developing a rattle. That didn't sound like bees!

Then the source came into view: a cloud of things that jumped and fluttered and descended. There seemed to be thousands of them.

"Locusts!" Orlene exclaimed. "I thought those were abolished decades ago!"

"The rules are different here," Jolie reminded her. "I think we'd better hide."

"But locusts eat only plants!"

"Among the mortals." Jolie headed for the bushes beside the path.

Orlene hesitated, then followed her example just as the vanguard of the swarm arrived.

The insects landed and began to chomp. The foliage of the bushes disappeared. In a moment the locusts were dropping onto Jolie and chomping at her clothing.

She couldn't help herself; she was revolted by the contact. "Away!" she cried, brushing frantically at them. "Off! Off!" She hated to touch them, but hated worse to let them touch her. She heard Orlene exclaiming similarly in the next bush.

Then the locusts began to bite flesh. Jolie screamed, and Orlene echoed her. Both leaped out of their bushes, flailing at the horrible creatures. The locusts clung, continuing to bite; their feet hooked in, making it as easy to crush them as to remove them. More descended, cloaking the women with their loathsome bodies.

"The wand!" Jolie cried. "Try it now!"

"I invoke you!" Orlene screamed, waving the wand violently.

A cloud of darkness formed around the tip of the wand. It spread rapidly, enclosing Orlene and the locusts, then Jolie. It became night around them, complete with stars.

There was a wrenching of the cosmos. Jolie felt herself turning around and over and inside out, painlessly, but with vertigo. The biting stopped. The locusts were gone. The vertigo was evidently too much for them.

The cloud of darkness dissipated. Light returned, penetrating as the thickness of the darkness eased.

Jolie found herself on a slope—but the mountain had changed. It was now alien. No—it was a mountain-sized depression! They were standing on the slope of a roughly conical pit. Yet, oddly, it wasn't dark in its depths; it was lightest at the base and darkening at its rim.

Rim? Jolie looked upslope—and spied a giant dome. This was not a pit, it was a closed cave!

Beside her, Orlene was gazing around with equal wonder. "Like the inside of a tremendous diamond!" she said.

Jolie had to agree. The walls of their prison were faceted, and the whole was like an elegant cut. How had they come here?

Again Orlene fathomed it first: "The dark cloud—it phased us into the mountain!" she exclaimed. "We are inside the mountain!"

"But then it's upside down!" Jolie said. "Narrow at the base and broad at the—"

"It isn't, *we* are!" Orlene said. "We were climbing toward the point; now we are descending toward the point. We're inverted—inside and upside down."

Indeed, it seemed to be so. "That was one impressive bit of magic," Jolie said. "The wand got us away from the locusts by phasing us into the mountain, where they couldn't go."

"Well, you did tell me to use it at need!"

They contemplated each other. Their clothing was tattered but still serviceable. Their skins were abraded, but not seriously damaged. The locusts had not been able to do a lot of damage in the few seconds they had had.

"Do you suppose the wand can conjure us back outside?" Orlene asked.

"That seems likely. But maybe we should descend to the peak of the mountain first, then go out. That will save energy and danger."

Orlene nodded agreement. They resumed their travel, following the same path they had, but from the other side: a slightly raised surface. Indeed, all of the local contours seemed to be the same as those of the outside of the mountain, with the exception of the living portion: the grass, brush and trees. The outcroppings of rock were pits here, and the depressions were mounds. On the larger scale this was an evenly faceted surface, but on the immediate level it was highly varied.

In fact, it seemed to be such a perfect inversion of the outer surface of the mountain that increasingly Jolie wondered about it. She had thought the mountain was a shell, with an inside and an outside, and that the wand had phased them through that shell and put them on the inner surface. But such a mold had no need to be identical on inside and outside, and indeed was unlikely to be. In fact, it might be close to impossible on a scale like this; such a thin film, following the exact surface of a mountain, should quickly collapse unless soundly buttressed on one side or the other. This one wasn't buttressed outside *or* inside.

"Something funny about this," Orlene said. "I'm not sure we're inside a hollow mountain; I think we're part *of* it."

"We'd be embedded in it!" Jolie said, laughing.

"No, somehow we're reacting to the rock and earth—the solid inanimate parts—as if they are air, while the air is like rock to us now. Gravity is reversed too; we're trying to fall away from the planet, but the air is stopping us. Normally we're trying to fall into the center of the planet, but the ground stops us."

"But we're not on the planet," Jolie pointed out. "We're at the verge of Purgatory, which is nowhere in relation to the planet, but might be pictured as a two-dimensional plane somewhere between Earth and infinity. We seem solid here because our ghostly state has better definition; it's an illusion, for we have no three-dimensional solidity."

"Oh, I forgot about that! I'm still thinking in mortal terms. Sometimes it's hard to believe I'm really dead."

"Your body is dead; your soul lives on. But I think you have helped me answer a confusion I was having. I thought this big diamond structure should collapse because it isn't supported on either side, but of course I was thinking in mortal terms. The rules here are those of Purgatory and illusion; this structure is as Nox made it, and there is no point questioning it."

"So it really can be us assuming a solid semblance, because

if Nox defines the rules of interaction, that's how it is. A dream world."

"Yes, it really can be." Jolie glanced at her, bothered by something else, but not sure what. Orlene didn't seem quite the same, but Jolie wasn't certain that she had changed. Maybe it was just this altered perspective again.

They resumed their descent, but were shortly interrupted by something new. The ground, such as it might be, was shuddering.

They looked around, alarmed, and spied motion across the pit. Something was moving, sliding across the surface like flowing water. The effect spread around the pit, toward them.

"Avalanche!" Jolie exclaimed. "Or a snow slide, or something."

"Maybe water?" Orlene asked, peering at the stuff. It seemed to sparkle.

"We've seen no water here before," Jolie said. "But it does seem to move like it."

Then the effect reached them. Fine powder sifted down by their feet, and by the sound of it, more was on the way from above.

"That's not water," Orlene said, bending to scoop some with a hand. "It's dust, or—ouch! It prickles!"

"That's glass!" Jolie exclaimed. "Ground glass! Or diamond dust! Don't breathe it!"

Orlene dropped her handful with alacrity. "But in a moment it will bury us!"

"Use your wand! We have to get out of here!"

Orlene whipped out the wand and waved it. "I invoke you!"

The darkness formed, expanding as it had before. In a moment it encompassed them. The vertigo returned.

It passed. As the cloud dissipated, Jolie saw that they were back on the outer mountain, amid the bushes, but higher than they had been. Their progress inside translated into progress here.

Orlene rubbed her fingers cautiously together. "No more

glass," she said gruffly. "Or diamond dust. Wish I'd had a bag to save some of it!"

"That's a relief! Apparently the things of the inside can't follow us out, any more than the things of the outside can follow us in. The wand is attuned to us alone, by Nox's order."

"Must be," Orlene agreed in that same gruff voice.

Jolie looked at her. Now she was sure: the woman had changed. She was using a lower tone, and she seemed a little larger than before. Indeed, her body was more robust. What was happening to her? Jolie decided not to comment until she had a better notion. It might be part of the strangeness of this mountain.

They proceeded up, following the path. But before long there was another threat. A giant bird was coming down the slope, standing taller than either of them, with muscular legs and a thick, ferocious beak.

"What is that?" Orlene asked, taken aback.

Jolie was amazed. "I've had opportunity to do some research into this and that, over the years. That looks like one of the big flightless predator birds of prehistoric times—*Diatryma,* maybe."

"Is it friendly?"

"Unlikely. They were fearsome hunters."

Orlene glanced to the side. "Maybe I can fight it off with a stick."

"Don't try it!" Jolie cried, aghast. "They strike forward with their legs, to disembowel! Use your wand!"

Orlene hesitated, then brought out the wand. As the bird charged, she invoked it.

There was a harsh, angry squawk. The bird plunged at the expanding darkness. For a moment the malevolent head projected next to Jolie's own. The great beak turned to orient on her face, but Jolie was already ducking down into the cloud. She felt the vertigo.

In a moment they were back inside the mountain and the big bird was gone. Now it was certain: only those for whom the wand was intended could use it. Orlene was the only one who could touch it or invoke it, and Jolie was the only other one it transported. Otherwise the bird would have come with them, for most of its body had been within the cloud.

"I'm going to find a weapon," Orlene said. "I don't want to be caught short again."

Jolie looked at her, dismayed. Now her face was changing, losing its beauty. The jawline was stronger, and there was a shadow at the chin. Was she reverting to some primitive form? Still, it seemed best not to comment, for there was nothing positive Jolie could say.

Fortunately there was nothing suitable as a weapon. "Damn!" Orlene grunted. "Well, when we go back outside, sure as hell I'll get something."

She was swearing now. She never had before, being indelibly feminine. That suggested a personality change keeping pace with the body change. Was something similar happening to Jolie herself? She didn't feel different, but then Orlene didn't seem to feel different either. It was surely Nox's doing—but why?

As they descended, with Orlene setting a brisk pace, Jolie continued to ponder the matter, ill at ease. Nox was the Incarnation of Night, really an ancient goddess, mistress of secrets and dreams and all things hidden. This was surely a type of dream, crafted for the two of them. But why should Nox bother? It would have been easy for her to make herself entirely unapproachable, or to manifest before the visitors at the outset. Why set this strange mountainous challenge for them? What was the point?

Maybe it was a mischievous game. Parry, now Satan, had mentioned her with a certain awe; it seemed that Nox had a way with men that was not to be denied. Maybe the Incarnation was having idle sport with the two women, seeing fit neither to tempt them nor to banish them. If so, it was getting cruel.

Something was happening, again. There was no sign of the ground glass they had fled before, but as they got farther down, the air was becoming warmer. Jolie saw Orlene sweating, but her pace did not diminish. The woman now had more muscle, and it seemed functional; she was braving the discomfort of the heat as she might a private challenge, showing that it could not daunt her. Jolie would have preferred to avoid any such challenge, but saw no alternative.

"Sheesh, it's hot!" Orlene remarked, wiping her brow with a handful of her tattered blouse, which she carelessly yanked out of her waistband. That exposed her chest.

Jolie was appalled. Orlene had been full-busted, her endowment masked only by her demure manner and conservative mode of dress. Jolie had helped get her dressed after her recovery from her predeath emaciation. Niobe had been the most beautiful woman of her generation; her daughter Orb had fallen not far short of that, and her granddaughter Orlene was close enough. Now Orlene's bra was oddly shrunken. At the same time the muscles of her arms were larger. There was no longer any question: she was changing.

There was a swirl in the air ahead. Dust was being sucked into a whirlwind. Jolie recognized the phenomenon, because of her association with Gaea: it was a heat vortex, part of the mechanism for generating a quick storm. Gaea controlled the elements, and could bring wind or rain or draught to any region she chose. Uncontrolled use of the tools of weather could be hazardous, especially to those in the immediate vicinity.

"We'd better get out of here!" Jolie said. "We don't want to get burned."

"What's *with* this place?" Orlene demanded rhetorically. "It's one damn thing after another! Let's just see about this twister!" She forged ahead, right toward the vortex.

"Wait!" Jolie cried, alarmed. "That thing's dangerous!"

Indeed, the vortex wasn't waiting to be approached; it was moving right toward them, its winds screaming. Orlene's hair whipped about, and she almost fell as the blast caught her. The wand fell from her pocket and bounced on the ground.

"The wand!" Jolie screamed. "Get the wand!"

Orlene saw it. "Christ!" she grunted, diving for it. She caught it. "Invoke!"

The dark cloud formed. The raging wind had no effect

on it. Soon they were both within it and wrenching back to the exterior realm.

They were closer to the summit, but Jolie was no longer concerned about that. She was in serious doubt whether this mission should proceed. Not only were the dangers getting worse, Orlene was still changing. Now she was not at all feminine. In fact—

"Orlene!" Jolie exclaimed. "Have you looked at yourself?"

Orlene glanced at her with irritation. "What are you talking about?"

"You've been changing! The farther we go—no, it must be the wand! Everytime you use it, it—"

"Quit stuttering, woman! What's the matter with the wand?"

"It makes you more like a man," Jolie finished, horrified as she realized the direction it was going.

"For chrissake, girl, stop talking nonsense! We've got to get on with this before something else happens."

"Didn't you hear me? *That wand is changing you into a man!*"

"And you into a monkey!" Orlene retorted, laughing. She started up the path, striding strongly. Her hips had narrowed and her feet grown, making her better at this. Apparently her shoes did not bind.

Jolie stood for a moment, appalled. Orlene refused to recognize how she was changing!

They were looking for Nox, Mistress of Night. This must be a dream sequence, where the most outrageous situations were accepted as given. It was Orlene's dream; Jolie was merely an observer. Thus it seemed that only Jolie could see what was happening.

Should she urge a retreat from this mission? That would probably be wasted effort; if Orlene couldn't see the problem, she wouldn't act to abate it.

Jolie hurried after, soon panting; *she* certainly wasn't changing! She lacked the muscles and imperative to stride boldly onward. But she was afraid of letting Orlene walk into Nox's den alone.

Another menace appeared. It looked like a mountain

44

goat, but it had three horns—and three legs. Two in front, one in the rear, in each case. Others of its breed followed; there was a flock of them. There was no way to avoid them on this narrowing mountain.

"I've had just about enough of this crap!" Orlene snapped. She stepped off the path, took hold of a struggling sapling, and wrenched it down. Its roots twisted out of the ground, spraying dirt. Orlene gave it another jerk and the remaining roots snapped. She had a serviceable staff.

She turned to face the tri-bucks. "Now charge me, dog-meat!" she cried. "You'll get roots up your nose!"

Jolie, breathless from running, was unable to speak. She was amazed at the strength Orlene had shown in ripping out the tree, and at the sheer aggression she was showing. But there were too many of the odd creatures to fight!

The first creature charged. True to her word, Orlene countered it with the rooty end of her pole. The front pair of horns rammed into the roots and shoved the pole back. Orlene, at the other end, was pushed down the path, cursing. The creature tossed its head, throwing the staff clear, and resumed its advance, the others close behind.

"The wand!" Jolie gasped.

Orlene's lip curled into a snarl, echoed in her throat, but she did bring out the wand. She evidently wanted to fight, but appreciated the odds against victory, so gave way grudgingly. That was, of course, the man's way.

The cloud appeared. In due course they were back inside the mountain, on the descending slope.

Jolie didn't want to look, but had to. Her fear was confirmed: Orlene was another stage more masculine than before, being larger, hairier, and now proportioned like a man. The exposed bra hung pointlessly; there was muscle rather than mammary flesh there now. Was her genital anatomy changing similarly? Jolie was sickly certain that it was.

"Well, come on, cutie, we're almost there," Orlene barked. She forged on down.

Cutie? Jolie liked this least of all. What was Nox trying to do here? What was the point in turning a nice young woman into a brutish man? Was it a joke? It certainly wasn't funny!

45

Near the bottom of the pit they encountered another hazard. It was cold here, the heat of the prior session gone as if it had never existed. Ice appeared—but it did not stay in place, it moved. Glaciers were developing in the angles between facets, flowing as if liquid, but they were solid. Ice was coming down behind them and wedging together ahead of them. They tried to climb over it, but it was slippery and numbingly cold.

"Damn it!" Orlene exclaimed, slamming a fist into it. A slight patina of cracks appeared at the point of contact, signaling the power of the blow, but that was all. "What is the point of this interference?"

She perceived the external threats but not the internal one! "Nox is playing with us," Jolie said. "Incarnations can be cruel."

"Well, I want to tackle her face to face!" Angrily, Orlene invoked the wand.

When the cloud cleared, they were almost at the peak. The bushes surrounded a small bare region. That was all.

Orlene was now completely male; no vestige of femininity remained, except for the tattered and incongruous clothing. She even had a light beard. But she—Jolie found that designation anomalous, but refused to concede the inner reality of the change—still refused to acknowledge her situation.

Orlene tramped on up to the top. "Well, at least there're no monsters this time," she muttered with rough satisfaction. "But where's Nox?"

Jolie followed. "She may not be here at all. This may merely be her diversion for us, a dream sequence that expends our energies but leads only to futility. The Incarnations can have unusual ways to—"

"Don't give me that noise! I came here to see the bitch, and I'm going to see her! Where is she?"

What an ass her companion had become! But it was pointless, and quite possibly dangerous, to dally here longer. They were in Nox's power, and if they affronted the Incarnation, things could get much worse.

"Nox won't see us unless she chooses to," Jolie said

carefully. "I think we should accept the fact that she's not interested, and get off this mountain before we annoy her."

"Listen, doll, whose side are you on?" Orlene demanded. "I didn't come here just to quit! Where the hell is Nox?"

"This isn't wise!" Jolie said pleadingly.

But Orlene turned with masculine arrogance and gestured at the sky with a fist. "A pox on Nox!" she bellowed. "Get your ass down here, Incarnation!"

Horrified, Jolie grabbed at Orlene's arm. "You mustn't!"

Orlene turned, trying to shake her off, but Jolie clung. She had to get them away from here before something terrible happened!

Then Orlene's eye fell directly on Jolie. Her mouth pursed appraisingly. "Say, I never realized what a piece you are. C'mere, girl." Her muscular arm came around to catch at Jolie's free arm.

Suddenly Jolie was being hauled in and lifted by a body much stronger than hers. "What—?"

"Gimme a kiss!" And their faces were together.

"Stop that!" Jolie cried, amazed and dismayed. She fought to get free, and managed to twist one arm away.

But Orlene didn't stop. She grabbed again, this time catching at Jolie's skirt. Jolie tried to spin away, but the hold on the skirt inhibited her motion, and she fell.

Orlene went down with her, pinning her to the ground. There was no longer any question about the hidden anatomy; it was male and functioning. Jolie realized that the situation was already beyond protest; she was unable to dissipate in ghostly fashion here, and she had either to fight free or fail to. Why hadn't she taken warning when she saw the changes occurring in her companion?

She could, of course, revert back to her drop of blood. But would Orlene come with her—and if so, would she revert back to her original form and nature? Jolie didn't dare risk it. She fought, but knew she was losing.

Then a cloud formed, not black but white, its vapors swirling internally. «What is this?»

"Nox!" Jolie cried, recognizing the strange, soundless way

47

the Incarnation spoke. She had never seen Nox before, but Parry had described it.

Orlene paused, looking up. "The bitch is here?"

«Come to me, man-thing.»

Orlene got up. She stared at the Incarnation. The mists formed into a phenomenal woman-shape, naked and beckoning, with writhing tresses of vapor and two compelling dark eyes.

Orlene walked into the shape, embracing it. Her loins thrust and thrust again, and the form wrapped itself about her. The face kissed her ardently. The merged forms floated from the ground, not noticing in their preoccupation.

Jolie's amazement was admixed with disgust. Orlene had tried to rape her, and now was having sex with Nox! How could she ever forgive either of them for such a thing? She had only tried to help a woman find her lost baby!

«There is much you do not understand,» Nox said to her directly.

"There is much I do not *care* to understand!" Jolie retorted, made bold by her shock.

«Here is part of it.»

Then Orlene emerged from the white cloud, her female form restored. She stood there, her mouth opening in an O of wonder, horror and dismay.

Simultaneously, Jolie felt herself change. Suddenly she lusted after the woman who stood before her, her passion so compelling that it admitted of no interference. She strode toward Orlene.

Only to be intercepted by the cloud. «Love me instead,» Nox said. Her female aspect was the most utterly arousing and inviting thing imaginable, making any human body hopelessly crude and clumsy.

Jolie stepped into it, her member stiffening. She plunged into Nox—and found herself floating, unable to achieve the culmination. The frustration was maddening.

Then the cloud dissipated, depositing her on the ground. «Remember!» Nox cautioned.

The two women stood looking at each other. Both were fully female again, each appalled.

"Oh, Jolie," Orlene said. "I don't know what—I cannot ask you to forgive me—I am so ashamed—"

Understanding was coming. "Nox made you into a man," Jolie said. "And you were overwhelmed by male passion."

"But you were my companion, my friend! How could I—"

Jolie would not have understood, except for the brief lesson Nox had given her. If Orlene, unwarned, had run rampant, what of Jolie, who had seen it all—and run rampant herself the moment the Incarnation afflicted her with the same complaint? She was the one who truly knew better, yet she had been helpless before her abrupt desire.

"It seems that men have passions that women do not," Jolie said. "I have indulged those passions in my own man without ever really understanding their nature—until now."

"But men do not—" Orlene faltered, unable to say the word.

"They have learned control. We did not have time. Like a fire which burns out of control when untended—"

«Remember,» Nox repeated, her semblance returning.

"How can I endure this shame?" Orlene exclaimed—and collapsed.

Jolie ran to her, finding her unconscious. For the moment, that was a relief. "Why did you play with us, Incarnation of Night?" she asked, no longer concerned about manners.

«You have much to learn.» That, it seemed, was the extent of the answer they were to have.

"She came to recover her baby, Gaw-Two," Jolie said. "Please, Incarnation, return him to her, now that you have humiliated us."

«I have her baby,» Nox agreed. «I lent her his semblance as he will be when grown.»

Orlene, stirring, reacted as if struck. Jolie, appreciating her horror, interceded. "A man—like his father."

"No!" Orlene cried in anguish. "Norton is not like that!"

"Like Gawain!" Jolie exclaimed, catching on. "His genetics were changed!"

«Like Gawain,» Nox agreed. «As he will be, grown naturally.»

49

"But he died of a genetic malady!"

«Which continues in his Afterlife.»

Orlene was horrified anew. "My baby—still diseased! Out of control!"

«Leave him to me,» Nox offered. «I can control him.»

That was yet another horror. Orlene fainted again.

"Not that way!" Jolie protested. "Give him back to her; we will cure him somehow!"

«Not readily. His soul has been tarnished; he can never exist free without extensive revamping.»

"She'll do whatever needs to be done!" Jolie cried.

«Then you must obtain items from each of the current major Incarnations,» Nox said. «Fail in any, and it is lost.»

"She won't fail in any!" Jolie promised.

«Here is the list. From Death, a blank soul, that the spoiled one may be reimplanted on a clean sheet, lacking the fatal flaw. From Time, a grain of sand from the Hourglass, that time may be reversed for the transfer. From Fate, a thread of life, to realign the one spoiled. From War, a seed, to generate the violence inherent in man as a healthy competitive spirit. From Nature, a tear, to restore animation in the newly implanted soul. From Evil, a curse, to put the fear of evil into the soul. From Good, a blessing, for this can be done only with that blessing.»

Jolie listened, aghast. That was an impossible list!

But she couldn't give up on Orlene! "And when she gets these things, then you will restore her baby to her?"

«Then will I restore him,» Nox pledged.

"She'll do it!" But Jolie, experienced in the ways of Incarnations, knew that it would be the miracle of the millennium if she succeeded. No wonder Nox had sought to discourage Orlene, by physical and emotional challenge; it would have been better if she had given up on her quest.

Then Nox faded out, and after her the mountain, too, and great dark mists swirled up to mask everything. When they cleared, the two were standing back at the fringe of Purgatory, just before the path diverged from Clotho's path. In fact, the path they had followed no longer existed.

CHAPTER THREE

Vita

JOLIE LITERALLY DRAGGED ORLENE BACK TO Purgatory proper, for the woman had reverted to inchoate soul form, intent only on drifting down to damnation. Her balance had been good, and she had fought to remain as a ghost; now her balance had shifted bad, and she no longer fought. But Jolie refused to let her go—not until she had consulted with Gaea.

Once firmly in conventional Purgatory, Jolie was able to make the jump directly to the Treehouse. She laid the limp soul on the bed—but the moment she let go, it began to sink through the bed, starting its journey toward Hell. She had to grab it again and maintain her hold.

How could this have happened? Souls weren't supposed to change their balance in the Afterlife! Not suddenly, like this! They could have their evil ground out slowly in Hell, or leached out gently in Heaven, but that took centuries. It seemed that Nox had done more than merely tease the woman!

Soon Gaea returned. "You seem to have a problem," she remarked, noting the flaccid soul.

"Nox teased us cruelly," Jolie explained. "She caused my companion to become a man, who was then overcome by his passion, and he tried to ravish me. For a moment she changed me, too, and I too was overcome. I have been attacked before, and have sinned before; I was able to endure it. But my companion—"

"It isn't like Nox to tease without reason," Gaea said. "She seldom concerns herself with our activities, and seems to have little interest in them. There may be more here than we understand."

"She did agree to help the baby—but gave an impossible list of requirements. We would have to get something from each of the Incarnations."

"It is also unlike Nox to bargain in such fashion. This is strange indeed."

"Now this soul is weighted down with evil, and I dare not let go. I feel responsible, for I was with her, encouraging her to visit Nox, thus bringing this humiliation upon us both. I don't want to let her go to Hell on such basis, after she fought so hard to avoid Heaven so that she could help her baby."

Gaea hesitated a moment. If she did not know the identity of Jolie's friend, whom Jolie had carefully avoided naming, she surely suspected. She was being circumspect in her comments, speaking generally rather than specifically. "Do you wish help in this matter?"

Here was the crux. Gaea could not help without discovering for certain that it was her daughter at issue. How could Jolie confirm that at this stage? Not only would it bring personal grief to the Incarnation, it would represent a conflict of interest.

"Forgive me, Gaea. I think I do need help, but I prefer not to ask for yours. You have been generous in giving me leeway here, and I do not want to inflict the consequences of my error on you." Which was true, as far as it went.

"Perhaps another Incarnation?"

"Have I the right to ask?" What she meant was that

though Gaea would help because of Jolie's closeness to her, other Incarnations might be more cynical. Jolie knew them all, except God, and they all accepted her, but this was a matter of courtesy rather than respect. They were apt to consider her request seriously only if Gaea asked them to—and Jolie didn't want to ask for that, either. What a predicament she had gotten into, unawares!

"My mortal cousin Luna is an understanding person," Gaea said. "She might be able to advise you."

Jolie hadn't thought of that. Luna was the one, of all mortals, most in touch with the affairs of the Incarnations. She was related to several of them in one way or another, and kept company with Thanatos. She was a Senator in the mortal realm, and so had considerable power in both the mortal and immortal spheres. She would be ideal for the kind of advice Jolie needed.

"Yes," Jolie said gratefully. "I will ask her."

Luna lived at an estate guarded by a fence of iron spikes and two hungry griffins. "Hello, Griffith!" Jolie called to the red male. "Hello, Grissel!" to the female. The two reared up on their hind feet and struck at the air in salute; they remembered her. Because she was a ghost, they could not have hurt her anyway, but she never made a point of that.

She floated through the door, dragging Orlene's soul. "It's me, Muir!" she called, for the guardian within could touch her. Muir was a moon moth, a ferocious flying spirit Luna's magician father had tamed for her before his death. Like some demons, he could manifest physically when he chose to, but he was mainly a protection against supernatural threats.

Muir recognized Jolie and folded his wings. They formed a black cloak around his insectoid torso, hiding his formidable talons. Woe betide the one he attacked! He remained hovering in the air despite closing his wings, because he was not subject to mortal gravity any more than Jolie was.

"Is Luna available?" Jolie asked.

Muir flickered. That meant he had darted to find Luna and returned here so swiftly that the motion was barely evident. He nodded his head briefly forward, his antenna flexing: she was available.

Then Luna entered the room. She was a beautiful woman of about forty, with brown hair. Jolie had wondered before how the two almost-sisters, Luna and Orb, could be so similar in other respects but differ in this one—and suddenly, for the first time, she realized that Luna had dyed her hair, or magically changed its color. All the women of her family had honey hair of one shade or another, similar to Jolie's own, through three generations; Luna must have, too, as a child. Why had she changed it?

"Why Jolie," Luna said. "With a lost soul. You must have come to see Zane." That was the private name she called Thanatos.

"I have a problem," Jolie said. "I need advice, and I think help."

"And not from Orb?" Luna inquired, lifting an eyebrow. Her eyes were gray, like mist over a placid lake; these at least were natural.

"May I speak in confidence?"

Now Luna realized that this was no casual matter. "You know I cannot commit to that in any matter that affects my objective. Does this?"

Her objective was to thwart the efforts of Satan to take over either the mortal or immortal realms, and it was generally known that there was a major crisis coming in perhaps four years, where her action would be critical. Satan had been trying desperately to nullify that situation before it occurred, and all the Incarnations had battled him to preserve it. Jolie, as the consort of Satan, therefore had to be treated cautiously; she understood that. Her relations with Luna and the Incarnations were positive, but she was technically an agent of the enemy. Thus it was necessary that Luna qualify any offer to help; she wouldn't help Satan win against God.

"I don't think it does," Jolie said. "Not directly. But if nothing is done, it could bring mischief to both sides."

"Will you trust my discretion, if you tell me without my prior commitment to confidence?"

"Yes." For Luna cared about Gaea as much as any mortal could, having been raised with her in Ireland before the one became the companion of an Incarnation and the other became an Incarnation herself.

"Then tell me as much as you need to, as quickly as you can." This was Luna's first indication that she had pressing other business, but of course she did.

"I watched over Orb's daughter Orlene," Jolie said. "She was doing well, raised by an adoptive mortal family. She married a ghost and had a child by her lover, in the ghost's name; this is a legitimate device among mortals today, though technically sinful."

"Of course," Luna agreed. "I remember that Orb had a child but could not marry the father; I am glad to learn that that child did well."

"Not well enough," Jolie said, plunging on. "During my inattention her baby was afflicted with a fatal malady. After he died, she suicided, determined to join him. But she was good and bound for Heaven, while he was in balance and went to Purgatory, where Nox took him. I helped Orlene's spirit go to seek Nox, but Nox turned her into a man who tried to rape me and then had relations with Nox herself. Now Orlene is burdened with evil and will not struggle to stay out of Hell. I cannot tell Gaea, and dare not let the soul go lest it be lost. I am convinced that Orlene is not evil but was overwhelmed by the mischief of the Incarnation of Night. I need some way to keep her here, as a ghost, until she realizes this and will resume her quest for her baby. Then she may be all right, and I can tell Gaea without bringing her more grief than is warranted."

Luna nodded. She possessed the lawmaker's ability to grasp complex matters quickly. "This is not Satan's doing?"

"It is not his doing. It was his bidding that sent me to Orlene when she was a child. He—when he and I were married, as mortals, we had no child, and—" Then Jolie was crying, caught off guard by the tragedy. Orlene had been much like a daughter to her, as she watched her in the way that Gaea would not. She cursed herself again for relaxing at what turned out to be a critical time.

55

"It occurs to me that our interests may coincide," Luna said gently. "I am organizing for the issue to come, what may be the final showdown between Good and Evil of this sequence. I have need of a soul to animate a mortal who is in a similar state to Orlene's, for different but sufficient reason. A soul that animates a mortal host cannot descend to Hell until it leaves that host. Would Orlene be willing to animate that host until the host recovers?"

"No. It is my will that holds her here, not hers."

"Then would you be willing to keep Orlene in that host, and animate the host yourself, until you can persuade Orlene to do it? This action would have a devious but significant effect in the war between Good and Evil, so you would be serving Good."

"But I am Satan's consort!" Jolie protested.

"Even Satan knows the meaning of honor—and so do you. Satan cannot openly support your action in preventing that soul from descending to him, but the forces of Good have no such conflict of interest. Can you serve Good to this extent, in order to buy time for Orlene to recover her initiative?"

Jolie saw how cleverly this offer was designed. Satan indeed did not want Orlene in Hell! He wanted her in as good a situation as possible before Gaea learned of it. So, just as Gaea would not openly consummate her marriage to Satan, Satan would not openly support Good. But his interest in this particular matter was the same as Gaea's—and Jolie's.

"Yes, I can do this," Jolie agreed.

"It will not be easy," Luna warned. "I think it best not to tell you the manner this relates to my interest, but you will be charged with serving that interest as it becomes apparent to you, until you leave that host."

"I agree to this," Jolie said.

"And I see no need to acquaint Gaea with what you have told me, until there is a better resolution," Luna said. "Now I must go, but Zane will be along presently, and he will take you to the girl."

"I'll have to tell Gaea where I'm going."

"No need; she knows." Luna left.

Jolie stood, bemused. How could Gaea know? Then she realized that Gaea's suggestion had not been offhand, about seeing Luna. She must have cleared it first, or at least have known that Luna had such a need. The Incarnations had levels of communications that others hardly fathomed, and Luna was in certain respects like an Incarnation.

She remembered, too, the first time she had animated Gaea's physical body and gone to make love to Satan. It had been nominally Parry and Jolie, as it had been so long ago in life, and as such, wonderful. But it was also the secret, forbidden consummation of Satan and Gaea, the Incarnations of Evil and Nature. There had been only one direct evidence of that which an outsider could have recognized: when Satan had asked Jolie to thank the one whose body she had borrowed, and Gaea had said in her own voice, "She knows."

Luna had been similarly certain. But she had also agreed to keep Jolie's information private, for now. So Gaea knew that Jolie's business was serious and in good hands, and that was enough.

She waited, hanging on to the limp soul, and in an hour there was a sound outside. She looked out, and there was Mortis, the beautiful, pale death-horse, trotting down through the air toward the yard. The two griffins set up a squawking of welcome. Mortis landed, the hooded figure dismounted, and the animals sniffed noses.

Thanatos strode to the house. Jolie stepped through the closed door to meet him. She was, of course, used to his skull visage; he was actually a living man, become the Incarnation of Death when he killed his predecessor, and his appearance was only his costume. "Luna said—"

"Yes. Are you ready?"

"Yes." There was that hidden communication again!

"It is not far from here. Ride with me."

Jolie followed as he returned to Mortis. The horse became a pale car, somehow knowing his master's desire unspoken. His master? Mortis had outlasted several Officeholders! Jolie tried to enter the car but could not pass through the substance; Thanatos had to open the door for her, in seeming gallantry

57

which was not mock. The associates of the Incarnations had special qualities too; Jolie had not realized that Mortis was ghost-proof, but it did not surprise her.

"I understand Nox is involved," Thanatos remarked as the car moved smoothly out of the grounds, self-guided.

"She made this person into a man and caused him to attempt rape," Jolie replied. "Now her evil overbalances her good and she is sinking, but I don't think it's fair."

"Her balance is positive, not negative," Thanatos said. "She sinks only because she believes she is evil, but no guilt should attach for a burden imposed by another party. Is this not the one for whom you interceded so recently?"

"Yes, she is. I learned that the Incarnation of Night had the soul of her baby, so I guided her there—and Nox played a cruel game before agreeing to help. Even then, she set horrendous conditions."

"That is not like her. She has been indifferent to mortal and immortal affairs throughout my tenure. What conditions did she set?"

"An item from each of the active Incarnations, to facilitate correction of the malady of the baby's soul."

"What item from me?"

"A blank soul."

There was a pause. Then the skull turned toward her. "If that is typical, the chances of completing that list are minimal."

"But better that Orlene try, than that she give up hope," Jolie said, hoping it was true.

"Perhaps it is a deliberate diversion, intended to be an endless quest for her."

"But why would Nox do that? She could have denied the interview entirely if she didn't want to give up the baby!"

"The Incarnation of Night is excellent at keeping secrets."

He said no more, and Jolie didn't dare pursue it. She had mentioned the item listed for him, and that was as far as she could go on her own; Orlene would have to pursue it herself, when she was able. Jolie's task was to enable Orlene to resume her quest; then the decision would be Orlene's.

The vehicle halted. They were in a bad section of the city

of Kilvarough, where rundown tenements were scheduled for demolition in favor of modern megabuildings. Thanatos led her to a grimy chamber where a teenage girl lay sprawled asleep on a flimsy cot. "This is Vita," he said. "She is a harlot being addicted to Spelled H. Her individual volition is almost gone; she responds merely to the voice of authority supported by force."

Jolie was aghast. "Luna has need of such a one?"

The grinning bare teeth seemed to grin further. "There is a rationale. We did not feel free to ask any other to undertake this task, for there is much discomfort in it, and you may avoid it also."

"No, I said I would do it, and I will," Jolie said. "But I can see that I won't enjoy it."

"True. I leave you, then, to your devices." He turned and walked back the way they had come, in a moment fading from view. Jolie knew that he had not truly disappeared; rather, he was not visible or memorable to anyone who did not have reason to see him, and her reason had passed. As a ghost she could perceive him far more readily than living mortals could, but even so, it was only because he permitted it.

She walked to the sleeping girl, dragging Orlene's soul. Prostitution and Spelled H—a combination for disaster! She would have to do something about that immediately!

"Very well, Orlene," she said. "I will carry it at first, but it is for you I am doing this." She embraced the soul and stepped into the body.

She felt the effect of the drug immediately. The girl was not in a natural sleep, but in a stupor. Jolie was not conversant with the cycle of Spelled H, for the drug had appeared centuries after her time, but she understood that its effects varied with the dosage and the time following the dose. Once a person was habituated to it, she depended on it to be functional; there was a certain euphoria followed by depression, which could be abated by another dose. Properly managed, it could keep a person in the pleasant in-between state during the waking hours. Too much made the addict hyper; not enough brought an agony that was not merely of the body. Gaea had cured several musicians who had been addicts, but short of direct intercession by the Incarnation of Nature, few broke free. This would require iron willpower!

Orlene settled into the host and found the mood compatible: hellbound. Jolie, freed of the need to hold on to Orlene constantly, got to work on Vita.

"Up, girl," Jolie said, using the host's sodden lips. "We're going to work off this high, or low, as the case may be." She forced the limbs to move and the flaccid stomach muscles to contract.

The host groaned and sat up. Jolie felt the spinning of the senses and the pounding at the temples. This was definitely a low! But she pressed on, making the host rise unsteadily to her feet and stagger to the grubby toilet nook. She ran water and splashed it on the face. Vita had vomited recently, by the taste of it, and there were bruises on her body: someone had been hitting her.

Jolie decided to go the whole route. She stripped off the dirty clothing, then stepped into the shower cubicle. Cold water blasted down, shocking her body. She gritted her teeth and washed both body and hair as thoroughly as possible without heat. The discomfort was more important than the cleanliness, at the moment.

When she couldn't stand it anymore, she got out. The water cut off automatically. Shivering, she went to stand before the pane of glass that served as a full-length mirror.

This host was nubile, with hips and breasts that would have been on the way to provocative fullness had bad eating and bad living not interfered. The hair, too, could have been lustrous, but seemed to have been hacked off at shoulder level and otherwise mistreated. Bruises showed on the arms and shoulders. By the feel of it, the men this prostitute served had been urgent and rough and had not necessarily confined their ardors to the genital region. There were no scars or punctures on arms or legs, but of course that proved nothing; there were oral, nasal and optic variants of the drug.

The lethargy of incipient withdrawal remained. Jolie spread the bedsheet on the floor and tried exercises: sit-ups, leg lifts, curls and stretches. The body protested, way out of shape for this, but again, the point wasn't health but effort. Could exercise burn off the traces of the drug? She was going to try it.

Actually, this was helping Jolie, too, for she was not used to living flesh. She had been seventeen when she died, and though that was considerably older then than it was today, she had been long out of body. Gaea lent her body for special occasions involving their common interest, but the body of an Incarnation was in stasis and invulnerable, not truly mortal. Vita's body was all too evidently mortal, with the discomforts and weaknesses of mortality. Jolie had to accustom herself again to keeping the body balanced when she stood, so that it would not fall over, and to the needs of ongoing processes.

That thought clarified one problem. She walked back to the toilet and used it. Ghosts had no natural functions, but mortals had to be constantly aware of input and outgo, or their systems got into trouble.

Then she went to the food-storage section to find something to eat. That was a waste of time; there was nothing. Evidently this girl ate outside.

Jolie checked next for money. There was none of that, either. Then she tested the door. Sure enough, it was locked, and she had no key or admittance card. She was a prisoner.

She wished she had paid more attention to the nature of mortal life in the slum sections. As it was, she had little notion how to proceed. How had this host come to such an involuntary situation?

Jolie tried to contact Vita, but the girl's mind was satisfied to let someone else do it. The drug had dulled her awareness, but that was only part of the story; Vita had little interest in facing reality. Perhaps that was just as well, for now, because had she objected to Jolie's control, it would have done her no good. The soul in charge of a host had command and could not be involuntarily displaced. Had Vita not been in a stupor, Jolie could not have taken over.

She checked next on Orlene. The case was similar there. Jolie remained on her own; if she didn't do something, neither of the others would.

Still, there might be something to be gained here. *Orlene, this is Vita, your host,* she said internally, hauling the spirit of the girl up. *Vita, this is Orlene, who will be animating your body for a while. She lost her baby son, and died of grief, and suffered again after death. She can tell you what it is like.*

Who cares? Vita demanded, retreating.

Why don't you just let me sink to Hell, where I belong? Orlene asked.

What do you know about Hell? Vita retorted. *It has no fear for me, after what I've seen on Earth.*

You haven't experienced what I have, Orlene said.

Yeah? Well, I don't want to know about it!

That ended the dialogue. Jolie shrugged her host's shoulders. At least it was a beginning.

She had two ways to ascertain Vita's situation. One was to establish enough of a rapport with the mind of the host to learn it from her. The other was to pick it up from ongoing experience. The latter seemed to be the choice.

She returned to the main chamber and resumed her exercising. This time she ran in place, using the large muscles of her legs to give her heart and respiration a workout. It might be wishful thinking, but she thought the body's tone was improving and the brain becoming more functional.

There was a sound at the door. Then it burst open. A neatly dressed thug stood there, staring at her with brute disapproval. "What the hell you doing, running around baretit?" he demanded.

Oops! Jolie had forgotten to don clothing after her shower, that being another detail that ghosts did not have to worry about. As a ghost she could assume any form, clothed or unclothed, that she desired, merely by concentrating on it. Once she had learned how to do that, she had done it so routinely that she was always garbed appropriately. But the physical host needed artificial garbing.

The man was staring at her exposed torso, which was an embarrassment. His face showed disgust, which was a further embarrassment. Who was he—her captor?

Now the man strode forward, one hammy hand reaching

out to grab her shoulder. "Answer me, brat! What you think you're doing? I didn't tell you to dance, I told you to sleep it off."

"Sleep what off?" Jolie asked, twisting away.

Immediately the hand swung up and clipped her on the side of the head, stingingly. "Don't sass me, blackass!"

Jolie was stunned both by the blow and the words. What had she done to deserve the first, even assuming this man had authority over her? What was the meaning of the name he had called her?

"Now get dressed good," the man said gruffly. "Got a special john tonight, likes 'em young and lean and hurting, so you can scream and cry all you want, but no claws and no kicking. You get a sniff of H before so you can act lively, and more after if you make him happy. But first you eat; got to get more meat in your dugs so you can work up to the big time." He strode to the shallow closet and checked the dresses there. "This one—make you look as young as you are. And a ponytail, and not much makeup. Look like some jerk's niece. *My* niece, maybe. But don't never forget you're just a whore. Come on, get it grinding." He shoved the dress at her.

At last it was coming clear. This was what was called a pimp—a man who procured women for deviant customers. Vita was young, and it seemed there was an illicit market for sex with underage girls. The pimp was serving in lieu of a parent—a bad one, to be sure, but perhaps doing better for her than she would do alone on the street.

The first thing Jolie had to do was get Vita out of this trap. But she realized that this would not necessarily be easy to do. With no information and no money, and under constant lock or guard, her options were quite limited. So she would have to play along for the time being, watching her opportunity to make her break.

She dressed. The man actually did her hair, his fingers surprisingly skilled. He did know his business, however low that business might be. He wanted her to look childlike and innocent for this role, so that the client would be satisfied and pay well and return again on other days. It was all quite close

63

to the reality, except for the significant detail of the sexual element.

She checked herself in the mirror. Now she realized that Vita was of mixed blood, her skin light brown rather than white. That explained one remark. To have any evident black heritage was to be defined as all-black, logic to the contrary notwithstanding. The Negroid element was slight and showed not at all in the hair, which was brown and straight, or in the facial features; makeup could have eliminated it entirely. But to the pimp she was "blackass"—as if it were literally true, and as if there would have been any fault if so.

"Looking good," the pimp conceded grudgingly. "Now you get your sniff, and I'll take you to meet him at a classy joint. Eat what you can; you won't get more till morning."

He brought out a small package of something. Jolie realized it was the Spelled H—the magically enhanced variant of an ancient addictive drug, far more potent than the original. She couldn't afford to take that!

She sought to turn her face away as the pimp brought the package up, but suddenly Vita's soul stepped in, seized control, and sniffed deeply. Jolie wrested control back immediately, but it was too late; the drug was in the host's system. Already the exhilaration of it was spreading out from her nose, encompassing her brain, and giving her entire body a tingle of joy.

This is disaster! Jolie thought at Vita. *You can't afford this stuff! It will kill you!*

But the girl, having gotten her fix, was satisfied. She retreated into near oblivion.

Jolie intended to be on guard in the future. The addiction was not yet complete; she should be able to fight it off despite this setback. If she got the girl out of this situation, there might be no further opportunity to take the drug. Perhaps this slip was just as well; it had shown Jolie how canny the seemingly passive girl could be, pouncing during Jolie's momentary inattention. She would be on guard against that henceforth. Also, it would have made the pimp suspicious if she had refused the fix.

"Now we go," the pimp said. "Remember, any trouble, no more H. That goes double for when you're alone with him."

The system was clear enough. The drug kept the girls obedient, and the pimp supervised every aspect of the business so that there were no errors. It was a living, of a sort.

They walked out of the room and down the narrow hall. Jolie could have run for it, but several things restrained her. She did not know her way around this neighborhood, so would not be able to hide quickly. The pimp was robust, and could probably outrun her, and certainly could subdue her when he caught her. Others here were more likely to help him than her. And if she did win free, what would she do alone on the street? Until she learned where Vita's home was, and got money to travel there, she would be entirely on her own resources, and they were forbiddingly meager. So she still had to play along; her time was not yet.

There was a limousine waiting. It seemed the pimp lived in style, even if his girls didn't. They got in and rode to what was indeed a "classy joint"—a quality restaurant. They were guided to a table already occupied by a fat, extremely well-dressed man of middle age.

"This is my niece, Vita," the pimp said, nudging Jolie, who smiled obligingly. "You show her the sights, call and I'll pick her up, okay?"

The man nodded, his porcine eyes taking in the young body. This was what he had ordered, certainly!

The pimp helped Jolie take the opposite seat. Helped? His grip on her elbow was warningly firm. She would behave, or suffer more than H deprivation! Then he left the restaurant, but she noticed that the limo didn't drive away. He was still watching, making sure that she was committed. Later, when her addiction to H was complete, he would be able to relax, but this was still the training stage.

The meal was excellent, and she was famished. The sniff of H had restored her appetite and evidently made her sparkle, physically. The client seemed happy to have her eat her fill; it was part of the avuncular role he relished. He talked to her, telling her how he had always wanted a girl of his own like her. Jolie realized with a shock that he wasn't actually a bad man, but rather a man with an illicit hunger for young flesh that he could indulge only in this manner. Some slight and perhaps reasonable liberalization of the laws would place him within the normal spectrum.

Ha! Vita thought from the depths. *He's a closet pederast, wants a boy but doesn't have the nerve to go for it, so goes for young girls instead.*

Jolie realized with another shock that Vita could be right. She would have to make her break before they got to the man's hotel.

They completed the meal. Her belly was full; she had eaten too well, after too long a hiatus. "I better go wee-wee," she said girlishly.

"In my suite," the client said. "I'll watch."

Now Orlene took note. *What is this?* she asked, horrified out of her retreat.

They get a big thrill out of watching you do it, Vita replied. *Sometimes they take the stuff and smear it on you. Anal fixation, it's called, or something. All I know is, it stinks, but the H fixes it so you don't care.*

And I thought rape was perverted! Orlene thought with revulsion.

Vita laughed. *Man can't rape a girl, when she needs the money. Better to get it done fast, before he works up to weird ideas—but not so fast he feels cheated.*

But that makes it seem as if men are mere sex machines! Orlene protested.

So what else is new?

Jolie realized that this was working out well, in its strange way. Both Orlene and Vita were benefiting from their limited dialogue, being drawn out of their private miseries. But there was a long way to go before either would be ready to resume normal functioning.

They left the restaurant. The client spoke to the doorman, who whistled down a taxi carpet.

Jolie knew that once she got on that carpet there would be no escaping, for it would deliver them directly to the client's suite, which would be forty or more stories high in a megabuilding. She really did need to use the toilet, but not with him watching or perhaps participating! So, bloated or not, she had to make her break now.

The taxi carpet sailed down and hovered at knee height. It was shaped: the rear of it curled up to form a backrest, while the front descended in an S curve to accommodate the legs. Magic would hold them firmly in place while it was in motion, as required by safety regulations. There was no danger of falling off—and no chance to jump off, no matter how low it might fly. The client sat on it, then heaved his legs around and up to the front. His weight was such that even the sturdy levitation spell gave way slightly and the carpet dropped closer to the curb.

The doorman put out a hand to help Jolie board. Instead she ducked under his arm and ran down the sidewalk. She didn't care where she was going, as long as it was away.

"Hey!" the client cried. "Stop my niece!"

The doorman, ever obliging, lurched after her. Jolie dodged around an approaching couple and ran into the street. Tires squealed as a limousine braked to avoid her.

No—that was the pimp's limo! He had anticipated this effort and was intercepting her. She was in trouble now!

I could've told you that, ninny! Vita thought. *You've got to go along to get along. They know all the angles.*

Now she was effectively boxed, the limo on one side, the doorman on the other, and the carpet behind. *If you're so smart, how would you escape?* Jolie demanded, not expecting an answer.

But the girl surprised her. Apparently the urge to show her superiority in this respect overrode her desire not to aggravate the pimp, whose wrath would surely be fearsome. *I would fool them by scrambling under the carpet, then run into the restaurant and out the back.*

Jolie couldn't improve on that! She feinted to the front, and both limo and doorman lurched that way to cut her off, while the carpet advanced to close up the gap, hovering at waist height. She reversed course and plunged toward the carpet. She dived down below it, scrambling on hands and knees in the gutter. That was good for neither her pretty dress nor her knees, but excellent for surprise.

67

She regained her feet beyond it and bolted for the restaurant door, which was now unmanned. She shoved in and charged along the carpeted entry hall. The maître d' called to her, but she ran right on, seeking the back.

She found the passage the waiters used, and leaped through it. Then she found the door that accessed the kitchen and shoved through that. Now she was amidst the tables and ovens where the food was being prepared.

"Get out of here, gamin!" a cook cried. "This is a restricted area!"

She saw a door labeled EXIT and ran for that. She pushed through and found herself out in the back alley, surrounded by old-fashioned garbage cans and a Dumpster. *Where next?* she thought, knowing that the pursuit would soon appear.

Hide, Vita advised. *The Dumpster, maybe.*

But those get picked up regularly and taken to compactors and furnaces! Orlene protested.

That's why nobody'll think to look there, dummy!

Jolie accepted the logic. She hadn't much choice. She was panting, and felt ready to burst, and was afraid she could not run much farther and would soon be caught if she tried. At least she could rest in the Dumpster.

She climbed up its irregular exterior, heaved herself over the top and dropped inside. She landed on a pile of fresh garbage; the thing was half full. It seemed to be mostly large lettuce leaves and fruit rinds, but there was a good deal of semi-liquid meal leavings collected in the bottom.

But they might look, Vita warned. *Better cover up.*

Jolie gritted her teeth, knowing that this was more good advice. She squatted in a low spot and hauled in a pile of watermelon rinds to cover her. She hated to do it to her dress, but she was committed now.

She heard voices outside, muffled by the walls of the Dumpster and the garbage around her. That would be her pursuers, searching out her route. In a moment someone poked his head over the rim of the Dumpster. "Just garbage in here! What a smell!" he called, and moved away.

The sounds died. *Don't get out yet!* Vita warned. *They'll hang around awhile, waiting to see if we come out when we think they're gone.*

You're very canny, Jolie remarked.

I learned a lot in a hurry, after I ran away from home.

You ran away? Why? Here was key information!

None of your business. Vita retreated.

So much for that. Jolie was animating the body, but it would take her a lot more time than she could afford to access the memories on her own. She depended on the host's cooperation, and this had been invaluable as far as it went, but it was limited.

But now, waiting, she became aware again of her need to relieve herself, after the big meal. She didn't see how she could remain quietly here for any length of time without taking care of this detail.

Do it here, Orlene suggested. *We can't get any dirtier.*

Apt notion! Jolie shifted that minimum necessary to get her panties down, and proceeded to add to the garbage. Certainly the smell would not betray her here!

When about half an hour had passed without further commotion outside, she burrowed cautiously out of her noxious cell and hoisted herself up to peek over the rim. The alley seemed to be clear.

She climbed out and tried to clean herself off, but it was hopeless; the fluids of the garbage had soaked through almost every part of her dress, and solids adhered here and there. She would be an obvious figure wherever she went!

Maybe I should take off my dress, she thought.

And become a spectacle for every juvenile hood in the area, Vita retorted with a certain grim relish.

Yet again, the voice of street experience! *But where can we go?* Jolie asked.

Why didn't you think of that before you skipped out on that date? I could've handled the fat man.

"Listen!" Jolie said aloud. "That man wanted illicit sex with a child!"

What else! That's how I pay my way. Maybe it's not the best life, but it's better than what I had before.

69

"What did you have before?"

This time Vita answered. *Only a little incest.*

"Only a little—!"

Before I bugged out.

"But surely your mother—"

Didn't want to know.

And I thought rape was bad! Orlene echoed.

It was rape all right! Vita thought. *I fought him, but I couldn't stop him without making a commotion Mom would hear, so in the end I had to grin and bear it. I had asked for it, after all.*

"I don't believe that!"

You don't? Genuine surprise. *Want me to show you how it was?*

They were standing outside the Dumpster, soaked in garbage. This was hardly the time for a prolonged internal dialogue! But Jolie realized that the girl was being much more forthcoming now, and might not soon again be so. "Yes, show me." She sat down by the Dumpster; this was as good a place as any, now that the chase was over.

Vita opened up the memory. Vita was propped on her bed in a pleasant room, watching a holo show. She was wearing a loose light shift that fell somewhat provocatively across her torso. A man entered: her stepfather. *No—my natural father,* Vita corrected Jolie's assumption.

Your genetic father! Orlene thought, shocked again.

He just had a fight with Mom and was mad. Wish I'd known! He saw up my nightie—I never thought—I mean, we used to sort of wrestle, and sometimes his hands—I thought it was just, you know, accidental feels, but he was getting hot for me and I shouldn't've led him on. So when it went too far—

Suddenly the man was on her, pinning her to the bed, one hand yanking open the top of her shift so that it tore. His other hand opened his own clothing.

Amazed, she struggled. *I thought it was some kind of game. I mean, we'd tussled before, and he always let me win, 'specially when he got his hand on my ass. But this time he really held me down and—*

There was no art, no mercy. The man spread his body on hers, driving in between her kicking legs. It was over in a moment, and he got off and lurched out, closing up his clothing. There had been no speech at all.

I didn't know what he'd done, at first, Vita thought. *It was so sudden, mostly I felt my breath being squeezed out, I thought it was just his weight, pinning me, and something accidental jamming into me, like an elbow, only it wasn't. Maybe I didn't want to know! I could've screamed, and I guess I did know, because I knew if I screamed, he'd be dumped in jail and Mom'd never forgive me. So I asked for it, really, by letting him feel me before, and see up my—by not trying to scream—* Now the soul was crying.

"That was rape," Jolie said firmly. "Child sexual abuse and rape."

But I must've lured him on, spreading my legs like that! I didn't know that it's like a red flag to a bull, a man goes crazy, he can't help it—

It was rape! Orlene repeated. *His guilt, not yours!* Then, as an afterthought: *Bulls are color-blind.*

"I agree!" Jolie said. "A man can be overcome by lust— but not when he has had time to learn control, not when he's your father! Why did he come to your room at all? He had it in mind before he ever saw you."

Anyway, after that I packed up my stuff and got out of there. I knew I'd done wrong. I almost starved, before the pimp picked me up, and since I was already worthless, what did it matter, you know? So he took care of me, and I did what he said, and I guess I didn't want to live much. But the II made me feel better, and pretty soon the rest didn't matter.

"We'll have to get you help," Jolie said. "You can't just go home. But you can't stay on the street, either."

That's why I stayed where I was. Nowhere to go.

Jolie pondered alternatives. She could walk the girl to Luna's estate, which wasn't a great distance away. But Luna had sent her here, which meant that Luna knew Vita's situation. She could have fetched the girl herself, if that was the solution. Probably Luna had concluded that Vita needed to be treated from the inside, so that she could come to terms with her situation and return home voluntarily.

Home—to a father who had raped her? Definitely not that! So it was still Jolie's problem, hardly closer to solution

71

than before. Homeless, garbage-laden, without money or other resources—what was she to do with this host now?

Well, there were homes for runaways. One of them should do as a temporary measure. All she had to do was locate one, or find someone who knew the address of the closest one.

She started walking. But now the back alley was becoming inhabited, as the evening approached. "Hey—get a smell of that!" a juvenile boy exclaimed.

In a moment there was a circle of boys: too young to work, old enough to have bad ideas. They soon tired of exclaiming and making gestures of nose-holding, and worked up to more serious notions. "Open a hydrant! Hose her off! Strip her naked! Then—"

"Look, I'm trying to find a runaway house," Jolie said, and realized her mistake even as she spoke.

"So nobody knows where she is!" a boy cried happily. "Haul her to the water, then into our hideout. We'll have a hot time tonight!"

We're in for it now! Vita remarked. *You and your big reform ideas. This is the real world!* Then, as an afterthought: *But maybe they've got a little H! For that I'll take them all on!*

You'll do nothing of the kind! Jolie thought. But she was very much afraid that the alternative would be gang rape, which did not seem like much of an improvement. This was indeed the real world!

But as they closed on her, a police carpet floated down. Immediately one boy leaped for her, a knife showing in his fist. "Say it's nothing!" he whispered, holding the knife in such a way that the police could not see it, but ready for stabbing.

Jolie thought fast. "I'll do better than that!" she said. She scraped some garbage from her dress and threw it upward toward the carpet. "Take that, flatfoot!" It had been decades since police had sported flat feet, if ever, but the name clung.

What are you doing? Orlene asked, appalled.

I'm getting us arrested!

The garbage, inadequately thrown, missed, but the surrounding boys laughed. Jolie realized that she needed something more solid. Quickly she reached under her dress and hauled down her sodden panties, while the boys gawked appreciatively. She wadded these into a ball and hurled it at the carpet. "And that, jerks!"

But they'll lock us up! Vita protested. Streetwise, she knew better than to taunt police!

Yes—away from your father—and your pimp!

This time her aim was good. The ball smacked into the uniform of the leading cop. The boys almost fell down laughing.

"That does it!" the cop said. "You're coming with us, gamin!" The carpet dropped all the way to the pavement, while the boys scattered.

But won't they send us back home?

Not if we tell our story first.

"Phew!" the cop exclaimed, jumping off. "What you been in—a garbage dump?"

"Right," Jolie said. This was exactly what she wanted: to be arrested. When the police heard Vita's story, they would put her in a runaway house or the equivalent. She had taken a roundabout route, but she had gotten Vita out of a bad situation and into a better one, with the girl's consent.

CHAPTER FOUR

Judge

IN THE MORNING, CLEAN AND IN CLOTHING provided by the detention center, they were shown into a pleasant office. Vita, suffering H withdrawal, refused to participate, and Orlene, appalled at what she had learned, had retreated to passivity again. Thus it was up to Jolie to handle this interview.

A man of middle age sat in an easy chair. He stood as they entered. "Please make yourself comfortable," he said, indicating another chair. "This is a preliminary interview, informal, and if you wish, off the record. I merely wish to learn something about you."

Jolie found herself disarmed by his manner; he hardly resembled a callous bureaucrat! She sat, and the man sat again. He had a receding hairline which he did not bother to mask, and an expanding waistline, yet he seemed healthy overall. His eyes were gray-brown, as if the pigment had smeared. There were smile lines framing both eyes and mouth, but also frown lines.

"Now, when we ran the routine identification check on you, we discovered that you are a local resident—but there is no lost-person report on you. Indeed, there is a qualifier: your identification remains invalid unless you corroborate it. We are legally bound not to report you, without your permission. This is unusual, to say the least."

It was also interesting! Certainly Luna knew where Vita was, for she had sent the two of them to her. But what connection did Vita have to Luna, and why was it so important to get the girl straightened out?

I sure don't know! Vita thought irritably. *And care less. Ask him if he's got any H.*

So the mystery remained—unless this was merely a convenient case, to keep Jolie occupied and Orlene from sinking to Hell. Well, it certainly was doing that!

"I had a bad experience at home," Jolie said, speaking for Vita. Internally, she asked: *May I tell him?*

Go ahead, I don't care. But I won't go home.

"This is often the case," the man agreed. "In past times runaway children were routinely returned to their homes. Then it was discovered what they were running from, and policy changed. Abuse?"

"Perhaps," Jolie said cautiously.

"Would you like information on what constitutes abuse, legally? We want to understand your situation, and to have you understand it yourself."

Jolie glanced at the matron who had brought her here, and who remained standing at the door. That might be for her protection, or the man's. "Are you trying to get me to incriminate myself? I'm willing to do that; I did throw garbage at the police carpet, so they would arrest me."

"So that you could win clear of the youth gang that was closing in on you," he agreed. "I understand—and so did the arresting officers. But there are other aspects of this case that cause us to be reluctant simply to turn you loose again."

"I don't want to be turned loose!" Jolie said, alarmed. She knew that this host would be far better off in custody than on the street.

"We have little choice, as you have committed no significant crime and you can not be classed as a runaway. But we are willing to help in whatever way seems appropriate."

"This doesn't sound like a police interrogation!" Jolie exclaimed. "Who are you? What do you really want of me?"

The man smiled. "I apologize for neglecting to introduce myself. I am Judge Scott, and this is a preliminary hearing before our formal meeting in court. I prefer to know something about those who come before me, so that my ignorance does not lead to bad decisions."

Jolie was amazed. "I thought you were just a functionary! Someone to take evidence to use against me."

He smiled again. "That, too, perhaps. But the roots of my involvement are curiosity and a desire to do what is right, which is not always merely what is legal."

Jolie realized that her encounter with this man could be a stroke of luck—or perhaps had somehow been anticipated by Luna. She decided to put her cards—not merely Vita's—on the table. "May I speak privately with you, Judge Scott?"

"The matron is here to ensure that I take no unseemly advantage of you," he reminded her. "This is standard policy with juvenile females."

"I understand that. But what I have to say is private and I think not at all what you expect."

"There is also a recording of this interview being made, for my protection as well as yours, so I can not guarantee you privacy."

"That recording can be sealed as proprietary material."

The Judge raised an eyebrow. "You sound uncommonly knowledgeable for your years."

"I am. Please let me talk to you alone."

He nodded to the matron, who quietly retired.

"I am not merely a runaway fifteen-year-old girl, H addict and prostitute," Jolie said. "I am a more mature woman who is animating her body as a temporary host—and a still more mature woman who is operating during the incapacity of the other one. Can you grasp this?"

"Certainly this is possible, if the host consents. What would be the purpose in such a grouping?"

"The host is important to another person, who does not

wish to interfere directly. The other ghost is important to me, so I brought her to this host in order to prevent her soul from sinking to Hell, where it does not belong."

The Judge gazed at a spot on the ceiling. "Allow me to remind you that the charge against you is limited to abuse of an officer of the law, in the circumstances a misdemeanor. You have not been charged with substance abuse or with prostitution, and may not wish to volunteer such information to the court."

That's for sure! Vita put in. It seemed she was monitoring this dialogue.

"Oh, but I do," Jolie said. "In fact, I am prepared to turn state's evidence in exchange for treatment and witness protection."

You're crazy! Vita protested. *The pimp was bad, but not as bad as prison. You know what happens to girl prisoners? I wear a null-preg, null-VD charm to keep me clean, but in prison they get mean, and the charm won't help.*

Startled, Jolie glanced at the girl's wrist. There was the magic band, matching her light brown skin, which she hadn't noticed before.

"I am not certain you understand what such action would entail," the Judge said. "You would have to remain in protective custody, and with our present limited facilities, that means an adult prison. I believe I would prefer to return you to the street."

Jolie smiled. "My host would prefer to return to the street too. But I am proceeding on the assumption that she would only become fully addicted to Spelled H, would be mercilessly exploited and abused by her pimp, and would come to a sad end. I also believe that there was reason that we were sent to her, and that she must be restored to her family."

No way! Vita snapped. *My band's no good against that either.*

"To which she does not wish to be restored," the Judge said. "I would suspect that she has been abused there, perhaps sexually molested. But prison is not the answer."

"Neither is the street," Jolie pointed out.

His eyes came down to focus on her face. "Tell me more

about yourself. Not the host; I mean you the ghost. When did you live, and why did you not go to Heaven?"

"I don't think that's relevant."

"It is if you are in control of the body. It is your responsibility that will determine the host's overt actions, and this will help me make a decision."

Jolie nodded. "Stop me when you've heard enough. My name is Jolie. I was born in southern France in the year 1191 A.D. of common peasant stock. In 1205, when I was fourteen, I was summoned to the house of the local sorcerer, a young man a year my senior but of infinitely greater experience and education and power. He fed me and talked to me and said he wanted my love, and in due course he had it, and I married him. I was killed by a crusader in 1208, but there was enough evil in my situation to put my soul in balance, and I remained with my husband as a ghost. He became a friar, but when he was of middle age, I animated a living woman and tempted him into sin, and thereafter he was prey to a demoness sent by Lucifer, and I could not approach him."

"Lucifer?"

"Satan's predecessor. When my husband died, he replaced Lucifer and became Satan. Today I keep company with Gaea instead of with Satan, but I still love him and visit him when I can. Now I am trying to help Gaea's daughter, and—"

What?

Jolie bit her lip. "Oh, I said too much! She didn't know, and it wasn't yet time to tell her. I got carried away by what I was telling you—"

"Some might suppose a person who told such a story was either inventive or crazy," Judge Scott remarked.

Jolie nodded. "So I might as well finish it while you're still listening. Gaea sent me to Luna, and Luna sent me to help this host. I do not know what her interest in this host is, but I do know the girl needs help, so I am trying to help her. Most immediately, I am trying to get her off the street and off H, and this is where I beseech your help."

The Judge seemed undisturbed. "Since you are a long-term ghost, you will have mastered the tricks of the trade, as it were. You will be able not only to animate a willing host, but to manifest directly to those who are interested enough to perceive you."

"Yes. Do you wish me to?"

"Yes, please."

Jolie drew herself out of the host and floated in the air beside her. Then she intensified her image until she manifested in her natural living guise: a seventeen-year-old French villain girl. Even so, few could have seen her.

The Judge looked directly at her and nodded. "Can you speak also?"

"If you can hear me."

"I can hear you. Who remains in charge of the host?"

There was a pause. Then Orlene spoke. "I suppose that's me. I wanted to sink down to Hell, but now I am uncertain. This girl does need help, and it may be my penance to bring her out of her slough."

"And you are?" the Judge inquired.

"Orlene. My baby died, and I committed suicide and am trying to reach him in the Afterlife. But the Incarnation of Night played a cruel trick on me, and I can not forgive myself for what it brought me to."

"Will you, also, vacate the host?" the Judge asked.

"But she'll sink to Hell!" Jolie protested.

"Perhaps not, now," he replied. "She cannot be condemned to Hell for evil inflicted on her by another."

"But she doesn't believe that!"

"I am coming to believe it," Orlene said. "Certainly I understand now that others have problems as bad as mine, and it behooves me to do what I can to help them, instead of merely giving up." She moved out of the body and floated.

"Who remains in charge of the host?" the Judge asked again.

Vita looked around craftily. "Look, Judge, this is all a big mistake. If you'll just let me go—"

"You would be back on the street in a moment, looking for H," the Judge concluded.

"I didn't say that!" She glanced at him appraisingly. "I can pay, if you like young flesh." She shaped her hair with her hands and inhaled, trying to enhance her figure in the plain prison dress. "Anything you want, just don't put me in prison or ship me home."

The Judge nodded again. "Point made. Return to your host, ghosts, and we shall discuss ways and means."

"But they won't let me have—" Vita protested. Then Orlene approached her from the left and Jolie from the right. She tried to bat them away, but her will was not in it; she knew that only Jolie was competent to deal with the Judge at this stage. So after token resistance, she allowed them to reenter her and resume control.

The Judge considered for a moment. "I want your commitment, Jolie, that you as the dominant personality will remain with this host until her situation has been clarified."

"Well, that depends on Orlene, and on Luna. If Luna asked me to leave—"

"You are referring to Senator Kaftan?" he asked sharply.

"Luna Kaftan, yes. But I wouldn't want her name brought into this until I know more about her interest in this person."

The Judge touched a panel on the arm of his chair. "Senator Kaftan, please."

In a moment the air between them flickered and a holo picture of a young man appeared. "Senator Kaftan's office," he said. "Oh, hello, Judge Scott! She's in conference at the moment, but I'll have her call you back."

"No need, Joe," the Judge said. "Merely inform her that I propose to assume jurisdiction over one of her clients, with her permission."

Joe's eyes moved around until they spied Vita. "No problem, Judge; her permission is noted."

"Thank you." The image faded.

"What's going on?" Jolie asked, amazed.

"When you mentioned Luna Kaftan, I knew this was no ordinary case. So I verified that you are what you claim to be, and that this girl, your host, is indeed a concern of Luna's. She wants the matter handled discreetly, so I am assuming personal jurisdiction. But I am not about to take an errant

81

juvenile girl into my home unsupervised. I must have your commitment to remain with her until this matter has been resolved."

"Your home?" Jolie still was struggling over the Judge's evidently close acquaintance with Luna.

"There are no appropriate facilities for such a project. My housekeeper will see to your comfort. I will release you on your own recognizance, and you will report to my residence immediately. There you will be able to tend to your host's needs without harassment. Will you make that commitment, Jolie?"

If Luna knew this man and trusted him, Jolie realized she could do no less. "Yes."

"Very well. You will be conducted back to your cell. This afternoon you will appear before me formally. Thereafter you will go to this address." He gave her a card. "I will provide a carpet, as the girl's pimp may be on watch for her release. Avoid him."

"Thank you," Jolie said faintly. What was she caught up in here? The Judge seemed so direct and understanding— but taking an underage prostitute into his home? If it wasn't for Luna's involvement, she would distrust this overwhelmingly; as it was, she distrusted it only significantly.

The matron returned. The interview was over—and what an interview it had been!

So he does *want young flesh!* Vita thought.

Jolie, you can't put her into his power! Orlene thought. *You know the sexual imperative of the male!*

Who cares? Vita retorted. *He can't be as bad as the pimp was. If I do good, maybe he'll let me have some H.*

No sex! Orlene thought.

No H! Jolie thought at the same time.

We'll see, the girl responded smugly.

If your father molested you, Orlene asked, *why are you so eager for sex with strangers?*

I'm not eager, in fact I don't like it. But it's not incest, and if anyone finds out, it won't put my father in prison and break up my family and break my mother's heart. It's the only currency I've got now, so I might as well make it count. The H makes it okay, and it can really make a man jump. Sex is power.

They reached the cell. "Here is your headache pill," the matron said, proffering a capsule.

"Headache?" Jolie asked, surprised. Then she realized that the Judge must have ordered it, so she accepted it. "Thank you."

They were alone. *Is that H?* Vita asked eagerly. "I'm near dying for a sniff."

"You aren't dying," Jolie said. "I can feel your body, now, remember. It's only a moderate withdrawal discomfort; you really aren't addicted yet, and you aren't going to be. This pill is to ease even that symptom." She put it in her mouth, and it dissolved immediately into sweet juice, which she swallowed.

Maybe it's just a symptom to you, but it's one hell of a craving for me! Vita retorted. *If I were on my own now, I'd be out hustling for it, you bet.*

You will not have it while I'm in charge, Jolie retorted.

Vita subsided sullenly. It was obvious that she was biding her time and would go for the H the moment she had opportunity. Even though they shared the body, they did not share the craving.

Gaea is my mother? Orlene asked.

"It is true," Jolie said, subvocalizing. "I'm sorry I said it like that, but it is true. She birthed you when she was mortal and could not marry, so gave you up to a Gypsy woman, who gave you to the family who adopted you. When she assumed the Office of the Incarnation of Nature, she had the power to influence your life, but felt that would be a conflict of interest, so she made no attempt to locate you. Instead a friend asked me to watch over you, and that I did, visiting you in your dreams. When you died, I couldn't tell her, but I still tried to help you, so that you could achieve some satisfaction. I hoped that I would be able to tell her that you died but were satisfied, but it got complicated."

It got complicated, Orlene agreed. *Jolie, how can you still try to help me, after what I did?*

What did you try to do that was so bad? Vita asked.

"It wasn't her fault," Jolie said.

I tried to rape her.

Vita made a thought-whistle. *How could—*

"She was turned magically into a man, whose passion then overwhelmed him," Jolie explained before Orlene could get into more guilt. "I am still trying to help you, Orlene, because I know you, and know that you would never have done such a thing in your normal state, either living or dead. It was the cruel prank of the Incarnation of Night, making you pay for your audacity in wanting your baby back."

Some prank! Vita thought admiringly. *But you know, men do like to do it to women, and you can't trust any man who denies it. That's why I know what to expect from the Judge.*

I don't think so, Orlene thought. *The Judge glowed.*

He had a glow on?

What?

"She means was he intoxicated or under the influence of some drug," Jolie clarified.

Oh. No, I mean I can see when a person is right for another, and the Judge is right for anyone. He's a good man, a very good man.

Jolie had forgotten about Orlene's talent. Some people had individual magic, such as Gaea's for enhanced music, and Orlene's magic was to be able to orient on any person or people and tell by a glow she perceived whether they were suitable for each other. It was interesting that she endorsed the Judge. He had struck Jolie as a good man, but such impressions could be mistaken.

Well, we'll see how he is when he gets me alone in his house, Vita concluded. *You know, I can see why you'd be sent to watch Orlene, she being related to an Incarnation, but I'm sure not related! What's so important about a black teen whore?*

"I wish I knew," Jolie said.

They relaxed, feeling the lethargy of the pill. It did seem to be countering the drug withdrawal pangs for Vita.

In the afternoon they were conducted to the formal hearing. Judge Scott sat at his tall desk, in the traditional robe of the office. The clerk read out the charge, and the

Judge dismissed it, with a warning to Vita not to repeat the offense. It was all done in a minute, and the next defendant was brought up.

They walked out of the courtroom and to the carpet access. Immediately a carpet sailed up, recognizing Vita. They boarded, and it took off.

Vita peered down. *There's the pimp's limo!* she thought. *So he was waiting for me!*

"He was waiting for you," Jolie agreed. "With Spelled H in one hand and a club in the other."

God, I want to go to him! I mean, for the H.

You are off the H! Jolie retorted.

You offered to testify, Orlene thought. *You could have gotten that beast locked away. Why didn't you?*

"It's almost impossible to make it stick," Jolie said. "And new pimps and drug runners come in as fast as the old ones are taken out. It's hardly worth dealing with the minor criminals; it's the big ones the law wants."

The carpet sailed up and over the city, following the established carpet routes. Jolie peered down, noting the activities on the tops of the megabuildings. Some were set up as parks, with shrubs and trees growing, and garden paths, and even fair-sized ponds. Others were set up for sports, with tennis courts, running tracks, game fields and swimming pools. Some were residential, in the archaic sense: little country villages set amid winding roads. The best way to get away from the bustle of the big city was to live on top of it—if you could afford the rentals. Jolie always looked with longing at such developments, because they reminded her of her origin in medieval times, when isolated villages were most of what there was. Were she alive again . . .

You really are from long ago, Vita thought, picking up the thought.

"Yes, I really am," Jolie agreed wistfully. "I would have been long since dead and gone, if I hadn't died." She smiled, realizing the incongruity of that statement. But it was true: but for the crusade, she would have lived out her life with Parry, learning magic and growing old, perhaps having children and grandchildren. Yet she might also have died of one of the periodic plagues, or in childbirth, or some accident. The average lifetime had been short then. So there were ways in which she was better off now, as a ghost.

And I thought ghosts were always moaning! Vita commented. *You two ghosts aren't spooky at all!*

Jolie laughed. "Not at the moment!"

The carpet approached an isolated megabuilding. This one was restricted, meaning that the average person couldn't enter it without a special pass. People in sensitive positions normally lived in such buildings: those subject to assassination or harassment, such as government officials, company presidents, prominent entertainers and, of course, judges. Luna—Senator Kaftan—was exceptional in her residence in the heart of the city. But, of course, she had special magic protection.

Jolie hoped that the Judge would live on the roof, but was disappointed; his suite was buried deep inside the building. The carpet accessed it by descending into a central court and flying along a tube that curved like the inside of some giant serpent. *You'd think a judge could do better than this,* Vita remarked.

Not an honest one, Orlene replied.

That seemed to be the key: Judge Scott was not rich. But this residence would be quite secure from characters like Vita's pimp. It was also not the kind of place from which it would be easy to run.

At last the carpet halted at a spherical chamber. There were several doors, one of which listed the name ROQUE SCOTT.

Roque! Vita thought, with a giggle in the background.

I like it, Orlene thought.

Oh, I like it too—I just think it's funny!

They got off the carpet, and it flew away, following whatever orders it had been given. They approached the door, and it opened. A grandmotherly woman stood there.

"You must be Vita," she said. "I'm a V too: Vaasta. Your room's waiting."

She glows too, Orlene thought.

Now, tuning in, Jolie began to see it: a gentle radiance

that surrounded the woman. This evidently meant that she was benign. That was comforting to know.

The suite was spacious enough, its aspect enhanced by strategically placed mirrors. It had no windows to the outside, but a magic picture showed a scene of thick foliage and a small puddling stream with tiny fish. The leaves of the trees moved with the breeze, and it was even possible to reach into it and touch things, though not to remove them. Vita found it fascinating; she had never had access to gentle magic like this. Orlene was nostalgic; she had had pictures like this during her life, and shared them with her lover Norton.

Vaasta showed them the room and found several dresses for them; evidently she had been sent word to order some in the appropriate size range. Jolie looked at her host in the mirror and approved; she now looked much more like an innocent girl than a prostitute. As far as Jolie was concerned, that would be the reality henceforth.

In the evening the carpet brought the Judge home. Jolie presented herself, neatly dressed. "We thank you for providing us this refuge, Judge Scott," she said.

"Roque," he replied. "Here I am Roque, and you are—which one?"

"Jolie," Jolie said after a momentary hesitation. She had no mortal identification, so that was better.

"You understand, this is an unofficial arrangement," he said. "I freed you in court, and you are not required to remain here. But I feel it is better for you to be here until your internal questions are resolved."

So he has young sex on ice, Vita remarked.

"Thank you, Roque," Jolie said. "What may I do to earn my keep?"

"Why, I really hadn't thought of that," he said.

Ha!

"I am sure that one of the three of us has some knowledge or ability that you might find useful," Jolie said.

He smiled. "Unless you can look at a suspect's face and accurately read his innocence or guilt, I have no use for you at court, and Vaasta is quite adequate to maintain the residence. So you should consider yourself—yourselves—guests, as my favor to Senator Kaftan, whose motives and judgment I deeply respect."

I can do that, Orlene thought. *All I would have to do is orient on a person's suitability for release into society, and the good ones would glow.*

"As it happens, Orlene has a magic talent, and could do what you describe," Jolie said. "We should be happy to go to court with you."

"I was speaking facetiously," he said, surprised.

"I wasn't."

He considered a moment, in the way he had. "You really wish to do this?"

Certainly, Orlene thought.

I'd rather lie in bed and watch holos, Vita thought.

"We have a difference of opinion," Jolie said. "But the vote is two to one in favor of going to court with you."

"Then perhaps we should wait for a unanimous decision," the Judge said.

"No need. I govern the host, and I feel it is better to earn our keep."

Listen, it's my body! Vita protested.

Which will be out on the street and back with the pimp, without Jolie, Orlene returned. *She agreed to remain for the duration, which is why he's willing to have us in his home. He knows she's a responsible person, while you aren't.*

"Justice is not always served by the governing party," he said. "The host should not be coerced."

He's taking my side? Vita asked, amazed. *He must want flesh real bad!*

No, he's glowing, Orlene reported. *He is really trying to do what is proper.*

Oh, all right! But I'll kick up a storm if it gets boring.

"Make that unanimous now," Jolie said, smiling wryly.

He smiled again, this time with increased warmth which added to his presence. "As you wish. Now let us see what Vaasta has for dinner."

Vaasta was good at her business, and it was an excellent meal. They had carrot casserole and pseudolobster salad, which caused Vita to tune out in disgust, but she returned for dessert: rainbow wafers. It was inexpensive fare, but nutritious. Then the Judge retired to his study to review upcoming cases, and Jolie settled down to watch the evening holo shows. To Vita's disgust, she insisted on watching the news first. Then she tuned in to an entertainment program for Vita's benefit. It was full of violence, lust and humor, in that order, with virtually no social significance, and Vita loved it. Then to their chamber, where they slept undisturbed, to Vita's expressed surprise and unexpressed annoyance.

It was a new experience for Orlene, who had not occupied a living body this way since she died, and for Jolie, who had not been away from Gaea this long since coming to her. But it was pleasant enough for all three of them. Their dreams were a mélange of all their minds and experiences.

In the morning they joined Roque on the carpet and flew into the city. They entered the rush of commuter carpets, so thick that at times it was easy to lose track of the fact that they were high in the air. It was more like being part of a river current, with other carpets above and below and on all sides.

"By the way," he murmured, "in court I should be addressed as Judge Scott."

"Of course," Jolie agreed. She was in a formal suit which was somewhat baggy on Vita's slight frame but made her look a trifle older.

In the courtroom she was given a seat next to the steno, so that she seemed to be an apprentice or assistant, and no one questioned her presence. Orlene watched each case, and Jolie saw the glow she saw. She whispered to the steno, "Guilty . . . really guilty . . . innocent . . . doubtful," and the steno signaled the Judge by some obscure means.

Vita, far from being bored, was fascinated. *I never saw such a line of creeps!* she thought. *They all want the Judge to think they're good guys, but we're seeing right through them!*

There came a recess, and the Judge summoned steno and assistant to his chambers. "I happened to be versed in most of the morning's cases," he said. "Many are repeaters, or have records elsewhere. You had no prior knowledge of them?"

89

"None," Jolie said. "We had never seen or heard of any of them before; we went only by the glow."

"You called them with complete accuracy. I am amazed."

"It is Orlene's magic; she had a lifetime to master its use. She can tell who is right for whom, and who is good or bad, or who is telling the truth or lying."

"I am often required to make judgment calls, and when the evidence is inconclusive, I try to err on the side of leniency. It bothers me greatly to err too far, and to receive news of a crime that was enabled by my misjudgment. I want you to sit in on a preliminary interview and to inform me of your impression."

"Without the steno? How should I do that?"

"Sit quietly with your hands in your lap, moving nervously. When the indication is good or true, let your right fingers be exterior; when it is bad or false, let your left fingers show. I will not remark on this; merely keep them appropriately positioned throughout."

"Yes," Jolie agreed. "Like this for good, and this for bad." She cupped her left hand with her right, then reversed it.

"Precisely. You may be far more valuable than I had anticipated."

This is sure more fun than turning tricks! Vita thought.

I should hope so, Orlene responded dryly. This immersion in the ugly side of society seemed to be helping her; Jolie wondered whether it was because it was now evident how few living folk were perfect or even really good.

The in-chambers case turned out to be a suave businessman, a rather handsome individual with a commanding presence. There were diamond cuff links on his shirt, and his tie clip was a sparkling opal.

"So nice to see you, Judge Scott," he said genially, proffering his hand.

The Judge did not take it. "This is not a social meeting, Mr. Bronx."

"Call me Cheer," Bronx said. "I don't believe in standing on formality."

"I do," the Judge said coldly. "As you know, this is a private preliminary hearing to determine whether formal charges of embezzlement should be brought against you. Are there any factors you wish to have placed in evidence?"

"You know, Judge Scott, I really admire your unusual technique. They say you can tell more about a case in an informal hearing than a prosecutor can bring out in a week of witnesses."

Despite the man's open attitude, his nature was thoroughly evil. The glow about him seemed black. Jolie's hands were set firmly in the negative position.

"Is there any reason I should not remand you to a criminal court specializing in racketeering?"

"Apart from lack of evidence? You know I would not soil my hands on that sort of crudity, Judge Scott."

To Jolie's surprise, the glow changed. This man *was* innocent of that particular charge. She changed her hands.

"Extortion?" the Judge asked.

"You know such charges are unfounded!"

And it seemed they were.

"But you do gain considerable illicit wealth by cheating on contracts with state agencies," the Judge said. "I believe the term for this is 'skimming.' "

"How can you say such a thing! I am a regular business-man!"

The hands reverted to the "guilty" position.

"The evidence is inconclusive," the Judge said. "But I believe it is best to determine the accuracy of any charges made. I shall direct that a thorough investigation be made into your business practices. You will present your books to this court next week, for review by a qualified accountant."

"But my books will show no wrongdoing!" Bronx protested.

"I was referring to your private set."

The glow around the man became like a bottomless pit. Now Bronx knew that Judge Scott knew what to look for, and rage and fear surged in him. Yet his face remained bland. "Of course."

After the interview the Judge nodded to Jolie. "Your hands were invaluable."

"But you seemed to know the answers already!"

"I suspected; you confirmed. Now I am able to eliminate the false leads and concentrate on the true one. Bronx will shortly be out of business in this city."

Gee, this is fun! Vita thought. *He's really socking it to those toads!*

So it went, and their day was a success. "Little did I know that you would prove to be so useful," Roque said as they returned to his residence on the carpet in the evening. "For the first time, I was assured of making no errors."

"We are glad to help," Jolie said.

He's just warming us up for the night, Vita thought, but she was less certain than she had been.

"Do you care to tell me more of the background of the girl?" Roque asked.

Does he glow? Vita demanded.

Yes, he means well, Orlene replied. *He is a good man.*

I guess he is. Okay, tell him about my father.

"She was raped by her father," Jolie said. "Rather than make an issue that would destroy her family, she ran away, and was taken in by a pimp who dosed her on H and prostituted her to wealthy clients with a taste for what she calls 'young flesh.' She felt that this was better than what she faced at home."

"It is unfortunately routine. Is she willing now to testify against her father?"

No!

"She is not."

"Will she trust my discretion if she gives me the name?"

"But you already have the name! You said there was a—a note in her file."

"Yes. We know her identity unofficially, but it must be corroborated before we are allowed to report it. Unfortunately this restricts my action, and I can not make a further investigation into the matter without that corroboration."

That's the way I want it! Vita thought.

"No."

"Let me explain my interest here. Vita is the daughter of Senator Kaftan's chief researcher. Her absence has made her mother unable to function effectively, and it seems she is the

92

only one able to pursue a critical line of research that relates in essential business. Senator Kaftan must have that information."

But they'll put my father in prison! Vita thought in anguish. *That'll really break up Mom!*

"I feel that a man guilty of a crime like that should receive the full impact of the law," Roque continued. "But circumstances are seldom clear-cut. Would it suffice if her father voluntarily separated, and took up residence in another city, and was denied visitation rights?"

You mean I'd never see Dad again—and no scandal?

That is what it means, Orlene agreed.

And Mom—she wouldn't know?

"Would her mother know?" Jolie asked.

"Not unless Senator Kaftan told her—which the Senator might do, if asked."

I guess . . . Vita thought uncertainly. *And me—would she know about me? I mean, the H and all.*

"Vita doesn't want her mother to know about her recent situation, either," Jolie said.

"She could call the Senator's office and leave a message for her mother, stating only that she is safe and will return later," he suggested. "I think that would be a great relief to her mother."

The Senator's office! Vita thought. *I never thought of that!* Her feeling of relief and elation flooded through them all.

The carpet pulled into the megabuilding. When they reached the apartment, Roque placed the call. In a moment he was talking to Luna herself, while Jolie watched from just outside pickup range. "Luna, the girl would like to leave a message for her mother, no return address, her father not to know. Can you go along with this?"

"I can, Roque," the Senator said. "Put her on; her confidence will be protected."

Roque stepped away, and Jolie stepped into pickup range. She relinquished the body to the girl.

"Uh, Mom, it's me, Vita," she said awkwardly. "I, uh, I got into some trouble and couldn't come home. But I'm okay now, doing real well, in fact. I, uh, I've got a job, kinda, and it's real nice. I—Oh, Mom, I love you, and I'm coming home soon's I can!" She cut off the contact, unable to continue, overwhelmed by her tears.

Roque returned. "That will mean a lot to your mother, Vita," he said.

Vita turned and hugged him tightly, catching him off guard. He stood there somewhat helplessly, patting her shoulder. Then she retreated, and Jolie took over.

She released Roque. "Thank you; this is Jolie again," she said, stepping away. "It was very kind of you to do this."

"Well, there is a practical aspect, of course," he said, embarrassed. "Luna needs the services of her mother, and this will facilitate the return of those services."

But he did it because he didn't like grief in either Vita or her mother, Orlene thought. *He glows of goodwill, not practicality.*

"Of course," Jolie said, agreeing with both Orlene and the Judge.

They had supper and watched the evening holos. As they retired for the night, wearing a silken nightie Vaasta had shopped for during the day, Vita had further comments.

I hugged him, and he never put a move on me!

He is a decent man, Orlene agreed. *As decent as I have encountered since dying.*

I thought sure he'd grab a feel, at least a little one, but he didn't.

He didn't, Orlene agreed.

I mean, he doesn't have a woman, so unless he's—

He isn't. He glows normal.

I think I love him.

"Now, wait!" Jolie murmured.

I mean, every man I ever got close to, including especially my father, wanted to get into my pants.

"Well, your pimp didn't."

You kidding? He had me first thing! Said he never put flesh in the field 'less he knew it was tight.

"There goes another bastion of morality!" Jolie said with irony. "If you can't trust your pimp—"

Oh, come off it! It was just business to him. But he sure put me through the grinder! I learned more in fifteen minutes—

"We really don't need to review it," Jolie said, though she would have smiled had Orlene not been present. It was evident that the girl was resilient and would not suffer emotional crippling from that particular aspect of her experience. At the same time, it wouldn't have bothered Jolie to see the pimp roasting eternally on a spit over a fire in Hell. For every truly decent man, there seemed to be two truly unscrupulous ones who would take advantage of any girl they could catch, regardless of age.

But Roque's different. I mean first he gave us a nice place to stay, and then he helped me talk to Mom, and he's not hot for my flesh. What's more to ask?

"Time. Experience. Maturity," Jolie said.

He's got them in spades!

"Not his. Yours."

Pooh! Maybe for you old women that's okay, but I'm young and alive. I want to love!

And some day surely you will, Orlene put in. *But not illicitly.*

That's the only kind I know!

They slept—and suffered through Vita's dreams of hugging a man who didn't grab feels. Her emotion, unwarranted and unrealistic as it was, was nevertheless overwhelming. Perhaps it was a long-dammed reaction to her need for respect for an older man, lost when her father betrayed her. The thing was, Roque really was a good man, one worth loving. But there was no way he would love an underage girl.

The next day something alarming happened in court. They were sitting as before, beside the steno, when one of the cases turned out to be the pimp. He was there on an accurate charge: soliciting for prostitution.

Oh, my God—if he sees me . . . ! Vita thought.

Jolie agreed. She tried to cover her face with her hands, but couldn't do it effectively without becoming obvious.

The pimp's gimlet gaze caught her and lingered for a moment. There was no question: he recognized her. Vita felt doomed, and Jolie couldn't argue. That pimp would blow the whistle on the whole thing if he didn't get his way!

Then the judge's head turned, following the pimp's gaze, and he realized what had happened. Abruptly he called a recess. "You will consult in my quarters," he told the pimp.

In a moment, it seemed, they were there: Judge, Jolie, and pimp. "I gather you recognize this woman," Judge Scott said abruptly.

"I sure do, Your Honor! That's one of my gals! What's she doing in your court?" He stared penetratingly at Jolie.

The gall of the man! How could he think to get away with this? He was talking himself into prison!

No, he figures to blackmail the Judge, Vita thought. *Figures the Judge won't want to be exposed with a whore.*

The Judge turned to Jolie. "Is this true?"

You're no whore! Orlene thought fiercely. *Whatever you were into before is past now.*

And there was the key. "I am not his creature," Jolie said, speaking with her own voice. "I despise his breed."

The pimp's jaw dropped. He did not know that Jolie had taken over Vita's body, and her words were not at all what he had expected from a cowed, H-addicted girl.

"The lady seems to disagree with you," the Judge remarked. "What basis do you have for your claim?"

He called me a lady! Vita thought, thrilled.

The pimp realized that he was in trouble. If the girl had found courage, she could testify against him and put him in a lot more trouble than before. Still, he made the attempt. "You know I've got what you want, girl."

"Are you by chance alluding to an illegal drug?" Jolie demanded imperiously. "Certainly I want none of that, and none of you, you despicable whoremaster! I shall be happy to provide information—"

The pimp raised his hands in a surrender gesture. "Suppose I just get out of town in a hurry, Your Honor?"

"I would have no objection to that," the Judge agreed.

That concluded the session. *But how come the pimp backed down so fast?* Vita asked. *He knew I never could tell him no!*

"He discovered that he wasn't dealing with you anymore," Jolie explained. "Had it been just you, he would have taken you with him, and the Judge would have let you go rather than be compromised and have his reputation sullied. Or so he thought. But he found himself up against a fearless judge and a fearless woman, and knew the odds had turned against him. He did the most expedient thing: voluntary banishment. You'll never see him again. The Judge let him go because this is more effective than sentencing him on a misdemeanor charge."

Gee! And that about covered it.

CHAPTER FIVE

Roque

ON THE WEEKEND, ROQUE TOOK THEM FOR A
walk in the park. Jolie had requested it, because the host, as
a minor, was not granted free access; she had to be accompanied by a responsible adult. Vaasta had no interest in
parks, but the Judge liked to take weekly strolls. His suite was
about halfway high in the megabuilding, by no means a
favored site, so he did feel squeezed at times.

They took an elevator and zoomed up sixty stories to the
roof. They stepped out, and were deep in a forest. Indeed,
when they turned, their elevator was gone; there was no sign
of civilization except the marked path, which curved out of
sight both forward and back.

But where did it go? Vita demanded, amazed.

Magic, Orlene replied, laughing.

You're teasing me! Let me ask Roque.

Jolie turned to the Judge, who was inhaling the fragrant
air with evident satisfaction. "I am turning the body over to

99

the host, who finds this a novel experience. Since there is no expedient escape from this level, I believe she will behave."

"As you wish." He evidently had a notion of Vita's question. "However, I shall expect you to remain resident and to take over if she misbehaves."

Jolie nodded. She did not fully trust Vita, but believed that the girl's burgeoning crush on the Judge would cause her to stay in line. She vacated.

"Now I know I'm just a street-level city girl who's never been nowhere," Vita said. "But we just came out of an elevator and now it's gone, and I know they don't waste magic on regular folk. What happened to it?"

Roque smiled in the way he had, and Vita felt a thrill of emotion that worried Jolie. Crush? Jolie had forgotten how potent the passions of youth could be! The girl had said she loved him, and indeed, in her way she did. But she had rather direct ways of expressing herself. That would have to be watched, until it passed in favor of some other interest.

"It is not magic," Roque said. "It is merely camouflage. This is not a real tree; it is the mask for the elevator." He touched the bark of the huge tree trunk the path curved around, and a panel slid aside to reveal the elevator chamber within. In a moment the panel slid quietly across again and the tree was whole and seemingly natural.

"Oh!" Vita squealed, delighted. "It tricked me!"

"We must labor hard to maintain seeming naturalness," he remarked, walking down the path. "These parks are restricted to responsible adults because irresponsible folk have no proper appreciation for them, and may litter or damage them. It might be taken as an analogy of society: only those who have achieved a mature viewpoint are capable of appreciating what it offers without abusing it."

"You make it so sensible!" Vita said, thrilling again. She had had little interest in parks before, and none in maintenance, but she was an instant convert.

"I should; I am one of those charged with the enforcement of society's standards."

"Yeah, my pimp would just spit on this path."

"Oh, perhaps he would not descend to such depravity."

She glanced sidelong at him, trying to fathom whether this was humor. He saw that, and allowed his straight face to quirk. Then she felt free to laugh. She was learning social nuance, too, in a hurry. Jolie was amazed at the potency of this association. Roque had treated Vita with courtesy, and she had responded in a manner Jolie hoped was not embarrassing him too much.

"Oh, look at that!" she exclaimed farther along, stooping to peer at a delicate flower. "It looks just like a—"

"Lady slipper," Roque supplied. "Indeed, that is its name. It is one of many ornamental plants cultivated here and in other roof parks."

"Gee, I wish I could be here forever!" she exclaimed.

"I understand the feeling. When I am amidst a hard day at court and I feel my temper fraying, the image that pacifies me is this one, especially the pond ahead."

"There's a pond?" Vita literally skipped ahead, casting off five years in her delight.

I walked such paths with Norton, Orlene thought wistfully. Her own nostalgia and emotion were riding along with Vita's joy.

And I with Parry, Jolie agreed, similarly charmed.

The pond was lovely. It had mossy banks and clear water, and ducks glided on its surface. The males had heads with iridescent green. They turned and swam toward the visitors.

Roque touched another tree trunk. A panel opened to reveal a chamber containing slices of bread. He took out two, handing one to Vita. "You tear it into bits, like this, and toss it to the ducks. Only one slice per person, per visit, so that the birds do not become obstreperous." He flipped a piece to the leading duck.

A mother duck with four little ones appeared. "Oooo!" Vita cried, tossing her fragments to them. The ducks took them eagerly, but headed back into the water the moment they were gone. They knew better than anyone that it was no use importuning a visitor for seconds.

"They don't really like us, just our bread," Vita said, disappointed.

"This is another truism of life. I, as a judge, find few who

101

like me personally, but many who cater to me because of my position. You, in your past life, found many who cared nothing for your personality, only for the passing use of your body."

"Gee—you mean a judge is like a whore?"

"I would not have expressed it quite that way, but perhaps that is the essence."

"And both are like ducks!" she concluded. "No, wait, that's backwards. The ducks are the others, the ones who just want something, and you gotta be smart and catch on to them and not be flattered, no matter who you are."

"Agreed." And with that simple indication of approval of her rationale, he sent her floating again.

They walked on. "There is something I have been meaning to mention," Roque said.

"Me too!"

No! Jolie thought, alarmed by the girl's swell of excitement and love.

"Oh? You have a concern, Vita?"

But the girl, heeding Jolie's threat to take over, demurred. Vita now respected Jolie's judgment and would give her the body on demand, rather than risk in some way offending the Judge. "You first, Roque." She liked the privilege of calling him by his first name.

"There has been a grace period, but now it is necessary to arrange for your resumption of schooling," he said. "By law you must remain in school until you are sixteen, and it would be better if you continued until you are qualified for adult responsibilities. Your time as an outlaw is past."

"Gee, was I an outlaw?" she asked, intrigued.

"You certainly were. Had you been arrested in the course of your business, I would have had to fine you and remand you to the juvenile authorities."

"My pimp would have lied about my age and gotten me off."

"True. But *I* shall not misrepresent your age, or allow you to be mistreated while you are in my charge. You must undertake schooling."

"I can't go home for that!"

"Not yet. But there is an adequate local school in this building."

"You mean I'd have to quit going to court, and go sit in dumb classes all day instead?"

"I am afraid so."

That prospect did not appeal to Jolie or Orlene any more than it did to Vita. This was a temporary situation for them, which was extending because of the difficulty about getting Vita back home, and they did not want to suffer through material with which they were long since familiar.

"Say—maybe Jolie could tutor me!" Vita suggested. "She's lived forever and knows a lot, and so does Orlene."

"Tutoring—by a pair of ghosts? That had not occurred to me!"

"And they could do it all the time! You could test me, or something, to be sure I knew the stuff! And I'm learning a lot in court, really I am! Maybe if you got them registered as tutors—"

"This is irregular, but you may have a point. Are they amenable?"

Yes! Jolie and Orlene thought together.

"They say yes. Should I put them on?"

"No, I will accept your word."

"But my word's no good! I lie all the time, to get what I want. You can't trust me!"

"Are you lying now?"

"No! I wouldn't lie to *you,* Roque!"

"Then perhaps your word to me is good. You are developing a new standard, in keeping with your present situation."

She was taken aback. "Yeah, I guess maybe so."

"I shall see what can be done."

"Gee, thanks, Roque! I love you!" As she spoke, Vita threw her arms around him, hauled herself in and up, and planted a kiss on his startled face.

No! Jolie thought, way too late. She had been caught off guard.

But Vita, aware that she had transgressed, retreated, leaving Jolie in charge by default.

She quickly disengaged. "Jolie here," she said. "I must apologize for allowing—"

"Jolie, we must talk," he said, frowning. He led the way to a park bench and sat.

She joined him. "I can assure you that this will not happen again."

"What is the girl's emotional state?"

"Roque, she's young, and she has not had experience with a truly decent man before. You have treated her neither as a juvenile nor as a black prostitute, but as a legitimate person in her own right. She is recovering from H addiction, and I think has sublimated that discomfort in emotion. It is hardly surprising that—"

"She was not speaking figuratively, then."

Jolie sighed. "She was not."

"This places me in an awkward position. You know I cannot afford to have an amorous, underaged girl in my household."

Now, that's not fair! Orlene objected. *We agreed to remain in charge while she remained here.*

"You know that these things happen," Jolie said carefully. "Schoolgirls get crushes on their teachers, but the classes go on, and in due course they graduate to more serious involvements."

"I am not a teacher in a classroom with many students. I am a judge, and this child is residing in my suite. Considering her history, it would be inappropriate for such an arrangement to continue."

No! Vita thought in anguish. *I can't live without him!*

Jolie considered the complications of moving the host to some other facility and of dealing with the host's hurt. She wished she had intercepted Vita's rash action in time, so as to have avoided this problem. But now she had to tackle it directly.

"Roque, I deeply regret that this thing happened, but it is a reflection of the existing state. I feel that it is best for all concerned that the arrangement we had just settled on be allowed to stand. Orlene and I will tutor Vita and see that she qualifies to the necessary standards. We will remain in charge so that you are not embarrassed by this sort of foolishness again. You will not be left alone with the girl."

"Still, it is essential for a judge to avoid the appearance of impropriety, as well as the reality."

"I think you are being as foolish as the girl," Jolie said tartly. "The appearance is in the eye of the beholder. Your behavior has been impeccable, and hers will be so in the future. The impropriety occurred, as it were, offstage—and what was it? A girl impulsively kissed her guardian, who in no way sought or encouraged such attention. Even a judge should see no impropriety in that."

"What does she say about this?" he asked, wavering.

"I shall put her on again," Jolie said. Then, as she did so: *Vita, just sit straight and apologize for embarrassing him, and be in control. That will show him that you have learned your lesson.*

Jolie returned the body to the host. "Vita, here. I, uh, I wish to apologize, and—oh, Roque, please, please don't send me away! I love you, I want to be with you always, I want to have sex with you, I want to be your mistress for ever and ever, but I'll behave just perfectly, I'll do anything you want, only I beg you, please just let me stay!" Her tears were flowing as if turned on by a faucet.

Ouch! Orlene thought.

Vita tried to retreat again, but Jolie refused to take over. *Get yourself out of it this time!* she snapped.

Roque was looking at her, his face neutral.

"I'm, uh, not adult," Vita continued with difficulty. "I know I've got a lot to learn. I'm just a silly juvenile girl. I know my emotions get out of control. But with Orlene's guidance, and Jolie's, and yours, I hope to become what I should be. I really respect you. So—whatever you decide."

"If I allow you to remain . . ." he said.

She bowed her head, her shame at her outburst bringing her the control she had lacked before. "Whatever you decide," she repeated.

He nodded. "I think I perceive improvement already." He stood.

Don't question him! Jolie shot. *He's testing you.*

Vita, chastened, continued their walk, silent.

105

* * *

The Judge let it pass. Jolie and Orlene maintained strict control, and there were no other untoward incidents. Vita labored assiduously, and did indeed make progress in her education; she took standardized tests, and Jolie and Orlene refused to help her at all, but she gained. She was a bright enough girl, as should have been the case, considering her mother's proficiency as a researcher.

Time was passing pleasantly enough, but Jolie knew it could not last. Orlene recovered her equilibrium and resumed her interest in recovering her baby, but that had to wait until their present mission with Vita was resolved.

Orlene took it with surprising grace. *I know my baby is safe with Nox, and there is no aging in the Afterlife, so it can wait. When we finish here, I will be better prepared to resume that quest.*

It was not that she had lost interest in her baby; Jolie could tell by the ghost's thoughts that it remained strong. There was something else—and one day that other thing manifested to Jolie's considerable dismay.

Judge Scott was due for his annual vacation. He planned to go to the northern mountains, where a section of wilderness had been preserved as a giant park. "Have no concern; Vaasta will see to your needs, as usual," he told them.

I want to go with him! Vita thought urgently.

"I don't think that's wise," Jolie murmured.

I wish to second the motion, Orlene thought. *I identify with the wilderness, because of Norton. That's over, of course, but the delight remains. If we could accompany him, perhaps tending to the cooking or other chores that Vaasta does here . . .*

Roque glanced at her. "Your brow is furrowed, Jolie. Is there a problem?"

"I'm afraid there is. The other two want to go with you."

"I doubt that would be appropriate."

"I agree."

Now look, fair's fair! Vita thought. *Isn't Orlene supposed to be the one helping me, and you're just along to help her?*

"True, but—"

So Orlene should have a vote, shouldn't she? I mean, she's adult, she knows what it's all about.

Jolie looked up. "They wish to put it to a majority vote—and they are two to my one."

His mouth quirked. "Perhaps I should talk to Orlene."

Jolie turned over the body, uncertain what would come of this. "Orlene, here. No offense to you, Roque, but Vita and I feel that you do us an injustice by leaving us behind. We would be prepared to handle routine chores and try to pay our way, for the pleasure of the experience and your company."

"But much of this will involve hiking and camping alone. There would be an impropriety in having along a female below the age of consent."

"The host may be so, technically, but I was of age when I died; indeed, I was married and had borne and lost a baby. I am adult, regardless of the body."

"But it would be impossible to avoid the suspicion that we were in some manner involved with each other!"

"I hope you do not take this amiss, Roque, but I would not be averse to that suspicion."

What are you saying! Jolie thought, aghast.

"I am not certain I follow your implication," the Judge said carefully.

"Then I will clarify it. I have come to hold you in deep respect, and though it would be inaccurate to say that I care for you in the fashion that Vita does, I would by no means object to getting to know you better. I hope this is not cause for alarm on your part."

It is cause for alarm on my *part!* Jolie thought. *How can you, responsible woman, make such a proposition?*

The Judge considered. "I fear I may regret this. But it is true that I am not apt with the details Vaasta normally handles. You may accompany me if that is your sincere desire."

I'll have no part of this! Jolie thought. Orlene, at first bewildered by the circumstance of her death, and then by Nox's cruel trick, had now recovered astonishing poise and assertion. *You are doing it for Vita's sake—so that she can indulge her passion for the Judge!*

"Jolie does not approve," Orlene said.

107

"I would not wish either to interfere in your internal arrangements or to cause any of you three discomfort," Roque said. "Take time to consider among yourselves, and I will accede to your decision."

They did that. It was obvious that Orlene did indeed intend to accommodate Roque in more than routine matters, in part at Vita's behest, but also in part because of her own developing interest. But what was worse was Roque's willingness to go along with it. Apparently there was a majority of three for this excursion.

I will take a break, Jolie thought, her nose out of joint. *You do as you deem fit, Orlene. I will return when your party does.*

"We shall miss you," Orlene said sincerely.

Jolie departed as the others did, but in a different direction. She returned to Gaea and made her report on the weeks she had been gone: how Luna had sent her to Vita, who was now staying with the Judge while her home situation clarified.

"And not only the girl, but the woman, too, attracted to the Judge?" Gaea inquired.

"Girl and woman, each in her fashion," Jolie agreed. "It is my concern that they mean under this cover to let the girl have at the Judge."

"Why do you feel that this is wrong, considering our own arrangement with a man?"

"The girl is underage!"

"Only by society's definition, which is seldom honored in practice. She is evidently cognizant of her true interest, as is the woman. I see no harm in it. Do you have another reason?"

Jolie realized that she did. Of course her concern about Vita was spurious; the girl had had plenty of sexual experience already, so had no illusion about that aspect, and the Judge was not a man to take unfair advantage. "I hadn't realized, but I do. It relates to the man, but I'm not sure—"

"You have an interest in him yourself?"

"Not a romantic one; there has only ever been one for me."

"Whom we shall see shortly; I confess to having been out of sorts during your absence."

"I want to see him too! But the Judge—"

Then Jolie paused, the realization coming. "I see him as a candidate for an office!" she exclaimed. "He's such a good man, yet with considerable experience with the human condition. I don't want to see him sullied or disqualified!"

"Romance should hardly do that!"

"But with an underage girl, knowingly? That would certainly be a sin."

"Not by my definition, if it is truly voluntary by both parties."

Jolie thought back to her own days of life, when she was in love at age fourteen. She had waited until marriage before indulging in sexual activity, but that had been most unusual for that time. Certainly it seemed in retrospect that she could have indulged sooner, and now she wished she had. She had had so little time with Parry!

"But what about God's definition?"

"Interesting that you should raise that question at this time. Are you aware of the nature of Luna's research, with which you are indirectly helping?"

"What does that have to do with God? We were never told—"

"It is time you knew, Jolie, but I am not at liberty to tell you. Therefore I shall compromise: I shall tell you, then seal it off from your awareness until a more appropriate time. It is not my purpose to tease you, but to prepare you subconsciously for what could be a significant role you will play."

"What are you talking about? I am just a ghost!"

"The final confrontation is coming upon us, and all the Incarnations including Satan are girding for it. But it is not of precisely the nature even the Angel Gabriel anticipated."

"The confrontation between Good and Evil? But I cannot be involved with that, because of my conflict of interest!"

"No more than mine, my friend!"

"No more than yours," Jolie conceded. "We both love Satan; how can we be discussing this?"

"We have concluded that the issue can not be settled with the present cast, because as far as we can ascertain, God has not involved Himself with mortal or immortal affairs in several centuries. Therefore it behooves those who support Good to arrange for a change in the Officeholder."

Jolie was aghast. "Replace the Incarnation of Good?"

Gaea nodded. "Install a new man—one who will at least pay attention to mortal matters."

"But is that possible? Surely if the present Officeholder does not step down, no other force can make Him!"

"No other could—were he defending his turf. But in the absence of such defense, it becomes the prerogative of the other Incarnations to elect a replacement, by unanimous vote. The lesser ones support the greater ones, and outside ones like Nox do not concern themselves in this. So we are planning to hold a conclave and elect the replacement."

"But Satan will oppose that!"

"Of course. Because it is to his interest to maintain an inactive Incarnation of Good. A new one would be active, greatly complicating Satan's drive for power."

"Unless it were Satan himself. He really isn't evil."

Gaea smiled. "You and I might vote for him, but I doubt that a majority of the Incarnations would, let alone make it unanimous. It will have to be some other man."

"Some other man," Jolie agreed, still awed at the prospect.

"So Satan's defenses will be two: first he will try to prevent the vote from being taken. Since it requires the accordance of a clear majority of the mortals who believe in God, the first battle will occur in the mortal realm. It is in preparation for this that Luna is researching."

"Her key vote!" Jolie exclaimed. "To bring her constituency in line!"

"Even so. This is the help you have been rendering her. She requires precise information as to the sources of mortal opposition, so that she can neutralize as many as possible. Fate has been able to read ahead this far: it will come down to one vote, and that vote will be hers, but she must do it with the support of her mortal constituency. Satan will do his best to deny that support. This issue has been building since Luna entered politics, and perhaps longer. But it is only the first; the second will be the decision on the man."

"And that man may redefine the standards," Jolie said, seeing it. "So that there may not be automatic sin for consenting love, or for voluntary death, or a hundred other things."

"Yes. Those standards may once have been appropriate, but their relevance has eroded. We can not know how they will change, but we must try to select a man who will change them for the better."

"So the candidates I have been watching—"

"May be for that Office."

"And the Judge—"

"May be a candidate."

"But a unanimous choice—Satan will veto any man the others agree on!"

"True. But once the conclave is assembled, it will continue until the selection is made. Eventually there must be a compromise."

"But that almost guarantees that the best man will not be chosen!" Jolie protested. "That he'll be a compromise choice, with at least some evil—how can that be?"

"It evidently was so the last time. The evil in that choice manifested as indifference or vanity. Just as there is some good even in Satan, there is some evil even in God. But that will be better than nothing—which is what we have now."

"What we have now," Jolie echoed. What a development!

"So now you can appreciate the importance of your observation. You must understand the Judge well enough to be able to recommend him for such an Office—or to eliminate him from consideration. We must not have any mistakes in our nominations! You must retain awareness of the critical nature of your mission, but not of the mission itself. I regret putting you in such a position, but believe it must be so, for the present."

"I understand. I would not have believed it otherwise."

Gaea looked at her—and abruptly Jolie forgot what she had been told, retaining only the imperative to study Judge Scott with excruciating care and objectivity.

"Now let's go consort with the enemy," Gaea said.

Jolie was relieved to shift from the perplexity in which she found herself. She was aware of having discussed something of transcendent importance, but could not recollect what it was. She floated into Gaea and animated her body, conforming it to her own.

She rejoined Vita and Orlene as they returned from the Judge's vacation. Vita looked tanned and fit and satisfied, though of course her tan was permanent. Roque seemed pensive. Jolie dreaded to conjecture what that meant, despite Gaea's assurance about the morality of the situation.

We were naughty, Orlene thought.

Jolie had washed her hands of the matter, but now she had to know: exactly what had happened on that trip north? The other two were glad to fill her in, running a chain of vivid selected memories. It was as if Jolie herself were living it.

An airplane, for the scientific devices tended to be better than the magical ones for massive or long traveling. Arrival at the northern airport, where megabuildings were sparse. A carpet to the campsite, with supplies for several days. A foot hike to the local sights: huge old pine trees, jagged natural slopes, and a freezingly cold untamed river.

Evening at an unheated cabin. They cooked their staples over an open fire of burning wood, an amazing novelty, complete with choking smoke. Both Vita and Orlene loved it.

Then the night in the cabin. They had separate sleeping bags, but Orlene balked. "We are alone now, Roque, and there is no need for confusion. You are a gentleman and will not force the issue, but we deem it our prerogative to do that. Unless you protest, we shall merge our bags and join you for the night."

"I must object," Roque said.

"You have reservations about the age or race of the host?"

"No, it is the age of the controlling person that counts, and it never occurred to me that race should be a factor. But—"

"You have difficulty relating to women?"

"No! But—"

"Objection noted. Overruled."

He had to smile. "I can not stop you, but it should also be noted that I did anticipate something like this, and am resolved to take no advantage of anyone. If you wish to talk, I shall be glad to do that, but that will be the extent of it."

Orlene put the bags together and got in with him. "I shall be happy to talk, Roque, if it does not deprive you of sleep. Of what nature is your concern?"

"Merely the question of propriety, which you have now answered satisfactorily. But I have the impression that there is something I do not know of you and your motive, and I would like to understand that. Vita has expressed interest in me of a certain, shall we say, personal nature, but you have not, so your interest in accompanying me here, and in establishing such propinquity, is obscure."

She snuggled close to him in her nightie. "I want you to understand the manner in which you have done me some singular good. I was an adoptee, raised by good folk, but always with the knowledge that I had been born to other parents. Even though there was never any discrimination of any kind against me, that awareness always set me just a bit apart. Perhaps it was that which led me to avoid true marriage and agree to a ghost marriage, wherein I married a ghost and agreed to bear a child who would carry his inheritance. The ghost, Gawain, was a dragon slayer who had in turn been slain by one of his quarry, technically an allosaur. I never knew him in life, and he was unable to manifest to me in death, so there was no love between us. Indeed, I was satisfied that it be so, for I think I felt unworthy of love, because of my anonymous parentage. Gawain solicited men to come to me, but I had the right of veto, so that I would not have to endure sex with an inappropriate male. I was not being coy; I have the talent of judging people by the glows of their auras, as you know, and I judged each prospect by his glow as a father and lover. I was actually relieved when the first ones had inadequate glows. If the truth be told—and this is the time, I think, for telling it—I really did not believe the ghost existed, and thought that the men who came were mere opportunists.

113

Only later did I come to accept the validity of it and that Gawain really was active on my behalf.

"Then Gawain brought Norton, a wandering environmentalist, and the sight of his glow overwhelmed me so that I could hardly speak. He and I faltered through an introduction, but I knew from the outset that he was the one. Indeed, he came to live with me, and we were lovers, and he fathered my baby, and then—" She found herself crying.

"I know the history," Roque said gently. "I regret that such tragedy came to you."

"So now I am a ghost, having followed my baby," she continued after a while. "But when Jolie and I went to see the Incarnation of Night, and I became a man and attempted to rape her, that was such a blow to my self-esteem that I retreated entirely. I had seen most men, other than Norton, as crude, lecherous animals, but now I knew that I was no better, for I had been worse than they, when given their imperative. I had never dreamed that sex could be so powerful a force! It entirely overwhelmed me, and all ethical scruples ceased to have meaning. I simply yielded to the imperative to *do* it, and damned be all else. Only Nox's intercession, her offering of herself to sate my intemperate lust, aborted my effort. I wronged my friend Jolie, but that was only the half of it, because my confidence in my own quality of character was shaken. How could I condemn any man for yielding to his passion, after that? How could I consider myself in any way superior, or even equal to others, in the moral sense? And so I gave up my quest, finding myself unworthy of it, and let myself sink toward Hell, where it seemed I belonged. Only Jolie saved me, by refusing to let me descend, though she was the one I had wronged.

"She brought me to this host so that I would not sink the moment she let go of my soul. Here I became immersed in the horrors of a girl of the street, and realized that it was not enough merely to condemn myself for my fall; I had to try to do something about the evil that was around me and in me. Then the host came to you, and I came to know you, Roque. I had forgotten that there are differences in men, as there

114

are in women. Forgotten that I had known and loved a good man, Norton. Indeed, now I saw that I had not loved him enough. When my baby died, all I could think of was the baby, and I went to join him. Now I see how badly I wronged Norton, who loved me. I could not save my baby, but I could have saved my relationship with Norton. So I was doing wrong before I went to Nox. I had been intemperate in my narrow vision, and came to understand it and rue it too late.

"But now, for a time, I am alive again, borrowing the body of a girl. Temporary though it may be, I am resolved to acquit myself better than I did in my own life. My crime was to neglect the importance of the personal relationship, to underrate love. You have helped show me that, by being what you are: a fair and generous man. Vita loves you, Roque, and I am not sure that this is a fleeting fancy. It is my wish to intercede in what manner I may to facilitate the consummation of her love during the window that is available to it. Soon she will return home and that window will be closed. I am aware that you do not wish to have an untoward relationship with a girl who is below the legal age of consent. But if you will have one with me, in the knowledge that she is present—"

"I will not," Roque said firmly. "I will deal with her directly, invoking no surrogate."

"And this is the other aspect of what you have done for me," she continued, unperturbed. "You have shown me that it is possible for a man to withstand temptation. I know the forces that are in you, for I have experienced them myself. But what overwhelmed me, you control so consistently that never by word or glance or deed do you yield to it. I envy you that control, and I admire you for that and all that you are. You are another man I could love, Roque; I do not do so because it is no longer my prerogative. I cannot make up in death what I squandered in life. But now I have the assurance that to be male is not necessarily to be evil, and I thank you for restoring that perspective to me."

"I thank you for your candor," Roque said. "I wish I had known you during your life. Perhaps I wish that I could have been the man to approach you, in your ghost marriage, for there is much that I like about your attitude. Of course, I might not have glowed the way your lover did—"

"You do glow, brightly," she said. "You would certainly have qualified. In fact, you would qualify for almost any woman. How is it that you are not married?"

"I really am not apt with women," Roque confessed. "Somehow it seemed that each woman in whom I might have taken an interest was taken by a more aggressive or endowed man. Justice was always my passion, and the girls had other interests. So I never married, to my regret."

"Had any woman come to know you as we are coming to know you, things would have been different."

"It is kind of you to say so. In fact I very much appreciate the sentiment."

"Perhaps we should sleep now," she said, closing her eyes in the darkness, half expecting him to make some sort of a move, for she was very close to him.

"Of course." He made no move, though his glow showed his desire.

Next day they took another hike, admiring the scenery both great and small. Roque had an interest in all things natural and was happy to discourse on it, and Orlene and Vita were happy to listen, for their separate reasons: Orlene remembered Norton's similar interest, and Vita thought that anything to do with Roque was fascinating.

At night Orlene turned the body over to Vita. Vita approached Roque. "Vita, here. Tonight is my turn. May I be with you?"

Roque smiled. "I said I would deal with you directly, invoking no surrogate. I rather suspected this confrontation would come."

She put the bags together and linked them, joining him in her nightie. "I promised to behave, and in these weeks with you, I have come to understand what discipline can be. Orlene and Jolie taught me a lot, and not just about school subjects. You taught me a lot, too, Roque, and not just in court. So I think this time I can be near you without going haywire, but if I lose my grip, Orlene will take over so you won't be embarrassed."

"This is commendable," Roque replied.

"You know how I feel about you, and I know you have no interest in juvenile girls, but would it be too far out of line if I asked you to sort of put your arms around me?"

"You are in error about one of your assumptions, Vita."

She froze. "I'm sorry, I guess I asked too much."

"No, your request was reasonable in the circumstance." He put his arms around her, bringing her close to him.

She was almost afraid to move, lest he change his mind. "Thank you, Roque. It means so much to me. After the experience I've had, it's really been neat to be with a man who didn't want to, you know. I'm really sorry I came on to you the way I did before. I guess control and restraint are the biggest things I've been learning. I just somehow thought that the only way to please a man was—"

"Please desist, before you embarrass me further."

"Sorry," she said, chagrined.

"There is something I must tell you," he said gravely. "Aspects of it may not please you, and if that is the case, you have my apology, and I will understand if you prefer to separate yourself from me."

"You're going to send me home!" she cried, stricken.

"No. Were you listening when I talked with Orlene last night?"

"Yes," she said faintly.

"Then you are aware that I have never married and never was able to develop a close association with a member of the opposite sex. There is an aspect I did not discuss, however."

"No! You can't be gay!" she exclaimed in horror.

He laughed. "No, that is not my situation. But certainly I have had a secret vice. I am, despite your impression, typical of men in my desires. In my private imagination for many years I have pictured an event of a nature I have never cared to advertise. In this vision an attractive young woman approaches me and states that she has conceived an inordinate passion for me and wishes to indulge herself with

117

me in the wildest of sexual orgies. This is of course forbidden, for she may not even be of legal age. Yet in my vision I am sorely tempted, assured that no other party would know."

Vita lifted her head. "You're joking!"

"Far from it. When you stated that you wished to be my mistress, you fulfilled that secret desire. I knew that I should send you immediately to some other facility. I knew that I was wrong in my failure to do that. Even then, I knew that in time you and I would find ourselves as we are now. I accepted the ruse of Orlene's control, knowing that she would free you for this encounter. Therefore, I can not claim any surprise; I wanted to be alone with you. This is the manner you have misread me; I am no better than any of the men who have used you in the past."

Vita was stunned. "You—You wanted me all the time?"

"I did. I fought against it, knowing how wrong it was to implement any part of my fell vision, and lost. But I assure you that this is as far as it will go. I have no intention of molesting you, and if I have repulsed you by this confession, I certainly understand."

"But last night Orlene was willing, and you didn't touch her."

"That was less nobility than expedience. My desire is not for Orlene, though certainly I would be interested if that were her wish. My desire is for you."

"But you knew I was watching! You could have done it with her, and I could've pretended it was me."

"She offered herself as a legitimizing personality, she being of age and experience to know her mind. She did not truly desire this kind of interaction with me, but felt that she owed it to you, for the use you have allowed her of your body. I find that a fine gesture on her part, but it is not one I care to indulge. My vision is illicit; my desire is for the body and personality of youth."

"Young flesh!" she exclaimed. "All day you put away pimps and women who do it, and you crave it yourself!"

"That is my secret shame. I regret destroying your image of me, but I felt you should know the truth."

"You don't really care for me, you just want young flesh!" she charged.

"The irony is that I do care for you. I have been impressed by the manner you settled down and worked at learning, and by your increasingly proper deportment. I know that many times at meals and during our walks in the roof park the others have relinquished your body to you, and that after your first declaration, you have not shamed yourself in your actions or words. You have been helpful to Vaasta; indeed, she has spoken favorably of you. You are becoming a fine young woman, and it ill behooves me to interfere with that. This is why my illicit passion for your flesh is such an evil; it spoils what would otherwise be an excellent relationship."

"But you know if you asked me, I'd be glad to spread my legs for you!"

"That is one reason I have not asked you. The willingness of the girl does not excuse sexual abuse."

"So you just figured to get me here like this, and tell me your desire, and that'll maybe turn me off, and it'll be over," Vita said. "You aren't one for force or rape or anything like that."

"I am afraid so."

"But you sort of hoped it wouldn't turn me off, and I'd dive right in with you anyway."

"It is the time for candor."

Vita thought about it, not moving from his embrace. "I guess I should ask Orlene."

"She well might have some sage advice for you at this stage."

"But I'm not going to. You know what I really wanted, when I said I wanted to be your mistress?"

"Love, security, attention."

"That's right! And the best way I ever knew to get it was to please a man, and the best way to please a man was by having sex with him. I didn't know any other way to win your interest, and I wanted it real bad."

"I think I was aware of that too. Certainly you are not obliged to prostitute yourself to me for—"

"Oh, shut up, Roque! *I want your love!* Now I know that it's not the same as your sex. Can you say you love me?"

Roque hesitated. "I cannot say I do not."

"Why not just lie to me?" she flared. "Say the magic word, and I'll do anything you want!"

"This is, of course, standard procedure with men," he said. "To tell a woman it is love, when the true object is merely sex. I would not care to deceive you in that manner."

"Why not?" she demanded.

"It would not be ethical. But apart from that, I am uncertain of my feeling for you. It would be foolish for a middle-aged man to love a child in that manner."

"Then tell me you don't love me!"

"I cannot."

"If I can't have your love, I'll give it to you for honesty. Nobody ever seemed to care much before how I felt about it, and you do."

"True."

"Oh Roque, could you maybe just kiss me and see how it is?"

"I am not certain that would be wise."

"So call me out of order!" she said, and turned her face to find his in the dark. She kissed him emphatically.

He remained passive for a moment, then his arms tightened around her. He kissed her back. It seemed to go on forever, and her feeling ignited, and she half climbed on him, trying to get closer than close.

"Oh, Roque," she gasped. "If that isn't love, I'll settle for it!"

"It is passion," he said. "Not to be trusted."

"Look, I know a girl's not supposed to get all hot and eager, especially when she's underage, but I've just got to have you! All those bad men I've had in me, let me get one good one and erase all the rest!"

"This isn't right—" he began.

"You have your vision, I have mine too! I want you to want me, to want me so bad you just can't help yourself," she said, clawing out of her nightie. "Maybe the world will end tomorrow if you do it, but you're so hot you don't care, you

120

just gotta have me, and I'm yours, Roque, I'm yours." Free of her clothing, she started to work on his. "Your vision *is* my vision, you crafted it just for me—that's what I want to believe!"

He could not withhold his mounting passion. "Ask Orlene!" he cried. "Ask her if she can tolerate this!"

You're doing great, girl! Orlene thought, feeling hot herself. *Maybe it is wrong, but it's got to be!*

"She says to go for it!" Vita panted, getting his pajamas open.

"We shall surely regret this in the morning," he said, his resistance crumbling.

Then they were kissing again, and merging, and Vita felt the thrust of his loin and the jet of his culmination, and she went into a feeling she had never had before in sex with a man, and clung to him and stretched to kiss him and touch his tongue with hers while the feeling spread through the rest of her body. "Oh, Roque! Oh, Roque!" she breathed, over and over.

"Oh, my darling," he breathed back. "Though I go to Hell, it is worth it!"

"I'll go there with you, my darling, my love!" she babbled, clinging to him, trying to keep the fading feeling, trying to hold him within her. But it was useless; they had to separate, lying beside each other.

"We have been quite crazy," he remarked.

"Yeah." Then she realized something. "Hey, you never felt me up!"

She felt the shake of his laughter. "I fear it is late for that."

"No, it isn't! Here, do it now!" She grabbed for his hand and hauled it to her breast. "Squeeze!"

He squeezed, gently. "Do you know, it does give me pleasure, even at this moment when my sexual urgency has been sated."

"So maybe you really do love me."

"So maybe I do," he echoed.

She caught his hand again, guiding it to her other breast. "Every one of my johns, he was hot to kiss me and feel me

121

before, but once he got his meat in, that was all, he just wanted to be outa there. How come it's different now?"

"Because we did it for love."

"Oh, Roque, can you say it now?"

"I think perhaps I can, foolish though I know it to be."

"Say it! Oh, say it!"

"I love you, Vita," he said.

"I love you, Roque." She had thrilled to his presence, and to their dialogue, and to their culmination, but the thrill she felt now was deeper and finer than any of these. "Promise me you won't change your mind in the morning!"

"You know I cannot promise that, Vita. In the morning the full realization of my folly will be upon me."

"Well, it won't be on me! I could stay here like this forever!"

"So could I, Vita. But morning will come despite us."

Morning did come. Vita did not remember sleeping, just lying there holding his hand to her breasts, but now the light was filtering in past the cabin curtains. Roque was in his bathrobe, clean-shaven, his hair combed.

He saw her stirring. "Perhaps I should absent myself while you clean up and dress," he said.

She felt her hair plastered to her face in sodden hanks. They had sweated last night! "I must be a sight!"

"You are beautiful." He walked toward the door.

She scrambled up, heedless of her nakedness, and ran to him. "Don't go, Roque! I've got this notion that if you do, you'll never come back! You'll realize it was all a terrible mistake, and you'll resolve to never let it happen again and I'll lose you forever!"

"Well—"

She caught him and tore open his robe, then plastered herself against him. "Please, please, please, Roque, this is all the time we have. I swear I'll behave when we're back in the city, let me be your nymphet now!"

"You are trying to seduce me!" he exclaimed with mock outrage.

"Anything you want, Roque! I've been waiting all my life for right now, and I'll never have another time like this. I've got to make the most of it! I love you, I love you!"

"And I love you—even in the morning," he said, and she knew she had won.

"Don't forget to feel me," she reminded him.

"You are amazing," he said, running his hand over her buttocks.

Soon they were into sex again. She didn't think of it as making love, because this entire experience was an unremitting making of love; the sex was only its most emphatic manifestation.

Jolie woke from the vision of the memory. "The whole vacation?" she asked, flabbergasted. "Solid sex? You were more than naughty!"

Solid love, Orlene corrected. *I thought I was going to have a limited affair with him, for the benefit of Vita, but she wound up doing it herself.*

You liked it too! Vita put in.

I liked it too, Orlene agreed. *I stayed out of it, overtly, but really I did participate. We were wanton! That poor man hardly got any rest at all. Now we leave the pieces for you to pick up.*

Jolie tried to be angry, but this vision was too fresh and strong, too full of the delight of abandon. She remembered her seduction of Parry when he was a friar. How sweet it had been—but with what a consequence!

Unfortunately this, too, would have a consequence. Now Jolie remembered something she seemed to have forgotten. "I must tell you something I learned," she subvocalized. "You must not repeat this to any mortal. We want to consider Judge Scott as a candidate to become an Incarnation. This means that I shall be observing him to decide to what degree he qualifies. But—"

Oh, no! Orlene thought. *And we just caused him to sin!*

"Gaea disagrees. She feels that natural, consenting love is no sin, and if it is to be considered such, then the definitions of sin need amending."

Yes! Orlene agreed. *He is a good man, he deserves an Office!*

But if he should become an Incarnation, Vita asked, *what would become of him?*

"He would step into an immortal plane and leave his ordinary mortal existence behind. He would no longer age, or be vulnerable to mortal mishap."

So then he wouldn't be interested in any nymphet.

Jolie saw her point. "You knew this could not be permanent, Vita. In fact, it could not extend beyond your one wild fling. So that wouldn't make any difference to you."

Yes, it would! I want to be near him always!

"However, if there should be any longer-term relationship, it is not unknown for Incarnations to retain them," Jolie continued. "I maintain a relationship with an Incarnation, though I am a ghost, and Luna Kaftan maintains one with the Incarnation of Death."

Maybe there's a chance for me, Vita thought, relieved. *Which Incarnation is he being considered for?*

Here Jolie drew a blank. "I—I think it could be any one of them. But each is so important that it is vital that no errors be made."

Vita was dismayed. *We made him sin—and now he won't qualify?* she asked.

He didn't sin! Orlene demurred. *Maybe we did, but he didn't. He tried to do the decent thing all along, but in the end he was human, and I am glad of it.*

"The question is, how does he feel about it?" Jolie asked. "If he feels it was a sin, then there is evil on his soul, and it will hurt him."

Perhaps you should ask him, Orlene suggested.

Jolie sighed, knowing she would have to do it.

She broached the matter as they rode the carpet to the city. "I understand the girls were active during my absence," she said.

"Exceedingly," he admitted. "I am sure you are aware that my interaction was with the child, not the woman, despite expectations."

He would not bend a bit to protect himself! "What are your intentions?"

"I shall report myself to the board of ethics, which I suspect will suspend me pending investigation and retire me thereafter."

She had been afraid of this. "Roque, I left because I felt that what was contemplated was wrong. But now I see it otherwise. There was no force, no coercion, no promises founded or unfounded. There was only love between man and woman. A young woman, granted, but old enough in experience and in guidance to know her mind. I don't believe that should be the concern of the board of ethics."

"The law is clear, and I am charged with the upholding of it. When I transgress, I must pay the price."

"When the board investigates, they will question the girl. She will testify that nothing untoward happened. What will then be the disposition of the case?"

"But that would be untrue!" he exclaimed.

"The girl is young and has a checkered history. She knows what would happen to you and to herself if she confirmed any intimacy between the two of you. Do you think she will indict you?"

He stared at her. "This is blackmail!"

"This is reason. In your heart you know that no crime was committed and that the lodging of the report you contemplate would only hurt each of you. What is your ultimate definition of justice?"

"You speak like a creature from Hell!"

"I am the consort of the Master of Hell."

He pondered. "The girl must leave my house. Only then may we be assured that the event was isolated."

No! Vita thought.

"She loves you, Roque."

"And I love her. But it must be."

Jolie sighed. "You are a good man, Judge Scott. You hold to higher standards than we do. We shall depart your residence at our earliest convenience."

No! I can't! I'll die!

125

Quiet, you silly child! Orlene snapped. *She has something in mind.*

"Thank you, Jolie," the Judge said, looking miserable.

"You are not welcome, Roque."

At that he had to smile. "I think it best that you not relinquish control until the departure is accomplished."

Jolie nodded. He was indeed a good man.

CHAPTER SIX

Death

JOLIE TOOK THEM TO LUNA'S OFFICE. SHE borrowed the Judge's personal carpet; it would return to him on its own when she got off and dismissed it.

So what's your plan? Vita demanded. *You know it's my body; you can't keep me away from him forever!*

"I can as long as I retain control," Jolie said. "But fear not, I am on the side of romance, having been the route myself. The Judge had to do what he did; it was his compromise after I threatened him with your noncooperation. If he couldn't pay the penalty for his deed, he had to make certain that no further abuse occurred. So he will not report the matter, and you are gone from his household. But that does not mean gone from his life. We shall be seeing him again soon enough, I'm sure."

When? How?

"We are about to determine that. Meanwhile, Orlene, I think it is time we resumed your quest for your baby. You have recovered your equilibrium, and can now exist as a ghost without sinking to Hell."

Oh, Jolie, of course I want to do that! But—

"But you are halfway in love with Roque yourself, and wish to leave him hardly more than Vita does."

It is true. I have not forgotten Norton, nor do I wish to encroach on Vita's interest, but—

It's okay, Orlene! I feel so much better with you along. Without you I couldn't have been with Roque on that vacation, and even when you let me do it with him, you were there, helping me not to make too much of a fool of myself. Without you I'd revert to H; I know you and Jolie are helping me get over the craving, and with three it's much easier than alone. I really need you! I have no jealousy of you; you're part of what Roque sees in me.

"So I believe that the three of us should remain together," Jolie said. "Working to accomplish both your desires, and mine too."

Yours too?

"I am highly impressed with Roque Scott, and not just because of the way you girls feel about him. I think he just might qualify to be an Incarnation, and I want to watch him closely with that in mind, so that I can make a full report when the time comes. So my job is compatible with yours; we can watch him, and sometimes be with him, and try to recover your baby, together. Of course we shall have to take some turns."

Agreed, Orlene thought, relieved. *I confess that when you said I could leave this host, I was afraid; I prefer residence in the living state to being a ghost, and I very much like Vita's company.*

You do? I thought you regarded me as an impulsive juvenile.

I do. You do things I would never unbend enough to do. The way you tore open Roque's robe—but I loved being along for the ride. You lend excitement to my life—I mean, my death.

And you lend maturity to mine, Vita thought, pleased. *When you two came, I thought, What the hell is this, spooks messing up my life even worse than it was, keeping me from the H. But you're better than H! You got me to Roque, and you're teaching me so much, I really think I can be something when I grow up.*

"So I think we are agreed," Jolie said. "We shall work

together, until it seems appropriate to separate, and perhaps we shall in time achieve all our desires." The truth was that she, too, rather liked experiencing the living state again. She had never had enough of it, the first time, with Parry.

We are agreed, Orlene thought.

Great! Vita added.

The secretary in Luna's office looked up. "May I help you?"

"I need to see Senator Kaftan," Jolie said.

"The Senator is away from the city this week. Do you wish to make an appointment?"

That wouldn't do; they needed a residence today. Jolie, in her concern with moving them out of the Judge's residence, had not anticipated this.

Maybe Mom . . .

Good notion! "Is Vera here?" The folk at Luna's office were all first names, as was Luna herself, normally.

"Why yes, you may see her if you wish."

"I will have to put you back in charge," Jolie murmured.

They were shown into a back office piled with books and papers and video screens: the research department. There was a woman who looked a lot like Vita, thirty years older.

"Mom!"

The woman looked up, startled, and burst into tears. Vita went over and hugged her, crying herself.

Before long they were comparing brief notes. It seemed that Vera had gotten a notion of the problem in the family, but didn't want to speak of it openly. She did not importune Vita to return home. Vita was at pains to explain that though something had caused her to leave, and that she had had some bad times, she was now much better off and perhaps even had a better life than she might have had.

"I've been staying with Judge Scott," she concluded. "He has a housekeeper who's nice, but you know he can't keep a juvenile girl in his house forever, it would look wrong, so I have to move out. I've got a friend with me, a ghost, and when I need to do something adult, she takes over. We're going to do some traveling, and we're helping in your research, maybe."

Vera's look indicated that she had a glimmer of why her daughter had to depart the presence of the Judge, but again she preferred to let it lie. It was obvious that Vita was physically healthy and emotionally sound, and that was an immeasurable reassurance. "You know of my research?"

"Some, Mom. The final confrontation between Good and Evil, when—"

"Enough! You are helping in this?"

"In part. Looking for candidates for—"

"Don't say it! Satan's minions are everywhere."

"Satan knows it's coming, Mom. Anyway, I sort of need a place to stay, for a while, until I travel. We thought Luna might know—"

"Let me ask." She got up and hurried out.

In a moment she returned, the look of surprise still on her face. "Luna left word: you are to go to her house immediately. It seems that Judge Scott notified her."

"The Judge is a great man, Mom."

"I am not sure I grasp all of what is going on here."

"I guess you know, Mom, it was Luna who sent the ghost to me, to get me straightened out. She wanted you to feel at ease. The Judge, when he learned about her involvement, decided to help."

"She is a great woman."

"I guess that's why she and the Judge understand each other so well."

"There seems to be a good deal of understanding," Vera remarked somewhat wryly.

A carpet took them to Luna's estate. The two griffins charged up as it came down. Jolie took over. "Griffith! Grissel!" she called. "Smell my soul!"

They recognized an approved visitor and relaxed. They stopped at the front door, cautiously. "Muir!" she called to the moon moth within. "It's me, Jolie, in human host."

Muir, too, recognized her, and she entered without challenge. *Gee,* Vita remarked, impressed.

They walked through the house, admiring the aura paintings on the walls. Luna could see auras, Jolie explained to the others, and so could judge people in much the manner Orlene could. Perhaps that was not surprising, for Orlene was very like a niece to her.

There was a note on the kitchen counter. WELCOME, TRIO. FOOD IS AVAILABLE. USE THE EAST ROOM. DRESS IN SOMETHING NICE.

"Dress in something nice?" Jolie asked, perplexed. "To stay alone until she returns?"

They checked the East Room. It was a beautiful suite, complete with a closet stocked with several lovely dresses of the appropriate size. There were slipper-shoes which fit Vita's feet perfectly. There would be no problem dressing nicely!

They made a project of it, taking a good bath, washing the hair and putting a slow curve in it by using a spellstone designed for that purpose, and donning a dress that was first cousin to an evening gown. Vita had filled out during her time with the Judge and now looked impressive in the low décolletage. *I think I've been turned into a princess for a night!* she thought admiringly.

There was the sound of a chime. They tripped down to the front door, uncertain who could be calling, but certain that Muir would allow no intruder.

Roque Scott stood there. He gazed at them, astonished. "Here?" he asked.

Jolie turned the body over to Vita. "Oh, Roque!" she breathed. "Don't go away!"

He stepped up and swept her into his arms. "This is not my house," he said. "I am not obliged to enforce standards here."

"Shut up and get on to the endearments," she said, lifting her face for a kiss.

"You are delightfully forward, my juvenile delight."

"I'm too young to know any better. How come you're here?"

"I received a message from Luna's office, asking me to check on an item of some value at her house. Naturally I came here after work, knowing that she would not ask such a favor capriciously."

131

"We didn't see anything," Vita said.

"Of course you didn't, my darling innocent." He stroked her hair.

She tittered, catching on. "Gee, it's fun to be innocent!"

Maybe we should depart for a few hours, Jolie thought.

"No!" Vita said.

Roque's hand, having proceeded beyond the length of her tresses and on down her back toward her rear, froze. "No?"

She laughed. "I didn't mean you, Roque! I *want* you to feel me. I was talking to Jolie. She wants to go away."

"She did before," he pointed out.

"With Orlene this time. So I can be all the way alone with you. But I'm afraid I'd screw it up."

"Well . . ."

"Oh, you know what I mean! I want to be good for you, Roque, and on my own I keep getting too wild. I'd get the shakes, for sure, and turn you off, and I sure don't want to do that! So I don't want them to go."

"In that case, I am certainly amenable to their continued presence. I must confess that I do feel easier knowing that a woman of adult experience is monitoring the proceedings, because it allays my concern about taking advantage of one who is young."

But I'm another man's wife! Jolie protested.

"Maybe you better talk to Jolie," Vita said. "Give me one good feel before I put her on."

His hand resumed its motion downward—at which point Vita gave the body to Jolie. He squeezed her buttock. Jolie clamped her teeth, trying to look neutral.

"The gamin!" he exclaimed, realizing. He was now able to recognize them separately, by their manners.

Jolie disengaged. "As we know, she is young," she said. "And full of mischief." She walked to a couch and sat down, crossing her legs demurely at the ankles.

He took a seat across the room. "Perhaps your reasons for bringing Vita to me were mixed. As you know, I succumbed, and you and I agreed to do the appropriate thing. I think you were aware that I did not truly wish to separate from her, and I think you are not averse to our meeting in a situation like this. Your absence is thus a mere formality or courtesy which need not be invoked at this stage."

"I am the wife or consort of Satan," Jolie replied. "I do not care to be present in the body of a woman who is making love to another man. Orlene may certainly remain, but I prefer to absent myself."

"I am minded to debate the issue," he said, "if you are willing. If you do not approve my liaison with Vita, you can not excuse yourself merely by being absent in a manner you know will facilitate it."

"That isn't what I said!" Jolie said, stung. "I did have doubts, but subsequent thought has eased them, and I now feel that the two of you should be allowed your love. My presence or absence shouldn't affect that. But my own—"

"Yes. You do not wish to engage in the appearance of impropriety. I understand this consideration rather well. But this, too, I question. If I understand it correctly, your marriage to the man who is now the holder of the Office of the Incarnation of Evil dissolved when you died. He subsequently remarried, and you now join his present wife in amorous engagements. Thus the experience of joint involvement is not foreign to you."

He had it exactly! A thought had been growing beneath Jolie's level of consciousness, and now it surfaced. If she was to study this man as a potential candidate for the Office of an Incarnation, she could hardly do so by deliberately not observing him in moments of his passion. She had to understand him fully. She also needed to know how he approached matters of ethics and questions of propriety. Also, how he related to the underlying questions of Good and Evil. That meant she should remain.

Still, she had a problem. "It is more than the appearance, Roque. I do not love you and do not wish to be embraced by you, even in surrogate. I would feel extremely awkward about returning to my husband—or, if you will, consort—after—"

"There is also this to consider: Satan surely has been intimate with a great many women over the course of his tenure, yet you still love him and wish to join him at every opportunity. Do you hold to a standard you do not expect of him?"

Ouch! The days of Jolie's sexual innocence had been left behind centuries ago. She no longer believed in a double standard. She knew Parry had had long and extreme affairs with the likes of the demoness Lilah and the damned soul Nefertiti, yet had returned gladly to her when she remanifested. What counted, in the end, was not his dalliances during her absence, but the way he felt about her, and she about him. He had never loved the demoness or the damned soul; he had loved Jolie. Now he loved Gaea—and still loved Jolie. Was she so much less certain of her love for him?

"I think you have made your case, Roque," she said. "I will remain."

He smiled briefly. "As you wish."

"But one more thing, before I submerge. How do you feel about Satan?"

"I suppose that is a fair question, from one who loves him. I am adamantly in the opposite camp, and wish to support the forces of Good in every respect. Yet I see the need for a repository of damned souls, until they can be redeemed, and therefore I concede the need for a supervisor of that repository. As I understand it, Satan is not actually evil, just as Thanatos is not actually dead; he is merely a human person handling an unusual and often unrewarding job. I think you would not love him were that not the case, just as Luna would not love Thanatos."

A fair answer indeed! "Suppose you ever found yourself in a position to—to negotiate with Satan on some matter. Would you do it?"

"Of course. I feel that I am already, whenever I decide whether a given person should be punished or rehabilitated or go free. Satan is attempting to evoke the Evil; I am attempting to evoke the Good. It is, in a fashion, a continuing exercise in classification and treatment."

This man was certainly, to Jolie's way of thinking, a prime prospect! "So you, knowing that one who is close to Satan is with the woman you love, do not feel threatened."

"Satan never threatened any person whose convictions and practices were good."

"I think Luna might disagree."

"Luna is perhaps an exception," he admitted. "She is pivotal. But I think it is not her soul he threatens, only her political power."

"You impress me, Roque."

"Jolie, you impress me also. I thought I was dealing with a wayward girl, and then you manifested, and the case became inordinately more interesting. I had no intent to take Vita into my residence, until I became aware that you were in control. Then I realized that rehabilitation of the girl was not only possible, it was already in progress, and I did my best to facilitate your effort. Certainly you have been in no sense a malign influence. My subsequent relation with Vita, though unintended, was thus a direct result of your involvement. For that I must thank you. However wrong it may be technically, I now believe it is right ethically. You have brought light into my life, and I shall always be grateful."

"I, too, am glad it happened," Jolie said. And she wondered: could Luna have known this too? That Judge Scott was a worthy prospect to be an Incarnation, and that Jolie would discover this by the time she shepherded Vita through her problem? It seemed likely, now.

She returned the body to Vita, who promptly jumped up and flung herself across to Roque. "What were you trying to do, pinching Jolie like that?" she demanded, plumping into his lap.

"By your mischief," he said. "What is this delight you have in being impertinently handled?"

"I hated it when my johns did it," she confessed. "I hated everything about them. But I did catch on to what men like. Now I've got a man *I* like, I want to be sure I'm giving him a good time." She drew up her knees so that her dress fell away, and guided his hand to her inner thigh.

"I trust you realize that this is shameless exploitation." But his hand did slide along her skin caressingly.

"You can do better than that," she said. "Come on, what are panties for, anyway?"

135

"For dirty old men's delight," he said. "Still, I would not want to spoil your pretty outfit."

"I'll take it off!" she said eagerly, and began scrambling to do just that.

All that effort we made, dressing her—gone! Orlene thought with resignation.

"But this sheer enthusiasm on your part continues to amaze me. How did you come by it?"

"I guess I just so much wanted to be wanted," she said. "Not just used and thrown away, but loved and needed forever. Maybe when I get older I'll really like just to talk with you, the way Jolie and Orlene do, but right now I just want you so hot for me you can't think of anything else." She was bare, now, in record time.

"Perhaps we should retire to a more appropriate place," he suggested.

"Like a bed. This way!" She bounded off again and hauled him along after her.

Soon he joined her there, unclothed. He kissed her and held her and squeezed her in intimate places, exactly as she demanded. *I wish I had thought of this sort of thing when alive,* Orlene thought.

Jolie had to agree. Vita's passion was not feigned; her body was humming with desire, and it affected all of them. She recalled the saying that a man gave love for sex, while a woman gave sex for love. This was certainly true here, but each aspect was so intense and pervasive that the dividing line ceased to have meaning. The two were giving passion for passion, reveling in it, delighting in its grandeur and its naughtiness.

So it was that Jolie was along for the ride, as Orlene had been before, and the revels of the couple became her own. She knew that next time she merged with Gaea and went to see their man, she was going to give him a show and an experience he hadn't had in years. There was much to be said for exuberance.

The next morning Thanatos appeared. "I understand you are ready to resume your quest," he said.

Vita screeched in terror and leaped out of bed. She was, as was her wont after sex, naked; Jolie had left her alone.

That's Thanatos, Jolie explained. *He brought us to you. We have nothing to fear from him.*

"Oh." Vita hastily turned the body over to Orlene, who as hastily wrapped a sheet about herself. They had been lying abed late, after the strenuous activity of the early part of the evening, and he had come upon them unawares. That, of course, was often the way of Death.

"I, yes," Orlene said. "Thanks in part to you, I am no longer in danger of descending to Hell. But when Jolie talked with you before, you told her it was impossible, or nearly."

"The quest must continue, regardless. From me you need a blank soul?"

"So I understand. To transfer—"

"Come with me."

Orlene hesitated, remembering how Thanatos had come for her when she died and she had fled him. *Have no fear,* Jolie thought. *He is a good man, as well as a good Incarnation.*

"May I dress first?"

"Dress," he agreed.

She paused, but he did not retreat or disappear. *Just go ahead and do it,* Jolie urged. *He doesn't even realize there could be a problem, after all the naked souls he's seen.*

Orlene went to the closet, snatched down a decent dress, and grabbed for the rest of what she needed. She carried them into the bathroom and got herself in order as quickly as she could. Thanatos waited impassively, seeming not to move at all.

"I'm ready," she said, emerging. But he was already on his way, and she had to run to catch up. She didn't dare ask where they were going.

In the yard the death-steed Mortis was grazing. *Oh, look at that!* Vita thought. As with many girls of her age, she was thrilled by the notion of a horse, any horse.

Thanatos glanced at his deathwatch. He turned and put his hands at Orlene's sides. He lifted, and the horse came up and stood before them, so that Thanatos could set her on.

Then Thanatos mounted behind her, putting one arm around her in an impersonal way to keep her secure.

The horse took off. There was no wind, no tilt, but suddenly they were riding upward through the sky, leaving the city below. *Ooooo!* Vita squealed in awed delight.

"Mortis likes you too," Thanatos remarked.

You can hear me?

"I hear your soul, Vita."

I like this too, Jolie thought.

"Women do," he agreed.

They peered down to see fluffy cotton-ball clouds below. Mortis was galloping on air, moving far faster than any mortal animal could. On occasion his hooves kicked up divots of cloud dust, which dissolved behind them. The scene was beautiful, with the morning beams of the sun spearing out from the east, lighting the near sides of the clouds.

I begin to get a notion what Luna sees in Death, if he takes her on rides like this! Vita thought.

"On occasion," Thanatos agreed.

Then the steed was moving down to another city. They had no idea where it was; the speed and magic had been such that it could be anywhere. They had departed at dawn, local time; here it was afternoon.

They landed on a city street amidst traffic. Orlene flinched as a car charged toward them—but it passed right through them as if they were ghosts. Yet of course they were not ghosts, exactly; Vita's body was alive and solid, so that meant that Thanatos and Mortis had to be solid, too, to lift and carry her as they had.

Magic, Jolie reminded her.

"True," Thanatos agreed. "Mortals can neither perceive nor affect us unless we wish it."

The horse walked across the street and into a solid wall. They passed through the wall and into a lighted factory region at the base of a megabuilding. "This man is about to die of a rare internal electrical imbalance," Thanatos said, dismounting and approaching one of the workers. Sure enough, the man paused before his equipment, and fell back, looking startled.

Thanatos stepped in and reached out to the man—but not to help support him. His hand passed into the man's body without resistance and out again, holding the man's soul. The soul came out in a translucent skein, mottled by black patches and white, distorting out of shape. The body sank to the floor, its eyes staring as if still startled.

"But you never gave him a chance!" Orlene protested. "He might have recovered had you not swept out his soul!"

"He would have endured until I took his soul, but not for recovery. I acted promptly so as to spare him unnecessary pain. When a soul is in balance, a person can not die until it is removed, no matter how hopeless the physical case." As he spoke he was folding the soul like so much gossamer, until it was wadded into a ball, which he placed in a little bag.

He returned to Mortis and mounted. The horse walked back through the wall, then galloped into the air again.

"How can you just take lives, all day?" Orlene asked.

"It is a necessary part of human existence," he replied seriously. "Without death there could soon be no new life. The old must be cleared away for the new. Even as it is, we are threatened with overpopulation."

Orlene was silent. She hadn't thought of it that way.

Soon they came down in another city, somewhere in the world. Mortis halted at a Dumpster similar to the one they had hidden in when fleeing Vita's pimp, so long ago. "Your turn, Orlene," he said abruptly.

"What?"

"Within that Dumpster is a newborn infant who will die within hours if unattended. No mortal knows of his presence except his mother, who is beyond compassion in this respect, having such serious difficulties of her own as to be unable to return. My attention is not necessary, as the baby is unsullied and will go to Heaven, but to avoid subjecting him to avoidable agony as the next load of garbage is dumped, crushing him, I am interceding. You are looking for a blank soul; this one is close enough. Climb in and take it."

"But I can't do that!" Orlene protested.

139

"You are with me, sharing my power for this event by my extension. Do with him as you saw me do with the last case, and the soul will come out for you."

Orlene waited a moment, flustered. "But—"

"I understood that you wished above all else to recover and cure your own baby," Thanatos said emotionlessly. "This is the way to obtain one of the seven elements required. How serious is your quest?"

Tight-lipped, Orlene got down and approached the Dumpster. Now they heard it: a faint mewling from within. They climbed up and peered in.

The baby was there, half swathed in dirty rags, grease and blood splotched over his body, short dark hair matted to the tiny skull. "Oh, my God!" Orlene breathed numbly.

So little! Vita thought. *I never realized how small they were. His ankle is no bigger around than my thumb!*

Orlene reached forth with a shaking hand to take the soul. Her teeth were clenched.

No! Vita thought. *Don't kill him!*

She has to, Jolie thought. *It would be cruel to let him suffocate in garbage, or to die slowly of exposure. Thanatos is right: it is an act of mercy to take this innocent soul now.*

But he's just an eensy baby! He never did anything to anyone! He shouldn't be killed, he should be held and cuddled and nursed and everything!

Those are not his options, Jolie returned, realizing that they were in effect Orlene's inner voices, her conscience debating while she hesitated. *It is wrong, we know, but the world is not governed by right, it is governed by circumstances, and all we can do is alleviate the most egregious cases. Sometimes the choice is between evils.*

You must be good at that! Vita shot back.

"That's not fair!" Orlene protested. "She's not evil, she's—"

Oh, damn, I'm sorry! Vita thought with genuine contrition. *I didn't mean that, Jolie. It's just that I never was into killing, and this poor baby—*

I know, don't I know! Jolie replied. *I died before I had a baby of my own, and then when I came to watch Orlene, it was like—*

I guess we better stop; I don't think we're helping.

140

Jolie had to agree. This was Orlene's decision, hard as it was. Thanatos had given her a cruel lesson in death and souls!

Orlene reached again for the baby. He took a ragged breath and cried a little louder, as if aware that death was upon him.

"I can't!" Orlene cried. "Oh, I just can't!" She put both hands down and picked up the baby and held him close.

Jolie and Vita maintained thought silence, not knowing what would come of this. Probably she had forfeited the soul she so needed; Thanatos would take it himself and put the dead baby back. But how else could she have reacted—this woman who had already lost her own baby and died herself because of it? What Thanatos had inflicted on her had been more than cruel, it had been diabolic. Jolie knew it was not her place to judge him, but she could not accept this thing he had done.

Orlene climbed out of the Dumpster, managing to bring the baby along. She came to stand before Thanatos as he sat on Mortis. She held the baby protectively. "Maybe I have no right to ask this, but if there is any way to save this baby, I've got to do it," she said, the tears coming. "I'm a mother, not a killer."

"That is not your baby," Thanatos said. "You can gain nothing by interceding."

"I know. I expect nothing. Please."

"But you can salvage the soul, for your purpose."

"I cannot, though I lose my own baby. Please."

"I ask you again to consider just how serious you are about your quest for your own baby. If you will not do what is necessary—"

"Oh, Thanatos, I would give my own soul to save my baby, if it were only clean enough instead of hopelessly soiled! But I cannot sacrifice this innocent one to my purpose! This baby should have his chance to live and to make his own decisions about good and evil as he grows. I am grief-stricken over the loss of my own, but I cannot help mine by denying this one his chance. I beg you, I beg you—spare him, if you possibly can!"

141

The death's head nodded. "I can, to a degree. Mount."
He extended a bone hand.

Orlene grasped it, holding the baby close with her other
arm. Her weight diminished and she was moved effortlessly
to the front of the great horse.

A short gallop through the air and buildings brought
them to a hospital. "Take him there," Thanatos said, lifting
her down.

Orlene walked into the hospital. She approached the
front desk. "I found this newborn baby in a garbage dump,"
she said. "Please take care of him and arrange for his
adoption." She held out the baby.

A nurse appeared and took the baby. "You will have to
make a statement," she said. "Where he was found, what
time—"

"I can't do that," Orlene said, turning away.

"But you must! It is a crime to—"

Mortis walked through the wall. Thanatos reached down.
Orlene caught his hand and was set back on the horse.

The nurse stared, holding the baby. "She disappeared!"
she exclaimed. "She just disappeared!"

"Sometimes they come like that," the girl at the desk said.
"So there is no legal claim on the baby. We'll take care of
him."

"Yes, we'll take good care of him," the nurse said.

Mortis leaped, passing through the ceiling, through the
various chambers of the hospital, and on out the roof.
Orlene, her effort done, sank into renewed grief. Jolie
understood the temptation that had been on her: to try to
keep the baby herself. She had resisted that, but it hurt. *You
did right!* she thought.

You did right, Vita echoed.

"Yes, you did right," Thanatos said. "I will save an
otherwise lost soul for you, from a baby whose situation is not
subject to salvage, and deliver it to you when you have
obtained the artifacts you require from the other Incarnations. You are worthy, in my estimation."

You mean this thing was a test? Vita thought, outraged.

"A soul is infinitely precious," Thanatos replied, unperturbed. "I would not yield one to a person who failed to appreciate its value, not merely as a convenience for a purpose, but as an entity in itself. This was a necessary determination. Orlene refused to do what she believed was wrong, even to achieve the thing she most desired."

But did you have to make her hurt so? Jolie demanded. *Knowing that she had lost her own baby?*

"The ultimate proof of character is not lightly achieved. A lesser proof would have been valueless. Incarnations do not deal in valueless matters."

The understatement of the century! Jolie realized that Thanatos had been correct in his action, however cruel it had seemed. Orlene had won her soul not by taking what was proffered without conscience, but by maintaining her standards of decency and compassion despite the seeming cost.

I think maybe I learned something, Vita thought. *I couldn't've done it myself.*

Jolie wasn't sure she could have, either. *We thank you, Thanatos, for this hard lesson,* she thought.

"You are welcome, Jolie," he replied.

Mortis landed back in Luna's yard. Orlene got down. "I, too, thank you, Thanatos," she said. "I will try to get the other things I need."

"We are not yet finished," Thanatos said, dismounting. He accompanied her into the house.

"I don't think I understand," Orlene said.

Thanatos took a seat on the same couch that Judge Scott had used the night before. Jolie was glad that they had thought to return to pick up Vita's scattered clothing before sleeping! "The shifting of the course of a life cannot be accomplished by a single Incarnation unilaterally," he said. "A life is too important for that. In my early days in Office I sometimes declined to take the souls that were due. I once saved a drowning man, for example, instead of allowing him to die. I learned later that both Chronos and Fate had had to make adjustments to accommodate my action. They had not spoken of it to me, making allowance for my inexperience in Office. Now I am more careful, just as other Incarnations are careful of my prerogatives. Orlene, you will have to present

143

your case for the baby you saved to Fate, so that she can decide whether to alter his thread of life."

"But Fate is—"

"Your natural grandmother," he said.

"My *what?*"

Thanatos paused. "I apologize. I see you did not know."

I did not tell her, Jolie thought. *I thought it best to let her follow her quest without the complication of that knowledge.*

"My natural grandmother!" Orlene repeated, dazed.

"That may complicate the picture," Thanatos said. "Nevertheless, it was at your instigation that that baby's thread of life was rerouted, and it is your responsibility to obtain the authorization for it. Jolie will be able to guide you to the Incarnation of Fate, of course."

"I will do it," Orlene agreed. "I agree it is my responsibility." But she remained shaken by the revelation of her ancestry.

"You should also check with Chronos."

"The Incarnation of Time? Why?"

"In order to fit this special session into my schedule, I borrowed time. This has actually been a rerun of time I am spending in my normal duties, so that I have not sacrificed them or been rushed. Chronos is tolerant of such occasional borrowings on my part, but it would be better if you approached him and explained directly."

"I need to see him anyway, to get a grain of sand," Orlene agreed. "I shall do that forthwith."

"However, in fairness, I must advise you that your interview with Chronos will not be easy."

Jolie remembered the key thing about the Incarnation of Time: he lived backwards. That complicated things for every person who interacted with him, mortal or immortal!

"I will do what I must," Orlene said.

"I think you do not yet grasp the nature of the problem. Not only does time reverse in his residence, he is a man you knew in life."

"I knew him? But how could that be? I've only been dead for a few months! How long has he had the Office?"

"That depends on perspective. By my reckoning, it has been perhaps twenty five years; I had not thought to verify the precise length of his tenure. By his reckoning, it might be as little as two years."

"Either way, then, I cannot have known him!"

"I believe his given name was Norton."

Orlene stiffened. "Oh, no!"

Thanatos stood. "It is not my concern how you may handle your interview with another Incarnation. Certainly I do not wish to interfere in their activities that do not relate to my proper business. But you seem to be uniquely related to or involved with more than one Incarnation, in which number I am included because of my interest in your aunt Luna, so I have brought this matter up to you. I bid you good prospects."

"My aunt . . .?"

"I think I have made another error," he said.

That, too, is true, Jolie thought. *Maybe I should have told you all of it at the outset, but—*

"But I was in no condition," Orlene said.

Yes. Then the business with Nox—

Orlene, shaken again, walked to him. "I appreciate your information, Thanatos." Then she lifted her face and kissed him on his lipless mouth. The expressionless skull face managed to look startled.

Two days later Luna returned. "I trust you were not bored, being here alone?"

Jolie was back in charge. "By no means, thank you. We have been tutoring Vita, and getting to know Muir and Griffith and Grissel, and looking at your wonderful pictures, and we had visits by Judge Scott and Thanatos."

"The moon moth and griffins seldom have company they appreciate; I'm sure they have been most pleased. I am glad you like my paintings; I really have little time to paint now, but on occasion I still do it, to relax. As for Roque, he is a good man," Luna said, with an oblique smile that suggested that she well understood that situation. "Thanatos is a good

145

Incarnation." Jolie wasn't certain how she meant that, knowing that Luna had been Thanatos' mortal lover for well over a decade.

"We are grateful for your generosity in allowing us to stay here during your absence," Jolie said. "Now I think we should find some other lodging, so that—"

Luna looked seriously at her. "I would not think of it. You, Jolie, are a good friend and incidental liaison with the enemy. Orlene is family. Vita is the daughter of my employee and friend Vera, whose situation is still clarifying. It behooves me to facilitate your various interests. I understand that you, Jolie, are now also doing an observation of the Judge as a prospect for an Incarnation."

She was really current! "Yes. But it would help if I know which Incarnation was the most likely prospect. The Offices are so different—"

"We do not feel free to advertise that at this stage. But we do need candidates who might be acceptable to all of the Incarnations."

"But Satan will not agree to any completely good man!"

"And the others will not agree to any completely bad man," Luna agreed. "Therefore our most likely prospects will be compromises—people with both good and evil. In truth, the current Incarnations are similar compromises, brought about by chance and circumstance, doing the best they can. But we distrust chance, and wish to upgrade prospects, with no affront intended toward any current parties."

In other words, she wasn't letting any secrets slip. Jolie was increasingly curious about this matter. She tried once more. "When we were with Thanatos, we thought he was acting cruelly, but it turned out that he was merely clarifying the gravity of the matter of taking a soul for any purpose other than its own. We conclude that he is doing a good job. Yet he must have had a lot of evil on his soul, to encounter his predecessor, because Thanatos normally goes after only those souls that are in balance between good and evil."

"True. He was in balance, with as much evil as good. So was I, when we met; we compared notes. He has been doing

146

a good job, and surely changing his balance slowly positive, and I hope my own is similarly changing. Certainly it is possible for such folk to perform well. But if there were a better system of selection, we might guarantee that future Incarnations will be better prepared for their Offices."

It did make sense, though Jolie had little confidence that a real upgrading of Incarnations would come of it, because unanimity among the Incarnations was virtually impossible.

"We shall be glad to stay here, if it is really all right with you," she said, returning to the earlier subject. "But Orlene does wish to resume her quest, and we have decided that the three of us will remain together to see that through. That means that we hope to go physically to see the remaining Incarnations. So if we have to travel—"

Luna laughed. "You will not have to travel! All the Incarnations have residences in Purgatory."

"But in mortal form we can't get there," Jolie pointed out. "As ghosts, Orlene and I can go, and indeed have already been. But Vita—"

"Oh, you need to leave her unchaperoned for a time! Certainly she may remain here; Muir will watch her and prevent her from leaving, and the griffins will be happy for company."

You know, that might not be so bad, Vita thought. But Jolie could feel her disappointment; she did like the animals and the house, but she very much wanted to participate in the larger adventure. Also, she was aware that Roque might not visit her alone, and feared that if he did, she would make some romantic blunder that would turn him off. She wanted to remain with Jolie and Orlene, but was afraid she couldn't. She was trying to be nice about it. That, for her, was significant progress; she was learning self-sacrifice, perhaps inspired by Orlene's example.

"We intend to do it together," Jolie said firmly, and felt the thrill of Vita's joy. "We two ghosts like the experience of being alive again, and Vita likes our company. We have a viable combination, and will keep it as long as all of us agree."

Luna nodded, unsurprised. "It is possible for mortals to visit Purgatory; indeed, the Incarnations are mortal in certain

147

respects, such as their normal solidity. But you will need the intercession of an Incarnation to get there."

"As it happens, I am on good terms with an Incarnation or two," Jolie said. "I happen to know that Satan doesn't use his residence in Purgatory, so it would be available for a temporary stay. But if we were to ask his aid . . ."

Again there was a knowing nod. "I would not forbid you this earthly residence, in that case. Though it is true that I oppose Satan, and expect to be instrumental in defeating his major ploy not far hence, it is also true that we must have his cooperation for what we intend in the longer run. In earlier days I believed that the conflict between Good and Evil was absolute, but with time and experience I have learned that it is relative. It is as if we are playing an important game, with each side wanting very much to win but both sides agreeing that without adherence to certain ground rules, there will be no game to win. Even enemies need to cooperate in certain respects and to honor each other's prerogatives."

"Thank you," Jolie said. "We shall remain here, except when visiting Purgatory. May the game continue."

"May the game continue," Luna agreed, smiling.

CHAPTER SEVEN

Time

LUNA GAVE THEM FARE FOR A COMMERCIAL
rocket flight to another city. While they waited for the taxi
carpet to arrive, Vita went out to give each griffin a farewell
hug, then came inside to do the same for Muir, who put up
with this in gentlemanly fashion though it evidently wasn't
his idea of fun. Orlene then embraced Aunt Luna. In her life
she had known none of her blood ancestry; now it was
sustaining her in death.

The carpet arrived, and Jolie took over, because she knew
where they were going. "Rocketport," she announced, and it
sailed up, carrying them away. Jolie looked back and waved
to Luna, feeling sentiment herself. She had known Luna for
many years, and liked her, but this was the first time in
mortal guise, and it had a special impact. The considerations
of food and lodging and physical protection loomed far
more important in the living state. Living was so *physical*! In
a few days she had come to a much more acute appreciation
of the woman's qualities. Luna was very like Gaea, who had

149

been her sister-cousin Orb, but significantly different too. She seemed older, because she had aged normally while Gaea hadn't, but that wasn't it. She was in many respects what Gaea would have been had she remained mortal, and that was a precious insight.

She was also like Orlene in her former life: quite attractive, and sensitive to the feelings of others. Jolie knew that she had seen Orlene in her worst stage, that of emaciation, death, horror and despair. But she remembered how petite and lovely she had been in her life and happiness, and how nice. Now those qualities were returning, though she was in a different body; Vita was becoming pretty in the ways that Orlene had been. Luna showed how Orlene would be in later life, and that was attractive too.

I really regret having died, Orlene thought. *I acted hastily and thoughtlessly. Only now that it is too late do I appreciate what continuing life had to offer.*

"Perhaps I should have told you your heritage," Jolie said. "I tried to avoid interfering in your life, other than watching you and being your dream-friend, and now I regret that."

Had I known, I might have acted quite differently, Orlene agreed. *But I cannot blame you for leaving me my freedom to find my own way.*

Vita did not chip in. She was dreaming of Roque.

The carpet arrived at the rocketport. They entered at ground level and rode the carpeted belts to the interior ticket counter. Then they took the old-fashioned escalator to the launching area at the roof.

The rocket was sitting there in its harness. Jets of steam hissed from nozzles, making it seem like a monstrous hot dragon. A ramp led up to a tiny mouth in its base.

Vita took an interest. *Science is so scary!* she commented.

Jolie could not argue. Back in her days of life, science had been relatively backward, while magic, for some few practitioners, had been advanced. But she had to admit that science had its place; it nicely complimented magic as a way of getting things done. Both had their liabilities, of course, but that was a concomitant of power.

They rode the ramp up to the mouth and into the maw of the monster. Inside it was like a small, cramped building, much higher than wide. A moving ladder hauled them up to their berth, about midway along the length of the rocket.

A harness awaited them there. *Just like the big one!* Vita thought.

"For different reason," Jolie explained. "The big harness holds the ship vertical and above the building, so that no actual landing field is necessary and there is room for the rocket jets to flow. Our small harness is to hold us in place for the pressures of the takeoff and landing. Springs allow it to give way, cushioning the worst of the acceleration. This will be a short, violent hop."

That's my kind of trip, the girl agreed.

They got into the harness and clamped it on around arms, legs and torso. There was a brace for the neck, and a helmet to hold the head secure.

In due course there was a shrill warning beep. Then the rocket took off. First they felt the rising power of its jet, causing the entire vessel to shudder. Then the motion commenced, slow at first, but rapidly accelerating.

Hooo! Vita thought, feeling their jaw, breasts, and stomach sag with the abrupt increase in weight.

A vision screen came on, showing a fisheye-lens view of the outside. They were rising, the building and surrounding city of Kilvarough dropping down. In moments they had a panoramic view of the region.

I like Mortis better, Vita announced.

Neither Orlene nor Jolie cared to argue with that.

The rocket blast cut off. Their harness bounced up, its springs recovering their compactness. They were in free-fall.

Wheee! Vita thought.

But in a moment the rocket spun about, its business end pointing forward. Then the blast resumed, just as if they were still rising. But now they were slowing and descending, as the screen showed. The rocket was efficient, which meant the ride was short.

"I would have preferred a modern saucer," Jolie said. "They are as fast, but they use antigravity instead of jet propulsion, so are a lot easier to ride, I understand. Of course, as a ghost I never had occasion to ride one."

Maybe on the way back! Vita thought eagerly. She loved experience of any kind.

The ship backed down to its rocketport and dropped into its harness. The safe-to-debark gong sounded. They got out of their harness and waited for a vacant slot on the moving ladder. Naturally, all the other passengers were trying to leave at once, so they had to wait some time.

A slot appeared. Jolie grabbed a rung and swung her feet across. She glanced up and found herself peering up the skirt of another woman. It was foolish to wear such clothing to travel!

Then she looked down and spied the man below looking up her skirt. Ouch!

They should make men wear skirts, Vita thought.

Orlene, silent so far, caught that and went into a mental giggle. Jolie tried to contain it, but a peep leaked out. "Maybe we can get Luna to pass a law," she murmured between suppressed heaves. "But who would want to look at that?"

That, of course, was the problem: turnabout was not fair play, because women had little interest in looking at men the way men looked at women. Life was inherently unfair.

No it isn't, Vita thought. *It gives us power, because we've got what they want.*

At the bottom they let go and rode the ramp out and down. At the roof of the rocketport they transferred to the express escalator, which took them down at a slant to the main door. They had no baggage, so beat most of the crowd out.

The taxi carpets were lined up. Jolie took the first one. "Mock Hell," she said.

Soon they were there: at the megabuilding devoted to the follies of damnation. Satan had set it up decades ago as an exhibit, in an attempt to show mortals that Hell was really a fun place. This had been successful, and it had become a major tourist attraction. People of all ages flocked to sample evils that were not encouraged elsewhere.

Jolie walked through the gambling den, where the customer always won. Piles of silver and gold coins abounded. *Sure looks like fun!* Vita thought.

"Wait till you see the next level!" Jolie replied. She was, of course, long familiar with this setup; it was an excellent initial sorting place for potential evil. Satan got early warning here of forthcoming clients.

The next level was devoted to gluttony: clients were stuffing themselves with all manner of pastries and confections and tasty beverages. *Ooooo!* Vita thought.

Jolie approached one of the chefs. "May I borrow your glasses a moment?"

"We don't let clients—" he began.

"Pierre, don't you know me?" she asked, extending her ghost face in front of the host face.

He did a double-take. "Of course, Mistress of Satan!" he agreed hastily, extending his glasses.

Jolie put them on. They were not prescription lenses, but magic spectacles, and what they showed was a spectacle indeed: the reality behind the fostered illusion. The clients were eating garbage, literally, and drinking reeking sewer dip. For this privilege they were paying not with money, but with percentages of their souls. They were committing themselves to Hell by stages, for pleasures which were no more genuine than those of sin itself.

Ugh! Vita thought, her gorge rising.

Jolie quickly removed the glasses, as it was she who would vomit if this went too far. "The wages of sin are garbage," she said, returning the glasses. "Thank you, Pierre; this client is not going to Hell anyway."

"I don't know why Satan keeps company with the likes of you!" Pierre said, smiling.

"There's an ineradicable bit of good in the worst of us," she responded. "His bit of good relates to me. But don't worry; I happen to know that he's having an affair with an Incarnation."

"But that's even more extreme!" Pierre protested. "She's bound to be good!"

"But think of how far he can drag her toward evil!"

153

He nodded, seeing the point. Jolie walked on.

Is Satan really—? Vita asked, her interest quickening.

"He really is," Jolie said. "It's a terrific scandal."

Gee, she thought, awed. *Who*—?

"Oh, I wouldn't blab her name to just anyone."

You're teasing me!

Jolie laughed. "I am, dear! But see, we're here." For they had come to the Infernal Elevator, which served as a convenient conduit between Purgatory, the mortal realm, and Hell. This was what she had been headed for all along.

She touched the entry panel, again extending her ghostly identity. The panel recognized it, for she had free access to all Satan's works, in any form, if she could handle them. It slid aside and the steamy interior of the Hellevator showed.

She stepped in. "Purgatory," she said.

The panel slid across again. Flames erupted from the edges of the floor. The elevator moved up in a cloud of smoke which somehow didn't choke. It was mostly illusion, to provide the proper flavor for an artifact of the nether region.

This is more like it! Vita thought enthusiastically. *Where else does this crate go?*

"It connects everything except Heaven," Jolie said. "For some reason, Satan couldn't get God's permission to put a stop there."

Fancy that, Orlene thought dryly.

"Something you should keep in mind about the supernatural realms, Vita," Jolie said. "They are not quite like the mortal one. They are not actually physical, they are two dimensional, and cannot normally be detected or interacted with by living mortals. But to those in them, they seem three or four dimensional, and therefore solid. The folk there will seem alive, but they are not; all are spirits except the Incarnations, who are of neither the natural or supernatural realms. The folk of Purgatory don't need to eat or sleep, and anything we eat there will not sustain us. Only by special dispensation can mortals enter any of the supernatural realms."

How come this elevator is taking us there, then?

"It is really a mechanism for translation," Jolie explained.

"The Incarnations don't need translation, but your body does. We seem to be rising, but we are instead changing, becoming two dimensional. Such a process represents a strain on the system, so is seldom authorized. But because I am close to an Incarnation, I am allowed to do this, and I am taking your physical body to Purgatory. While there I will never depart from your body, for that would leave you there without authority, which would be extremely awkward. I will turn the body over to Orlene for the duration, for this is her quest. You may observe and comment, but you will not be put in charge."

Yeah, I can see why. I won't pester you for anything.

"And Orlene—are you going to be able to handle an encounter with your lover, in his new role?"

I have no choice, Orlene replied grimly.

The Hellevator flamed up again and stopped. The panel slid aside. They were at the fringe of Purgatory, its seemingly natural landscape opening out before them.

Jolie stepped out. Behind her the device disappeared in another dramatic gout of flame and smoke, leaving only a brooding fumarole. Ahead was a path leading windingly toward a mansion in the distance. "That is Chronos' residence," Jolie said. "It will take us at least an hour to reach it, and we won't hurry; in fact we may be best advised to take a nap before we start."

No, I am ready to tackle this now, Orlene thought.

"You misunderstand. It is not your courage in question, but the nature of the structure. Time runs backwards within it. You will thus emerge before you enter. Rather than meet yourself and get fouled up, it is better to allow sufficient time around the edges, before and after, so that you are not put in difficulty. We can proceed with a series of scheduled pauses, during which we sleep or at least pay no attention to what is around us, so that whoever may pass before us knows what times and places to avoid."

This is crazy! Vita thought.

I don't care about any of that, Orlene thought. *I just want to get there and explain about the time Thanatos used on my behalf, and beg for a grain of sand.*

155

"But this man was your lover!"

Her what? Vita asked. *Did I miss something juicy when I wasn't paying attention?*

I will apologize to him for leaving him as I did. I see no reason to delay; it will only erode my nerve.

"As you wish," Jolie said, realizing that one way might be as good as another, and if not, that the woman simply had to go her own route. She released the host body to her.

Orlene took over and began walking briskly toward the castle. Jolie realized, belatedly, that the last time they had been to Purgatory, on their way to see an Incarnation, Orlene had become a man and horribly embarrassed herself; she could be nervous about such experience and want to get through as quickly as possible.

Because this was Purgatory, the body did not tire. Orlene, discovering this, picked up her pace, and soon she was almost running. Thus it was that she reached the castle in half the time Jolie had estimated. Flushed with nervousness rather than exertion, she lifted the ornate door knocker and let it fall.

In a moment a butler opened the door. "And who may I announce to Chronos?" he inquired.

"Just a supplicant for a favor."

"Please wait in the foyer."

She entered and waited, while the butler departed for the interior. There was a scenic mural on the wall that looked almost real enough for her to walk into. The furniture was comfortable, and the floor was polished hardwood. *You're right,* Vita thought. *This seems awfully real and solid!*

Don't be deceived; its reality is on a different plane from that of the living host.

The butler returned. "Chronos will see you now."

She followed the man to the main chamber. Her breath caught in her throat. There stood Norton, exactly as she had known him in life!

He turned and looked at her. "May I ask who you are?"

He did not recognize her—because she wore Vita's body! Her appearance was that of a pretty teenage black girl. "I will tell you—but first let me plead my case. Thanatos took me to

156

see how he drew out souls, and he had to borrow time from you to do it. I hope you will approve this, for I did learn something significant."

"Thanatos was kind to me before I assumed this office," Chronos said. "I have no quarrel with his use of time, and will not question it."

"And—And I am told I need from you one grain of sand from—"

"What?" he asked, astonished and dismayed.

"I—I know it is very valuable, but I really need it. You see, I lost my baby, and the Incarnation of Night told me that I could only cure his malady by getting something from each Incarnation, and—"

"If I knew a way to cure a baby's malady, I would have cured that of my own baby before he died, and so saved his mother, whom I loved. Certainly one grain of sand will not—"

This was getting awkward! She should have told him her identity at the outset. "I know. It was a terrible mistake, and I made it worse. I see you still wear Sning."

He glanced at the ring he wore, which was in the form of a tiny snake curled around the finger. "How could you know about that?" he asked, surprised. "The only one who knows is dead. Not only that—"

"Dead," she agreed. "And trying to save her baby."

He was not a stupid or unperceptive man. "Can it be you, Orlene?" he asked, amazed. "In other form? I mistook you for a mortal!"

"Oh, Norton," she said, her tears starting. "I did not mean to deceive you! I just forgot that you would not know my mortal host, and then I thought I shouldn't try to influence you by—oh, how I wronged you when I died! I didn't think of you at all, just the baby, and if it were possible to undo that evil, believe me I would, but I can't! I loved you, Norton, and love you still, but was blinded by my folly! I can't ask your forgiveness, I can only proffer my apology for what cannot be undone. I shouldn't have come here!"

He came to her as she spoke and took her in his arms. "Have you come to stay with me, Orlene, this time?"

She was taken aback. "Stay—here? Oh, Norton, I cannot! This host is a living girl who must return to the mortal realm. I am here with her, and with Jolie, who is—"

"Ah, Jolie, Satan's consort. I have my differences with Satan, but she is a nice woman."

"Yes. So I'm not here alone, and can't remain."

"But you are a spirit. The mortal girl could return, and Jolie is already a ghost, and you could remain, assuming your natural likeness here. If you do not leave this mansion, the problem of time will not exist, and we can be together for decades, never aging."

Orlene was wildly tempted. This possibility had never occurred to her. To be back with Norton, in seeming life and comfort, indefinitely!

Then she remembered Gaw-Two. "My baby—could he be here too?"

"No. A person can exist here only during the span of his natural life. In thirty-seven years I will fade out and have to pass the Hourglass on to my successor, in mortal terms my predecessor, for I will then be passing beyond the time of my birth. Gaw-Two would come up against his limit in mere days."

"And then have to exist forward," she concluded. "Oh, Norton, I cannot give him up! I do love you, but I love him, too, and his need is greater. I must rid him of that terrible malady of the soul and see him safely on the way to Heaven before I can rest." She felt terribly guilty saying this, but it was the truth.

"But if you could save him, and be with me?"

"Then I would be at peace, and nothing else would matter."

He nodded. "I learned from Sning—the demon ring you gave me—that you were yourself given up for adoption as a baby. I can see that it would be very important for you not to do that to your own baby."

"Yes. I knew I was adopted, but I didn't know my true parentage until after I died. I think it does affect my attitude. I always wanted to be the very best mother I could possibly be, and I still want to, even though my son and I be ghosts. I want my baby to know me, even after death."

Chronos paused, thinking, then came to a decision. "Orlene, I can take you to see your adoption, if you wish. I never went back that far in your life myself, as my concern was to forget you, not enhance my awareness of you, but now I think it would be appropriate. You are younger than I; your adoption will be within my tenure of office. Would you like to see it?"

Orlene was amazed. "I can go see that? But wouldn't there be paradox or something?"

"My activities are normally immune from paradox, a necessary concomitant of the Office. But in this case there will be an extra precaution: we will not be visible or audible to the folk of that time, or able to affect them in any way. We will merely watch."

"Oh, yes, then!" Orlene exclaimed. "I would love to go back to that scene! Even earlier—I would like to see my mother give me away. Can we do that?"

Chronos glanced at his ring, which had been hers, and she knew he was asking Sning and being answered by yes-no squeezes. "Yes, Sning can direct us there; he was present throughout. I will follow his guidance and show you your life from the outset. Take my hand."

She took his hand, feeling strange. They had been lovers, and now she was dead and he was an immortal of a sort, but still there was that love between them. What memories lay in that simple contact of hands!

He lifted his great Hourglass. The fine flowing sand within it changed color, becoming an intense blue. Then he tilted it slightly—and the mansion misted out. There was a flickering, almost too rapid to detect, which she realized was the cycle of days and nights, going backwards, hundreds of them, thousands of them.

Then they were floating across an unfamiliar landscape. Chronos questioned Sning, using a "twenty questions" technique he had evidently refined with practice. "India," he announced. "A traveling circus, or something similar."

"A circus in India?" Orlene asked. "I originated there?"

"So it seems."

Now they came to a caravan of wagons drawn by dragons. Indeed, it was a traveling show! One wagon held a mermaid in a tank, and another a giant serpent, and there were assorted other animals and freaks and performers.

They entered one of the better wagons, which was closed in like a house. There a man and woman lay together, evidently lovers.

"War! Nature!" Chronos exclaimed, astonished.

"What?"

"I recognize these two! He is the Incarnation of War, called Ares or Mars. She is the Incarnation of Nature, called Gaea, when she assumes her natural likeness."

He's right, of course, Jolie thought. *They are your natural parents, Orlene.*

Orlene stared at the two figures, her emotions churning. These shocks of discovery were coming at her with cruel suddenness! But in a moment she rallied, showing more courage and control than Jolie had seen in her before. She was definitely learning to cope.

"Yes, I learned of this after my death," Orlene said, omitting the crucial detail of the timing of her learning. "But this must be before they became Incarnations."

"I think so, for certainly they are not together now."

"Oh, why did they separate and give me away?" Orlene cried, feeling the pain of it in a way she had not before.

There was a sound of horses, and a commotion outside. The to-be Incarnation of War got up to see what it was—and was met outside by an elaborately garbed officer. "Prince, we have come for you!" the officer called. "The Prince, your brother, is dead."

"He was a prince?" Orlene asked, amazed.

Indeed it turned out to be so. Not only that, he stuttered, avoiding it only by going into a singsong mode of expression. The officer had come to fetch him back, and would not be denied, though the Prince even threatened to behead him. They gave the to-be Incarnation of Nature a bag of precious gems and told her never to seek the Prince again, for the Prince would marry a Princess of his father's choosing.

But before he left, the Prince gave her the ring: Sning. Then he departed—and she fainted.

They carried her into her wagon, and a snake charmer tended to her. When she woke, the snake charmer said, "My dear, you are with child."

"She hadn't known!" Orlene exclaimed. "None of them knew!"

"None of them knew," Chronos agreed, verifying it with the ring. "That child was you."

Guided by Sning, they skipped ahead. The woman, then known as Orb, left the traveling show and went to France, where she settled and hired the service of a blind, maimed, yet beautiful Gypsy girl as a maid. The girl was Tinka, and Orb had known her before; indeed, she had taught Orb the Gypsy language of Calo, and Orb had helped the girl to find a husband, so they were fast friends. They sang together, for Tinka had similar magic, making the music wonderful, and practiced the wicked Gypsy dance the *tanana*.

Will you look at that! Vita thought. *I thought I'd seen some sexy dancing, but that is the granddaddy of sex! God, I wish Roque was here!*

Even Jolie herself was impressed. *I knew that Satan helped save the Gypsies; now maybe I know why! I never saw a more expressively erotic dance!*

The two women visited Tinka's father, the old Gypsy Nicolai, a man of distinction in the town. It seemed that Orb had done his daughter a favor by teaching her how to use her power of music and by making her beautiful despite her truncated fingers and club feet. Nicolai did not forget favors, and now Orb was treated with respect by the villagers. No word of her pregnancy escaped; the Gypsies protected their own from scandal.

Nicolai danced the *tanana* with his blind daughter, and the impact of the dance was doubled. He was a master, and it showed in his every glance and gesture. *I'd give anything to learn that dance!* Vita thought. *What a man!*

Jolie had to agree. There could be art to eroticism, and the *tanana* was that art, and Nicolai was the master of the dance. He looked to be about sixty years old, but it didn't matter; he was ageless when he danced. He also played the fiddle, beautifully; Orb brought out her little harp and they played together, and it was awe-inspiring.

Chronos skipped ahead again, and the baby was born. Orb was unable to use medication to alleviate the pain, because she had a protective amulet that fought the medicine, but a Gypsy midwife helped her instead with a Spell of Analogy. She gave birth and named the baby as a variant of herself: not Orb, but Orlene.

Soon, advised by the ring, Orb had to leave. Her father was dying, and she had little time to see him. She left the baby with Tinka, with instructions to give her for adoption to a well-to-do tourist family. She removed Sning. "When you find the right family, put this ring on Orlene's finger." She also gave the Gypsy girl a great ruby, from the bag the Prince's people had given her, so that she would never be poor again. Then she left, tearfully.

Tinka took perfect care of the baby. She was married, but her husband spent much time away, so she rejoined her father. Nicolai, evidently remembering Tinka's babyhood, was good with Orlene; he held her and talked with her and sang to her and danced with her, holding her aloft while his feet moved cleverly. The baby loved it; she seldom cried when Nicolai was near.

"This child has magic," he said. "A rare and good talent, fit for a Romani soul! She can see and judge auras."

"He knew!" Chronos exclaimed, astonished. "The glow you can see—he knew, even then!"

Orlene, grown now, watched, the tears streaming down her face. "I always liked dance and music," she said. "Now I know why. I almost remember—that marvelous man—that wonderful, blind Gypsy girl! Surely I saw them glowing brightly and was reassured."

Then the ring guided Tinka to intercept a passing tourist couple. She was blind, but she could get around, especially with Sning's help. She spoke only Calo, while the tourists spoke English, but it didn't matter. She showed them the baby, and they were smitten, and it was done. She put Sning on the baby's finger, where it fit magically well, and departed, trying to hide her tears.

"Oh, Tinka, I didn't know!" Orlene said, watching. "You wanted to keep me and could not!"

Orb returned, as Gaea, and cured her blindness, Jolie thought. *And made it possible for her to bear children.*

"I'm glad! My life was good; my adoptive parents treated me very well, and I was never in want. But this discovery of the people in my past—how it joys and hurts!"

"I wish I had known this about you," Chronos said. "You were so much more than I guessed. But I loved you regardless, and had I known what was to happen—"

"I acted foolishly," she said. "Orb could not keep me, so she did what she had to and went on. Tinka could not keep me, so she, too, did what was right. But I—when I could not keep my own baby—oh, I failed you, and myself, and all of those who sacrificed so much to give me my good life! I am ashamed!"

"Orlene, you may lack the power to undo the past, but this is a power I now possess. Come with me." He put out his elbow.

Bewildered, excited, she took his arm. With his free hand he lifted the great Hourglass that suddenly appeared. The flowing sand in it turned bright red as he tilted it.

Then they slid through the wall of the room and out of the village, much the way Mortis moved through substance. The flickering came again.

They approached a megabuilding Orlene recognized: it was the one containing Gawain's apartment—the one she had occupied in life, as the wife of the ghost. It had not been long in objective time since she had left it, by dying, but it had been an eternity subjectively.

They came to rest immediately outside her door. "We are in that period when you were gravid," Norton said. "But before Gawain obtained Gaea's gift. You must approach your prior self and warn her of the danger. She will then warn my prior self, who will warn the ghost. That should do it."

"And the malaise will never come upon Gaw-Two!" she exclaimed, suddenly seeing it. "He will not sicken and die, and I will not suicide, and we will be together in life!"

He merely waited.

"Yet I hesitate," she said. "I made such a bad mistake before, I don't want to make another. I must not be hasty. If I do this, and Gaw-Two is saved, and we are happy—what happens to Jolie?"

"Jolie? She merely returns to Satan; she has no problem here."

True, Jolie thought. *I would much prefer to see you alive and happy, Orlene! It would relieve me of enormous guilt, and I would not have to tell Gaea how her daughter was lost.*

"And Vita—that's the mortal girl, my host—what of her?"

"Why she would return to whatever her life was before you joined her. Probably the two of you would never interact, since you encountered her after you died."

"But Vita was on the street! A—She was subject to the sexual appetites of strange men, and getting hooked on a bad drug. She would most likely have proceeded in a descending spiral to depravity and death if Jolie and I hadn't come to pull her out of it!"

"I am afraid that would be the case."

Roque! Vita thought. *You mean I wouldn't meet Roque?*

"Oh, Norton, I don't think I can do this!" Orlene said. "I couldn't let that other baby die, when Thanatos took me there, and I can't do this to Vita, who is my friend. There has to be some other way!"

"If you live, what you did in death will not occur," he said. "That cannot be altered. You must live or die, not both."

But you could leave yourself a message! Jolie thought. *Vita's address, so you could go and . . .* But she lost it, the ramifications and complications becoming an impenetrable thicket. How could a white stranger with a baby go and rescue a black prostitute in a stupor from H? How could Vita be introduced to Judge Scott and go to live with him? What had been feasible from within hardly seemed so from without!

"And if I live, then what of you?" Orlene continued. "Will you go on to become the Incarnation of Time?"

"And there you have it, Orlene: paradox. I cannot do a thing that changes my own past, in that fashion, for if I did, I would not obtain the Office and therefore could not do that thing. In all other matters I am immune from paradox, but in this one I am not."

"So it is impossible, after all!"

"It is impossible. But I wanted you to understand in your own fashion, so you would not think I was being argumentative or callous. Our relationship is finished, because you must go forward, even as a ghost, and I must live backwards as an Incarnation. Now let me judge your plea on its merits." He lifted the Hourglass again, angling it as the sand turned pink.

They sailed up through the building, ghostlike, and into the sky. Chronos needed no magic elevator for his conversions! Soon they were back in his mansion.

"How did you come to assume this Office?" Orlene asked, partly from curiosity, partly because she wasn't quite ready to discuss the merits of her case.

"After you died, Gawain felt guilty, and he tried to find some better setup for me. He remarried and invited me to impregnate his new wife, but I thought of you and would not. Later he learned of the coming vacancy of this Office and persuaded me to assume it. I admit I was moved by the notion that this might provide me the power to do what we have seen I could not do: change your past and mine so that you would survive. I discovered better, but by that time I was committed. And I admit this is no ill existence. And, lest you feel guilt for depriving me of love life, I am accommodated there too."

"You have a lover?" Orlene asked, relieved but not completely pleased. "Then why did you suggest that I remain here with you?"

"I would prefer your company. I don't love the other woman. She merely accommodates a particular need."

Orlene remembered her experience with the urgency of the need of the male, and could not condemn him. "Who is she?"

"Another Incarnation. Only Incarnations understand."

165

"An Incarnation? Which one?"

"Fate."

"But Fate's my grandmother!"

"What?"

He doesn't know your ancestry, Jolie reminded her. *He just learned of your immediate parentage, as you did, and has not yet made the connection to Lachesis.*

"I'm the daughter of Nature and the granddaughter of Fate," Orlene continued. "That's why they sent Jolie to watch me. I didn't know while I lived, but now I do."

Disgruntled, he gazed at her. "Which Aspect?" he asked after a moment.

"Aspect?"

"Fate has three Aspects: Clotho, Lachesis and Atropos, of ascending generations. I believe each originates with a different mortal woman. They share the body, but they are three distinct personalities. Which one is your grandmother—Atropos?"

Lachesis, Jolie prompted.

"Lachesis," Orlene said numbly. She hadn't realized that Fate was so complicated!

"I indulge with Clotho, the youngest," he said, relieved. "Voluptuous, bouncy, midnight-black hair—of course, she can change her form, they all can, but I think that's her rest state."

"What does Lachesis look like?"

"Somewhat like an older edition of Gaea, actually, with light hair—sometimes she buns it up and makes it brown, but, well, it's not far from the shade of yours, really."

"That would be my grandmother," Orlene said, relaxing. She understood how three separate women could share a single body, even when one indulged in sexual relations with a man not of the others' choosing. "It really isn't my business."

He seemed glad enough to let the subject change. "Now, how did you come to encounter Nox?"

"She has Gaw-Two. She took him when he came to Purgatory, and says she will give him to me if I can obtain the items I need to cure his malaise, which remains with him in death because it is of the soul, not the body. From Chronos, one grain of sand, apparently because one soul cannot be transcribed to another without a hitch in time, or something—I don't quite understand it, but am sure that it is so."

"It is so," he agreed. "But you would not be able to use such a grain that way. Time is a tool that only the Incarnation of time can wield. What the sand would actually do is summon me to itself—that is, to its possessor, you—at need, and I would then manage the hitch in time and take back the grain. But this, too, has a complication. At what time do you anticipate this operation?"

Years! Jolie thought, knowing that it well might not be done at all.

"Years hence, I fear."

"Then likely before my tenure. That would explain why the sand is necessary, because I cannot go tangibly beyond my own term of Office. I can go intangibly, and observe certain aspects of reality, but I cannot affect them. If, however, you carry such a grain with you to that time, I will be able to go to it and act in the limited way that relates to its purpose." He paced the floor, considering. "Since I may not commit my predecessor—you would think of him as my successor—to such an action, I think I must give you the grain of sand. I think I would have agreed to do this were you not my lover in life, and the baby not mine, so I can justify it now."

"Thank you, Norton," she said. Again she remembered her brief, horrible experience as a male. Did he expect her to . . . surely she did owe him that, considering. "Do you wish—"

"Here is the grain," he said abruptly, cutting her off. He touched the Hourglass and the grain appeared on his finger. "Do not lose it. I regret that I have other business now and must ask you to leave."

She took the grain, holding it tightly between thumb and forefinger. It tingled. "I . . . thank you, Norton."

"Welcome." He ushered her out.

167

Moments later she stood at the front door, alone, be-mused by the suddenness of the conclusion. *There is a generous man,* Jolie thought.

Yeah, he was really hot for you, but he wouldn't let on, Vita agreed. *He just hustled you out before he could give in to it.*

"But I would have—if he had let me ask—I owed him so much—"

He didn't want you to buy that grain of sand, or pay for it, Jolie thought. *He wanted to give it to you. He did.*

"After what I did to him!" she said. "I had no business dying like that! I should have stayed with him and had another baby, but I just—" She choked herself off.

Let's get out of here before we meet you coming in, Jolie thought. She was impressed by Chronos' behavior, but now was not the time to dawdle.

"You do it," Orlene said. "I'm hurting again."

Indeed she was. Jolie resumed control of the body and walked briskly away from the mansion in the direction opposite to the one from which they had approached.

"Tomorrow we can tackle Fate," she said. "But today we had better get established in Satan's residence, so that we have a suitable base for operations."

It was a fair walk, and in this mortal body she was unable to turn a page in the fashion of Gaea to reach her destination instantly, or to fly ghost fashion, so it was afternoon by the time they reached it. Actually, Purgatory did not have days or seasons; time was meaningless here. But they were on Vita's living internal clock, and didn't fight it, thinking of time as they did in the mortal realm.

Satan's domicile, as perceived through their mortal eyes, was impressive, even awesome.

From outside it resembled the most forbidding of castles, with huge stone blocks forming a wall rising to an alarming height, enclosing a cylindrical central turret extending even higher. From the apex extended a pole which branched into a three-tined fork, from which flew a flag with the shape and color of a flame. Outside was a moat on whose surface fire danced, forming fleeting figures of demons who alternately beckoned and made obscene gestures.

Horrible! Orlene thought, though not really shocked.

Great! Vita thought, delighting in naughtiness.

"Isn't it a marvel?" Jolie inquired, pleased. "For centuries Satan's Purgatory residence was unmaintained, and Lucifer's before that, because he had no interest in this region and no undamned souls had interest in contacting him. But when I returned to animation as Gaea's companion, I did not deny my connection to Satan. I couldn't go to Hell on my own, only in her company, because I am not damned, but I wanted to maintain some liaison. So with the permission of the Incarnations of Nature and of Evil, I made a project of renovating the Purgatory Presence in my off moments. I made it a point to include all the classical symbols of the Office. When Satan saw it, he laughed so hard he sank through the ground and disappeared."

They walked the path to the moat. Now the flame figures became quite clear, putting on a show for the visitor. Male flames pursued female flames, caught them, and indulged in vigorous acts of fornication.

Appalling!

I wish Roque were here!

The main entry resembled the mouth of a dragon, gaping wide, as if in expectation of excellent prey. Small flames flickered within its dark maw. "Fresh meat!" Jolie called.

The dragon's mouth opened wider. Smoke billowed out. Then a huge red tongue rolled down to extend across the moat, its tip landing at the brink of the path. The flame figures retreated in alarm, except for one couple still engaged in amour. "Drawbridge," Jolie explained. "I gave it the password."

They crossed the drawbridge and approached the giant, ugly portcullis. It resembled enormous teeth projecting down, syrupy saliva dripping from their polished tips. As they passed under it, the teeth started down—and stopped, well above head height, after giving Orlene and Vita a scare. "Just a little extra fun," Jolie explained. "The mouth can't

169

close without reprogramming, but it can give entrants a bit of a jolt."

Inside, two little demons appeared. One was male, wearing little trousers with a hole in back for his tail to emerge, the other female, with a skirt and a flamelike bow in her hair. "These are Dee and Dee," Jolie said. "Our poster models, for the lascivious recruitment campaign. They're not really demons, merely borderline damned souls who elected to work here. They were experienced; they'd been in Gaming before they died."

Oh, I've seen them! Vita thought. *I remember the billboard with him peeking under the skirt of a luscious woman, and the legend "You Won't find THAT in Heaven!"*

"Yes, that has been one of our most popular numbers, dating from before my restored time," Jolie agreed. "And quite true too; God doesn't believe in fornication, once a soul has been Saved, so those who are interested in that sort of thing have to see to it as mortals, or in Hell."

I'm not sure I want to go to Heaven, Vita thought. *I mean, bad sex is awful, sure enough, but good sex is great, with the right man. I know Roque's going to Heaven, and if I can't join him there and give him an even better time than as a mortal, what's the point?*

"That's not for the Bride of Satan to say," Jolie said, smiling.

They followed Dee and Dee through the castle, getting the introductory tour. There was a central court with a garden of bloodsucking flowers and a pit of fire, with erotic statuary strategically placed. There was an excellent kitchen in which all manner of delicious foods were being prepared. There was a chamber for the storage of wealth, with gold and silver coins piled high, and buckets of gems: faceted diamonds, rubies, emeralds, and sapphires of many colors nested in beds of garnets. Pearl necklaces hung on racks, and iridescent opals sat on shelves. "Symbolic of the vices of man," Jolie said. "Gluttony, and greed for money."

But like the stuff in Mock Hell! Vita thought.

"No, actually these jewels are real. But their threat to man's virtue is the same. Wealth is perhaps Satan's most potent tool for the evocation of the evil that lies in mortals.

But they cannot take it with them to the Afterlife, while the evil on their souls does indeed go with them. That is the disastrous nature of the choice they make."

You mean the food here isn't garbage?

"It isn't garbage—but it won't sustain your body, either. However, your body can exist for an indefinite time here in Purgatory, in much the way the souls here do; we don't need to eat."

I don't get it. What happens if we do eat here?

"The danger, if we were going back and forth between Purgatory and the mortal realm, and only ate here, would be in thinking that it was pointless to eat there when all this excellent free food is available here. The body might feel satisfied, but it would be illusion; it would be running out of sustenance while in the mortal realm. So it is better to eschew the food here and eat only when in the mortal realm; that way natural hunger is a good guide."

Too bad, Vita thought sadly.

They settled in the family room. "You should find Purgatory video interesting," Jolie remarked as the screen came on. "But it can be disquieting too."

A neutral announcer appeared. "Two ghosts and a mortal woman have taken up temporary residence in Hell's Acres," he said. "One ghost is Jolie, the former wife of the man who later assumed the Office of the Incarnation of Evil; she is unable to visit him in Hell, though it is rumored that she has found a way to get around that restriction. The other is Orlene, who committed the sin of suicide after losing her baby. Her history is becoming more interesting. She seems to be seeking out each Incarnation in turn, beginning with the nebulous Nox, who may have played an unkind prank on her."

What is this? Orlene demanded.

"The Purgatory News Service is always current and personal," Jolie explained. "It relates to whoever is watching it. So when Thanatos relaxes, he gets news of his doings, and when Gaea watches, she receives news of hers. I have never quite understood its mode of operation, but its targeting is always perfect."

But it didn't mention me, Vita fussed.

"As for the mortal, she is Vita," the announcer said immediately. "She is the fifteen-year-old daughter of Vera, a leading researcher for Luna, the central figure in the approaching confrontation between Good and Evil. Raped by her father, she fled home and was driven to prostitution. Her mother was too upset by her unexplained absence to concentrate, so Luna arranged to have the visiting ghosts animate Vita's body and extricate her from a developing drug habit and life of sin. This was only partially successful; she instead became the mistress of a leading local judge, encouraging him to walk in the path of the unrighteous."

That's a lie! Vita thought, furious. *Roque's a good man!*

"The threat of scandal caused the judge to expel her from his residence," the announcer continued, unperturbed. "But her hold on him was too great, and the affair continued. It is difficult to tell at this stage how much harm will be done to the judge's reputation, let alone the balance of evil on his soul."

Damn! Damn! Vita thought, rage and pain mixing. *I wouldn't hurt Roque for anything! They make it seem so—so sordid!*

"Of course, the encouragement of such behavior might have been expected from the Bride of Satan," the announcer said smugly. "But it is a mystery why Orlene, a relatively chaste woman at the time of her death, should—"

Turn it off! Orlene thought.

"You mustn't take it too seriously," Jolie said as the screen went blank. "It speaks from a very moralistic view, because Purgatory is the place of moralism, where borderline souls are sorted for destination. Some of us disagree with this attitude, but it is best to be aware of it."

You're right, Orlene thought after a moment. *We should hear it through.*

Yeah, Vita thought. *We shouldn't let it get to us. It's just twisting things.*

Jolie turned the screen on again. ". . . support such mischief," the announcer continued, picking up precisely where cut off. "Now the three of them have taken the extremely unusual step of coming physically to Purgatory and staying at Hell's Acres. It will be interesting to see what activity they indulge in on the morrow."

Yeah? Well, you'll just have to wait, gossip monger! Vita thought fiercely.

"But we can tune it in to anyone we wish," Jolie said. "Ozymandias, for instance."

The dour face of the erstwhile King of Kings appeared. "A greeting, Jolie," he said, recognizing her despite her current host. "Satan is out at the moment. May I take a message?"

"We are borrowing Hell's Acres while interviewing Incarnations," Jolie said. "Our next interview will be with Fate, and it could be awkward, because one of her Aspects is Orlene's grandmother. Is there anyone there who could give us good advice?"

He frowned. "This really is not the locale for good advice. However, evil advice is available. Here is the Magician."

A new face appeared on the screen: that of an aging, worn man, the set of whose jaw suggested a determination that mere death had not eclipsed. "Hello, Jolie; do you know me?"

"You're Luna's father!" Jolie exclaimed. "You spent a lifetime opposing Satan, only to finish in Hell! What an irony!"

"I did what I had to do," the Magician said. "Black magic is less limited than white magic, and the task was great, so I knowingly garnered evil on my soul in order to serve the greater good. I succeeded in guaranteeing the continued life of my daughter, so that she will be able to balk Satan's final ploy of this sequence, and I am satisfied to pay the price."

"But all that you did was for the cause of Good! To have you confined to Hell for that—"

"The end does not justify the means. I used unauthorized means. I do not protest my fate."

"I think I'd better put Orlene on," Jolie said. "She was left as a baby, to be adopted by others, and only after her death did she learn of her natural ancestry." She turned the body over to Orlene.

"So you were left as a baby," he remarked, interested. "So was I. It must run in the family."

173

"Magician, if you are Luna's father, what are you to me?" Orlene asked, flustered.

"I am in a manner your uncle," he replied. "And Luna is in a manner your cousin, despite the differential in your ages. You see, your mother Orb and I had the same mother: Niobe, who is now Lachesis, the central Aspect of Fate. Orb and Luna thought of each other as sisters or cousins, but they were of different generations. Orb's parents were Luna's grandparents: Niobe and Pacian. Certainly we are close kin."

"Uncle," Orlene said, fastening on that. "Then you will give me apt advice, though you are damned?"

"I will. What is it you intend to ask of Fate?"

"I need a thread of life, so that my baby's Afterlife can be changed and he will no longer have his malaise."

"You ask for a lot!" the Magician said. "She may be your grandmother, but she will not give you that without excellent reason. You will have to persuade her that it is somehow in the interest of the larger framework to do it."

"But it is only in my personal interest!"

He frowned, thinking. "You ask for this, for your baby? I think she will understand that, having had to leave her own baby and then having seen her daughter leave her baby. You represent the third generation in the family with problems with babies. Perhaps she will be moved." But he did not look confident.

"Thank you, Magician," Orlene said.

"I am glad to have seen you, Orlene, however late." He clicked off.

The announcer reappeared. "There is an interesting development in the case of Orlene, who it seems is unashamed to contact Hell itself to—"

The screen went blank as Jolie took over the body. "Why don't we retire now? We don't need to sleep here, but we can if we choose, and I think it would help. We may have a big day tomorrow."

The other two agreed.

CHAPTER EIGHT

Fate

THEY DID SLEEP, UNNECESSARY AS IT MIGHT BE here, and were refreshed in the morning, pointless as that designation might be, here. Then they set out on foot for Fate's Abode.

Jolie was familiar with it, of course, but it was new to the others. It was in the form of a huge spider web, with the residence fashioned like a cocoon of webbing.

"Fate is a triple entity," Jolie reminded them. "I believe that Lachesis would not try to interfere with any person's thread of life for purely personal reasons, and probably neither told the other Aspects which thread yours was nor paid any special attention to it herself. So the chances are that she won't recognize either Orlene or Vita."

So do we make our identities clear at the outset, or wait? Orlene asked.

"I'd better identify myself first, and explain why I'm in a living host," Jolie said. "Then I'll introduce the two of you and turn the body over to Orlene."

175

They approached the structure, treading carefully on the huge web. Vita had nervous thoughts about big spiders, but Jolie reassured her: any spiders here were sure to be manifestations of Fate.

Jolie knocked on the web door. The surface yielded and sprang back as her knuckle touched it, but there was a sound, and in a moment the door was opened from inside.

A voluptuous black-haired girl stood there, her lustrous hair literally sparkling. "Oh, you're not an Incarnation!" she exclaimed, surprised.

"No, I'm Jolie," Jolie said. "In a mortal host. Hello, Clotho! Do you have time to—"

"Oh, Jolie! I didn't recognize you, but now I do! No, actually this isn't a good time; we have an emergency and are just about to go to the mortal realm."

Jolie hadn't anticipated this. Of course, she couldn't interfere with the business of an Incarnation. Yet it was in her mind, and the minds of her companions, that after this interview they should return to the mortal realm, to eat and to assimilate what they had learned. It would be awkward to come here a second time. "Maybe if I state my business quickly?"

The woman blinked into middle age. "Jolie, we really are too pressed for courtesy at the moment. I am sorry."

"I bring your granddaughter, Lachesis."

The Incarnation did a double-take. "Oh, my! Very well, come inside while we prepare. We can talk while I orient on the appropriate threads."

Jolie entered. The Abode inside was fashioned of web also, with floor, walls, ceiling and even furniture all of the grayish material. She turned the body over to Orlene.

"Hello, I am Orlene," Orlene said awkwardly. "I lost my baby, and died, and now—"

Lachesis spun on her. "You what?"

"You didn't know?" Orlene asked, taken aback. "I assumed I was only reminding you."

"My dear, I know nothing of your activities. This is deliberate, so that I will not play favorites with mortal threads. I did know that Jolie was keeping track of you, and though she associates with Satan, she also associates with your mother, who likewise does not follow your activities. We have been satisfied that Jolie would notify us if something important came up in your case, and I assumed that this visit represented such a notification. But—you *died*?"

"Yes. When my baby died, I—I committed suicide. I realize I shouldn't have, but—"

Lachesis plumped into a chair, appalled. "I hoped I had misheard or misunderstood. Where was Jolie while this was going on?"

"She was observing a candidate for a future Incarnation, and I was doing well—there was no indication, because it happened fairly quickly, and—"

"So now she brought you here, in an effort to make up for the oversight that allowed you to die?"

"I don't blame her!" Orlene exclaimed. "I was responsible for what I did. Now she is helping me seek my baby, and I thank her for that."

Lachesis paused, as if listening to an inner voice. Then she stood. "I can see this is going to be complicated, but we really are busy, and can't take the time to investigate your thread. We shall simply have to take you along with us and discuss your situation as we go." She made a curious motion with her hand, and a length of thread flung out, lassoing Orlene. "This will keep you close; don't be concerned if strange things happen."

"Oh, I have already seen some pretty strange—" Orlene started. But she broke off as Lachesis became a huge spider.

The spider jumped through the wall of the Abode—and Orlene followed, drawn by the thread. There was no jerk or vertigo, just an abrupt change of setting, as they passed through the wall without resistance and hovered over a giant tapestry in another chamber. The tapestry was fashioned of many thousands of brightly colored threads, and each of these followed its own course without regard to the patterning of the tapestry as a whole. Yet, overall, it was a marvelously unified construction, and beautiful in its variety and depth.

"This is the Tapestry of Life," Lachesis explained. "We

are about to search out several particular threads, each of which represents the life of one mortal person." They floated down—and instead of landing on the Tapestry, they approached it as if from an enormous distance, and it seemed to grow larger with changing perspective.

Awed by this vision, Orlene for the moment forgot her own quest. "If I may inquire—what is the emergency you are in? I thought Fate controlled the destiny of all things, so would be the last to suffer a problem."

"True and false. We handle the lives of mortals, but we operate within a framework of rules that greatly limits our leeway. We must also be careful of the interactions within the Tapestry; if, for example, we carelessly remove one thread, that may affect others, which in turn affect others, in the end damaging the larger pattern and requiring spot correction. We also may be subject to the interference of Satan. We also on occasion do make errors—of which you may be an example. But this particular emergency relates to none of these. Atropos is retiring."

"Your—One of your three components?" Orlene asked, surprised.

"Our eldest Aspect, yes. She who cuts the threads of life." Lachesis was abruptly replaced by Atropos, a large grandmotherly black woman. "As Fate, we don't play favorites," Atropos said. "But we do watch. Lachesis refused to watch you, but I see it differently, and I watched my friends. Suddenly one is in trouble, because of a distant thread I had to cut, and I feel responsible. I can't ethically help her as Fate, but I can step down and then help her all I want as a mortal, and that's what I have to do. So there has to be a replacement for me. This business came up so quickly, I hadn't lined up a successor—but if I don't step down before today is out, it will be too late for my friend. So we're in a real hurry."

Orlene was coming to appreciate the fact that not even the powerful Incarnations had easy existences. Their responsibilities expanded with their powers, and the complexities of their Offices could lead to hectic moments.

The Tapestry of Life was looming closer. Now the individual strands looked like cables, stretching from horizon to horizon (though there wasn't any horizon here), sometimes brushing by others, sometimes spanning regions alone. The network had looked flat from a distance, but now was clearly three dimensional, with many layers of threads, and the weave was increasingly intricate.

"Jolie might have a candidate," Orlene suggested. "She has been observing prospects for Incarnations."

"Any smart grandmothers who want to leave the mortal realm?" Atropos asked.

No, Jolie thought. *Mine are all younger.*

"No," Orlene echoed.

"Well, we do have a couple of prospects," Atropos said. "There's a woman who has had an immense amount of life experience and we think could do an excellent job, if she wants to. We're going to ask her now."

They had reached the Tapestry of Life and were flying between the huge cables. They oriented on one that extended a long way back. It had been twined closely with several others, but those had terminated, and now it continued in isolation.

They flew right up to it—but as they came within touching range it changed, and became a woman, in a dusky room, sitting alone, crocheting.

Atropos came to stand before her. "May I talk to you, Mrs. Forester?" she inquired politely.

"Why not?" the woman replied. "I can't see you well, but I can hear you. You're supernatural, aren't you?"

"Yes. How did you know?"

"Because you never came in the door. I never heard it open, or the floors creak. You coming to take me out of Mortality?"

"Maybe. Mrs. Forester, I am an Aspect of Fate. I cut the threads of life. I need to step down, and I would like you to take my place. I have observed you, and believe you are qualified to handle this Office."

"You are the one who ends lives?"

179

"Who sets their limits, yes. It is, of course, not a casual decision; I spend as much time as I need to determine the appropriate point for each."

"I can't see well enough to read, which is why I'm not looking at a book now or watching a holo. How do you think I could see a life well enough to judge when it should be stopped?"

"You will assume a new body," Atropos said. "Then you will be able to see perfectly. You will also be in perfect health and invulnerable to physical injury. You will be immortal, as long as you want to be. But you will be one of three, never alone, never completely in charge."

Mrs. Forester sat for a while and thought about it. Finally she looked up. "I don't want it."

"Do you know that you do not have long to live, as you are? This would effectively extend your thread of life indefinitely."

"I know it. But it's my turn to go, and I'm ready for it. You have cut the lives of my husband and my children and my friends, so that now I am alone. All of them should have had more time to live. Maybe you had reason—but I know I don't want to do that to anyone else. I'd rather just finish my term and rejoin my folks in Heaven. I will not serve as judge on any other person's life."

Atropos nodded. "Mrs. Forester, I thought you would feel that way. I am stepping down because I am needed in the mortal realm, and will not interfere with the lives of those who don't deserve it, for my own personal reasons. I will not live long after I step down, but I will do what has to be done. I came to offer you this position because I knew you were competent and not power hungry. But it is true that Fate makes decisions on the lives and deaths of mortals, and you can not avoid these decisions if you assume the Office. I thank you for your time, and I respect your decision."

Mrs. Forester picked up her crocheting. "Come and see me, when your business is done and you are mortal."

"I will try to." Atropos faded out.

Away from the thread, Atropos vented her spleen. "Damn it! Some of these white women have too much pride! It's hard to get the best, because they aren't moved by the idea of power or immortality."

They were moving through the cables, toward another prospect. Lachesis remanifested. "Why did you come to me now, Orlene?"

"When I met Thanatos, I prevailed on him to spare the life of a newborn baby. We took it to a hospital instead. Thanatos said you would have to adjust its thread. I—"

"I have already remeasured it," Lachesis said. "Thanatos has compassion, and I would not second-guess it. I handled that the moment it occurred, without investigating the case, because I knew he would have reason."

"Thank you," Orlene said, relieved. "The other thing—I went to Nox to recover my own baby, but she said I had to have an item from each Incarnation. From you, a new thread, to—"

Lachesis was replaced by Clotho, the lovely, youngest Aspect. "That is my department; I spin the threads of life. But this is no minor thing you ask! For one thing, what is the point, if your baby is already dead?"

"My baby died because he had come upon an incurable malaise of the soul. That malaise continues after his death and will prevent him from ever being a truly good spirit. I must free him from that."

Clotho looked at her. "I sympathize with your need, but each thread I spin represents a potential life. I cannot sacrifice any one of them without excellent reason. I know you are the granddaughter of Niobe—I mean, Lachesis—but we cannot do favors merely because of such a relationship."

"If there is any way I can earn it," Orlene said. "Any thing I can do—"

"We really do not stand in need of anything a mortal might offer, and even less of anything a ghost could do. Certainly we can consider the matter, and if anything occurs—" She shrugged.

Orlene felt the weight of defeat. She knew she had nothing to offer but her plea. Clotho was treating her fairly; she could not claim otherwise.

They reached the next thread. This one was amidst

181

several others; it was evident that no close associates of this person had died recently.

They approached—and were in the presence of an old woman on a convoluted carpet. "Miss Ember," Atropos said, reappearing.

The woman jumped! "Oh, I didn't see you coming! What can I do for you? I have some nice knickknacks for sale—"

"I am Atropos, an Aspect of Fate. I have watched you, and know that you are a good woman. I want you to take my Office and cut the threads of life."

"Is this a joke? I may be old and crippled, but my mind is sound. What are you trying to pull?"

"I can prove my identity, if you wish. This is not a joke."

"Very well: prove it."

Atropos flung a line of web. It settled around the woman. Then Atropos flung another line, up through the roof of the house. She became a giant spider. She hooked onto the line that secured Mazie Ember's carpet with one leg, and used the others to climb the other line.

The climb was rapid. In a moment they were passing through the roof and rising up into the sky. Atropos/spider hauled the cargo up to a local cloud. Then, perched on the top of the cloud, Atropos resumed her human form. "This is part of the power of an Incarnation. Do you wish to see more?"

Mazie was evidently shaken, but not convinced. "Yes."

Lachesis reappeared. "I am the central Aspect of Fate, Lachesis. I measure the threads of life." Then Clotho: "And I spin them. The three of us share this body, and you would share it, too, being immortal until you chose to leave."

Mazie was becoming persuaded. "I never thought that I would ever be offered such a job! But I can't move my limbs at all; that's why I use a medical carpet. I would be useless."

"No," Clotho said. "You would join our body, leaving yours behind. Atropos would assume your body, and it would assume her likeness and mortal capabilities, and she would use your carpet to fly away to her pressing business among the mortals. You would regain full use of your limbs."

"Oh, my!" Mazie exclaimed, astonished. "What a dream!"

"But you would have to share time with the other two," Clotho said. "Lachesis and I would be your constant companions. Our duties are pressing; it is no holiday we offer you. Merely a new mode of existence."

Mazie shrugged. "No."

Atropos reappeared. "You do not wish to take the Office?"

"Oh, I would love the Office! But not the responsibility. I could not ever trust myself to decide when a life should end. I am sure I would make mistakes, and that is too important to allow mistakes. So I know I must not do it."

"We all have had to learn our Offices," Atropos said. "We all have made mistakes. But we keep striving to do better."

"But I don't trust my own judgment," Mazie said. "I have always been dependent on the decisions of others. To be suddenly free of pain, of paralysis, and to be making decisions for others—no, I know I would make a mess of it. So I thank you for the offer, and I make the one decision whose correctness I can be sure of: not to take what you offer."

Atropos gazed at her, then faded out. The carpet slid back down the line, into the house, and resumed its former position, no harm done.

"We can't force a person to take the Office," Atropos said. "But it leaves us up the crick. I don't have any more good prospects."

Clotho reappeared. "Are you sure you have to go, Atropos? You know we'd rather have you stay with us."

"I have to go," Atropos said, manifesting again. "What I have to do, no other can do for me. I guess we'll just have to shop for any woman who'll take the job, even if she isn't the best. I hate this, but that's the way it is."

Lachesis manifested. "It is your prerogative to end your tenure when you choose. We must support you in this, just as we supported Clotho's predecessor when she decided to marry the Japanese martial artist. It will work out somehow; it always has. It is not as if your successor will be alone or unguided." But she did not look happy.

"If I may ask—" Orlene said hesitantly.

183

Lachesis glanced at her. "Oh, Orlene—I forgot you were with us! Of course we shall return you to the Abode!"

"No, I mean, I have a question about your change of Aspect. Does it have to be a woman?"

Lachesis paused. "Why no, of course not," she said. "No Incarnation is fixed by sex. But during both my tenures—no, it doesn't have to be a woman."

"I think I know a man who might be good, and who might accept it," Orlene said. "If you were willing to consider him—"

Jolie and Vita, hitherto satisfied to leave it to Orlene, came alive together. *You don't mean—* Jolie started. *Roque?* Vita concluded, with horrendously mixed emotions.

"Who is this man?" Lachesis asked sharply.

"His name is Nicolai," Orlene said. Jolie and Vita relaxed, amazed. Orlene, pretty much lost at her death and after the encounter with Nox, was now really taking hold! "He's an old Gypsy widower, whose only daughter is married and gone. I don't know if he is still alive, actually, but—"

Lachesis spread her hands. Between them a webbing appeared: a section of the Tapestry of Life. She peered closely into it. "He is alive." She put her hands together and the webbing vanished, except for a single strand.

Then they were moving rapidly along that strand. All else blurred past.

They came to rest in a village in southern France. The old Gypsy man's refuse hovel remained almost unchanged—and so did he. He had been about sixty years old; now he was eighty, and slower, but still doing for himself in the Gypsy way.

Atropos appeared to him. "Nicolai," she said.

The old man's gaze swung to fasten on her. "I hear you, Mistress of threads! What do you want with me?"

"How are you at judging folk?"

"Excellent!" he said. "I can tell almost at a glance how much money a man is worth and how much he will yield for a trinket."

Atropos smiled. "All Gypsies can. But suppose you had to make decisions on their lives?"

"A man does what he has to. But we do not like to kill. That is seldom necessary."

"I will be direct. I am Fate. I have three Aspects, one of which I must replace before the day is out. We are considering you to replace that Aspect, but we are uncertain whether we want a male, and whether you should be that male. If you are interested, you must persuade all three of us, and we may not be kind in the investigation. We can not give you time to consider; our deadline is hard upon us, and if you do not wish to be considered, we must go elsewhere immediately."

Nicolai hardly blinked. "The Romani are quick to assess any situation. Answer me three questions, and I will answer yours."

"Ask."

"Which Aspect?"

Atropos touched her ample bosom. "Me—Atropos. I cut the threads of life."

"Will I have complete discretion about which threads to cut?"

"No. You must always consider the benefit of the entire Tapestry of Life, and the interests of the other Aspects and the other Incarnations. The cutting is never random or careless. But within those guidelines, you do have discretion. No one else will second-guess you."

"Will there be occasion for music or dancing or storytelling?"

"If you wish."

"Then I am interested."

Atropos gazed at him. "You didn't ask about magic or immortality or power."

"I didn't need to. I know what Incarnations are. I know the power they wield. I know they are immortal as long as they want to be. I know they can choose their forms and that at least one aspect of Fate is always young and lovely."

"That won't do you any good," Atropos warned. "Only one Aspect can assume form at a time, the other two becoming mere thoughts. You will never be able to touch Clotho."

"But what joy to be near her!"

"Then let her be the first to question you," Atropos said grimly.

Clotho appeared, deceptively young and bouncy. "So you like to dance," she said. "How can you reconcile that with the serious business of cutting threads?"

"What is life worth without merriment? Serious matters constantly beset every mortal person. We can seek reprieve only in the innocent pleasures of life, such as music and dance and the appreciation of luscious flesh like yours."

Clotho was not much moved. "If you faced death tomorrow, would you dance today?"

"Yes! I face death every moment of my life, especially now that my years are almost done, so every moment I make the most of it. There can be no better death than with a fiddle in my hands and a song in my throat and beauty in my eye."

She remained skeptical. "Let me see you dance, then."

"Give me a partner."

Clotho hesitated, obviously not wanting to be diverted by getting into it herself.

I'll do it! Vita thought. *I think his dancing is terrific!*

"Do it, then." Orlene turned the body over to her.

"I'll dance with you!" Vita cried. "But I don't know the *tanana!*"

"Then learn it," Nicolai said, assuming a formal position. He seemed unsurprised by her appearance from nowhere. "Stand opposite me, look me in the eye. Now respond as I move, so." He demonstrated—and as he moved, he seemed to lose forty years.

Vita followed his directions, haltingly at first, then with greater confidence. Soon she was doing a bit of the *tanana,* and becoming extraordinarily sexy in the process. The dance left barely enough to the imagination to differentiate it from abandoned lovemaking, yet that caused the imagination to run rampant. Her hips flung out, and around, and forward in unmistakable emulation of vigorous copulation. Her breasts stood up and shook independently. But it was the movements of the head that had the greatest effect, particularly the eyes. She shot dark glances sidelong at her partner, those looks barely passing her tousled hair, and Nicolai met them with such burgeoning implication that even in the midst of her own effort she blushed. Jolie knew that the Gypsies were supposed to be lusty folk; now she knew that it was no exaggeration. They made sex appeal into an art, and it was truly shameless: they had no shame in it. Jolie felt Vita's increasing delight in the forms of it; this was almost as good as making it with Roque!

Meanwhile Clotho watched, her cynicism slowly becoming interest, and her interest excitement. Her body mirrored in diminished scope the motions Vita was making. Finally she could stand it no longer; she stepped forward, joining the dance.

Clotho was good at it; obviously she had had experience dancing. She quickly picked up the motions Vita had struggled over, and her voluptuous body gave her a head start. Orlene, watching, had a thought: *She is Norton's lover?*

You died, Jolie reminded her. *He still prefers you, but you can not join him.*

I have no business being jealous, she agreed. *All the same . . .*

Nicolai adapted without a hitch. Now he danced opposite two young women, and courted them both, and made both feel helplessly wanton. He could have stripped the clothes off each and done whatever he wanted with them, and neither would have objected; rather, they would have joined in with enthusiasm. They were captive of the *tanana,* and reveling in it. They had lost the social limitations they had come with, for the abandon of the dance.

Nicolai brought it to a halt. With the termination of his motion, his age returned. "That is the way I want to die," he repeated. "With lovely, panting maidens surrounding me. I have no fear of death when I have the dance. It is even better to the music, and with costume."

Clotho and Vita looked at each other. Indeed, they were panting, more from excitement than from the exertion of the exercise. "I must learn that dance!" Clotho said. "Eighty years old, and he can do that to me—I must learn it!"

Then she was replaced by Lachesis. "You have one vote, Nicolai," she said. "But I am not frozen at twenty; I have more on my mind than physical expression."

Nicolai squinted at her. "Orb!" he exclaimed. "You are her mother!"

"Now how would you know that?" Lachesis asked, startled.

"I am of the Romani. I see the family favor. Orb, she was beautiful, and she had a talent with music. She said once that her mother had been the most beautiful woman of her generation. I have seen none lovelier than Orb. You—what were you like when you were her age?"

Lachesis changed, becoming abruptly younger, and stunningly beautiful. "When I was Niobe," she said.

"Ah, she was right!" he breathed. "And can you also make music like hers?"

"No. She derived that from her father's side. Now stop trying to flatter me, and we'll see whether you qualify for our position."

"I was not trying *to* flatter you!" he protested innocently. "You know I spoke only truth."

"And a Gypsy can charm anyone!" she said. But she did not revert to her older form. She had been charmed, despite her caution.

"What would you have me do?"

"Can you relate to the problems of women, as well as to their sex appeal?"

He smiled. "In your presence, this is difficult—no, do not change!—but I will try. I sired but one daughter, and she was blind and lame, but I loved her as I loved none but her mother, and I treated her as a princess, and she was beautiful, but others did not find her so, and that was my abiding grief. What is there for a girl of the Romani who can not dance? But she had magic, and I wished I could teach her to use it, but I could not, for all I knew was the fiddle.

"Then Orb came, and she played and sang, and she had the magic. I sent for her, and gave her Tinka, and Orb taught my beloved to use her magic, and garbed her prettily, and was her friend, and brought her to the dance, and now Tinka could do well what was halting before, for her music gave her strength, and she was lovelier than any save her mentor, and the young men clustered around her, and soon she was married. From that moment Orb had no enemy among our kind, and I loved her for what she had done for my beloved child.

"Always before, I had seen in every woman the shadow of what was the great darkness that blighted my daughter, for without beauty a woman is nothing. Always thereafter I saw in every woman a hint of the brilliance of my beloved, and no woman was ugly to me, and I loved them all. If a woman has a problem, it is my problem too; if she hurts, I hurt too. Now Tinka is a grandmother, for generations come fast among our kind, and she can see, and I thank the world each day for the occasion that brought her salvation. That was your daughter, Niobe, who blessed mine, and I would do anything for her or for you." He abruptly stepped forward, swept Niobe into his arms and kissed her.

Jolie watched, caught between a laugh and outrage. What an impertinent gesture! But she saw that Niobe wasn't resisting, and indeed was cooperating. *Two down,* Orlene thought, and Jolie had to agree. The old man certainly knew how to make an impression on women, young or old, and all of them were women.

Niobe broke, gently. "It occurs to me that we could use talent like that, on occasion," she said. "But Fate has been traditionally female, and there could be complications if one of our Aspects was male. For example, we have been having an affair with another Incarnation, and I think it best that he not know that there is any male involvement. How are you at emulating a woman?"

"I would regard it as an exercise in costume," Nicolai said. "In my youth, I dressed in skirt and stuffed blouse and thieved from a rich household, undiscovered, though the master stole a kiss from me. But I fear my whiskers would give me away now."

Niobe laughed. "You would be able to don fully female flesh, of any age. That is not the problem. It is the attitude: could you act female for any length of time without becoming angry or ashamed?"

"Perhaps you misunderstand the nature of Romani pride," he said. "It is not in being male or female, but in

189

being apt at what one does. If I emulate a woman, my pride is in being so good at it that not only does no one suspect, but any man I encounter cannot keep his eyes and his hands off me."

The mature Lachesis reappeared. "You are a rogue, Gypsy man!"

Nicolai smiled. "You knew that before you kissed me, Irish woman."

"Indeed I did! Were you not so winning, I would urge Atropos to cut your thread immediately. But we are in need, and it may be better to have your persuasive nature working for us, for those times we must deal with others of your nature."

Atropos appeared. "And it is my turn. I'm no young pretty thing, and never was one; I'm an old black woman who's seen your kind before. You want to take my place, you rascal, then you sell me, and a kiss won't do it."

"If I can't sell you, I don't deserve to take your place, you magnificent creature," he said.

"I think this is going to be fun," Vita murmured.

"We have a case now for some thread cutting," Atropos said grimly. "We had hoped to find the new Atropos before this, but have taken too much time already, and it will have to do for an examination exercise. Come and see how you see it, because this is the job you would have to do." She flung a web, and it settled about Nicolai. Then she became the huge spider and raced through the roof and into the sky, hauling the man along, with Vita trailing.

Nicolai looked back at Vita. "I never thought I would go to Heaven; the Romani really don't believe in it, though we profess whatever religion is current and convenient. But if it happened, I didn't think it would be like this!"

"We aren't going to Heaven," Vita said. "Purgatory, maybe, but not Heaven."

"You do not seem to be an Incarnation. I did not see you until you stepped out to dance with me. Why are you here?"

"I came at a bad time, so they took me along. I'm just a street girl, with two ghosts to set me straight. This is fun!"

"The Romani could teach you much."

"Yes, but I'm supposed to steer clear of that stuff!" Vita said, laughing.

"Perhaps we shall meet again."

"Gee, I hope so!"

The spider halted. Atropos remanifested. They were in a chamber, and something was going on.

"We cannot be perceived," Atropos said. "We are as ghosts to the mortals here. This is a large saucer, about to be hijacked by terrorists six hours hence, as it orbits the Moon. We must manage events to minimize needless loss of life. Mishandled, the saucer will crash, costing two thousand innocent lives and several guilty ones. But the skein is already tangled, and now we must choose which threads to cut, and to what length. What is your judgment?"

Vita whistled silently. "That old lady, she doesn't fool around!" she murmured.

Nicolai swayed a moment, evidently set back by the suddenness and force of this challenge. Then he took hold. "Are there any stops between here and the Moon?"

"No," Atropos said.

"Any intercepting craft?"

"No."

"So all crew and passengers are aboard, and cannot leave?"

"Yes."

"May we warn the Captain about the coming hijacking, so he can prevent it?"

"No. Fate may not interfere overtly in the Tapestry of Life. It has long since been established that to do so leads to unmanageable complications and snarls that have worse effect than any good done by the interference. You might liken it to performing surgery on a man by poking him with a long needle: the harm in the doing exceeds the harm of inaction."

"So we can neither kill the hijackers early nor warn of their plot?"

"We can't kill them at all," Atropos said. "See, here is the skein." She gestured, and the endless complex pattern of colored threads appeared, superimposed on the chamber,

191

passing through it. Six threads glowed. "These are the hijackers. One of them enters a tangle at the start of the hijacking; that one we *can* cut. But the others—see where their threads are destined."

Indeed, the glowing five remaining threads wound back into the Tapestry to interact with many hundreds or thousands of others. It was plain that if any of these were cut prematurely, there would be extraordinary changes in the fabric and a major unraveling could occur.

Fate has to manage the entire Tapestry of Life, Jolie thought in explanation. *Normally her staff in Purgatory, and her field agents in the mortal realm, handle the details, but in serious cases like this one she takes a personal hand. She's not about to wreck the pattern they have labored to smooth, by interfering grossly here.*

Nicolai peered at the Tapestry where the tangle was—the one that marked the hijacking. "Why is this fuzzy?"

"Because I have not yet decided how to manage it. There is the potential to have a few threads cut and straighten the tangle, or to ignore it, in which case most of the threads will be unable to continue. There are about two thousand of them. But as you can see, this is an intricate knot, with many possibilities, and if I mark the wrong threads for cutting, instead of simplifying the knot it may only make it worse, and many more will be lost. I believe I can bring it down to fifteen cuts, but I would prefer that it be even fewer."

Nicolai inspected the pattern closely. "I have been good at tangles in the past," he said. "The Romani learn what we have to, including the artistry of tying and untying many kinds of knots." He traced the lines that skirted the tangle. Five of them glowed. "The hijackers are on the saucer with the victims, yet do not tangle?"

"The Tapestry of Life takes only peripheral note of geography," Atropos explained. "What is important is how lives interact with each other. Those five remain largely aloof and in charge; they will take a lifeship away from the saucer if they encounter trouble, and will hold the passengers hostage otherwise. Only the crew and passengers are at risk—and almost any or all of them can be cut off here, unless I act to alleviate it."

"These threads here and there which almost merge—what does that signify?"

"A very intimate interaction," she replied gruffly. "Romance or lovemaking. That normally occurs when a new thread is started in the Tapestry. On entertainment voyages such as this one, a lot of it goes on. That is a portion of the appeal of planetary tours."

He nodded, and continued looking closely.

"Sometimes there is a key strand which, when pulled or cut, frees the entire mass," Nicolai said, peering closely at the thick column of threads that represented the interaction of all those on the saucer. The six hijacker threads were mixed in, until the tangle began; they were merging with the throng, concealing their nature and purpose. They were evidently experienced—and this success would enhance their influence in the mortal realm, as their subsequent interactions indicated. "Satan has a hand in this?"

"Of course," Atropos said. "He stands to gain by the disruption of the orderly skein. The more disruption there is, the more evil surfaces, and he gleans that evil."

But the evil is there already; Satan merely finds ways to evoke it, Jolie thought. *That helps separate evil from good, which is the point of mortal life.*

But what if that separation occurs at the cost of many lives? Orlene inquired.

They go to Heaven or to Hell, as the case may be; their souls are immortal.

But their chance to change their status ends prematurely. That is not fair.

That is not fair, Jolie agreed.

"I believe I can cut it down to six lives," Nicolai said, looking up from the skein.

"Impossible!" Atropos exclaimed. "How do you propose to do that?"

"By saving this one," he said, pointing to the lone hijacker thread that entered the tangle.

"But that will only help the hijackers!"

"I think not. Note the close association with this victim thread, which also enters the tangle. Are they not lovers?"

Atropos looked. "Yes, certainly. What of it?"

"One is a hijacker, the other a victim."

She pursed her lips. "Now that is interesting, I agree! But of course the hijackers conceal their natures until the moment comes to strike. He would take advantage of what offers, male fashion. It can hardly affect the outcome, since he is the one who doesn't make it through cleanly."

"But if he survives, and loves a victim, what then?"

Atropos peered at the configuration. "You sly dog! You just may be correct! In fact, I think you are!"

"Satan usually leaves a way out, does he not, in case a project sours? This is the secret key he has left, intended only for his own use if he chooses. We had but to find it."

"Only a rogue would find it!" Atropos said.

"Agreed."

They poked into the tangle, analyzing the implications of the added thread, each making objections and answering them. "Let's play it through," Atropos said at last. "Remember, we must not influence him directly, but if an indirect nudge will do it—"

We can do it! Vita thought eagerly.

"We might help," Orlene said.

"Yes, I could use you," Nicolai said. "You do not count as Fate; you are ghosts."

Atropos frowned, but did not debate the matter. She obviously wanted to see whether the loss of life could be cut down to the level Nicolai suggested. She made an adjustment on the webs that had brought Vita and Nicolai here. "These will maintain you in unperceived status for the duration. I shall return; at the moment I must see to business elsewhere."

They understood: if this did not work out, Fate needed another prospect for a quick exchange, and could not afford to wait six hours to set it up. They were on their own for this event.

Orlene, perceiving the nature of what the Gypsy had in mind, elected to bow out. She turned the body over to Vita, though it was now very like a ghost. Vita was young, but she had the necessary experience.

It was a six-hour wait, for they could not jump forward

the way Chronos could. Vita followed the female passenger, while Nicolai followed the key hijacker.

The girl was Obelia, an heiress and socialite, making one of her frequent trips to the moon for entertainment and gambling. She was reasonably pretty and well formed, and made the most of it by wearing expensive jewelry and eye-catching clothing. She was frankly bored, and looking for excitement.

The man was Basil, of a good family fallen into hard times. He had the graces of royalty, but he had joined the hijacking plot because it promised to bring him restored wealth. The others were fanatics, but Basil was not; he simply knew what he wanted, and wasn't scrupulous about how he got it.

The first meeting of the two was coincidental: they were both unattached and attending one of the dances arranged by the saucer line. Saucers were the luxury vessels of the day; they had inherited the mantle of the old ocean cruisers, and it was truly said that many an illicit affair began on them. So, in this case, needing partners, the two of them came together. There was a certain air of elegant mystery about Basil that appealed to Obelia, and there was no mystery about the qualities she had that appealed to him: diamond earrings and a well-tempered cleavage.

So they danced, and it was fairly clear from the outset what each desired of the other: attention and excitement. They proceeded to their first sexual encounter with almost flawless point and counterpoint, in the manner of bidding hands of a card game, the object being not so much the culmination as the challenge of achieving it with proper flair.

But this was to be more than that, thanks to the influence of Fate's minions. "Let me clarify this," Nicolai said, as he and Vita watched the couple stripping down for sex. "They will have a whirlwind fling—by the threads it seems perhaps three episodes in five hours—but each knows it is only a passing diversion, and they will part when the saucer docks at the moon. He will be wounded in the takeover struggle, and she will be the fifth hostage executed before the saucer Captain caves in and gives the hijackers command. We must

195

intensify their passing passion into burgeoning love, so that neither can tolerate the death of the other."

"But how will that change what happens?" Vita asked.

"She will be near the Captain when hostilities break out; their threads indicate this. She may be able to save Basil, and he in turn will save her. But their love must be true, or events will overrun them both. We cannot tell them this, but we can enhance their feelings subliminally. We must be like Romani, deceiving the eye and mind to move our subjects to our will without their knowing. Can you do this, girl?"

"You mean, sort of get inside her and make her love him more?"

"Yes, as I must do for him, using the ghost-power Fate has lent me."

"Gee, I've done sex with a lot of men, but love with only one," Vita said, abruptly reconsidering. "I don't think I could do it with another. But maybe Jolie could."

But I love Satan! Jolie protested, appalled by this sudden shift.

"Or Orlene," Vita said.

Orlene considered. *I loved Norton, but must let him go. I like Roque, but would not interfere with you. I think this is an exercise I must attempt.*

"Great!" Vita exclaimed, relieved. She turned the body over to Orlene.

"I am Orlene, one of the ghosts," Orlene said. "I have assumed control. I will try to enter the woman and enhance her love."

"That is good. This element is essential, for it is the only way we can accomplish our purpose."

Orlene approached the woman and tried to enter her the way she had Vita. To her surprise, she succeeded. Apparently her occupation of a physical host did not prevent her from animating another, in this special circumstance Fate had set up. Nicolai disappeared similarly into the man.

So this is what it feels like to animate another body! Vita thought.

Don't distract Orlene, Jolie warned. *Lives are at stake.*

They had entered the host barely in time, for Obelia was

just coming together with Basil. She was about to say something like, "Let's see just how good you are, stud!" but Orlene put forth a powerful thought, and it came out, "Oh, what a handsome man you are, Basil!" Obelia was startled to hear herself say this, for she was jaded about sex and generally preferred to make her men squirm a little even during the height of their passion.

"Any man must be handsome in the presence of such beauty," Basil replied. Jolie had to suppress her laughter, which might become perceptible and interfere with the mood. There was the smooth Gypsy man talking!

Obelia felt a small thrill of pleasure at the unexpected compliment. This thrill somehow magnified, well beyond what was called for, as Orlene threw herself into it. As a result, instead of simply spreading her legs and getting on with the sex, Obelia kissed him passionately.

He seemed surprised, but quickly responded, flattered that she should take such an interest. Maybe she wasn't the hardboiled socialite he had taken her for! She responded to his response. As a result, what both had expected to be a fast, wild encounter became more extended and tender. He forgot her diamonds and noticed her eyes, while she found greater appeal in contact than there had been in mystery.

After the early passion abated, they remained together and talked, discovering common interests that would otherwise have remained undiscovered. Their three almost competitive episodes became two far more meaningful ones. Love was dawning, amazing them both.

They separated at last, for each had other business. She had a formal dinner with the Captain, for her family was a significant investor in the saucer enterprise, while he had to participate in the hijacking. She wanted to cancel the date to remain with him, and he wanted to warn her to stay in her cabin for the next hour, but could not without imperiling his mission.

The ghosts emerged. "That was very nice, Orlene," Nicolai said.

"You are an expert!" she replied. She felt a certain shame for the passion she had engendered and participated in, for she had felt it as if it were her own. But she knew she would do it again if the occasion arose. It was a pleasure evoking the positive aspects of people, rather than letting the negative ones dominate.

An hour later it started. The hijackers brought out make-shift weapons and laid siege to the control room and the Captain's quarters. The saucer's crew was helpless; the only laser pistol was the Captain's, and nothing else could overcome the clubs made from furniture that the hijackers wielded.

"Give up, Captain!" the spokesman for the hijackers called, standing at the doorway. "Or we will—"

The Captain drew his pistol and fired. But Obelia, seeing her lover about to be cut down, leaped across and pushed his arm, fouling his aim. The beam missed, ricocheting off the wall, as Basil dived for cover.

"You kill one of them, there'll be no limit to what they'll do!" she exclaimed, though in truth she would not have acted if she hadn't come to know and appreciate Basil so well. She was shocked that he should turn out to be a hijacker, but that did not erode his appeal. He was like a bold robber who loved a captive lady. It was downright romantic, in a way.

Outraged by her interference, the Captain pushed her away and retreated to his bastion: the cabinet where he kept the master spell that enabled the saucer to defy both gravity and inertia so that it could fly comfortably between the Earth and the Moon. Without that spell, the hijackers could not operate the saucer—and they could not approach it as long as the Captain had his laser ready.

The hijackers knew they had just two hours to gain that spell and move the saucer before a police ship came to complicate things. Their bargaining position would deteriorate sharply after that. "Send out an emissary!" their leader called.

The Captain's eye fell on Obelia. "You're it," he said gruffly. "You like them so much, you go talk to them!"

Obelia was nervous about going out there, but had no choice. She went. "What do you want?" she asked the glowering hijacker leader. Basil was gone, no doubt to see to guarding the crew or passengers, and she was just as glad, because she didn't want others on either side to know of the relationship between them.

"We want the master spell, you ninny!" the hijacker barked. "Tell him to hand it over!"

"But you know he won't do that!" she said, afrighted.

"Tell him that we will kill one hostage every five minutes until he does."

She returned to the Captain, who was covering the door with his laser; any other person who tried to enter would get shot. "They say—" Obelia faltered. "They say they will—will kill a hostage every—"

"And they'll take the whole ship if I give them the master spell!" he replied. "I'll never do it!"

"I don't like the look of this," Orlene said. "Are innocent people really going to die?"

"They really are," Nicolai said. "But fewer this way than otherwise. We had to choose between evils."

Obelia returned the Captain's message to the hijacker. "I thought he'd say that!" the man said. "Bring up the first hostage!"

Two other hijackers brought up an elderly man who looked frightened and bewildered. Without ceremony, the leader clubbed the man over the head, so hard that there was little doubt he was dead. Then he picked up the corpse and heaved it through the doorway so the Captain could see it. "Ask him again!" he cried, shoving her after.

Obelia, terrified and sickened, stumbled through the doorway to deliver the message.

The Captain was adamant, knowing that his only hope was to keep the master spell away from the hijackers. "If I give it to them, they'll have no limit to what they can do; all of us may die as they rob and wreck the saucer! I will not do it!"

Obelia returned to the hijackers. The leader nodded. They brought up a middle-aged female passenger, who screamed as she saw the club descending. It made no difference; her body joined the other.

"This is terrible!" Orlene exclaimed. "Can't we stop them some way?"

199

Nicolai looked grim. "We cannot. I think Atropos is showing us the worst of her dilemmas. I have seen death before, but I do not like this. I tolerate it only because I have seen the threads and know there is no other way."

"No other way!" Orlene exclaimed. "Where is God? How does He tolerate this?"

"That is a question to which I would very much like to know the answer!"

The impasse continued until four passengers were dead. Then the hijacker leader tried another tack. He grabbed Obelia and marched her before him to the doorway. "Tell him that you will be the next!" he snarled.

Obelia had seen the brutal deaths of the others and had become to an extent numbed and resigned. She went to the Captain. "I am to be the next hostage killed," she said.

"What do you think of them now?" he asked grimly. "Sorry you saved that one?"

She thought of Basil, and was hurt and ashamed. She had really been getting to like him, and all the time he had been a brutal hijacker, planning this slaughter! What she had taken for genuine interest must have been no more than a contemptuous dalliance on his part. "I made a mistake," she said dully. "Now I will pay for it." In fact it seemed to her that she was about to pay for her entire frivolous life. What had she ever done to benefit anyone except herself?

"You don't have to go back there!" the Captain protested, regretting his curtness. "They can't get you here."

"They will just murder someone else in my place," she said. She walked back toward the doorway.

"Don't go!" the Captain cried. "I forbid it!" He swung the pistol to cover her.

She hardly paused. "What will you do—kill me? Keep your conscience clean, Captain; they will do the job for you." She continued walking.

"I *can't* give them the master spell!"

"I know. I agree." She passed through the door.

The hijacker leader was waiting. "What's he say?" he asked eagerly.

"It wouldn't be ladylike to repeat his exact words," she said with the wannest of smiles. "But to paraphrase: he analyzed your simian ancestry in some detail, and described rather graphically a solitary vice you should practice to the point of expiration."

"Don't be cute, slut! What's his decision?"

Obelia, expecting to be clubbed momentarily, found herself at a loss for an answer, so Orlene prompted her: "When God kisses Satan and the Incarnations applaud, maybe then."

In rage, the man lifted his gore-soiled club. Obelia closed her eyes and clenched her teeth, determined not to flinch. This was her single stand for justice, decency and a worthwhile life, however brief; this much, at least, she could do with style.

There was a thud, but she felt nothing. She opened her eyes—and there was the hijacker leader, unconscious, with Basil standing over him. "There wasn't supposed to be any killing," he said. "But when it started, I figured I couldn't do anything about it. But when you—oh, God, honey, I don't care if I rot in prison forever, I couldn't let him do it to you! I'm through with this business!"

Dazed, she protested. "But the other hijackers—"

"Tell the Captain to come out here with his laser, and we'll take them one by one. They won't know what hit them!"

Obelia hurried in to the chamber. "Captain, Basil—the one I saved—he's changed sides! Come out and he'll help you take the others captive!"

"A likely trick!" the Captain snorted. "I'll not be fooled by that!"

"But he means it!"

"Then tell him to come in here!"

Obelia went back and told him. Basil nodded. "He's got no call to trust me. Tell him to hold his fire; I'm dragging this hulk in there."

She told the Captain, who watched alertly while Basil dragged in the leader. Then Basil stood. "Captain, I'm a hijacker, sure. But she saved my life, and I saved hers. If you

201

come out to where you can ambush the four others, I'll lure them in one at a time, and it'll be over with no more bloodshed."

"I'm not moving away from this cabinet!" the Captain said. "You mean it, you lure them into this room!"

"All right. Obelia, you go to the others one at a time, tell them Alex says the Captain's still holding out, and to bring in one more hostage each. Quick, before they start catching on that no one's returning!"

Obelia scurried out, still amazed at this turn of events. She *had* done right to save Basil! He *did* love her!

She approached a hijacker who was guarding the crewmen, locked in their barracks. "Alex says to bring another hostage."

"Damn! It wasn't supposed to come to this!" But the man collared a steward and hauled him toward the Captain's chamber, leaving the others locked up. Obelia followed, knowing the hijacker wouldn't trust her in the vicinity by herself.

The hijacker saw the four bodies. "Hey—where's Alex?"

"In there," Obelia said. "Now he wants them where the Captain can see them."

The hijacker seemed doubtful, but the bodies were evidence that Alex was busy. He pushed his frightened prisoner ahead of him.

As they entered the Captain's chamber, the Captain's laser covered the man. "Drop your club."

"But—"

"Drop it," Basil echoed. "You are now the Captain's prisoner. He'll hole you if you make a move."

The hijacker dropped his club and went to stand by Alex, who was now starting to recover.

Obelia went out for the next, and the scene was played again. It was surprisingly easy. The hijackers obeyed the word of their leader, and weren't unusually smart. In twenty minutes all of them were captive and the siege was over.

The total number of lives lost was six: the four murdered hostages, and one crewman who had been struck down during the initial phase, and an elderly woman who had suffered a heart attack when she realized what was going on.

"I was sorry I missed you," the Captain told Basil. "But Obelia was right; you did good work, and I will testify on your behalf. I don't think you'll spend time in prison."

"Thank you, sir. But I did get into this to make money, and I'll take my punishment."

"You may find yourself with money anyway," Obelia murmured, taking his arm.

Atropos reappeared. "We are agreed: you have good judgment, Nicolai. You may assume the Aspect." She stepped through the wall of the saucer, and Orlene and Nicolai were hauled after.

This time there was no transition; they were abruptly back at Nicolai's hut. "We shall set a golem to resemble you," Atropos said. "You will seem to have died naturally." She flung more webbing, and it formed into an image of the man, lying on his bunk, unmoving. "Do you wish to leave a message?"

"No. I am old; they know I am due to die soon. Let it be this way."

Atropos stepped through the wall again, and again they were hauled after, on the invisible web. They arrived in an apartment where a black woman was making a bed. Atropos gestured, and the great skein of the Tapestry of Life appeared. She reached out and touched one thread, moving it slightly. She nudged another thread so that it lay in the place just vacated. Then a little pair of clippers appeared in her hand, and she cut that second thread.

The clippers disappeared. She extended her hand to Nicolai. "Take my hand, take my Aspect," she said.

Nicolai grasped her hand. The two stood there for a moment, then let go. Then Nicolai began to change form, coming to resemble Atropos.

She glanced at Orlene. "We made the change, girl," she said. "It's his substance, become mine. He is with Fate."

Orlene looked, and saw the young Clotho, then the middle-aged Lachesis, then the old Nicolai. "But I must

203

masquerade as a woman," he said. He changed, becoming an old gray-haired woman, with a long dark skirt, antique feminine boots, a blouse that looked flat-chested, and a ludicrous little hat. "Will this do?"

Orlene smiled. "It will do. But watch the whiskers."

"Oops." The whiskers disappeared. "But I'd better give the body to one of the others, till I catch on better."

Lachesis appeared. "Yes, we shall have some adjusting to do. It will be strange for a while, hiding a man!"

The former Atropos glanced at them. "You folk better get out of here; there's going to be an ugly scene shortly."

"An ugly scene?" Lachesis asked. "You never told us exactly why you had to step down so suddenly."

"Because I saw something you weren't looking for, and it wasn't right to use my office to change it, but it had to be changed. My daughter remarried, and I thought he was a good man, but he turned bad, and started beating her, and now he's going to beat her too hard. So I switched out the threads. Go on, get out of here!"

Lachesis faded out, but did not leave. She had merely become invisible, and Orlene with her. "And give that girl her thread!" the woman called. "She earned it!"

The woman who was making the bed looked up. "What?" she said, as the magic surrounding the former Atropos faded, leaving her solid and visible. Then: "Ma! But you died ten years ago!"

"Not quite. I came back to do you one more favor, girl. Now you be sure to testify to what you see—and tell them the background too."

"The what?"

"That man's been beating you nigh to death! Think I don't see those scars? Tonight he's going to beat you too hard and kill you—only I'm going to free you from him."

"But—"

Then the man returned. He had been drinking, and he staggered, but he had plenty of energy remaining for belligerence. "Get out here, woman!" he yelled.

The woman started forward, but ex-Atropos blocked her. "He's going to *kill* you this time!" she warned. "He's going to hit you too hard and then claim you fell. You'll be better off free of him—and you will be, once he's in jail for manslaughter. Stay back." Then she marched out to meet her son-in-law. "You good-for-nothing drunken bum! You crazy wife-beater! You cheat on her, you treat her like dirt, and then you come home and mess her up some more! I always knew you were no good, and now you're worse! Now pack up your things and get your tail out of here, you slime!" She continued, getting more specific and more insulting, making it quite clear where he stood with her and how far away she wanted him to get from her daughter.

He hit her, of course. Ex-Atropos was old, and deprived of the protection she had enjoyed as an Incarnation, she went down without a sound.

"Time to go," Lachesis said sadly.

"But we must help her!" Orlene protested.

"No. She is dead. That was her own thread she cut."

Then Orlene understood. Atropos had substituted her own thread of life for that of her daughter—so that she would not have to cut her daughter's thread. Now the man would pay the penalty for murdering her, while her daughter survived to make a better life.

Vita had been correct: that old lady didn't fool around.

They arrived back in the webbed Abode. "You have seen more than outsiders usually do," Lachesis said. "You have seen our challenge and our pain. But you have also helped us in a significant manner, and you have earned your thread. We will hold it for you until you have the acquiescence of the other Incarnations. Now you must go, for we have much to resolve, and we prefer to do it by ourselves."

Orlene could well understand! That saucer hijacking, and that change of Aspects—and the sudden death of the woman who had been Atropos. "Thank you, grandmother," she said, and left immediately.

I think we'd better take a break, Jolie thought.

That's for sure! Vita agreed. *Those Incarnations—they've got real jobs to do! It isn't all peaches and cream for them, any more than for us!*

"Amen," Orlene agreed, shaken.

205

CHAPTER NINE

Cosmos

IN THE MORNING THEY CAUGHT THE Hellevator
back to the mortal realm, careful to get off at the right stop.
They didn't want to get carried on down to Hell by accident!

They emerged in Mock Hell and made their way out,
ignoring the temptations on the way. They took a carpet to
the rocketport—and discovered that it had been replaced by
a saucerport.

I don't want to get on a saucer! Vita protested.

Jolie laughed. "This one isn't going to the Moon! It
should be safe enough."

The girl was not completely reassured, but didn't argue.
Jolie bought a ticket by charging it to Luna's account, as she
had been told to do, and the charge was accepted.

The saucer was really preferable to the rocket, because it
had no need for acceleration restraints and its quarters were
generous. Indeed, they sat in an easy chair and watched
through a genuine window as it took off, lifting from the
pavement without a jolt and sailing over the city.

A man came over. "Looking for company?" he inquired in a tone that all three of them recognized.

Jolie turned the body over to Vita. "I'm underage, vacuumhead!" she snapped.

The man moved on. It was evident that he had judged her age correctly, but hadn't been bothered by that detail. However, he did not want the kind of scene she threatened to make.

"But you know, I don't feel underage when I'm with Roque," she remarked.

It is because he respects you as a person, Orlene thought. *He disagrees with the letter of the law, feeling that the maturity and discretion of those concerned should be the determinant, rather than an arbitrary figure. Your experience and judgment indicated—*

"Oh, pooh! He was just too hot for me to hold back!"

That too, Jolie thought. The girl did not want reason, she wanted passion. But the Judge would never have done it for passion alone.

"Anyway, he knew one of you two would scream if you thought it was wrong," Vita concluded. "And you didn't scream, did you!"

Not loud enough, Orlene agreed, laughing.

The saucer arrived in remarkably short order. Its velocity was deceptive; without inertia, it could travel at very high velocity without seeming to.

They took another carpet to Luna's estate. Luna was there to greet them. "Tomorrow is Saturday," she said. "I will be out for the morning, but I have asked Judge Scott to look in on you. Meanwhile, I am sure you can use a good night's rest, after your extended tour."

They discovered that they were indeed tired, emotionally as much as physically. They greeted the griffins, who seemed for a moment not to recognize them, and settled down.

They were, of course, ravenous; they had seemingly spent two days without food. Actually, only the time they had spent traveling to and from the Hellevator, here in the mortal realm, counted; still, there was a psychological effect.

"One thing I must be sure you understand," Luna said. "You may have been absent longer than you thought."

Vita was in charge at the moment. "Two days," she said. "But you know, in that short time they had changed from a rocket to a saucer. It—It was okay, but we'd rather have ridden the rocket."

"Two years," Luna said gently.

"What?"

"Unless special dispensation is made, the time that a mortal spends in Purgatory differs from that of the mortal realm. It may be extended or compressed, but normally seems to be a year here for a day there. I regret I did not think to warn you before; certainly I should have."

She's right! Jolie thought. *I knew that—but I forgot, because it doesn't happen to immortals. Only to mortals who go physically into Purgatory, which seldom happens. What an oversight!*

What an oversight! Orlene echoed, appalled. *What have we done to Vita?*

"But I feel the same," Vita said.

"You *are* the same, dear," Luna said. "You have aged only a few hours—the time you spent in traveling—for the aging process in the Afterlife is so slow as to be meaningless in mortal terms. But the time has passed here, and you are now legally two years older."

"You mean I'm still fifteen—but the law says I'm seventeen?"

"True, Vita. You are now that much closer to the age of consent, if that is important to you."

Vita chewed on a mouthful, knowing that Luna knew her situation with the Judge, and also knowing that it must not be spoken. "So if I went back to Purgatory for another couple of days, I'd be nineteen, and—"

"And legally of age to make your own decisions, in this region of the mortal realm," Luna said with the faintest of smiles.

"Gee." Vita's notions were stirring up like the winds of a tropical storm.

They had trouble falling asleep, because of amazement over the passage of two years and horrified reflections on the recent (or *was* it recent?) events of the saucer-jacking and

209

Atropos' change of personnel. So they turned on the commercial holo, and satisfied themselves that the news was indeed two years later. Then it went into a rather soupy romance, and they soon became oblivious.

In the morning, true to her word, Luna left on her errand, and they changed into something nice in anticipation of Roque's arrival. But not too nice, because Vita was determined that it not remain on her long.

There was a chime, and Vita sailed to the door. There he was, and indeed he looked a bit older. Vita didn't care. She leaped into his arms. "Oh, Roque!" she exclaimed between ardent kisses, "I didn't know it was so long! Can you forgive me?"

"Do I have a choice?"

She looked at him archly. "Have you found someone else?"

"No. It has been a legal and lonely period."

"Then you don't have a choice! Oh, my love, my honey, my grand man, I'm so sorry, I thought it was only two days, I never would have done it if I'd realized, I don't want you to suffer!" She paused. "You did suffer?"

"Horribly!"

"Then we have two years to make up in one terrific splurge of passion! Get your hands in gear—can you feel me while you're carrying me to the bedroom?"

"I can try." He picked her up, and she virtually curled around him, trying to get everything into play at once.

Talk of nymphets! Jolie thought.

One would think she was the one who had been waiting two years! Orlene agreed.

Roque staggered into the bedroom with the squirming Vita, who was kissing him all over his face and neck and shirt collar while she ran her hands around his body, pulling out his shirttail. His thinning hair was hopelessly mussed. They fell on the bed and indulged in a scramble of undressing in which Vita's hands did more feeling than Roque's did. Before it was complete, she wrapped her arms and legs around him and scrambled into the position of mergence, kissing him hungrily all the while.

«A moment.»

One might have thought it impossible for either to pause at this point, but this was a peculiarly compelling presence. They paused.

"Who the hell are you?" Vita demanded.

That's Nox, the Incarnation of Night! Jolie thought.

«True, ghost-woman,» the Incarnation responded. «Orlene must assume the body.»

But Vita's in the middle of— Orlene protested.

«Then I will change the form of that body to the masculine aspect.» Indeed, as she spoke, the change began.

Give me the body! Orlene thought desperately.

Vita, feeling the ghost's horror, yielded the body. Suddenly it was Orlene in conjunction with him.

"What?" Roque asked, aware of the change, and dismayed.

"It is Nox!" Orlene exclaimed. "She threatens ultimate horror! Oh, what an awful time for her to—"

"An Incarnation?" he asked. "What possible—"

«Now enter my dream.» Nox said.

"She is sheer mischief!" Orlene said. "I need her help, and she makes me suffer for it! I must do what she demands!"

Then the dream surrounded them. It was chaos.

"And the Earth was without form, and void," Roque said, actually sounding relieved to be in a changed situation. "We seem to be in the beginning of things."

"I'm sorry," Orlene said. "Nox does these things. I never would have gotten you involved if I had realized—"

"What is that you hold?"

Orlene checked. She was floating separately, with a sphere in her hands. It glowed, showing a scene of swirling chaos similar to the one outside, but with a single speck amidst it. "I don't know; it just appeared. A crystal ball?"

"Let me look at it." He drifted toward her and bent to put his face close to the ball. "The scene within seems to reflect our present situation, but not quite. There are two specks, and one of them is of two children, no, two people, a man and a woman—why, that's us! Our image is in there!"

"We're locked in a crystal ball?" Orlene asked, dismayed.

211

"I think the ball represents the vision we are in, in the manner an inset represents the scale of the larger picture. This shows where we are." He tried to touch the ball, to turn it, but his hands passed through it without effect. "The other speck—it is hard to see—seems to be a house, enclosed by a metal fence . . ."

Luna's estate! Jolie thought. *That's where we want to return!*

Yeah, I've got pressing business there! Vita thought. *We were just getting into it, when—*

"Could it be Luna's estate?" Orlene inquired. "Where we wish to return?"

"Yes! Yes, that is it!" he exclaimed. "Nox is showing us where we are relative to where we wish to go. Now I see a faint line, a thread—a connection between the two. But it winds all around the globe; it is a devious path, if that is what it is."

"Nox does not yield her secrets readily," Orlene agreed grimly. "I don't know why she sought me out this time, but I am sure we had better follow her directives, or we shall be most uncomfortable."

WHAT directives? Vita demanded. *There I was, just getting into it with—*

That would have become awkward, if she had changed you into a man, Jolie pointed out.

She can do THAT?

She can. That's why Orlene had to take over and learn her will. It would have been difficult if you had changed while—

I got the picture! Vita thought, appalled.

"It is apparent that Incarnations are not to be taken lightly," Roque agreed. "Even those we thought did not involve themselves in current affairs."

Such as MY affair! Vita thought violently.

"But what does she want of us?" Orlene asked. "She wouldn't take this trouble with us for nothing!"

Roque considered. "She has your baby, as I understand it. Is it possible that she thought you would not succeed in meeting the requirements for redeeming your son, and when you made progress, she decided to interfere?"

Now Orlene considered. "It is possible. But I doubt it. She

has only to tell me no, and I will be helpless. Instead she told me how to go about it. I don't think she wishes me ill. She may not have wanted to talk to me at first, so put the awful reverse mountain in my way, but when I won through that, she decided to help. Maybe this is her way of helping me further."

In the middle of my turn with Roque?! Vita thought indignantly.

Roque smiled. "I might question her timing, but perhaps it is so. Let's assume, then, that this is a necessary and helpful thing on her part, this isolation of us here. We must make every effort to ascertain what she wishes us to learn or experience, and to return to our starting point. This globe is certainly a hint. Presumably if we move, we shall be able to follow the line and return to the mortal realm, and resume our mortal activities."

"Nicely put," Orlene said. "But how do we move?"

"We shall have to experiment. Perhaps we can walk." He moved his legs, but his body did not progress. "That's odd; I was able to move before."

"You didn't walk, before; you drifted."

"So I did. It was my will that moved me, not my legs. So I shall will myself to move along that line toward our destination." He faced to the side, looking serious, but still he didn't move. "I'm afraid not."

"You moved unconsciously before," Orlene pointed out.

"So I did. But it is difficult to see how an unconscious act could be duplicated consciously."

Try a sneeze! Vita thought.

That's not unconscious, that's involuntary, Jolie thought.

"Maybe—Maybe it isn't what we want, but what Nox wants," Orlene suggested. "If she wanted you to look at the crystal ball, then you could."

"Perhaps. But what does she want me to do next?"

Orlene shook her head, baffled. "I suppose we just have to keep guessing until we come across it."

"That notion bothers me. We should be able to work it out logically." He stood for a moment, thinking. "If the globe is an accurate indicator of our position—that is, if we interpret it properly—we are far from home, and must trace a convoluted route there. If the journey is not physical, it may be mental. If we form the appropriate attitudes, we may make progress—"

He broke off, for they had both seen the globe flash. But that was all; the scene inside it was unchanged.

"I think that was a yes," Orlene said after a moment.

"I agree. That certainly is progress. We must see if we can make it flash again."

"I had a ring once," Orlene said. "I gave it to my lover Norton, who named it Sning. Sning would answer questions by squeezing once for yes, twice for no, and three times if neither answer was appropriate. Do you think the crystal reacts similarly?"

"I don't think so, because it didn't flash at all before, when we were evidently not doing what the Incarnation wished. I suspect it merely remains inert unless triggered by our progress toward Nox's goal. But this remains useful; no reaction is an indication that we are not making progress."

"And when you said that our attitude was the key, it flashed," she agreed. "Does that mean we shall have to change our attitudes on—"

The globe had flashed again.

"I believe we do have the key!" Roque said. "Now we shall have to determine to which attitudes it is attuned. Legal? Social? Political?" There was no flash.

"Ethical?" Orlene supplied, with no better success.

"Practical? Mathematical?"

Sexual? Vita thought.

"Vocational?" Orlene inquired.

Religious? Jolie thought.

The globe flashed.

They looked at each other. "That was Jolie," Orlene said. "She suggested 'Religious.' That seems to be it."

"Surely she does not expect us to change our religions!"

There was no flash. "Nox is from the old order, from the dawn of time," Orlene said. "I don't think religion means much to her. Maybe the subject just happens to offer the key to what she wants us to understand." And the globe flashed.

You're getting warm! Vita thought, her interest quickening. *And that bulb can hear Jolie and me too; it's pretty smart. Want me to think about how I don't think much of God because of what He let me get into? I mean, that sure didn't help my mother any, or Luna with her research, and that research was to support God!*

"The crystal didn't flash," Orlene said. "It must be looking for something else."

Should I think about how the world was made in six days? Jolie thought.

The globe flashed.

"Jolie thought of the Biblical creation of the universe," Orlene explained to Roque. "So that must be—"

That's crap! Vita thought. *It took millions, maybe billions of years to make the world!*

The globe flashed again.

"Don't tell me, let me guess!" Roque said, growing animated. "Vita thought of science! And what Nox seeks is a resolution of the debate between Creationism and Evolution!"

The globe flickered. "You may be warm, but I think not quite there," Orlene said.

"Then let's make it broader. Does Nox seek our exploration into the nature of ultimate reality?"

This time the flash was almost blinding. He had nailed it.

"But why?" Orlene asked. "Why should Nox care what we think? She has seen it all, long since!"

"Why should anyone care what anyone else thinks?" Roque asked in return. "Why should the Incarnations care which way souls go, or whether they are separated at all? Why should God care, or Satan? I think we just have to accept as given that entities of all types do care, and that Nox is normal in this respect. She now wishes us to explore the matter of reality and come to a conclusion. Perhaps she is aware of some interesting complication that this exploration will engender, and which will amuse her. So let's start by arguing the case of Evolution. Who will support that?"

"I support it, of course," Orlene said. "Don't you?"

He smiled. "You forget: I am a judge. I try to be impartial. I am not certain that the verdict is in, and in any event, it is not mine to make."

How can he be uncertain about Evolution? Vita demanded. *Everyone knows it's so!*

That's not true at all! Jolie protested. *God created the world in six days!*

"Our components disagree," Orlene said. "Vita says Evolution, while Jolie says Creation."

"Then we have our opposing views," Roque said. "We shall have to make trial of them. When we make a decision on the matter, Nox will let us return home."

The globe flashed.

"Let me be the narrator," Roque said. "I have a fair familiarity with both theories. I suspect that since you are the one, Orlene, who wishes a favor of Nox, you must make the decisions, after hearing the arguments." The globe flashed again. "So, in effect, I am the judge who keeps order, Vita is the apologist for Evolution, Jolie is the apologist for Creationism, and you are the jury who must come to a conclusion. The faster we complete the process, the faster we shall return."

"But I'm really not an objective jury!" Orlene protested. "I already believe in Evolution!"

"But can you honestly consider the evidence for another view? Are you able to change your mind if the preponderance of the evidence suggests that you should?"

"Well, yes, of course. But I really can't see that Creationism could—"

"That's enough," Roque said. "Reserve your conclusion until you have seen the evidence from both sides." He looked at the globe. "Now, as I make it, we are at the initial stage of the universe, the void, where all is chaos. What does Creationism have to say of the first stage?"

In the beginning God created the Heaven and the Earth, Jolie thought.

What do you mean, God? Vita retorted. *Where the Hell did God come from? Who created God?*

Roque smiled. "I can see by your expression that your advocates are already mixing it up. I wonder whether we can get them to manifest separately, so that I can see and hear them, and so keep proper order?" As he spoke, the globe flashed.

We can do that? Vita asked. *We can take separate form?*

Apparently so, here, Jolie agreed.

But it's my body! How can I exist apart from it?

Like this. Jolie withdrew her spirit from the body. She appeared as a ghost, clarifying her form. "Now you do likewise, Vita."

I don't know if I can! But she tried—and succeeded. She emerged as a diaphanous form, translucent and vague. *Gee . . .*

"Concentrate on your form," Jolie said. "Remember, this isn't a true situation; it took me decades to master ghost form, but you should be able to do it immediately, in this vision."

The form squeezed together and assumed human outline. The mouth opened. "And can I talk too?"

"Yes, in this situation," Jolie agreed. "It's probably just your thought, but we can hear it."

"But what about my real body? I mean, how can I—"

"Perhaps Orlene can assume a different form, for this," Roque put in.

"I'll try," Orlene said, surprised. "It is strange, being the only soul in this host!" Her form changed, becoming similar to her living one.

Before long the three of them were settled, each looking and sounding like herself, even though Orlene was actually using Vita's physical body. "It's weird!" Vita exclaimed. "Knowing I'm a ghost, and that Orlene is really my body!"

"That is not the least of the weirdness," Roque said. "But let us proceed with our business. Suppose I put questions to each advocate in turn, conducting this exploration in an orderly manner. Jolie, how does Creationism describe the beginning?"

"In the beginning God created the Heaven and the Earth," Jolie replied promptly.

"And I want to know just who created God, then?" Vita said.

Roque shook his head. "That remark is out of order. You must give the Evolutionist version of the beginning."

"Well, it—gee, I've got to remember stuff I forgot in school! But it's something like how the universe formed in a big bang about fifteen or twenty billion years ago, and—"

"Who created the big bang?" Jolie asked.

Vita looked nettled. "Well, I don't know, it just sort of—hey, isn't that out of order?"

"Yes, unless you wish to permit direct debate. For the sake of order, I will direct the question to each in turn. Jolie, who created God?"

"No one. He always existed. He is the Eternal."

"And who created the big bang?" he asked Vita.

Vita had evidently used the reprieve for some quick thinking. "I don't know how it started. But if it's okay for God to be eternal, then it's okay for the universe to be eternal too. So maybe it cycles, getting big and then squeezing together, and what we call the big bang is just this explosion. We can't go back and see, but we do know it's here, so why not accept that it's here, no matter how it started?"

Roque glanced at Orlene. "Have you been persuaded by either advocate?"

"I really can't choose between them," Orlene said, surprised. "Either God began and the universe began, or both are eternal. There really doesn't seem to be a conflict there."

The globe flashed—and their surroundings changed.

Vita was startled. "You mean that was it? The right answer was not making up her mind?"

"Or keeping her mind open, in the face of insufficient evidence," Roque said.

Jolie peered at the crystal. "I think we are closer to home! The specks aren't as far apart as they were."

"But still pretty far," Orlene said. "I see lightness and darkness, but it is still chaotic." She was breathing rapidly, trying to get air.

"Because this must be the second day," Jolie said. "When God made the sky to divide the waters from the waters." As she spoke, the scene seemed to separate into a portion above and a portion below.

"What are you talking about?" Vita demanded. "It doesn't make sense to divide water from water!"

"What is your version?" Roque inquired. "I must advise you that we of the flesh are finding this realm inhospitable, so a quick discussion would be appreciated." Indeed, he looked as uncomfortable as Orlene did.

"The Earth formed out of dust and gas and debris circling the Sun. The water was part of it, though I think at first it was mostly hot rock. So any water was mostly steam, then."

The scene around them changed, becoming red, molten rock, with clouds of vapor above. They hovered just above the surface, sinking slowly toward it. The heat was stifling.

"Say—it's showing what we describe!" Vita said. "That helps. You can see that this wasn't made in a day!"

"Certainly it was!" Jolie replied. "The day of the separation of the waters from the waters."

"What waters from what waters?"

"The waters which were above the firmament from the waters which were below the firmament. The waters of the deep universe from the waters of the Earth." As she spoke, the scene around them became one of deep night sky above and deep ocean below. The heat abated; now they were cold.

"And all this in just one little day? A billion years is more like it! I mean, molten rock doesn't cool overnight, you know."

Jolie shrugged. "Yes, that day could have been a billion years long."

"Oh, you don't mean one of our days!"

"The word 'day' means different things. A day of Creation means the whole stage, taking just as long as God needs to do it His way."

"There doesn't seem to be much difference between them, then," Orlene remarked. "I see no inherent conflict, merely ways of looking at it."

It was the right comment. The globe flashed.

"Then let's get on to the third day," Jolie said. "God

gathered the waters together in one place, in seas, and made the dry land appear."

The scene shifted again. Now there was land rising from the ocean, jagged and dark. It buckled and cracked, making great folds that were mountains. Storms raged, dumping water on the mountains, which wore them down. New ranges formed, in a constant, restless process.

"Well, maybe so," Vita said. "I mean, naturally the water settled to the lowest place, and what was left was high and dry. I say a billion years, you say you call that a day, so okay. But let's get some life here! I figure it started in the ocean—they call it the primeval soup or something—and after a while it crawled up on the land, the plants first."

"Yes," Jolie said. "God said let the Earth bring forth grass, and herbs, and fruit trees, each yielding fruit after its kind." As she spoke, a green carpet formed across the land and trees sprouted, grew, flowered, and put forth many types of fruit.

"And this day could have been another billion years long?" Vita asked, trying for irony.

"Yes."

The girl shook her head, bemused. "I can go with that."

"So can I," Orlene said. The globe flashed.

"And on the fourth day," Jolie said, "God made two great lights, the greater to rule the day and the lesser to rule the night." The Sun and Moon appeared, their light forging through the mists that had shrouded them before.

"Hey, wait!" Vita cried. "There were three days before there was any sun? Plants grew before—"

"There was light," Jolie said. "It just wasn't the Sun's light, until God decided that it should be so."

"Or until the Earth orbit stabilized. You do know that the Earth orbits the Sun, not the other way around?"

Jolie smiled. "I suppose if you stood on the Sun, and watched the Earth, it would look that way. But we're standing on the Earth and looking at the Sun, and we can see that the Sun goes around the Earth."

"There is a case to be made," Roque said with a smile. "Technically, bodies in space orbit each other."

"Viewpoint," Orlene said. "I still see no inherent conflict." The globe flashed.

"On the fifth day," Jolie said, "God created the great whales and all the fishes of the sea, and every winged fowl." Around them the creatures appeared, the ocean teeming with life, the sky showing birds.

"But are your days still a billion years long?" Vita demanded. "If you give them time, Evolution makes them evolve, so that's all right."

"The days can be that long if you wish," Jolie said. "God did it in the time he did it; it really doesn't matter."

"Then we still don't really have a conflict," Orlene said, and the globe flashed again.

"On the sixth day God made everything that was on the land," Jolie said, and all the creatures of the land appeared.

"Oh no you don't!" Vita cried. "Where are the dinosaurs?" A huge lumbering reptile appeared.

"You mean those bones God put in the ground to amuse scientists?"

"Yes, I mean those bones! The first creatures on land were the insects, and then the amphibians, and then the reptiles, and then the birds and the mammals. You claim the birds and whales came first, but whales aren't fish, they're mammals, and they couldn't have existed before mammals did. Even if your days are each a billion years long, you can't screw up the order of things like that!"

"But there were no dinosaurs," Jolie protested. "Life has always been as it is now, with all the present creatures and no others. God created them together, and then He created man in His own image to have dominion over them, and from that time to this it has been about six thousand years."

"What of the fossil record? It shows how the present animals evolved from the early ones."

"Do you mean that you have a chain of bones that shows an unbroken line from your dinosaurs to the modern creatures?"

"Well, not exactly. The dinosaurs died out. But the little mammals evolved after that, and we have their bones to prove it."

"You may have bones, but they are only what God put there. And I think even so, they do not have unbroken lines. For example, how good a line of bones do you have for human beings?"

"Uh, not too good, for people, I don't know why. But—"

"Because your notion that man evolved from animals is a fantasy," Jolie said, warming to her subject. "Foolish men see a few bones and think that proves Evolution, but smart ones see that the bones are only bones, put in the ground the same time man himself was put on the Earth. If it were otherwise, the bone record *would* be continuous—and it's not even close."

Vita was taken aback. "Gee, you really believe this stuff!" she exclaimed. "But you know, that doesn't prove anything. I saw a man once looking for a handful of change he'd dropped. He'd had to carry a bag of things into his house, then he came out later to round up the change, and all he could find was a few pennies. Know why? Because it was by a sidewalk, and some coins must've rolled into the gutter and gotten washed through the storm grate, and some fell in cracks between slabs, and some were lost in the grass—and there were people walking by all the time, and they would've picked them up and taken them away. So if you'd judged by what he found, you'd have said that all he dropped was two cents—but he really dropped over a dollar in change. Now you take those bones: some of them were dragged off and chewed to pieces by predators, some got washed into the sea, some got crushed by stones or just plain weathered away in the course of millions of years. Only a few ever got buried where maybe some scientist found them—and *that's* why the fossil record is so skimpy. I don't think God's a tease; He wouldn't put down wrong clues just to confuse people. He didn't do it at all; it happened by itself. We've found enough to show us the way of it, and that's what the fossil record proves."

"But God *could* have put down those bones," Jolie said. "Those bones don't prove how they were put down. You have one theory, I have another. Can we choose between them?"

Orlene shook her head. "I have to confess, I have my bias, but I can't honestly choose between them. It could have happened either way."

The crystal flashed. "We're much closer to home now," Roque said, peering into it. Indeed, they now stood in a setting that was almost modern, with a variety of broad-leafed trees nearby and fir trees in the distance. A deer was browsing several hundred feet away, and there was the sound of birds in the trees.

"But we aren't through with the subject yet," Jolie said. "You mentioned this soup from which life formed, as if this is easy. But the most primitive type of life is unimaginably complex! Even a single living cell has so many molecules, such intricate processes, that it would take a small library of texts just to write out the DNA code! The odds against such a perfectly functioning system coming together by chance are astronomical. Indeed, even your scientists will tell you that it would probably take longer than the whole age of the universe, as they figure it, from start to finish, for that to happen. It *has* to have been done by design—God's design."

"No it doesn't," Vita retorted. "There may be hundreds of billions of planets just like ours in the universe, all with their soups, so the chances of it happening on at least one of them aren't that bad. But Evolution doesn't claim that a single living cell just popped into existence from soup. It happened by easy stages. Maybe just two molecules came together by chance, at first, and that worked better than the loose ones, so they stayed that way. Then, maybe a million years later, a third one bumped into them, and if that worked better, it stayed. That's natural selection. All those molecules churning around all the time, banging into each other, some combinations are bound to work together better than others. It may be chance that brings them together, but once they are together, it's not chance anymore. So the key proteins were formed in that soup, bit by bit. When one combination produced life, it was only a little step—but it worked better, so it kept on, and made copies of itself, and then things really got going. Mutation—"

"But almost all mutations are bad!" Jolie protested.

223

"So those ones die. If one in a thousand mutations makes something better, then that's what survives. It just keeps going, getting better, because the worse ones either die or are less competitive. If more than one version works, then we get different species, and finally we have all the plants and creatures of the world today, including man. Mutation and natural selection, in little steps, with a lot of time—that accounts for everything. We sure don't need God to do it for us!"

Orlene shook her head. "It could have happened either way. God could have done it, or Evolution could have, or God could have used Evolution as His tool to do it."

The globe flashed. They now seemed to be quite close to home.

"We haven't settled this yet," Jolie said. "Even if Evolution could have done it, it still had to have an orderly universe. You claim that everything started in one big bang. How can an explosion lead to the systematic organization of galaxies and stars and planets we find? It could generate only chaos—and only God could have brought order out of that confusion."

"Not so," Vita argued. "In one of my math classes they got into computer-aided designs. You could start with any shape and keep changing it randomly, and if you selected for what you wanted, you could come up with just about any picture you wanted. It's cumulative. It might take a hundred steps or more, but it happened. I started with a V and made it into a flying bat, just by picking the right shapes the computer generated."

"But the universe had no one to pick shapes!" Jolie said. "Except God!"

Vita was taken aback. "You mean I'm arguing your case? No, I'm just saying that out of a random shape, order can come, if something selects for it. It doesn't have to be a person. In the case of the universe, I think it was gravity. When two bits of matter got together, they attracted others, just a little, and formed a ball in time. Eventually there were great stars, and when they got too big, they collapsed inward and made black holes, and they started sucking everything else in, making galaxies. We're just some of the fluff that hasn't gotten sucked into the hole yet. Some organization! I don't see it as any celestial design, just as part of the process. And life isn't all that great, either, it's really just the slime on the surface of our planet. But it's what we are."

"This is a horrible view!" Jolie protested.

"Well, it sure explains why mankind is so creepy!" Vita said. "Look at the way we're ruining the world, look at all the crime and sin and just plain grubbing for money! You think this is God's own image? Then God's a freak!"

"No, this is just the mortal testing God set up. But I agree, it isn't working very well, so any time now God will call a halt and settle accounts."

"We don't need God for that either! Pretty soon World War Three will come along and wipe us all out and it'll be done. We'll end with a bang, for sure!"

"That may be God's design," Jolie pointed out. But she did not look comfortable.

"Have we discussed this enough to enable you to come to a conclusion?" Roque asked Orlene.

"No, I can't decide either way," Orlene said. "They agree that the end of the world is coming."

Once more the globe flashed. But they still were not home.

"Evidently we are overlooking something," Roque said. "We seem to have brought the competing theories into alignment for our purpose, but Nox wants more of us. Unless we come to terms with that too—"

"The Incarnations!" Vita exclaimed. "Where do they fit into this?"

The globe flashed, and the scene around them changed. They were back in the early Earth, before life appeared.

The globe glowed, and expanded, and floated up to head height. It turned, and one side brightened while the other went dark. Water appeared on it, and land.

"It's the world!" Vita said. "The sea, the land, day and night! Just as we discussed them!"

225

Then the light of it intensified, flickering about the surface and making the depths glow. It coalesced at the ocean.

"That's life!" Vita cried. "It came from the planet itself!"

But the flickering was not done. Part of it collected at the dark side and part at the light side. The dark side remained constant, but the light side flickering separated into two, and then into seven nuclei, with a number of pinpoints as well. These remained.

"I don't get it," Vita said, when it was apparent that no further change was coming. "What's the point?"

"I suspect that is what we are here to determine," Roque said. "Nox is showing us something, making a point. We merely have to grasp it."

"Light and darkness, the light fragmented," Orlene said. "At the time when life appeared on the face of the Earth. Seven major fragments, like the seven—" She broke off, the realization coming, as the globe abruptly expanded farther.

"Incarnations!" Vita cried. "The seven major Incarnations—all on the Day side! And on the Night side—"

"Only the Incarnation of Night," Jolie said. "She never fragmented. She still governs the dark."

"But that means that they all formed together, and the lesser ones too," Orlene said. "When life came to the world."

"No!" Vita said excitedly. "The world always had its spirit! Like a hamadryad, the spirit of a tree, only this is the big original spirit for the whole planet! Life came when the world's spirit settled around its rim—and the Incarnations are another expression of it!"

"To watch it and guide it and make sure it goes right," Jolie agreed. "As you say, like the nymph of a tree, the Incarnations exist with it yet apart from it, too, protecting it—and if it dies, so do they."

"And there was so much going on by day, when the animals were active, that it took a slew of Incarnations to handle it," Vita said. "But the night shift, when they're asleep, isn't so bad, so Nox stayed just as she was."

"And she's not part of the day, so she doesn't have a say in it, but she still cares about the world," Orlene said.

Now the motion resumed. The globe had become the scene surrounding them. The Incarnations floated nearby, each glowing, but their outlines and features were shrouded. They could be distinguished by external hints, however; one was great and bright, another like red flame, and another seemed somehow inverted or backwards: Chronos, existing in reverse.

"They don't look human," Vita remarked.

"This is before human beings existed," Roque said. "Perhaps other creatures assumed the Offices."

"But there were no other creatures before man!" Jolie protested.

"Yes, there were," he replied. "We established that a Biblical day could be any length, and man was the last to be created. You can accept that."

She nodded, surprised. "So the Offices continued right up to the present, with human beings taking over all of them except for Night."

"And Nox may not be human, but she can assume the form when she wants to," Orlene said. "So now we understand the framework in which we exist: whether science or magic governs, Evolution or Creationism, the immortal Incarnations are with us. Human beings may step into the Offices for a while, but they are merely like the presidents of companies, doing what they are supposed to. The power is apart from the Officeholders. The Incarnations are immortal, though implemented by mortals."

"But why is Nox showing us all this?" Vita asked. "Why does she care about us at all? We are nobodies, even among mortals!"

"I think she is showing us why," Jolie said.

Indeed, the scene was changing as they talked. Modern buildings appeared around them, and cars and carpets and saucers. Then, abruptly, it ended in a blinding flash.

They blinked, trying to see. But as their vision cleared, all they saw was molten rock and horrendous cloud cover.

"Back to the start?" Jolie asked. "No life at all?"

"World War Three!" Vita exclaimed. "Oh, it's coming, and not too far off!"

227

"But can't the Incarnations stop it?" Orlene asked, appalled.

"Perhaps they can—but they will need our help," Roque said.

There was another flash, and they found themselves in a building. They were on a bed, the three women coalesced into one, with—

"Vita, take the body," Orlene said.

Huh? Then Vita caught on, and resumed control of her body.

They were back where they had started—in Luna's house, in the guest room, amidst the act of love. It seemed that no time at all had passed since Nox had interrupted.

When Luna returned, she found a chastened house guest. "Is something wrong?" she asked, immediately responsive to the mood.

"Not exactly," Orlene said. "But perhaps yes. Is the end of the world approaching?"

Luna paused, then abruptly took a seat. "What happened?"

"It is complicated, but the essence is that Nox visited and showed us a vision that explained a great deal—and suggested that World War Three is not far off."

Luna nodded. "Now you have a notion why our research is so pressing. We are trying to head off the disaster that is looming. Not even Satan wants that, but somehow it keeps building. If we don't find a way to head it off, in perhaps five years it will happen. But we know it doesn't have to happen—if we can do what has to be done."

"What is that?" Orlene asked, awed.

"I am not yet free to tell you that."

Jolie suffered a flash of something, perhaps a memory, but could not capture it. Had she once known more about Luna's research?

"But how can we help, if we don't know anything?"

"I suspect you can help, but it is vital that you not know the manner of it. I suggest that you go on about your quest, and after that we shall be in touch again."

228

"But how can I do something as personal as looking for my baby, when the world may end thereafter?" Orlene asked.

"Nox sent you on that quest, and Nox showed you the problem with the world," Luna said. "I suspect that Nox is no more interested in seeing the world end than we are, but your quest must in some way relate. Complete it, and perhaps then we shall understand."

Orlene gazed at her with mixed emotions. But there did not seem to be any better course to follow.

CHAPTER TEN

War

THEY RETURNED TO PURGATORY, USING THE Hellevator, knowing that another year would pass for every day and night they were here. Two days was their limit; they dared not risk more than that, because that was when the big event was to take place among the mortals, whatever it was. If Luna's effort failed, then the next three years would see the development of World War Three.

As they traveled, they discussed what they had seen in Nox's vision. Why had she done it? Why hadn't she gone to one of the Incarnations directly, or to God Himself? Not one of the three of them seemed worthy of her direct attention for even a minor matter, let alone World War Three!

Well, you know we weren't the only ones in that vision, Vita thought. *I thought Roque got dragged along by accident, because he was, well, close.* Jolie, who had the body for the trip, laughed at the understatement. *But maybe it was for him,* Vita continued.

"Because he's a judge," Orlene said. "Or—"

231

Because he's under consideration for an Office! Jolie thought. Again something nagged at the recesses of her consciousness, but could not be captured.

And maybe that Office could have some effect! Vita concluded, excited.

It did seem to make sense. "But what Office would that be? The one that relates to war?"

And we are going to visit Mars now! Orlene thought.

It did seem to make sense. If Roque were slated to become the Incarnation of War, the vision would ensure that he get right on the job of avoiding WW III. Nox evidently could not affect the events of Day directly, but this would be an excellent way to affect them indirectly.

"I think we had better observe Mars most carefully," Jolie concluded.

They presented themselves at the front gate of the Castle of War. The drawbridge descended immediately, and the portcullis lifted. Two lovely women came out, garbed in flowing gauzy outfits reminiscent of medieval royalty. One was in pastel pink, the other in pastel blue.

Orlene, in control for this visit, was taken aback. She was in contemporary street clothes: a conservative feminine suit, with hat and shoes. She suddenly felt dowdy, though the host was only fifteen years old in real terms. "Hello, I'm—"

"You must be Orlene," the lady in blue said. "I am Lila, and if I may, without offending you, I would like to talk privately with Jolie for a moment."

"And I am Ligeia," the lady in pink said. "I shall be happy to entertain you while Lila and Jolie talk. My husband is out at the moment, but will return shortly."

Orlene hesitated. "You mean—alone? Jolie could take over the host—"

I had better talk to her, Jolie thought. *Don't worry; you can trust these women. I know them both. I will leave you, and return soon.* She withdrew her spirit from the body and assumed her own form, as a ghost.

"Please come in, Orlene," Ligeia said. "I died abruptly myself, and not so long ago as to have forgotten what it feels like. I was so lucky to have been rescued by the Incarnation of War!" She took Orlene's arm, guiding her into the Castle.

Jolie was left standing with Lila. "Where to, demoness?" she inquired. "We are not enemies anymore."

"We never were," the demoness replied. "I had no share in your untimely death, and your man was merely an assignment to me—until I came to love him. Then I did what I could to save him, with your help. But before you returned, he had cast me off, and any onus between us was gone. He is yours now—as I think he always was, until he encountered the current Gaea."

"Understood. But we shouldn't remain here to talk."

"The high turret will do," Lila said. "Follow me." She rose into the air.

Jolie rose with her. They floated up to the highest turret of the Castle and in through its stony wall. This was a place of virtually guaranteed privacy!

They settled into two chairs that were set in the tiny chamber. "You haven't told him," Jolie said.

"What point? He doesn't want to be improperly influenced any more than Gaea does. But now that you have brought his daughter here, we shall have to brace the matter. My concern with you is how this should be broached."

Jolie considered. "Orlene learned after her death. Her mission here is coincidental—but yes, I knew that their relationship would have to be brought out. She already knows of her connection with Luna, and with Lachesis, and of course she was Chronos' mortal lover. I think she can handle it; she has gained poise since the trauma of her death."

"Ligeia knows; I advised her when I saw your approach. She will keep her own counsel until we return, but of course she is quite interested. How will Orlene react to the knowledge that her father has a wife and a mistress, neither of whom is her mother?"

"Oh, I'm sure she can handle that aspect! She has had a considerable recent education in human nature. But there is another aspect to this that could be a problem."

"That she comes begging a favor? He will not be moved

by the relationship between them. He has a will of cast iron when it comes to compromise. I should know; he saved me from extinction with that will!"

"So I have heard. She does come for a favor, but expects him to set what price he will, as the other Incarnations have. No, my concern is what we have learned along the way. You see, we were visited by Nox, who indicated that World War Three and the end of the world as we know it is approaching."

"That was supposed to be classified information," Lila said. "Mars is trying to divert it, but each fuse he extinguishes leaves another burning. For example, one of the first things he did when he assumed the Office was to eliminate the leading figure of Babylon, so as to abate the war between Babylon and Persia. But that reprieve was only temporary; factions rose up and the war was reignited, and now threatens to explode into a much broader and worse conflict. There just isn't any simple fix!"

"This bears on the problem. You see, I have been watching a mortal who may be a candidate to replace an Incarnation. It occurred to us that Mars might be the one replaced. That would account for Nox's intercession at this time, and for her alerting us to the threat."

"Now hold it!" Lila protested. "Mym is not due for replacement!" Her blue dress was fuzzing out, in her alarm.

"Mym?"

"Sorry, I forgot; that's his private name. I mean Mars, or Ares. He's a good Incarnation; there's no call to question his performance." Her dress disappeared entirely, leaving her naked and voluptuous in the manner only a demoness could be.

"None at all," Jolie agreed quickly. "This is nothing we seek! It's just that we were perplexed as to why Nox should intercede at this time—just before we were to visit the Incarnation of War. Why didn't she go to Mars directly?"

Lila settled back, and her dress reappeared. "I have known Nox for a long time. She always has reason for what she does, but that reason is generally opaque to mortals—and often to immortals too. I suppose if she knew that Mars was to be replaced, and there was something urgent involving his successor, she would act. But I distrust it. She would have known that her action would be conveyed to the current Incarnation of War."

"Maybe that's why!" Jolie exclaimed. "To warn him!"

Lila nodded. "I am sure he will take the warning to heart. I think not even your spouse wants that war."

"Agreed. Satan wants to rule, or at least to prevail, but that war would destroy his prospects as much as any of yours. But perhaps we should not rush to convey that warning, until the matter of the favor is settled."

"Yes. Let's keep both the relationship and the warning out of it until later."

Jolie smiled. "I will advise Orlene. Does that conclude our business?"

"I think so. I will advise Ligeia."

They floated down through the floor, orienting on the other figures.

Orlene and Ligeia were seated in the garden, which was about as delightful a setting as existed in Purgatory, with exotic flowers and statuary throughout. Jolie drifted into the host and immediately relayed a portion of her information. *So we concluded that it is best not to advise the Incarnation of War of our thought that he might be replaced,* Jolie thought. *Orlene must state her case and get his decision on its merits without undue influence by any other factor.*

"Agreed," Orlene murmured. "It is, after all, only conjecture."

The Lady Ligeia was serving tea. "I must say, it is a pleasure to have a living person visit," she remarked. "I was a ghost when Mars came to rescue me from Hell; later I animated a living body so that I could be with him, instead of going to Heaven."

"This is not my body, either," Orlene said. "I am with it only until I can complete my quest for my baby."

"Oh, you had a baby!" Ligeia said, interested.

They were soon into a discussion of that aspect, and Nox's strange involvement.

They were interrupted by the sound of horse's hooves.

"That will be Mym," Lila said. "I'll get him out of his armor and bring him here."

"Mym?"

"That's his private name. Here at home we aren't formal. Far from it! Li gets to tickling him sometimes, and he laughs so hard it wakes me."

"Li—that's Lila? The demoness?"

"His mistress," Ligeia said. "She assumes any form he wishes. Sometimes he teases her by making her assume my form. Then Li stands for Ligeia."

"And you don't mind?"

"Why would I mind? He is mine any time I wish—and I can sleep in peace any time I wish, thanks to her. You know how men are; they invariably want more than is convenient. It gets dull. Li is endlessly patient, and she has excellent experience."

"Since time began," Orlene agreed, impressed by Ligeia's tolerance. Obviously the woman had no doubts at all about her situation. But of course she wasn't just a woman; she was a princess, and that evidently made the difference.

A man appeared at the entry to the garden. He was not large; in fact he was a small man, quite ordinary in appearance, and fairly young. He was in a comfortable robe; the demoness had evidently seen to his change of outfit, as promised. There was something about him, as seen through Orlene's eyes; he glowed. Jolie had become used to this phenomenon when Orlene took over the host; most folk glowed to some extent. But Mars glowed with a peculiar, pulsing intensity, unlike any before. It was, she realized, because he was her natural father; had she not known before, she would have seen it now. The other Incarnations had not been like that.

Ligeia rose and walked to him. She kissed him, quickly and perfunctorily, but with such assurance that it seemed entirely in order. Indeed, his interest in her was quite clear; it was as if they had been together only a few weeks, instead of over a decade. Yet somehow their manner conveyed the truth; he was the master here.

"This is a ghost in mortal host: Orlene," she said, turning

236

within his embrace. "Orlene, this is the Incarnation of War." She turned again to him. "She has come to ask a favor of you."

Orlene approached, somewhat timidly. Mars put out his hand, and she took it.

The glow strengthened, becoming almost painful in its brilliance. Mars stared at Orlene, and she at him. Then they stepped into each other's embrace.

"My child, I did not know you in that body!" he said, squeezing her tightly.

"My father, I did not mean for you to know!" she cried.

So much for keeping secrets! Jolie realized that the Incarnation's talent for entering mortal hosts in the manner of a ghost, and Orlene's talent for reading auras, had combined at their touch, and all had been clear between them, though they had never met before.

"I had not known you had died."

"I had not thought about how you had become an Incarnation! I had forgotten—" Then she faltered. "Oh—they must not replace you!"

Immediately he read the conjecture in her. "I am not due for replacement!" he said. "You misunderstood."

"And now you have a wife, and a mistress, neither of whom is my mother!"

"I will always love your mother, and you. But she and I are no longer for each other."

"But how can you both be Incarnations and not to-gether?"

He put his hands on her shoulders and held her before him. "That is a separate story, my daughter. It was not what either of us chose, at first. I loved your mother, but I was required to marry a princess of another kingdom, and by the time I learned of your existence, too much had passed, and I was an Incarnation. It was better to leave her to her own course. Then she became an Incarnation herself, and I was glad for her. I think we understand each other, now, as well as any do, and there is something to be said for that."

"And how can I ask a favor of you, now that we know what you are to me?"

"Ah yes, the baby—my grandchild." Mars considered for a moment. "I cannot afford to play a favorite here. You will have to understand the nature of the thing you ask. You want a seed of war. I will show you the fruit of that seed."

Orlene was taken aback. "Now?"

"It had better be; you do not want to spend more time here than you have to, unless you leave your mortal host." In his brief contact with her, he had picked up everything.

"Now," she agreed.

He took her hand. "But what of us?" Ligeia inquired.

"Let the demoness assume my form and see to you," he replied.

Both women, in mock outrage, grabbed pillows from the chairs and hurled them at him. But the Sword of War had already appeared in his hand, and he and Orlene were moving through the wall and down out of Purgatory, toward the mortal realm.

"Where are we going?" she asked, impressed again by the facility with which Incarnations traveled. Thanatos had his pale horse, Chronos had his Hourglass, Fate her threads, and now here was the Sword of War, serving a positive function.

"The Babylon-Persia front," he replied. "When I was new in Office, I resolved a difference with Fate by eliminating the ruler of Babylon, and brought peace between them. But it turned out to be an uneasy lull, with periodic flare-ups, because the underlying ethnic antagonisms remained and there were unpaid debts from the war. Had one side or the other been victorious, the loser would have been largely annihilated, solving that problem. In our desire to stop bloodshed, we left those quarrels intact, and they continued to strike fire. Today the empires are nominally at peace, but there are continued incidents, and the interest and involvement of neighboring powers is growing, so that there is increasing likelihood of a larger conflagration. We Incarnations have concluded that we shall have to take serious steps to prevent this from escalating into World War Three."

"But can't you, as the Incarnation of War—"

"I am doing my best, and have succeeded in staving it off,

but in the face of the dereliction of another Incarnation, I am losing ground. I give it no more than five years, perhaps six, before the end. That is why we shall take action soon."

"To—To replace an Incarnation? But which one, if not you?"

"I have said too much," he said gruffly. "Here is the front."

It resembled a wasteland. The fields were scorched, with little of their crops surviving, and the buildings were mostly rubble. As they came to the surface beside a hut fashioned of bits of board, brick, cardboard and canvas, Orlene saw a plume of smoke on the horizon. She already knew better than to inquire what was burning.

"I will enter the man," Mars said. "You will enter the woman. You will understand the language and hear her name as your own. We will remain until the incident is done, which will not be long. Then you will understand what we face here."

"But—"

"It will be clear soon enough." He led her into the hut, walking through the wall.

She followed. Apparently he had extended his ghostly power to her for the duration. She was a ghost animating a living body, now to animate another host without leaving the first.

Inside, he turned to her. "Remember, you cannot be hurt, though you will feel what happens to your host. Now enter." He gestured to an old woman who was cooking something in a pot set above smoldering scraps.

Gee, I'm getting to find out about ghosts again! Vita thought.

Orlene stepped into the woman. Vita's physical body seemed to have no substance; it had indeed become ghostlike.

For a moment there was confusion, as they merged with the woman's foreign flesh and mind. Then focus returned, and Orlene was the woman. She was cooking a scrap of flesh she had found on her last scavenging effort; it was part of an animal that had been blown apart by a bomb. She hoped that if she cooked it long enough, it would become safe to eat. There was, after all, nothing else.

239

She glanced about. The hut was surprisingly comfortable, considering its nature. Paper from assorted packaging sealed most of the gaps between boards, and bits of foam from some vehicle's seats formed cushions for makeshift chairs. But there were no books, and there was no electricity; this was utter peasant existence.

"Orlene."

She jumped. Who was calling her name? Then she remembered what Mars had said: she would hear the woman's name as her own. She looked, and saw an old man lying on more foam fragments. This was the one Mars had entered.

"What is it, Father?" she asked. Rather, the host asked; Orlene had not willed the speech, being uncertain how to respond. The language seemed like her own, though she knew it was not.

"Outside."

Oh. She realized from the woman's thought that this meant he had a call of nature and needed help to rise. She set down her stirring spoon and went to him. She got her shoulder down, so that he could clutch it, and heaved him up. His legs were spindly and the rest of his body malnourished; it was hunger as much as anything that vitiated him.

No, it was more than that, her host's mind clarified. He had been exposed to a gas attack. He had been at the fringe, so he had managed to get away, though others had fallen and died. He had survived, but his lungs were damaged and his body weakened. Now he clung to life, but was slowly losing the fight.

She half held, half hauled him along out of the hut to the trench where refuse of all types was deposited. They had set up a box there that lent some support and some concealment, not really enough of either, but it was better than nothing. She left him there and returned to her pot inside. This was the extent to which she could still honor her father: to give him that little bit of privacy for this occasion. What a debasement it was for him, who had once been proud, the master of his field: to require a woman to support him in his weakness, so that he had no secrets of even that basest kind.

She thought about the grief that had come upon them as the result of this interminable war. She had once been proud herself, for a woman, having four sons and two daughters, and a husband who had taken the hajj. Then the war had come, and had not passed; year after year it had increased its toll. First the taxes, wiping out what little material gains they had made. Then her husband had been called to service to fight the infidel, leaving her father and herself and her children to manage the crop. They had managed—until the enemy had raided the village. They had quickly barricaded the house and hidden the children, but the troops had broken in, raped her, then beaten her father and knocked out the walls until they found the children. They had taken the boys away and raped the girls, though they were both under ten. For the first time she was glad that her husband was not there, for he would surely have been tortured and killed.

"Orlene!"

That was her father, ready to come in. She set down the spoon again and went out. She helped him stagger back to his mat, where he lay gasping. She did not like the thought, but could not help it: how much longer would he live? He had been caught by the gas when foraging, and had not realized at first how bad it was. He had thought himself charmed, because he had escaped what had brought others down, but the coughing had not stopped, and too often there was blood in it. His strength had ebbed, until even standing was an effort. She cursed herself for her realization that both her situation and his would be better when he died.

She stirred, and thought, remembering, not realizing that it was the ghosts within her who triggered the memories, so that they could learn more about her. She and her father and two daughters had survived, foraging in the burned fields for the roasted husks of grain left after the burning. Then the airplanes had come and bombed the village. Their house had been destroyed, and her older daughter killed, the younger one maimed by the collapse. They had fled to the outskirts and set up this hut from refuse, and now they were just hanging on until her husband returned.

241

There was a sound. She looked—and saw her father rolling off the pallet. She set down the spoon once more and went to him, though there was little she could do to ease his pain. He was gagging, the blood frothing on his lips. She tried to lift him up to a sitting position so he could clear his throat and mouth better, but abruptly he stiffened.

It took her a moment to realize that he was dead. She thought of making some effort to revive him, to pound his back or blow into his mouth to bring him back, but did not act; what would be the point? He was better off dead. At least his suffering had stopped, in this world.

There was another noise, this time from outside: irregular footsteps. That would be the child, back from her foraging. Maybe she had found something worth eating—or maybe she had grown too tired to continue. Would she be shocked to learn of her grandfather's death? Perhaps not; it had been obvious that it was coming. At this point emotions were muted, if not actually numb.

The child appeared at the door opening. Half her face was scarred, the hair gone, and the hair on the other side was ragged. She limped, but not badly; she had recovered from much of that injury.

"Mother, soldiers are coming!" she exclaimed.

The familiar hand of fear gripped her innards. Soldiers were bad news, whichever side they were on; the repeated tax shakedowns were almost as bad as the straight ravage by the enemy troops. She went out to look.

They were home soldiers, and their uniforms were clean. She felt relief: clean soldiers usually did not care to sully their uniforms with violence. Then she felt hope. Maybe her husband was coming home at last!

She stood outside, waiting for them. Her daughter, of course, was hiding; she had had experience with soldiers, and needed no more.

There were three: an officer and two men. "Orlene?" the officer asked.

She nodded, guarded until she knew their business.

"I regret to inform you that your husband is dead. He died honorably . . ." The voice continued, but she could not make out the words. Her emotion was not numb after all; her last hope had been dashed. She had hung on only for this, for his return, and now her support was gone.

The child came to the doorway. She had heard!

"Here are his medals," the officer said.

"We can't eat medals!" Orlene protested.

The officer was silent, holding out the medals.

Orlene glanced at her daughter, scarred and lame, any potential beauty she might have achieved destroyed before she matured, if she managed to live to adult age. With just the two of them now, without hope, and the fields remaining barren, and the war continuing interminably—what was the point in living at all?

But her daughter—she could still have a chance. "The suicide corps," she said. "You still need volunteers?"

The officer's eyes widened. "We do not ask this of you!" he protested. "Your family has suffered enough!"

"For a price," she continued grimly. "Surgery to fix my daughter's face, and good care for her well away from the front until she is grown."

"No!" the child cried, understanding.

The officer looked at the daughter. "You understand, you would not be able to go with her yourself? It is a life for a life, and the government does not ask—"

"What life is there for us here? We'll both die!"

The officer nodded bleakly. "You will have to come to the station and sign papers."

"We'll come now!"

"But Mother!" the daughter cried. "How can I—without you?"

"You'll die here!" Orlene said. "You have been weakening; I have seen it. They will feed you and fix your face, and you will be safe. As for me—my father is dead, my husband is dead, my sons are gone. I have no further need of life, only of vengeance for the ruin brought on us. Only you remain, and you can live—this way."

The girl had suffered much recently. She knew it was true. She did not protest again.

*　　*　　*

243

Orlene hauled a cart of fresh vegetables to the gate of the military base. There were a number of others like her, selling their produce each day, eking out their livings. But this was camouflage; under the vegetables was a bomb. It was her mission to take the bomb to the enemy headquarters and detonate it there. She would die in the explosion—but her daughter would reap the reward. This was the quiet, desperation strategy of the war effort.

The gate guard was bored and inattentive. He had evidently spent the night carousing or gambling or womanizing—any of which activities were forbidden by both military and cultural conventions—and wished he could be sleeping at this moment. His glance at her cart was cursory, and she herself was invisible: just one more poor widow among thousands. She did not even have to show her papers, though she had excellent forged ones, or to speak, though she had memorized several key sentences in the enemy's language. She pulled her cart on through, unchallenged.

Now she had to get to the HQ building. Whether the General would be there at this time was a gamble; his schedule was erratic, perhaps deliberately so, so that it was impossible to predict where he would be at any given time. But there was a fair chance that he would be, and certainly lesser officers would be there, so the bomb would have good effect. She regretted that she would never know the extent of her success. It would be nice to take out the man who had directed the strike against her village which had destroyed her house and killed her elder daughter. But she wasn't doing this for vengeance; she was doing it for desperation. Her government was meticulous about keeping its word, in this respect; when her bomb went off, her younger daughter would go to the hospital for surgery on her face, and then to a program for privileged orphans, and she might one day be a healthy, pretty girl. She knew better than to let anyone know about the rape she had suffered; that would count against her. But keeping that secret, and motivated to succeed, she would survive. That made it bearable.

Near the gate there were many women vendors. She moved away, supposedly seeking a region of the camp that had less competition. In fact she headed straight for the headquarters building. The officers had more money for good vegetables—and hers were the best. Superficially. She hoped nobody approached her to buy any, because she would very quickly exhaust her supply and expose the bomb. She would not be able to turn down a sale without arousing suspicion, unless the offer were plainly too low.

A boy approached. "Here," he called in accented urgency. He was raggedly dressed, evidently a peasant servant running errands for officers. Naturally they had sent him out instead of doing this chore themselves. She would have to get rid of him.

Then she paused. Could it be?

His eyes widened. "Mother!" he exclaimed.

It was her eldest son! Captive, he was serving in this military camp! At least he was all right; he seemed healthier than she was. But if anyone here caught on—

"You must go!" she whispered. But then, unable to help herself, she asked: "And your brothers—are they safe?"

He frowned. "One is. One is dead. And the third, I don't know; they took him to another camp, and—"

"Hey, boy, don't dicker with the hag!" a soldier called, spying them. "Take the cart to the mess hall, and the cook will give her its value."

"Right away!" he replied. He pointed, indicating the way to the mess hall. "We can talk while we go. How did you come to be here, Mother? I thought I'd never see you again!"

"I can't go to the mess!" she protested. "I'm here to blow up the officers' building!"

"But they'll kill you!"

"Never mind that. I'm doing it for you—and your sisters. Where is the officers'—"

"What's taking so long?" the soldier cried. This time he strode toward them, determined to make an example of some sort.

"That building!" her son said, indicating it with a flick of his eyes. "But you can't get there!"

"Yes, I can! Denounce me! Don't let them know you know me!" She started toward the building.

He hesitated as the soldier approached.

"*Do it!*" she hissed, moving faster.

He realized that this was the best course. "That woman!" he cried loudly. "I think she's a spy! She doesn't speak well!"

"What?" the soldier asked, confused.

"That woman—there's something funny about her! Stop her before she does something bad!"

"You're crazy!" the soldier said. But then, seeing Orlene running, hauling the cart behind her, he decided to follow up despite being told to by a servant brat. He broke into a run—and stumbled, because the boy hadn't quite managed to get out of the way in time.

That gave her valuable time. She expended what little strength she had racing for the building. Once she got there, it didn't matter who else was with her. The more the better, she thought grimly.

But as she came to the rise above the officer's building, the soldier caught her. She whirled and scratched his face, making him let go. Then she shoved the wagon and sent it rolling down the slope toward the building. Would it connect? It was supposed to detonate when the end of it was shoved in, and if it missed the building, or struck glancingly—

No, its aim was true! It was going to strike squarely.

Then a fist struck her from behind. The soldier was attacking her. She fell as he threw her down. She cringed as his boot swung at her body. It connected, and she felt something snap, and the pain flared. He kicked her again, this time in the face, and she knew her nose was smashed. He was beating her to death!

The world exploded. She thought she was dead—but it was the wagon detonating. It had destroyed the building!

Suddenly there were soldiers everywhere. She was hauled roughly up. "An assassin!" one cried, showing a knife. He thrust. She had thought she was beyond pain, but this was different. She tried to scream, but the blood choked it off.

"Come on out of there," Mars said. "It is over."

Orlene came out, screaming, before remembering that it wasn't really her. She saw the woman dropping, blood leaking from her chest and stomach. They were still beating her, foolishly, for she was already dead. Some distance away her son stood, watching, silent; he could not protest, for that would only lead to his death too. As it was, he would probably be rewarded, or at least commended, for he had cried the alarm—even if not quite in time.

Oh, God, what a mess! Vita thought, sickened.

Jolie agreed. It reminded her of her own death, centuries before. The horror of it never entirely abated.

"The fools!" Mars said. "They should have kept her alive. Then they could have tortured her for everything she knew. This way, they have nothing."

"Not even her son," Orlene said, still reeling.

"Right. I had to prod him to make him denounce her, but he did a decent job of it."

"You were in him?" she asked.

"First in the father, then in the officer, then in the boy," he agreed. "Now we go back. Don't want to keep the ladies waiting." He lifted his great red sword, and they sailed up into the sky.

"Waiting?"

"For most of an hour. They will chide me." He hardly seemed worried.

Orlene, numbed, focused on a peripheral detail. "How could I be in that poor woman for several days, and return in only an hour?"

"You were not in her that long. Only the conscious time. Perhaps half an hour at her hut and fifteen minutes at the base. I jumped you forward; it was pointless to go the whole route."

"But we can't remain in Purgatory several days!" she protested. "We'll miss the deadline for—I mean, if each day is a year—"

He smiled. "You had a year of mortal time to play with. We played with some of it. Only an hour of Purgatory time has passed. Fear not—I would not cause you to finish late. I have the same deadline myself, for that important meeting."

They arrived at the Castle of War. There were the two ladies walking in the garden. "Ho!" Mars called, landing before them.

Lila glanced at Orlene. "Did you learn the nature of war?"

Orlene burst into tears.

Ligeia stepped across immediately and put her arms around Orlene. "It is an ugly business," she said. "But he does not do it for spite. He wanted you to understand."

"I don't! I don't!" Orlene sobbed. "All that grief and death—what is the point of it?"

"There is no point," Lila said. "It is the nature of mortal man to fight. The pretext hardly matters. This flare-up was because one side accused the other of violating the truce. They had both been violating it right along, of course."

"Rights have to be wronged," Mars said. "Or so the mortals claim. In this case, they will keep on righting wrongs by committing new ones, until at last the entire mortal realm is righted and wronged in our version of Ragnarok."

"But this is preposterous!" Orlene flared. "Why doesn't someone do something about it? The Incarnations, I mean? Surely if all of you got together—"

"It is difficult for us to unify," Mars said. "Satan, for example, generally has a different agenda."

Satan doesn't approve this! Jolie thought. *He uses it to identify those souls that need earliest correction, but he doesn't like it!*

Why doesn't God, then? Vita thought.

"Why doesn't God do something?" Orlene echoed aloud.

Her father smiled in his grim fashion. "Perhaps you should ask Him, when you encounter Him."

Startled, she nodded. "Yes, I must see Him. I will ask Him!"

"I will give you the favor you came for," Mars said. He had read that, too, when he first touched her. "A seed of war. When you have similar commitments from the other Incarnations. I think this is what I would do for any person in your situation."

"Thank you," Orlene said faintly. She was aware that this Incarnation, like the others, had indeed put her through an ordeal before granting her favor. She had learned much that she rather wished she had not. What was the point in her quest to salvage her baby, when women were losing their whole families because of pointless wars? Yet what could she do except go on?

"You must stay the night here," Ligeia said, stepping away. She had held Orlene until she seemed stable.

"We must see Nature next," Orlene replied. "Then Satan and God tomorrow. We cannot rest yet, but thank you."

"Indeed, I see you cannot," Ligeia said. "But may we then help you to reach your next appointment?"

Orlene was tempted, but decided against it. "I have so much to assimilate, to settle in my mind! I think I had better walk."

"Of course. I am sure Gaea will treat you fairly."

Orlene made her partings and was escorted to the front gate. She hugged each of the understanding women, and then her father, knowing that no matter how the experience had hurt her, he had deemed it necessary. He had been fair with her.

CHAPTER ELEVEN

Nature

THEY WALKED DIRECTLY TO NATURE'S treehouse, letting their feelings sort out and settle. The horror of what they had just experienced of war was that they knew it was no isolated case. All over the world similar things were happening. Families were being destroyed, and heroic or unheroic sacrifices were being made, for pointless causes. It seemed that men just had a drive to fight, on any pretext, and that the women were unable to stop them. Why was it so?

Gaea was home. She came out to meet them as they approached. She was an older woman, heavyset, with a rather unflattering brown dress and green hat. "The *Purgatory News* alerted me," she said. "You are the ghost my friend Jolie has been working with!"

I never told her your identity, Jolie thought. *I would not have told you either, but Chronos made it known. Now you must tell her. She is your mother.*

"Yes, it is true," Orlene said, nerving herself. "I am

visiting each of the major Incarnations, to ask their help in recovering my baby. But—"

"But that is not lightly given," Gaea said. "Come in. I will listen to your plea, because I know Jolie would not be wasting her time. But I make no guarantee to help you."

They entered the house and sat in chairs of curving, living wood. The interior contours of the tree formed a central loop that had an odd quality: when she looked through it, she did not see the other side of the chamber, but clouds and sunlight.

That's her window to the world, Jolie thought. *Through it she can see anything in the mortal realm. She can also step through it and be there, if she chooses.*

Gee, that's great! Vita thought. *Can I look and see Roque?*

Orlene had other business, however. "I—I think I must tell you something else first," she said. "Because it doesn't seem to be possible to avoid it. I—I am your mortal daughter Orlene, and—"

Gaea was astonished. "I think you must be mistaken! Your body is no product of mine!" The fleecy clouds in the window were abruptly roiling.

"And I am dead," Orlene continued grimly. "This is a living host, not my own flesh."

The window went black.

Gaea appeared calm. "You understand, I can hardly take such a statement on faith! Where is Jolie?"

"She is here, with me. She has been all along—ever since I died. I—I acted without warning, so she did not know in time."

The window showed what might well be the worst and least forewarned storm of the century; the globe seemed to be covered by one big hurricane.

Then, abruptly, it cleared, and a somewhat eerie calm developed.

Gaea reached out and took her hand. "Yes, of course. I should have realized. I could have seen it directly, had I thought to. You *are* my daughter! But—dead?" She seemed stunned.

"I killed myself." Orlene had intended to explain the

circumstances, but was caught by a surge of grief that choked off her voice.

"But Jolie was watching you!"

Orlene nodded.

"One moment." Gaea's outline fuzzed. Then she was a young woman, beautiful, very like Orlene herself in her living state, with honey-blond hair and a most appealing figure. "I can handle this better in my natural form," she said. "My magic is going instead to insulate my emotion. Now you may tell me the story, and I shall relate to it in an objective manner."

"Oh, you look so much like me—when I lived!" Orlene exclaimed, amazed.

"I retain my appearance at the time I assumed the Office," Gaea said. "In twenty years I have not aged—but normally I mask it, so as to appear older."

"Oh, yes, of course! I am glad for you."

"But why did you do it?"

"My baby died. I—I had lived my whole life, to be the best mother it was possible to be, and when—"

"The kind of mother I could not be," Gaea said.

"Oh, that was not your fault!" Orlene protested. "Chronos showed me—you were deprived of—you did what you had to do!"

"Perhaps. And because of my responsibility to my Office, I wrote you out of my life. But indeed I missed you, my darling child! I compensated by trying to be the best mother to the natural world that I could be: the Green Mother. But I never looked at you, lest that awareness distort my judgment. I felt that if I performed well in my Office, you would do well in your life. Now I see that I failed."

"You did not fail! I had a good life, an excellent life! I ended it myself. I—"

The window turned dark, with a preternatural glimmer. "I remember an unfortunate case involving a baby. Were you—did you marry a ghost?"

Jolie, knowing what was coming, let no thought escape. There was nothing she could do to alleviate it.

"Yes. Gawain. I was to bear a child for him, an heir—"

"And I changed that baby, at his behest!" Gaea cried. "And destroyed my daughter!"

Orlene gazed at her with renewed grief. "You did not know."

"The ghost wanted his son to have his heritage," Gaea said. "I was busy, and granted the favor without properly checking, and so bequeathed to that baby the fatal regressive family malady. I was horrified at my error of carelessness—but now I am appalled. Look what I did to you!"

"No! I did it to myself! I was foolish and nearsighted and secretive, and brought grief to all those who had sustained me!" Orlene cried. "I could have let my baby go, and remained alive, and had another baby, and so fulfilled my commitments to both my ghost husband and myself, and not done the awful thing I did to my lover and my adoptive parents and to you! If I had it to do over again, with the perspective I have now, I would do what I know is right." Yet she paused, remembering Vita and the rest of it. "At least, I—I'm not sure. But then I did not know, and the blame is mine, and I curse myself for what I did in my ignorance. I know that it is right that I pay with my pain for—"

But Gaea was with her now, holding her. "No, no, my child, it cannot be! I gave you up by choice, knowing it was best, but you had no choice, your baby was dead by my hand, you could not adjust so suddenly! It happens to mortals all too frequently, because they lack the perspective, their lives are so brief and intense. I see it all over the world, all the time, and I cannot mitigate it despite all my power, for it is the human way."

The window had slowly brightened during this dialogue, and now the weather in the mortal realm seemed almost normal. Jolie was relieved; she knew the effect Gaea's emotions had on natural things. That was one of the reasons she had avoided telling Gaea of this matter directly. Gaea had surely suspected, but even so, the shock of confirmation had been formidable, and the climate of the world had been jolted. Now the worst was over.

"I thank you for your understanding, Mother," Orlene

said after a bit, wiping her face. "But I did not come here to speak this way to you. I came for a favor—which now I cannot ask."

"You must ask it, daughter—but I may not be able to grant it."

"It—I saw Nox, who has Gaw-Two, and she told me I had to get something from each Incarnation if I hoped to rid him of his malady."

"That must be true," Gaea agreed. "What is done by an Incarnation cannot necessarily be undone by that Incarnation, for things interact. I did the bad deed, but once it involved Thanatos and Fate—"

"And Chronos," Orlene said. "He was my lover, as a mortal. My death caused him to seek the Office of Time."

Gaea gazed at her for an extended moment, disconcerted. "Then this seemingly isolated error has had enormous consequence!" she said. "Perhaps only an entity outside the ordinary framework can perceive the full extent of it—and Nox is that entity. She lacks power in our realm, but her influence can be significant. Never before, in my experience, has she involved herself directly in our affairs. I find this more disturbing than reassuring."

"Surely she does not mean mischief!"

"We cannot be sure. Nox keeps her purpose secret—and she is the mistress of secrets." Gaea took a breath. "What is the thing you need from me, Orlene?"

"It is a tear."

Again Gaea gazed at her. The clouds swirled in the window. "That is not lightly granted."

"I know. If I had realized—if I had known what you have told me, I would not have come. It is not right to—"

"You must earn it," Gaea said abruptly. "As anyone else would. That will not be easy."

"None of this has been easy," Orlene murmured. "How may I earn it?"

"I have a problem whose solution may have bearing on the continued existence of the human species," she said seriously. "But that solution eludes me. I could use an opinion."

"But I know so little!" Orlene protested. "What could I possibly know about that you have not long since explored?"

Gaea smiled, not pleasantly. "It is a long shot, I agree. But Nox's involvement in your case suggests that you may have something. I will send you among the mortals on a research mission, and you will observe and form an opinion. For that opinion I will grant your favor."

Orlene was flustered. "But to provide a thing of such value, for an opinion of such little value—when I am your daughter! Who would believe—"

"I think you will have to weigh your opinion most seriously, to be assured that its value warrants its payment."

She's up to something, Jolie thought. *I know her. Don't argue, just get on with it.*

"What must I do?" Orlene asked.

"Leave your mortal host here. For this you must occupy another host, temporarily."

Don't leave me here! Vita protested. *I came to Purgatory with you, I want to go form an opinion with you!*

"Indeed, I want you with her, Vita," Gaea said, startling all three of them. They had for the moment forgotten how the Incarnations could perceive them individually. "You have experience that relates. Jolie does too. I am sending you to a teenage mortal girl who is very likely to get pregnant this day. Here is my concern: overpopulation is perhaps the greatest current problem in the mortal realm. The sheer increasing mass of human flesh is squeezing out all other creatures, rendering a record number of them extinct. It is depleting resources and destroying the environment for all. The competition for resources is generating pressure for war and bringing poverty to the majority of living folk. This is the thing I must deal with if the species is not to suffer grievously. But this problem is rooted in individual attitudes and acts. Responsible reproduction is essential for the perpetuation of the species, but irresponsible reproduction will destroy it. How can I cause all reproduction to be responsible, instead of the consequence of cultural or religious bias, or mere entertainment?"

The three of them were silent. Orlene was reminded of

her lost baby. Vita thought of her brief career as a prostitute. Jolie thought of the children she had never had, because she had died too soon. All of them had indulged in sex with abandon. None of them had succeeded in having families. How could they judge?

"In many regions of the world," Gaea continued, perceiving their doubt, "multiple children are needed to secure the welfare of their parents as they age. No importuning will cause those parents to reduce the size of their families; they would suffer if they did. In other regions, poverty eliminates most forms of entertainment; procreation, it is truly said, becomes recreation. In others, there are religious barriers to contraception or other means of family planning. I need a simple, practical, universal mechanism to make procreation responsible. I believe that a single case may provide the answer—if there is an answer. You will seek an opinion about the existence of such an answer."

It really was a critical matter! Mars faced the problem of a world-destroying war—and here was one of the roots of that war. Fate struggled with an increasingly tangled skein, and the sheer numbers of mortal folk contributed to that. The problems of the Incarnations were indeed linked. But how could they come up with an answer if the Incarnation of Nature could not? "We'll try," Orlene said.

"Lie down," Gaea said, showing her to the chamber she had used before. "The body will be safe here, and your spirits will not be in danger there."

Orlene lay down. Then Jolie linked hands, mentally, with Orlene and Vita, and the three of them floated out of the body. They had only vague human semblances, and their spirits overlapped each other, so that they seemed to be a single confused entity. They followed Gaea back to the window, which now showed a young, rather pretty black girl walking toward a building at dusk. She was in what was evidently her best dress for dancing, white pseudosilk with ruffles. The décolletage was low, and she wore a sparkling rose quartz necklace which rested across the slope of her nascent breasts.

"Follow." Gaea stepped into the window and appeared

beside the girl, who took no notice. They followed, and found themselves there too. "Enter her and observe. You may influence her, but that will change her situation and perhaps distort your observation. When you are satisfied, call me, and I will bring you back."

They floated as a tight group into the girl. Vita was still inexperienced, but Jolie was thoroughly experienced, so helped her get settled in. It was not the same as it had been with Fate on the saucer, or with Mars on the Babylon-Persia frontier; their technique was a magical pseudomergence of physical bodies, while this was actual possession of a mortal host by spirits. In the old days it had been thought to be possession by demons, but usually it had been spiritual, not demonic, habitation. When a demon did it, the demon normally took over completely, and usually destroyed the host before it was through. Spirits were far more gentle, and could not take over unless given leave by the host. They often, in fact, were benign—as in this case. But the popular prejudice against them remained.

That was the case while Jolie and Orlene were with Vita, and now it was the case with the three of them in the present host. They tuned in on the girl's mind, which was unguarded, and learned that her name was Ilka, and that she was fifteen years old, and that her name meant "hard worker." She did work hard, living up to it, and made pretty good grades, and did a lot around the house, too, but her mother still put her down as a child. She wasn't allowed to date, because she was too young, and anyway, all men were evil, her mother said, they just wanted to paw over a girl and put a baby in her and bug off. All her friends had boyfriends, and sure it was true about what those boys wanted, and two of her friends had abortions and a couple more were worried, but it sure proved one thing: they were women. She knew all about it: a girl could get a great good time from a man, if she got it before he managed to get into her pants, and if he liked her, he would be back next day for more, and if she got a baby, well, that was *really* proof she was a woman. She saw, she knew. She was tired of being dumped on by her mother; she wanted some romance, some independence, some respect.

So tonight she had dressed up and sneaked out: she was going to get into the big dance and have herself a time, no matter what!

She has trouble with her mother? Vita thought. *She doesn't know what trouble is!*

But if she is typical, she'll get pregnant—and we need to know what would stop her and all those like her, Jolie reminded her. *In my day we needed all the babies we could get, but today there are too many.*

I wanted my baby, Orlene thought wistfully.

She's a fool to want a baby! Vita thought. *I made sure to wear my charm, always! I mean, a baby would be fine, when I'm older and married and through with fun, but she's too young. She's my age!*

So you may understand her best, Jolie reminded her.

Yeah, I see the track ahead of her, to be a black whore like me, hooked on H! If you folk hadn't come and put iron in my willpower, I never would have thrown that off!

Ilka approached the dance building. It was brightly lighted, and magic flares in the form of dancing figures floated above it. Couples were arriving and entering.

That looks great! Vita thought. *I'd kill to get into a dance like that!*

But you don't know anything about it! Orlene protested. *And with no date—*

She'll get picked up, Vita said. *That's the idea. It's not as good as having a real date, but you do it any way you can.*

Indeed, Ilka was looking around now, trying to spot a likely man without a date. This was the tricky part.

There were several young men near the entrance, dressed to dance. One was fat, one was ugly, and one was neither. All were white.

Ilka nerved herself. She knew that white preferred white, at least to be seen with in public; she risked a crude rebuff. But if she got lucky, one of these would take her.

Sure enough, the handsome one spied her and stepped forward. "Lose your date, girl?" he called.

"Not exactly," she responded. "You looking for one?"

"Maybe. You got money?"

"Not enough."

"You expect to be paid for?"

"Maybe." She knew it wasn't smart of her to come right out and say it.

"Well, I've got the price of the dance. But it's not cheap."

"Didn't figure it would be."

"You want to go in with me?"

"Why not?"

"And come home with me?"

"Why not?"

He eyed her, looking down her front. It was a good front, pushed in and up for best effect; she had worked hard on that aspect, because she didn't yet have all the fullness she hoped for. "I think you're just looking for a ticket in, then you'll lose me."

"That's a lie!" But she knew girls did that sometimes. The thought had crossed her mind. What did she know of this character?

"Then come to my car first."

Nuh-uh! Vita thought emphatically. *He'll screw you twice: once in the car, again when he reneges on the deal!*

Ilka picked it up, for Vita had directed it at her. "After the dance!" she said.

He scowled. "Listen, you black bitch—"

You should talk, you white pimp! Vita thought. *You're trying to get some free ass!*

Ilka heard that thought. She assumed it was her own, and was surprised at her insight. "Forget it, pimp!" she snapped. "I'll go with one of these others."

"Yeah?" The boy's face turned ugly. He raised his voice. "Hey, this hooker's soliciting me! Isn't that against the law?"

"You liar!" Ilka exclaimed, furious. "You were trying to get me into your car!"

"I'm going to turn you in!" he said.

Brother! Vita thought. *They'll believe him too! Get out of here, Ilka!*

Ilka, responding to what seemed to be her own thought, turned and strode away. But she heard one of the others speak to the one who had approached her. "You fool, Frank—she'd've put out, if you'd played it straight!"

That's for sure! Vita agreed. *And gotten knocked up too. Crazy girl's got no amulet, no sense!*

But I wanted to go dancing! Ilka protested inwardly, the reaction setting in as she walked back along the street. *It was the only way!*

You'd have paid ten times what it was worth! Vita thought fiercely. *A hundred times! What would you want with a bastard baby?*

There was a shock in the host. Jolie thought it was Ilka, but then realized that it was Orlene. Orlene had been born to an unwed mother, and borne a son who barely missed similar status.

Who cares? the girl argued. *At least I'd love the baby—and it would love me. I'd be somebody!*

And there we have it! Orlene thought. *A baby would give her identity! A love relationship! As it did for me!*

But you were prepared, Jolie reminded her. *You were married, and had a good situation. Money was no problem. How would it have been on the street, with an illegitimate baby?*

Disaster! Vita supplied. *The girl's a fool! She'd get tired of that baby in weeks, and maybe leave it in a garbage dump.*

And she'd be starving herself, Jolie agreed. *But even if she kept it—even if her domineering mother let her keep it—she'd still be adding to the population. And it's because of her bad relationship with her own mother that she wants it. She wants to be a mother herself, to be the authority figure in her family. It's foolish, it's unworkable—but she'll still do it. And so will a million other girls!*

I'd get by somehow! Ilka argued.

Either way, it's mischief, Orlene thought.

At least we stopped one baby, Vita thought.

Tonight, Jolie concluded. They all knew that it was a hollow victory. The girl would probably get pregnant on another occasion. What opinion could they offer Gaea that wasn't already obvious? It would be impossible to have a ghost inhibit every wayward girl!

She was walking by a dark building. Suddenly a man appeared. He loomed up so quickly that she couldn't even scream before his gloved hand clamped over her mouth. She struggled, but then felt the prick of a knife at her side.

"Quiet, bitch, or I'll cut out your rotten heart!" the man hissed at her ear.

She had no choice; he was too strong, and the knife hurt. She walked where he shoved her: into the dark building.

Inside, he took her up a flight of steps and into a small room. He shut the door and turned on the light. Ilka blinked in the sudden brightness. This was evidently an interior room, without windows; no light would show outside. And what if it did? Surely the sound of her scream wouldn't carry, and if it did, neighbors probably wouldn't care.

He threw her away from him. Ilka stumbled, and tripped over a bed she hadn't seen in the brightness. She flopped on it, her fear increasing now that the immediacy of the prick of the knife was gone.

We've got to do something! Orlene thought. *We got her into this, by turning her away from the dance.*

We got rid of the creep, and brought on a horror! Vita agreed. *I've heard about this kind. Even my pimp steered clear of them. They rape and kill! It's called the slut/madonna complex or something. They hate women.*

It is a trifle more devious than that, Jolie said. *There are a number of them in Hell, all of them surprised to be there. To them, there are only two kinds of woman: the perfect, pristine, untouchable one, who is to be worshipped; and the dirty, evil and sexual one, who is to be condemned. Unfortunately, such men do have sex drives, which they can satisfy only with the evil variety of woman. At its extreme, they become serial killers of prostitutes. Jack the Ripper is the most notorious example, though by no means the worst perpetrator.*

I never felt easy about the purpose of Hell, Orlene thought. *Now I see that there are those who do belong there! This man—he glows a twisted black!*

"Strip, whore!" the man exclaimed.

Ilka rolled over on the bed. She opened her mouth to make a frightened denial—but Jolie put an overriding clamp on it. *Don't talk back to him!* she thought imperatively. *He will take that only as confirmation!*

So Ilka was mute, externally. But internally she was screaming. *He's got a knife! He's going to kill me! He just grabbed me, and—*

Stall! Jolie advised. *Move slowly. Sit up, start to remove your clothing, but have trouble with the snaps. Keep it slow, but don't stop. We shall try to help you.*

Now the girl realized that she wasn't talking to herself. "Who are you?"

Some visiting spirits, Jolie thought. *We stopped you from going with that cheap man at the dance. Now we will help you get away from this killer, because it is our fault you fell into his hands. Listen to us, and we will tell you how to escape.*

Ilka was doubtful. "I must be hallucinating!"

Listen to us anyway, Orlene thought. *Vita, you have had more experience with this sort of thing. Keep her moving slowly, while maintaining his interest. I'm going to check his mind for clues to how to handle him.*

Check, Vita thought. *We'll kick him in the balls if we have to.* She was not thinking figuratively.

Jolie drew herself out of the host and floated across to the man. She entered him. This was distasteful, because she had affinity neither with the male gender nor with the criminally insane mind, but she knew it was necessary. Only her long experience as a ghost, and with animation of mortal hosts, enabled her to do it.

She oriented on what she had expected: a twisted mélange of distortion and hate. The anonymous girl on the bed came into focus: her skin was dark, not because of her race, but because of the filth of her nature. She was a demoness, a succubus, a corruptor of man, evil incarnate: a creature to be used and destroyed. She evoked unclean lust in him, which proved both her power and her nature. By yielding to her lure, he corrupted himself—so he would expunge the guilt by killing her. Then he would be all right, for perhaps a month, until he encountered another corruptress.

Jolie was revolted by the narrowness and certainty of his perspective. He had not bothered to ascertain any part of the girl's true nature; he had simply assigned the evil to her. The evil of evoking lust in him. She could either admit that she was a despicable whore or try to deny it; in either case she proved it.

But Jolie had known this much about his view of women

before. It was an exaggeration of the view of many ignorant men—and every man was ignorant to some degree. Even Roque, as just a man as she had encountered recently, had this fixation: he related best to the forbidden fruit, the underage girl. Young girls were by this distorted definition better, because they were cleaner. They had not had time to indulge their whorish nature, so were more likely to be disease free, and less likely to talk back. Thus Vita's youth and adoration overrode Roque's knowledge of her life as a literal whore, and he accepted her without condemning her. But that was rare.

She had to explore the specific roots of this man's bias. There were always variations, and each case was unique to itself in detail. There had to be something that would provide the key to defusing the syndrome. She had to find it before things got violent.

Through the windows of his eyes, she saw Ilka slowly stripping, having trouble with a broken fastening. Her dress zipped up the back, and the zipper was difficult to reach, and evidently a thread had got caught in it. Usually girls had assistance in getting in and out of fancy outfits; it had not been anticipated that Ilka would have to remove hers alone. Actually, Jolie knew, she had put it on alone, so could handle it—but the man was not in a position to know this. The man did not try to help her; it was part of his fixation that the evil woman was using her unclean nature to seduce him, so she had to do it herself.

She was struggling, indeed, trying to get both hands on the stuck zipper. In the process she leaned forward, so that her breasts showed to his gaze as her décolletage hung low. Jolie almost smiled to herself; that was Vita's art. There really was some vamp in her! She knew that the man would watch as long as he was seeing something interesting, condemning her all the while but not acting. It was an excellent stall.

Meanwhile, Jolie was searching the man's mind and memories. She had had experience with this sort of thing, working with Gaea, but never so urgently in such a difficult case. The man did not understand his own motives; he had fashioned a construct of passion and illusion to justify and hide the ugliness beneath, and would not let himself view it objectively. She had to slip beneath that construct and see what he refused to see, without alerting him. He could readily clamp down on those nether memories and feelings, if he realized, and then she would not be able to reach them. She was an intruder here, unable to open any doors herself; she had to sneak through, like a thief.

There was a surge of conscious passion. Jolie was swept along, and looked out his eyes again. Now Ilka, having navigated the zipper so that the top of the dress was falling open to reveal her half-bra and stomach, was ready to pull it off over her head. But first she bent to remove her slippers, lifting her leg and bending her knee so as to reach her foot. In the process she showed her left leg under the dress to the thigh, all the way up to the juncture with her body. She looked bare beneath, but it was actually panty hose, shaded to make her legs appear lighter than they were, making of her crotch a perfectly seamless and hairless region. This, again, was Vita's doing; she knew precisely how to proffer a view without seeming to, so that the man would not press her while she struggled overlong with the slipper.

The effect of this view on the man was electric. He felt a phenomenal thrill of desire—almost immediately suppressed. A surge of guilt washed through him, and he wrenched his gaze away.

Jolie followed the guilt to its source—and suddenly had what she wanted. Those legs were clean—and it was not right, by his reckoning, to experience lust for a clean body. Bad women were dirty and hairy in their secret places, fit only for further defilement. The one good woman—the madonna—was absolutely pure in every part. Her proportions were perfect, but without hair or apertures; the madonna had no unclean processes. Her breasts had no nipples, her legs met without genital or excretory complication. She wore conventional clothing only from deference to the norms of society; she had no guilty secrets of body or of mind. Madonna, naked, would remain sylphlike, innocent of the incitement of any lechery.

Who was his madonna? She was Laurel, his older sister.

Jolie picked up the essence in a flash: the father had been a brutal man, given to violence on small pretexts, and the mother similar. Any slightest infraction brought a sharp slap from her, and any backtalk brought a beating from him. He was Kane, the clumsy and stupid child, seldom getting anything right. He was punished every time his grades came, and ridiculed in between. He had no self-confidence or self-respect. It was no better at school; he was known as a dunce, and had no friends. Once in grade school a girl had teased him, asking him if he wanted to play "Doctor," pulling up her skirt invitingly. Deceived, not realizing that she wasn't being friendly, and curious about what she might have under there that was supposed to be so interesting, he had agreed. She had led him around the corner of an outbuilding where there was a modicum of privacy, and told him that first he would have to show her his. He had opened his shorts—and immediately half a dozen other girls had popped up from hiding and screamed with wicked delight at his exposure. A teacher had overheard, and investigated, and the girls had blamed Kane. That had brought a suspension from school and a solid beating at home. Only Laurel, lovely Laurel, had defended him, saying that the bitchy little girls had set him up out of sheer mischief. It had done no good, but Kane was overwhelmingly grateful to her. Later, hurting, banned to his room without supper, he had heard a quiet knock. It was Laurel, sneaking some rolls and butter to him, the best she could do. He loved her.

Kane had learned early and painfully: all adults were brutal, all children were taunting, and all girls were garbage. Except Laurel. She alone was pure. Without her, his life would not have been worth living.

When he was ten, and she fifteen, she had run away from home. The father had beaten him, sure that he knew where she had gone, but Kane had not spoken. Indeed, he had known her plan, for she had wanted to take him with her, but had realized that it would be impossible to manage. So she had decided to go alone and to return for him when she could, so that they could both be happy. She had to get established, she explained; she had to get some money, and a house, because the street was no place to live. It would take time, but she would do it.

So Kane had endured, sustained by his faith in her. Laurel would come for him! That alone gave him strength. His life was nothing, but then it would be everything.

She had never returned. Thirty years had passed, and he had escaped by joining the military, and later by deserting that, and running drugs and anything else that offered; there was always work for the unscrupulous. He could never bring himself to condemn Laurel, for she was the one perfect woman, but his disappointment remained as a leaden weight upon his soul. When he could, he caught and punished bad women, hiding their bodies and moving on so that he was never caught. The police, he had long since learned, didn't understand about the need to punish bad women.

Time had passed during Jolie's investigation. Now Ilka's shoes and dress were off, and she was about to roll down her panty hose. Jolie now knew that this must not happen; the visible nipples were bad enough, but the rest would be disaster. She wrenched herself from the man and sailed across to the girl.

Leave the hose! she thought as she entered. *He must not see your flesh there!* For she now had a notion how to balk the killer. It would take some doing, but it was possible. *He sees the madonna as beautiful but sexless—no genitals. The whores have genitals. He won't kill you until he has sex with you, proving you are bad.*

But he'll kill if we stop undressing! Vita responded. *These freaks are touchy! Do one thing to balk them, and they explode.*

We won't balk him, we'll talk to him.

What about? Orlene asked nervously. *I think all he has on his mind is sex and murder, in that order.*

We'll tell him a story. I'll start it off.

"Get it off, bitch!" Kane snapped. He knew what panty hose was, of course; he had already forgotten, by involuntary suppression, the image of the madonna's clean juncture. It had been fleeting in any event; Jolie had been lucky to catch the thought. He knew this was a dirty woman, because they all were.

267

Give me the mouth! Jolie pleaded. *I know what to say!*

Ilka, still thoroughly frightened, retreated, letting Jolie assume control. She was very much afraid she was going to die; any promise of rescue, however farfetched, was welcome.

"You must let me say something," Jolie said.

Kane was startled, because this was the first time she had spoken to him. "That's right, bitch!" he agreed. "Talk dirty! Say the words! Prove what you are!" That was part of it, of course; the girl had to demonstrate her corruption, so that he felt truly justified in destroying her. She had to beg for sex in gutter language. It hardly mattered whether she cursed him or welcomed him, so long as she showed her nature clearly.

"In a moment," Jolie said. "I have to work up to it, you know." He hadn't known any such thing, of course, but since she was going along with his demand, only qualifying it slightly, and in the process extending the experience, he was able to accept it.

"Yes, work up to it!" he agreed. His right hand held the knife; his left hand went to his fly, opening it. He would not undress any more than he had to, so as not to be contaminated, but this much was necessary.

"There was once a girl," Jolie said. "She was different from all other girls, because she was nice. She was the only nice girl in all the world. Her name was—" She hesitated momentarily. Would it be too obvious to name his lost sister? Perhaps a close compromise. She had to hold his attention without invoking his critical faculty. "Her name was Lorelie. She lived in a bad family, with a cruel father and a mean mother. The only good thing about it was her little brother, who was the only person in the world who recognized her perfect nature. He worshipped her and did everything he could to help her, though their father beat him for it. She would have done anything for him, but they were both captive in the bad family, and it wasn't fun for either."

She looked at Kane. Was he buying this? It was pretty obvious, but his twisted emotion ran deep. He had built a philosophy on illusion, and she was tuning in on that illusion.

He was listening, his hands still. She had succeeded in getting his attention. He could identify with what she was saying.

"Sometimes the bad girls in the schoolyard teased her little brother," Jolie continued, elaborating now that her ploy seemed to be working. "Lorelie couldn't stop that, because she was in a different school. The bad girls made him show his thing, and then laughed at him. They didn't show theirs, but he knew theirs was bad, because they were bad girls." As she spoke, Jolie remembered her own childhood, in medieval France, when something similar had happened. The villain girls had at times been cruel in their games, in retaliation for the cruelty of the boys' games. Sex had been known, even in childhood; few made it virginally to maturity. Jolie had been one of the few, as much by chance as by design. She had been smarter than average, and so had had the wit to mask her dawning prettiness, and to stay clear of celebrations unless close to her mother. One of her friends had not been careful enough, and four boys had grabbed her and done it; she had pretended to like it, rather than get beaten, and then had kept her mouth shut, but the word had circulated anyway, and she had been blamed, not the boys. Jolie had escaped, but she well understood who was to blame for such things: the boys. It galled her to reverse the issue in this story, but it had to be done—and certainly some men were decent, and some girls were not. There had been Parry . . .

"So she brought him food, and comforted him, and tried to ease his welts," she continued. "There was little she could do, but she tried her best. She knew then that they could not stay in that family; they had to get away, to find someplace where there were no bad people. So she started making plans for them both to run away."

Kane was paying close attention, frozen where he stood. She was retelling his childhood, from the view of the madonna figure, offering a rationale that he had to accept. But would her story make him forget entirely what he had been about to do? The longer she stalled him, the more likely it was that someone else would come—but she had little confidence in rescue. She had to talk him out of it, and for that she needed a truly persuasive conclusion—and she didn't have one. She just had to keep talking, and hope that one of the four of them could come up with what was needed. A life was at stake!

"But there were so many things they needed. Money, to buy tickets on a rocket or saucer. Identification, so that the cruel father could not track them down. A place to stay. Food. Clothing. The list was endless. She wouldn't steal money, because she was pure and good, and without money she couldn't arrange the rest of it. Finally she realized that it could not be done; there was no way for the two of them to escape together. If they tried it, the police would catch them in no time and bring them back, and things would be worse than before. She realized that she would have to go alone, and somehow get some money and all the things they needed. Only then could she rescue her brother."

Kane's jaw was slack; he was mesmerized by the story, so true to his memory. But how was she to conclude it? The consort Scheherazade of Arabian Nights fame had told stories for a thousand nights, extending her life, but Jolie had no confidence that this would work here, even if her voice and imagination held out. *Think of a conclusion!* she thought to the others. *Something that will make him let us go!*

Meanwhile, she continued the story. "So she explained this to her brother, who was very understanding. 'I will wait for your return,' he said bravely. 'Don't tell them what I am doing,' she cautioned him, and he promised not to. Then she kissed the dear boy on the forehead and slipped out the window. She had only the clothes she wore, and a few dollars she had managed to save from baby-sitting, and a few scraps of food her brother had given her. She did not know how she would get them a good situation, she only knew that somehow she would do it."

She has no chance! Vita thought. *She'll have to whore, just to survive—and then what will her brother think of her? And this garbage about him being a "dear boy"—obviously he had the hots for her even at that age, but didn't know it.*

You are not being very positive, Orlene reminded her. *She has to succeed! Don't you see—this is this man's madonna!*

Who never returned, Jolie thought. *He was terribly disappointed, but he can't quite give up hope, even thirty years later. It's the one decent aspect of his sordid personality.* Then she had to resume speaking aloud.

"So she went quietly from that awful house, her eyes wet with tears for her brother, whom she knew would be treated even worse because of her absence, but she had faith he would endure, and give her her chance to elude the police search."

I'm going to throw up! Vita thought. *Her brother grew up to be a rapist and murderer!*

Try to help Jolie! Orlene thought. *Or this host is done for!*

And I'm the host! Ilka thought. *Will you tell me who you are, now?*

I'm Vita, a girl like you. The others are ghosts, helping me stay out of trouble. Now they're helping you.

"She walked a long way," Jolie continued, trying not to be distracted by the introductions going on in the background. She knew Vita was probably right about the fate of the girl, but she couldn't put that in the story! She had to show that Lorelie was still alive, still planning on returning. However ludicrous that might seem at this late date, it was necessary to the man's secret philosophy. "Her feet got tired, but she could not stop, because if she failed, it would be the end not only of her dream, but of her brother's. She could have endured her own humiliation, but the thought of doing that to her wonderful brother brought renewed tears to her eyes."

You know, I can see it, Ilka thought. *My pa's long gone, but my mother's pretty mean. If she'd just let me go to a dance, even! The way I sneaked out tonight—it's like Lorelie.*

That gave Jolie a notion. "Then a car stopped beside her. 'Can I pick you up?' the driver asked. She looked at him, and she wasn't sure, but she was very tired now and she still wasn't far enough away from the house, so she got in. The driver's name was Frank, and he was a handsome man. She didn't dare tell him that she was running away from home, so she said she was going to visit friends in the next state, but her carpet had gotten a glitch in its spell. Frank said he was going that way, so he zoomed along. But then he turned onto a desolate country road and drew to a stop in the forest."

"No!" Kane said, well knowing the sort of thing that was in store for her.

"But although Lorelie was a good girl, she wasn't foolish," Jolie continued quickly. "She opened her door and jumped out of the car and ran into the forest. Frank chased her, but couldn't see her in the darkness. Finally, disgruntled, he returned to his car and drove away."

Kane relaxed. He was really into the story. But where could it lead now? Jolie was running out of inspiration.

Snow White! Vita thought. *She finds the seven dwarfs in the forest!*

But less obvious, Orlene thought. *Make it one old man—no, better an old woman, no lechery there—who takes her in.*

But she is sick, Ilka added, getting into it herself. *Maybe so sick she loses her memory!*

That's it! Vita agreed. *That's why she doesn't return!*

What a relief! They had come up with a viable continuation. "Lorelie stumbled on through the dark forest, her tender flesh raked by the brambles. She had gotten some rest in the car, but not enough. She lost her slippers in the muck, and her pretty dress was torn, but she kept on, afraid that Frank would return with cruel friends and search for her. At one point she splashed through a stream. She didn't know it was polluted, and the pollution infected the scratches on her feet, starting a sickness in her. Finally she could go no more; she fell headlong, and hit her head on a rock on the ground, and was unconscious."

Kane remained frozen, avidly listening. He seemed to have forgotten the circumstances, or the supposed nature of the teller of this tale. He was lost in the vision of the perils of Lorelie.

"In the morning a kind old woman found her. The woman had been a sorceress of little note, and was now retired on a meager stipend. She knew immediately that this poor girl had been poisoned by the bad stream, and furthermore had hit her head when she fell. Fortunately the woman retained some ability with healing herbs and spells. She dragged the girl into her hut and ministered to her. 'She is like the granddaughter I never had and always wanted,' she said to herself as she undressed the girl and washed her clean. 'So lovely, so pure. Probably one of those mean young men was after her, and she got lost when she fled him.' She put herbs on the girl's bad scratches, and treated her as well as she could for the stream pollution. It was going to be a close thing, she knew, for the girl was very sick."

So sick she can't remember, Vita reminded her. *But how's that going to get us out of this scrape? I mean, when the story ends—*

We have to work on that, Orlene said. *Before Jolie gets much further, we'll have to come up with an idea for the ending. Now let's get to work!*

"The girl did survive," Jolie said, and Kane relaxed slightly. "But it was some time before she could sit up, and longer before she could speak. The old woman cared for her diligently, and slowly she mended. But when she was well enough to talk, another type of injury manifested. *She had lost her memory.* All she recalled was her name, Lorelie, and that there was something she had to do. So it was that she was unable to complete her promise, because she no longer knew of it. This bothered her terribly, because she knew what she had to do was important, terribly important, but it would take more magic than the old woman had to restore her memory."

"Lauric!" Kane said. "She couldn't come back!"

"Not then," Jolie agreed. "Not for a long time. So she stayed with the old woman, who fed her and clothed her and took care of her as she recovered. Years passed, and as Lorelie became stronger, the old woman became weaker, for she had been frail to begin with. Now it was the girl who took care of the woman. But though there might be a cure for what ailed the girl, there was none for what ailed the woman, because only very expensive magic can restore youth to a mortal person. Finally the old woman was ready to die, and she thanked Lorelie for making her declining years beautiful, for Lorelie was the nicest girl anyone could have for a granddaughter, and she urged her to sell the property, which the old woman had deeded to her name, and use the money to seek strong magic that would restore her memory. Because the old woman had no other relatives, and Lorelie knew she would not be able to abide living alone where the old woman had died, she agreed.

"The old woman did die, and Lorelie saw her soul float promptly up to Heaven, and arranged to have her body decently buried. Then she sold the property, and learned that it had increased greatly in value. The old woman had been poor, but this was one of the few deeply forested regions left in the state, and the state wanted it for a park. So Lorelie was now a reasonably wealthy woman. She could do what she had to do—if only she could remember what it was!"

I think I have it! Ilka thought. She identified readily with Lorelie, because they were the same age at the start of the story, and Vita felt a similar affinity. *She remembers, and she comes back—and he kills her!*

You dummy! Vita objected. *It's your body he'll kill! We don't dare suggest that to him!*

No, it may work, Orlene thought. *If her brother thinks she's a slut, then learns she's his sister, he won't kill her!*

Jolie had continued talking while this dialogue occurred. Would that work? Would Kane let Ilka go if he identified her with Lorelie—with his sister Laura? Maybe it would work!

"So she finally found a sorceress who specialized in memory-restorative magic," Jolie continued, having covered several prior contacts that hadn't worked out. "It had taken her an unconscionably long time to do it, and this was the most expensive one of all. It would take most of her remaining money. But she did go to the woman, and the woman worked her expensive spell, and at last Lorelie's memory was restored."

Kane was rapt. "How long—?"

"Suddenly she knew what it was she had to do," Jolie said. "But she was chagrined to discover that so much time had passed in the search that it now seemed pointless to do it. More than thirty years! She was now a woman of forty-five, pure and good as ever, but way too late to rescue her little brother. By this time their parents would be dead, and the little boy would be a grown man of forty. What a horrible mishap, that poisoning and fall that had taken away her memory. It was true that she had had a good life with the kind old woman, but if she had been able to remember earlier, she never would have waited. She would have returned immediately and brought her brother to the old woman's house, and they would have lived there happily, free of all the bad things of the world. Now it was too late!

"But *was* it? She thought about it, and realized that her good little brother might still be waiting for her return. Oh, he would be in a different house by now, perhaps even a different city, but she could still find him. Better late than never! What a joyful reunion they could have, even at this late date!"

But he doesn't recognize her, Vita thought. *He mistakes her for a whore, and is about to kill her—*

Before he recognizes her, Ilka concluded.

I like the way your mind works, Vita thought. *Can we be friends?*

Sure, if you like. If I live.

"She still had a little money left," Jolie continued. She was getting nervous now, because if this ploy misfired, they would have no other chance except a desperation fight for life. Fortunately Ilka had not been bound—but that might only be because the man was quite sure of his ability to overpower her. She didn't want it to come to that, though she had learned a thing or two about close combat in the course of her association with Satan, Gaea, and Mars. "She used it to have her brother located. Then she went to where he was, which was indeed in another city, for he had moved frequently, for what reason she didn't know."

Because it wasn't safe for him to stay close to where he had killed, Vita thought, having picked up most of the man's background from Jolie's thoughts. *Lorelie won't much like that!*

"At last she came to him, at night on a deserted street. 'O my brother, where are you?' she thought, her pure heart beating with anticipation and excitement." Now came the crucial part; she didn't know whether it would work, but it was all she had. "She walked along the street, looking,

275

somehow aware that he was near—and a man jumped out and grabbed her."

Kane jumped. "No, I wouldn't do that!" he exclaimed.

"He hauled her into the building, his hand over her mouth so that she couldn't scream—but it also prevented her from identifying herself," Jolie said, nervousness putting a shake in her voice. This seemed so obvious, so stupid, now that she was in it; how could it possibly work? "He thought she was one of the bad girls—"

"It's a lie!" he cried. "It's just a dumb story to fool me! You aren't my sister! You're just a black teenage slut!" He lifted the knife threateningly.

Jolie realized that she should have engineered the story to account for the color and youth. The sister could have been gravely injured, so had to use magic to animate a younger body. But it was too late for that now. "Lorelie tried to tell him, but he wouldn't listen—"

"You aren't her!" he screamed, throwing himself on her, the knife held up. "You have to be used and killed!"

Jolie, still in control of the body, tried to squirm aside, but he was too fast and strong for her. He held her down with his left arm across her throat, choking her, while his groin pressed against hers. But he could not make headway, because she still wore the panty hose.

He cursed and used his free hand—the one holding the knife—to reach down, to wrench the hose out of the way. He reversed the knife without letting go of it, so that it pointed up, while with two fingers he caught the waistband and yanked down. The material tore—and Jolie, in desperation, bucked her hips, trying to throw him off in this moment of his partial distraction. "Kane!" she cried. "No!"

Her left hip slammed into the butt end of the knife. She felt dull pain as it bruised her. But Kane cried out at the same time, in pain and horror, his body stiffening.

Then something liquid coursed down on her hip. Unable to think what it might be, she looked—and saw bright redness spreading out across her thigh and the bed below. He had stabbed himself! Or rather, her effort to buck him off had caused the point of the knife he held to ram upward into his body, right at the crotch. He had castrated himself.

Then he relaxed, his weight becoming heavy on her. He had passed out. She struggled to pull herself out from under, lubricated by the blood. It was messy, but possible, now that he was not trying to hold her. Soon she stood beside the bed, her left leg swathed in blood, staring down at him.

He's bleeding to death! Orlene thought, horrified.

He deserves it! Vita retorted. *He's a rapist and murderer!*

Jolie, more experienced and practical about this sort of horror, wasted no more time. She hurried to the apartment's little bathroom and hastily peeled off the panty hose. That left her leg almost clean, but she found a sponge and washed it anyway. Then she scrambled back into the dress, having no trouble with the fastenings. As she did this, she explained to the others: "He may be dying, or he may be less gravely wounded, and he could recover at any moment. We need to be out of here before he wakes. Then it will be in God's hands whether he lives or dies, not ours." She found the two slippers, and put one on. The second was blood-spattered, so she quickly rinsed it under the rushing tap and put it on wet. Details didn't matter!

She rinsed the soiled panty hose in the sink, then wrung it dry, wadded it up, and held it in a ball in her hand. She ran more water to clean the sink, so it would not be apparent that it had been used. She used the wadded hose to wipe her fingerprints off the handles.

The door wasn't locked. Had she realized, she might have distracted the man, led him a chase around the bed and made a break for the door and out! She went out now, running down the short hall and the stairs, and outside.

Then she slowed, deliberately, and walked on down the street in the direction she had been going. "I will return your body to you in a moment, Ilka," she murmured. "Are you able to proceed?"

No! the girl thought. *He almost killed me!*

"But you are alive," Jolie said. "When something similar happened to me, long ago, I died. This time I helped you avoid that—but I think in future you must stay closer to home, even though it may be dull."

Yes! Yes! I'll never go out alone again!

Jolie suspected that would be the case. The girl had had about as bad a fright as it was possible to survive. "I think you should say nothing about what happened. I have tried to eradicate the traces of your presence in his chamber. Go home, sneak back into your room, and pretend you were always there. Wash and dry your panty hose when you can. There will be a big splash of news when the man's body is discovered—or none, if he survives and flees the city. Stay out of it; there would be only mischief if they knew about you. Just make sure that you are never caught by such a man again. Are you ready to take over now?"

I think so.

Jolie returned control to her. *Now we must leave,* she thought. *We have corrected our error, and we have other business.*

"No!" Ilka cried. "I need you!"

No you don't, Vita thought. *We got you into trouble, so we had to get you out of it, but now you can get along okay yourself. But I'll try to visit you, when I'm back in my own body. Remember my name: Vita. Don't forget and try to kill me!*

Ilka began to laugh, hysterically, but managed to stifle it. "Then 'bye, for now," she said. "You sure did help me!"

They pulled out and floated beside her. Jolie shaped herself into visible ghost form. "Maybe you helped us too," she said, projecting her thought carefully so that the girl could receive it despite the separation.

Then they floated up into the night sky, fading from the girl's view. They saw her walking on toward her home, briskly, as if nothing had happened. It would take Ilka some time to recover equilibrium, but it seemed she would make it.

"Gaea!" Jolie called. She could have returned directly, herself, of course, but neither Orlene nor Vita knew how, so it was better to have Gaea do it.

The window opened immediately before them. They floated through and were back inside Gaea's Treehouse. They went to Vita's body and entered it, and Orlene animated it. It was her responsibility to report.

Orlene got up, paused for a moment to acclimatize, then walked out to the main chamber. Gaea was waiting for her. "What is your conclusion?"

Orlene sat down. "The girl was confused and dissatisfied with her life, I think with reason. She would have gotten pregnant without meaning to, but the notion didn't really bother her, because she thought she wanted a baby. She thought it would improve her life. So the root of it was deeper than mere accident or carelessness; she wanted someone to love, who would love her."

"It is in my power to abolish love, with the aid of some of my supporting Incarnations, such as Eros," Gaea said. "Should I do that?"

"Abolish love?" Orlene asked with horror. "Oh, no, that would be a horrible overreaction! It is love that makes life worthwhile when all else is ugly. There must be some other way!"

"What way do you suppose that would be?"

"Well, maybe—maybe if there was love, but not the ability to conceive unless all the considerations were in order. If a woman is healthy, and well-balanced, and economically secure, so that the baby would have a good home. If she couldn't have a baby until then, there would be far fewer babies, and perhaps no further overpopulation problem."

Gaea nodded. "I think your opinion is worthy of consideration. But such a course would require a judgment of female fitness that goes beyond the strictly natural. The social factor would have to be right. That sort of larger judgment is the prerequisite of another Incarnation, whose active cooperation I would need to make the policy effective."

"Who is that?" Orlene asked, excited by the prospect of such a significant step in the welfare of mankind.

"God."

Orlene stared at her a moment. She realized that this answer was obvious; she just hadn't been thinking in that context. "God must decide what is good, of course," she agreed. "But couldn't you approach Him about the matter?"

"I think not at this time," Gaea replied, with a strange expression.

"But in my quest to—I must approach Him!" Orlene said. "Would you mind if I mentioned this matter too?"

"Not at all, my daughter. I think that would be appropriate. If you gain the acquiescence of the final two Incarnations, I will grant you the tear you seek. You have, I think, more than earned it." Evidently Gaea knew about their siege with the murderer.

That made her think of something. They had caused the man's critical injury, or even death—but had it been only them? Or had a deeper part of Kane truly wanted to believe Jolie's story, despite his conscious denial of it, and caused that hand to turn in that critical way, placing the knife? What punishment would a man see as suitable for the one who attacked the one truly pristine woman in the world? The one who called him by his name at the very end, when he had never told it to his captive. Something very like the one he had received, perhaps.

"Quite possibly," Gaea said, reading her thought.

"But God—where was God when that awful man grabbed that innocent girl?" Orlene asked. "Why didn't He stop it? Why does He let this sort of thing go on all the time, all over the world?"

"You would handle things differently?" Gaea inquired, lifting a brow.

"Oh, I didn't mean to criticize God!" Orlene said quickly. "I just—there is so much I don't understand!"

"Perhaps you can ask Him that, too, when you see Him," Gaea said, unsmiling.

CHAPTER TWELVE

Evil

THEY RETIRED TO HELL'S ACRES, WHERE THEY spent a comfortable night. Theoretically they needed neither food nor sleep here, but the experiences they had had with War and Nature needed digesting. What a huge amount of misery there was in the mortal realm! So much of it appeared ultimately unnecessary, yet even the Incarnations seemed largely helpless to ameliorate it.

You know, I thought it would be fun, meeting Incarnations and all, Vita thought. *But each time, I get another glimpse of the awful stuff they have to deal with, and I wonder how they stand it.*

"It isn't always that bad," Jolie said, in charge of the body for the evening. "They do have their pleasures too. But with their enormous power comes enormous responsibility, and they all feel it. Every so often one gets too tired and retires, and then a new one has to be broken in. We saw how it was with an Aspect of Fate—but there, at least, there are always two experienced Aspects to help. It is worse with the others."

It must be! the girl agreed. *To have all that responsibility, and to know so little at first—I think I'm glad I'm mortal! At least I'm the only one I can mess up.*

Even our effort to deflect Ilka from getting pregnant almost got her killed, Orlene agreed. *I can appreciate better than ever why Incarnations don't like to interfere in mortal affairs. There are so many variables, so many ways for something well-intended to go wrong. Even God must get tired!*

"Well, it will be Hell tomorrow," Jolie reminded them cheerfully.

They let Vita peer out a turret window for a while, watching the cavorting flame figures on the moat. *Gee, I wish I was doing that with Roque right now,* she thought.

"What you call a hot time," Jolie said, smiling. But she understood; she wanted to be with Satan similarly, but knew this was not the occasion.

They slept, letting that bit of unconsciousness put some space between the horror of the recent events and their next challenge.

In the morning they made their way to the Hellevator and headed down, this time all the way to the basement stop. The mock flames of it loomed higher and fiercer as they descended past the mortal realm, until at last they came to a stop in what appeared to be a phenomenal bed of blazing coals. It was as if their precarious chamber were being flame roasted.

Jolie opened the door. "I will get us in, then Orlene will take over, as it remains her mission," she reminded them.

I never thought I'd get to go to Hell before I died! Vita thought brightly.

The door opened and Jolie started to step out. But a demon stopped her. It was huge and masculine, with hooves and horns, and its trident had sharp points. "Halt!" he barked gruffly. "Mortals can't come here!"

"I am a ghost," Jolie explained. "I am not evil, so can't come here in my natural state, but it is possible in a mortal host. We have come to see Satan."

"No mortals here!" the demon insisted. "Go back where you came from."

"But I just explained—"

"I have my orders. Go!" The trident moved menacingly.

Tell him to sit down hard on his pitchfork! Vita thought. *Endwise!*

Jolie considered whether to identify herself specifically. As Satan's consort, she was permitted in Hell. But this wasn't her mission, and she did not want to misrepresent it. Orlene had to be allowed to do it on her own, to the extent possible.

She stepped back into the Hellevator. "There is another way," she murmured.

"No way!" the guardian demon cried as the door closed. "First you die—then you come here!"

Go have a hotfoot! Vita thought back at him.

They trundled back up to Purgatory. "We shall have to enlist the aid of Gaea," Jolie explained. "But I think she won't mind giving it."

Gaea can help us get to Hell? Vita thought, surprised.

"She knows someone who can."

They exited at Purgatory and hurried to Gaea's Treehouse. Jolie explained how they had been balked by an ignorant demon. "I didn't want to identify myself, because this is Orlene's business. But I thought that if Natasha were willing to help—"

Who is she? Vita asked.

Gaea smiled. She fetched a small harp. She went outside and sat on the soft turf, setting the harp between her lifted knees. Her fingers caressed the strings, touching without playing. Then, facing the cloudbank horizon, she began to play.

The sound of it was exquisite. Jolie had heard this many times before, but was always entranced anew. She was Satan's first wife, and Gaea was his second; there had never been any competition between them, but had there been, Gaea's magic with music would have been decisive. Every note was perfect, and the theme was transcendent.

Then Gaea sang. The whole region seemed to come alive, resonating to the sound of her voice. The distant clouds turned color, passing through the spectrum of the rainbow. Dawn seemed to come, and sunset, and all between. No earthly voice could match this; it was the melody of the Incarnation, a fragment of what was called the Llano.

Both Orlene and Vita were rapt. There had been no hint of this potential before. Gaea had seemed like an ordinary woman in command of potent magic. Now, through Orlene's own magic, Jolie saw Gaea glow. More than that; her glow extended out into the environment—as far, in fact, as her music did.

After a brief passage, Gaea paused. All Purgatory seemed to wait with bated breath.

Then there came an answering song. It was a man's voice, without accompaniment, but so vibrant and feeling that all the world seemed to be the accompaniment. A few notes only, a few words, and then silence.

Gaea sang again, and accompanied herself on the harp. Again the region responded, joining her evocation. Then she paused a second time.

The male response came, closer now, stronger. It had seemed that in all the universe there could be no equal to Gaea's voice, but now it was clear that there was an equal in this hidden man.

After a momentary pause, Gaea sang a third time—and the man joined her. They made a harmony so beautiful that there was nothing for the listeners to do but be transported by it. The counterpoint was perfect.

Now the man came into view, walking swiftly toward the Treehouse. He was young and handsome, and he sang as he walked, still keeping time with Gaea. He wore ordinary slacks and shirt and shoes; were he not singing, he would have seemed to be just another man. Obviously he was not.

Jolie knew him, of course, but she kept her thought quiet. Let Orlene and Vita have this experience for themselves!

The man came to stand before Gaea. Their song climaxed and abruptly ended.

The plain before the Treehouse had been blank. Now it was covered with flowering trees, and a crystal stream wound through it. Warblers perched in the trees, listening.

Gaea set aside her little harp and stood. She had been middle-aged, but now she was in her lovely young state and her housecoat had become a summer dress which caressed her contours. Bright daisies formed a diadem in her hair. She was as lovely as a summer creature could be.

She stepped into the man and kissed him. They made a perfect couple, and they certainly seemed to be in love. Both Orlene and Vita were astounded.

I thought she was married to— Orlene thought.

Who the hell is this guy? Vita thought.

Now Jolie spoke. "Girls, meet Natasha, the handsomest man of the realm," she said as the couple broke from their close embrace.

Natasha's a MAN? Vita thought.

The man turned from Gaea. "Ah, Jolie," he said. "Come to me."

Jolie did. She stepped into his embrace exactly as Gaea had, and kissed him as ardently.

Holy refuse! Vita thought. Orlene, stunned, thought nothing.

"And Natasha," Jolie said as the kiss ended, "meet my present host, Vita, and Orlene, Gaea's daughter. I am turning the body over to her."

Orlene, suddenly thrust into control, stood in Natasha's loosening embrace. "How glad I am to meet you, Orlene," he said. "You are the daughter of one of the women I love."

"But Gaea's married!" Orlene exclaimed.

Natasha glanced at Gaea, smiling. "Oh, is she? So am I. Why should Mars be the only one with two lovely women?"

Orlene pulled herself away, actually spluttering. "I don't know who you are, but—"

"He is here to guide you to Hell," Gaea said. "I believe he knows a secret access."

Orlene realized that there was some kind of joke going on. "He's a damned soul?"

"Close enough," Natasha said. "Come with me; I believe we can get in unobserved, if we move quickly."

"But—"

Go with him, Jolie thought.

Why should she go with this handsome freak? Vita demanded. *He's two-timing his wife; how can we trust him?*

He is the world's greatest liar, Jolie agreed. *But we can trust him.*

Orlene, disgruntled, knowing that she wasn't quite catching something obvious, shrugged. "I will go with you, Natasha. But I would like an explanation."

Natasha put his hand on her elbow. "You shall surely have it. Tell me about yourself; I want very much to know."

Tell him, Jolie thought.

Bemused, Orlene started in. "I am Gaea's natural daughter, given up as a baby for adoption. I married a ghost—"

She broke off, for they were sinking through the ground. The layers of cloud were passing like the vapors they were.

"Continue," he said.

"And had a baby for him, but my baby died, and I killed myself. Now I am trying to recover him from Nox, and I need Satan's help."

"Nox? The Incarnation of Night?"

"Yes. She has my son. She set me a list of things I must get from each major Incarnation, and from Satan I need a curse. Only when the list is complete can I recover my baby and cure him of his malady of the soul."

The cloud dissipated. They stood in a stony cell. Ahead was a curving passage, lighted by guttering and smoky torches. "Follow this passage," Natasha said. "It will lead you to Satan's suite. I will conduct you back from this spot when you are finished with him."

"I have to walk alone through Hell?" Orlene asked, appalled.

"This is a privileged passage. No demon will molest you as long as you remain in it. Be sure you do not leave it, however." He urged her forward, letting go her elbow.

Orlene took a step, then turned. "I really don't—"

But Natasha was gone.

It's all right, Jolie said. *What he said is true: this is a passage only special guests may use. We are quite safe here, though it passes through the center of Hell to reach Satan's suite. We may pause and look at anything along the way, as long as we do not go astray.*

Orlene started walking. There were windows along the

sides, opening into assorted chambers. In each chamber was some activity, but the nature of it wasn't clear at a casual glance.

Orlene paused at one, in which a man sat, holding a wound in his chest. Blood was oozing, and he seemed to be in extreme pain. "Is he alive?" she asked, horrified. "I thought there were only damned souls here!"

The man heard her. "I am a damned soul," he gasped. "I am suffering what seems like eternal agony."

"What did you do to deserve this?" she asked, morbidly interested.

"I drag-raced a motorcycle." He seemed to be able to speak well enough, if haltingly, despite the wound.

"What?"

"I was in a pickup truck, on the nonmagic level of the highway. This motorcycle challenged me, so naturally I gunned my motor. I won—but I wasn't looking where I was going. I caromed off a slow car and vaulted into the opposite lane at high speed. I crashed head-on into a school bus, killing twenty-seven people. I died myself—and woke at the entrance to Hell. That was twenty years ago, and I still have a thousand years or so to work off."

"But that looks like a bullet wound!" Orlene said. "How could that happen in a highway crash?"

"It didn't. I was never shot."

"But—"

He made an agonized smile. "This isn't my injury I'm suffering. Nor is it that of any of the passengers who died in the crash. It is that of a dog."

"A dog!"

"You see, most of those passengers killed in the wreck were young—schoolchildren, in fact. They did not have a lot of sin on their souls, but they did have some. They would have been detained in Purgatory for a while, or somewhere, until they had absolved their sins and were ready for Heaven. But they weren't supposed to be dead yet. Probably they would have absolved those sins in life, before dying naturally at some later date. That's where I come in."

287

"Because you denied them that chance!" Orlene said, catching on.

"Right. I must endure their punishments, because they might not have had them on their records if I hadn't caused them to die early. It will take me centuries to catch up on all those sins of all those people, but it's worth it, because at least I am repaying some measure of what I took from them."

"But how does a dog—"

"One of them was a boy who was playing with a gun and shot his neighbor's dog. To cover up, he dragged the dog into a vacant lot and buried it. He was never caught; the neighbor assumed the dog had run away."

Orlene looked more closely at the man. "I see you are bleeding from the wound—but should that be over soon? How long did that dog take to die?"

"It wasn't a clean wound," the man said. "The dog didn't die from it."

"Didn't die! But you said the boy buried it!"

"Yes. The dog suffocated to death underground. I don't look forward to that part of it."

Orlene was appalled, despite the seeming justice of the punishment. "At least it will be over soon."

"In a few hours, yes," he gasped. "But, of course, that's only this replay."

"Replay?"

"I have to do it again, and again, until I have completely repented the act. That might have taken a hundred times, for that boy."

"But you didn't even do it! How can you truly repent what you never did?"

"I agree it is a problem," the man said. "I suppose that's why I haven't yet gotten beyond the first case."

"The first case? The first one killed in that accident?"

"The first significant sin of the first one killed," the man agreed.

"How—How many repetitions have there been?"

"So far? I don't know. I lost count at ten thousand."

"Ten thousand!"

"Several years ago, I think. But, of course, I'm not very

good at keeping time, here in this featureless cell. You are the first visitor I have had."

Orlene remained appalled at the thing he had done. She had no sympathy at all for those who took the lives of children, because she knew exactly what it felt like to lose a child. But this was ridiculous! The man would never succeed in expiating the sins of his victims, let alone his own. He was suffering pointlessly.

Now he was turning color, his gasping worse. He was going into the suffocation stage. "Is there anything I can do for you?" Orlene asked, feeling somewhat helpless and foolish, but compelled by her nature.

He wrenched a clenched eye open. "Maybe if you could ask Satan to let me get on to the next Atonement . . ." Then he went into a horrible shuddering, and she quickly moved on, unable to watch further.

God Almighty! Vita thought. *This sure as hell is Hell!*

It is a typical case, Jolie thought. *There are millions of them here. We can stop and interview any others we wish to.*

But Orlene faced straight forward, refusing to look left or right. She had seen more than enough of Hell.

It was a long passage, however, and she could not avoid hearing the piteous groans and seeing peripherally the struggles of those in unnatural agony. Truly, this was Hell.

At last she reached the end of it. There was a door, with a neat placard: SATAN. She knocked.

"Enter," a familiar voice called, and the door went up in flame. Beyond was a very attractive suite, with pleasant couches and pictures of green meadows on the wall.

She stepped in. A man came forward to greet her—or rather a demon came, with a grotesque face, horns, tail, and clothing formed of dancing flames.

Brother! Jolie thought, amused.

Alerted by this, Orlene looked more closely. "That's a mask!" she exclaimed. "And a costume!"

Satan shrugged. His tail fell off and the flames faded into a conventional flame-colored suit. He raised a hand to lift away the mask.

"Natasha!" Orlene cried, astonished.

"Which is 'Ah Satan' spelled backwards," he agreed. "You may also call Me Parry, after My mortal name, or Father, as you please."

"What silly joke is this?" she demanded, anger infusing her surprise.

Listen to him, Jolie thought firmly.

"I am Satan," he said. "I have many alternate guises. I wooed and won Jolie when I was Parry, and lost her when she died, and again when I was corrupted by the demoness Lilah—"

"Who?"

"You know her as Lila, Mars' concubine. She left Me for him. I was not pleased at the time, but it is true I had neglected her, and in any event I need no demoness now. In the present age I assumed the guise of Natasha, and wooed and won Orb before telling her I was Satan. She married Me nonetheless, as Gaea, but for a complicated reason we never consummated the marriage. So My ancient concubine now sleeps with your natural father, and I am your stepfather— the husband of your natural mother. This is why I asked Jolie to watch over you and to be your guardian and friend. It was not appropriate for Me to do it myself."

All true, Jolie thought. *I am with Gaea, but it was Satan who sent me to you.*

"I am—the stepdaughter of Satan," Orlene said, stunned. Yet she realized that she had known it, on a buried level; the intertwined relationships had been coming clear, following her death.

"And I love you as Jolie does," he continued. "As we would love the child we never had. I do not expect or require that this love be returned; in no other respect are you any creature of Mine. But I would do anything for you that a father would." He squinted at her. "But why don't you assume your natural form?" As he spoke, her body changed, assuming the aspect of her living state, rather than Vita's.

"I—I come to ask a favor," Orlene said.

"So I understand. Ask."

"I need a curse, to save my baby. To put the fear of evil in him, which fear he does not yet have."

Satan shook his head. "My blessing you could readily have, for it is worthless. But a curse—this is no minor thing. I cannot give you that; you would have to earn it."

"I will try." How well she knew that Incarnations did not lightly grant their favors!

"You see, by such a curse I would actually be doing the work of Mine Ancient Adversary, God. I would be causing a soul which would otherwise come to Me to go instead to Him. I would have to take equivalent value."

"If—If I could save my baby's soul, at the cost of mine, I would do that."

"No. Your soul is far too good for My realm! Besides, neither Jolie nor Orb would forgive me that. Ask something simpler, and I will grant it freely."

Orlene hesitated. "There is something—I know it is not my business, but—"

"Let Me be the arbiter of our business! Speak!"

"There is a man being tortured, in a chamber along the passage through which I came. He—I know he deserves punishment. But what he is suffering is pointless. He is in a closed loop, suffering for another person's sin, which he can never ameliorate. If he could just be nudged into the next Atonement—"

"You refer to the idiot who killed twenty-seven people and himself in a highway crash?"

"That one, yes. He doesn't ask for mercy, only for—"

"I agree. What he is suffering is pointless. The same may be said of many thousands of murderers who must suffer in lieu of their victims. But this is a thing I lack the authority to grant."

"But if you are the Master of Hell—"

"I am the Master of Hell. But not of the underlying definitions. The matter of Good and Evil can only be decided by a joint committee of God and Satan, and there has been no communication between We Two for centuries. I feel the definitions are long overdue for updating, if only to eliminate glitches such as this, but I cannot make that decision unilaterally. Only if God agrees may we work on this."

"But why doesn't God agree?" she asked plaintively.

Satan grimaced. "I fear you will just have to ask Him. He will not speak to Me."

"As it happens, I must go to Him next. Certainly I shall ask!"

"Lotsa luck," Satan murmured.

"And the curse—how may I earn that?"

Satan paced the floor, considering. "It occurs to Me there may be a way around that. You may not need My curse at all, or any of the other favors from Incarnations. I believe I can get Nox to release your baby, cured, now."

Ouch! Jolie thought to herself. *He's Tempting her!*

But Vita picked it up. *What do you mean? Is he going to renege?* They were communicating to each other, not to Orlene, whose attention was externally directed.

Satan is never that simple. Oh, I must not interfere, but I fear for her!

Well, then, I'll warn her!

No, you must not! She must endure it alone, or it doesn't count.

Orlene, meanwhile, hardly dared believe. "You can do this? How?"

"Anticipating your request, I availed Myself of the time you took walking the passage to visit the Incarnation of Night. She agreed to allow Me to try it my way."

"My baby!" Orlene breathed, her eyes shining. "Oh, how can this be?"

"You need do nothing arduous. A simple agreement on your part will suffice."

"An agreement?"

Now comes the kicker, Jolie thought. *He is so smooth, I hate it when he's doing such business. I never should have let her come here!*

"You are staying with the mortal Senator, Luna, are you not? You are friendly with her?"

"Yes. I am her niece, approximately. She has been most kind."

"She is to be engaged in a certain procedural matter which may be awkward for Me. If you would simply ask her to step aside—"

"I can't interfere in her political business!" Orlene protested.

Satan smiled warmly. "Please, do not misunderstand. I do not ask you to interfere, only to ask her to consider doing this small favor for you, so that you may help your baby, in accordance with My agreement with Nox. Surely Luna has no onus against your baby?"

I don't see what's so bad about that, Vita thought. *Considering what she has to gain.*

Just wait, Jolie thought grimly. *You never encountered as smooth-talking a rascal as Satan!*

I thought you loved him!

I do. But I also know him.

Orlene, almost overwhelmed by the offer, nevertheless didn't trust it. "Of course not! But—"

"Just how serious is your interest in helping your baby? I do not ask you to succeed in making Luna step aside, only to make the request, which she may decline if she chooses. For this I am prepared to arrange for the return of your baby to you. You need have no fear of this aspect; you will have your baby immediately, and your arduous quest will be over."

Orlene, increasingly distressed, found herself in tears. "Oh, Satan, for the sake of that love you profess for me, at least tell me the truth! I know this can be no simple matter, and I cannot decide on the basis of ignorance!"

Satan frowned. "Fair enough. I sought only to spare you details that might have distressed you. The whole truth is this: there is a critical issue coming up among the mortals, and Luna is to cast the key vote, deciding it. I will win by default if she does not vote."

"But what can this be?"

"It is the most important issue of our time. It will in effect decide the matter of which Incarnation shall wield the ultimate power. As you know, this is what I covet; for centuries My aspiration has been balked, but now at last it shall be decided."

"But how can Luna have any bearing on the power of Incarnations?"

"I see you do not yet understand. Very well, I shall be unconscionably direct. A number of folk have come to the conclusion that one of our number is not performing His

Office as He should. There will therefore be a vote to decide whether that Office should be declared vacant, so that a replacement Incarnation may be elevated to do the job. The importance of this matter to mortals is such that the deciding vote is theirs. If they, by the unanimous tally of their representatives, agree that the Office is vacant, then the remaining Incarnations, by unanimous agreement, may put a new person in that Office. It is of course to My interest to see that this does not occur."

"They want to replace you?" Orlene asked, amazed.

Satan laughed. "Me? Of course not! I have been arguably the most active and effective of the current Incarnations! No, it is the other in question: the Incarnation of Good."

Orlene stared at him, unable to speak.

Did I hear right? Vita thought.

You did, Jolie replied. *This is amazing! I knew, but had somehow forgotten. Now it comes back. They want to replace God!*

"You see, God has simply not been responsive recently," Satan continued. "Since we anticipate a formidable crisis— World War Three, to be specific, but there are also matters of overpopulation, exhaustion of mortal resources, global famine and disease and the like—we fear that humanity will be extinguished, and the world with it, in a few years, if action is not taken. Much of that action can be taken only with the acquiescence of all the Incarnations. So there is indeed a crisis."

Orlene found her voice. "How can you claim that God is—is not—"

"My dear, I am on the other side. I support the present God and want Him to remain in Office."

"But you are His antithesis! You oppose Him in all things!"

"Not exactly. I am competitive with Him. I rival Him for power. I wish to wrest dominance from Him."

"But you just said—"

"My dear, you are slow to appreciate the nuance. I agree with the other Incarnations that God is not doing His job. That has been My experience over the centuries. But I do not want Him replaced. I do not want His Office declared vacant. I have activated My minions among the mortals to oppose this declaration, and the decision in one leading nation is very close. In fact if Luna does not vote, it will be a tie, which will allow the prior position to stand, and therefore represent a defeat of the resolution, and God will not be replaced. So you can see that what I ask of you is not contrary to your belief or preference. I support the status quo, as do you."

"But if there is to be ruin—"

"Ah yes, we must not forget that. Action certainly must be taken. A new God would surely take it, and perhaps succeed in averting disaster. But if there is no new God, and the present inaction continues, the remaining Incarnations will have in the end to turn to the most effective remaining prospect. That, of course, is the Incarnation of Evil."

"You—You support God—because you think this will bring you ultimate power?"

"Now at last you have it, My dear. That is the essence of My motive. Certainly I will act to avert the crisis; the mortal realm will survive. But the power will be Mine."

"I just can't believe—God cannot be so—"

"And if you will merely express that same support to Luna, and encourage her to sit out that key vote, I will call Nox and she will return your baby to you now. I think this is a generous offer."

Orlene stood still, trying to come to terms with this. Satan urging her to support God—and offering what amounted to a handsome bribe to that end! Her entire quest could be completed this moment, merely by agreeing.

"I think," she said at last, "that you know more of this than I do. If you believe that my plea to Luna will be effective, then it may be. If you believe that this would give you ultimate power, then it must be. Therefore I must not do this. I must trust in Luna's judgment, trust in her to do what is right, even though it runs contrary to my instincts."

"Even though it costs you your baby?" Satan asked softly.

Orlene squeezed her eyes closed, trying to dam back her tears. "How can I weigh my baby—against the welfare of the world? I do want my baby, but not at such a price. I must do

295

what I believe is right, even though it pains me, even though I am uncertain what *is* right."

"Are you sure?" Satan looked grim.

"No, I am the least certain ghost in the world! But I think this is the way it must be."

"Then it shall be Nox's way," Satan murmured.

"Her way?"

"We made a deal, she and I. She would support My way, by yielding the baby, if I could make it work. I would support her way, if I failed. I have failed to Tempt you, so must honor the bargain I made."

"But what is that bargain?"

"If the Office of Good is declared vacant, there will be a nomination and voting by the remaining major Incarnations. Nox can neither nominate nor vote in that, because she is not of the forces of Day. But now she can act through Me. I will support her candidate."

"Who—"

Satan shook his head. "Nox is excellent at secrets. I must keep hers, until the time, lest the others marshal against it. No other is privileged to know her will."

"Her will has made endless mischief for me!" Orlene flared.

"So it seems. It may be that you would prefer to have the deal I proffered, instead of the alternative." He paused, but Orlene did not change her tormented mind. "But your options are not exhausted. What I proffered was a deal to shortcut your quest to My profit. You may still earn My curse, if you choose, and try to save your baby as you have planned."

"Oh," Orlene said, nonplussed. "I had forgotten, or thought you would no longer honor that."

"I honor every deal I make," Satan said. "Do Me My service, and I will guarantee your curse."

"Then I will do your service," she said. "What is it?"

"There is a new client who is uncooperative, as evil souls tend to be. I wish you to obtain his cooperation."

"But I know nothing of damned souls!" she protested.

"I believe you do know this one. His name is Kane."

Good God! Vita thought.

"Please refrain from using such language here, Vita," Satan said. "You must be aware it is out of place."

"We—We did kill him?" Orlene asked, disturbed anew.

"Technically, he killed himself. You were not truly at fault, and very little sin attaches to any of the four of you who were involved. He did, after all, initiate the sequence, and it was your right to defend the host. I will say that I regard your method as ingenious, however; seldom is a person killed by a story."

"I suppose we could try," Orlene said. "He can't kill us here, can he? I mean, Vita's body?"

"You will remain in the privileged passage, where no harm can come to you. Do not leave it, for a mortal host may not enter Hell proper. You will only talk to him, and persuade him to cooperate."

"What do you want from him?"

"The names of all the women he killed. There are, I believe, a fair number."

"You do not know them?"

"Orlene, Hell receives many thousands of souls every day! We process them in as well as we can, but we cannot pay close attention to all the details. In any event, the majority of the women probably did not come to Hell, so we cannot interrogate them. The information must come from the ones we do have: the murderers."

"But what good can that information do? The girls are already dead, and the murderer is already suffering!"

"But not as appropriately as he should be. Each damned soul should suffer the Atonements of his victims, according to the ancient convention. I cannot set these up until I have the identities of the women. With those, I can subpoena the records from Purgatory, and proper Atonement can begin."

"That never gets past the first one?" she asked sharply.

"That is not always the case. Sometimes they make it through a number before entering a closed loop."

"If I had any say in the matter, I'd get that fixed!" she cried. "I agree that they ought to do penance, but this only leads to bureaucratic gridlock! Nobody benefits!"

297

"Agreed. At such time as I have the final say, I shall make that little reform."

She sighed. "Show me the man. I'll do what little I can."

"Gladly. He is in the chamber nearest to this one, along the privileged passage. If you succeed in making him cooperate, I will know it, and I will reserve My curse for your use when the time comes. You may proceed directly down the passage to the other chamber, where you will be borne back to Purgatory. You will not have to face Me again."

She looked at him, uncertain of his slant. Then she turned and exited.

The chamber was right there—and within it was Kane, still in his clothing, lying on his stomach, blood flowing from his groin. Evidently he had bled to death, but here there was no relief of unconsciousness, and he had to suffer consciously.

You know, Jolie told the story, Vita reminded them. *Should she take over for this?*

"No, it is my favor I am seeking," Orlene said. "I must do it. But I confess to having little notion how."

The man heard her. His head lifted. He grimaced. "Who are you? Another bad woman, come to torment me?"

"I think you are already in sufficient torment," Orlene said. "But it is true that I am associated with one you thought to make your victim. Do you remember the last one?"

"The black bitch? How could I forget! Look what she did to me!" He squinted at her. "But you aren't that one. I don't remember you."

"I was with her, in spirit, with two others. We told you the story of Lorelie. We were the ones who orchestrated your demise. The living host-girl could not have done it alone."

"For sure!" he agreed, wincing as his exclamation triggered more pain from the knife embedded in his flesh. "I killed a dozen before her, and none ever came close to getting away, let alone killing me."

"It was time to stop you," Orlene said. The man bothered her, and his condition; she knew he deserved it, but she hated seeing the pain.

"Maybe. Now take off; I don't need any more whores to laugh at me. I'm sorry I didn't get rid of all of you."

"I am here to ask you to cooperate with Satan. He needs the names of the women you killed."

Kane laughed, wincing as he did so. "Go ram this knife up yourself, you damned slut! I know what happens when Satan gets those names! Think I want to suffer for the whores? I'd rather leave this knife in me!" But after a pained pause, he qualified that. "Gak, it hurts, though!"

"Gak?"

"We can't say the G word here; didn't you know? Now get out; I won't give you that last laugh."

"But you can't progress, you can't be absolved of your sins, if you don't do this," Orlene argued. "You will be locked at this initial stage, forever suffering the knife. Surely you can't want that!"

"I'm stuck—ha-ha—with it!" he gasped. "It's better than giving those bitches the satisfaction. Let them work out their own sins; Gak knows they deserve to!"

He was certainly recalcitrant. Orlene did not know what else to say.

What about Laurie? Jolie thought. *She's the one woman he worships. If she asked him—*

Say, yeah! Vita agreed. *Do you think she could be down here too? I mean, she must've whored just to survive, and she would've come back for him if she'd lived, so—*

"Let's ask," Orlene said. She returned to Satan's door and knocked.

Again the door went up in flame. Satan stood within. "You have completed your assignment already?"

"I may be making progress. I need to know whether a certain woman is here in Hell."

Satan snapped his fingers. Immediately Ozymandias stood beside him. "Her name?" Satan asked.

"Laurel. I don't know her last name."

Ozymandias frowned. "That narrows it to about half a million. We could line them up for your inspection."

Describe her from his memory, Jolie thought. She made a

mental picture of the madonna figure she had seen in Kane's mind.

"She is pretty—beautiful, really, even at age fifteen," Orlene said. "Perhaps not so when she died. Hair waist-length, dark, brown verging on black, figure slender, not pronounced. Eyes brown. She may have had to go into prostitution to survive when she ran away from home."

"About four thousand of that name answer that description," Ozymandias said, checking a notepad which appeared in his hand.

"She ran away about thirty years ago."

He flipped a page. "Three hundred."

"She has a brother named Kane."

"Twelve."

"Who is five years younger than she."

"Two."

"If I could interview those two—"

"One moment." Ozymandias disappeared.

"Good man," Satan said. "I bless, if you will pardon the expression, the day I rescued him from anonymity. Laurel is the client's older sister?"

"Yes. I think she will have influence on him, if we can put them together."

"That would be irregular."

Orlene repressed a smile. "Just how serious is your interest in the client's cooperation, Satan?"

He almost smiled in return. "No doubt a deal can be made."

Jolie knew that Satan was pleased, but she wasn't sure why. Normally he did not appreciate backtalk from the denizens of Hell. Of course this was his stepdaughter; he liked seeing her take hold. But Jolie wasn't sure that was all of it.

Ozymandias reappeared. Behind him stood two young women. Both were pretty, but both had had hard use. Neither quite fitted Kane's mental picture.

But Orlene didn't give up. "Which one of you promised to return for your ten-year-old brother?"

"What's it to you?" the left one asked.

"He is here."

She put her hands to her face. "Oh, the poor boy! I was sure he was bound for H—" she choked.

"Heaven," Satan said. "The damned cannot say that word."

"She is the one," Orlene said. "I must talk to her, and then have her talk to him. What can I offer her for her cooperation?"

"One minute per hour, with him," Satan said. "If she is instrumental in making him cooperate."

Get a load of his generosity! Vita thought.

Orlene decided not to argue. "May I talk to her alone?"

"One minute," Satan said. He and Ozymandias and the other Laurel disappeared, leaving only Orlene and the woman in the office.

"We have only one minute," Orlene said. "Laurel, your brother loves you, and I think will do anything you ask of him. You are his madonna figure, his perfect woman. He is a mass murderer who was knifed to death at age forty, but he loves you. His Atonement can proceed faster if he cooperates. You can spend one minute of each hour with him if you get him to do that. Will you?"

"No!" Laurel cried. "He mustn't know how far I sank! Let him keep his good image of me!"

"If you don't tell him about your life, I won't. Just tell him to cooperate. Then, every hour, you can console him. I don't think he'll ever ask how you died, or how you came to be here. All he will care is that you have returned for him, even here in Hell. For one minute each hour he won't suffer so much. You can keep your promise."

"My promise!" she breathed. "My one good hope—"

Satan reappeared. "Well?"

"I must take her to the client's cell," Orlene said. She took Laurel by the arm and guided her out the door and down the hall. "You can enter," she told Laurel. "I cannot. Talk to him. Get him to cooperate, and the reward is yours."

Laurel saw the suffering man lying on the blood-soaked

301

bed. Suddenly he assumed the form of a ten-year-old boy, uninjured. "Oh, Kane!" she cried, running in to him. Now she, too, was younger, fifteen and lovely.

"Laurel! You came!" he cried.

They embraced. "I said I would! But I cannot stay! You know this is Hell, Kane; you must do what they want, or you will never get out of it!"

"If you ask me—"

"We can be together—one minute each hour!"

"Then I will do it." His capitulation was that simple, once his deepest dream had been tapped. Orlene's effort of understanding and compassion had accomplished what Hell's torture had not.

Ozymandias appeared in the cell. "The names."

Kane, still held by his loving sister, started giving the names. Ozymandias noted them on a scroll with deft strikes of a quill.

Then he gestured. Laurel vanished, and Kane was back as an adult, with the knife. "She will return next hour," Ozymandias said, and vanished himself.

Kane gazed at Orlene. "You did this," he said.

"Yes."

He grunted something that almost sounded like "Thanks."

I still can't stand him, but I'm glad we did it, Vita thought. She spoke for them all.

Orlene turned away. She walked down the hall toward the exit. But when she came to the man she had talked with before, she paused.

"I asked Satan, but he said he couldn't change the rules. I am going to visit God next, and I will ask Him."

"I thank you," the man gasped, turning color. He was going into his suffocation stage.

"No, this isn't fair!" Orlene cried. "Atonement, yes, but not pointless torture!" She stepped into the chamber.

Halt! Jolie thought in desperation. *You can't go there! It's off the—*

But Orlene had already done it. Vita's mortal body came up against an invisible barrier and stopped, but Orlene's spirit went on. It was leaving the host, glowing.

What happens now? Vita thought, horrified.

We must pull her back! Jolie responded. *She must not be discorporate in Hell!*

They both grabbed at Orlene's spirit. But it stretched, the bulk of it going on into the cell. They were left holding the tail of the ghost, while the front reached the man.

Orlene put her faint hand on the man's head. The glow intensified, surrounding him. *Go on to the next!* she thought. *Break the chain! You must do it!*

The man stopped choking. He sat up, becoming gaunt. "I'm starving!" he exclaimed.

The joint pull exerted by Jolie and Vita finally prevailed. Orlene was drawn back into the host.

He's in the next torture! Vita thought, amazed.

"That boy—he stole money from a friend, and so the friend went hungry," the man said. "I am suffering that hunger. Oh, thank you, lovely spirit!"

I didn't know you could do such magic! Jolie thought.

"I can't," Orlene said, dazed. "He must have done it himself. I only encouraged him."

But Jolie had seen the glow. She knew that it required more than encouragement. Apparently there was an active component as well as a passive one to Orlene's lifelong magic.

Orlene went on, not quite understanding the significance of what she had done, at the dire risk of her soul. Had she not been hauled back, she would have been trapped in Hell, unable to escape despite her evident goodness.

They reached the end of the passage. The vapor closed about them. They moved upward, out of Hell.

CHAPTER THIRTEEN

Good

THEY EMERGED BEFORE GAEA'S TREEHOUSE. THEY heard the voice of the *Purgatory News* announcer coming from within; evidently the set was on. "All Purgatory is agog over the visit of one 'Natasha' to the abode of the Incarnation of Nature. Gaea is, of course, married to the Incarnation of Evil, and remains nominally faithful to him, though the marriage was never consummated. For her to entertain another man . . ."

Orlene smiled briefly as she knocked on the door. They knew who Natasha was, now, and why he had come. There was no scandal. The *Purgatory News,* like that of the mortals, was sensationalist and not too scrupulous about its implications.

Gaea opened the door. "You succeeded?"

"Yes. But now I must go to Heaven, and not with my soul alone, because I mean to return. I have no idea how to get there."

"I think Natasha will have to guide you again," Gaea said, with a smile similar to Orlene's own.

"I shall be glad to," Natasha said, appearing outside. "As it happens, I have a friend who knows the way through chaos."

Yeah, that bitch Nox! Vita thought.

"Oh? Perhaps I should come too," Gaea said.

I keep forgetting they can hear us! Vita thought, chagrined.

"By all means come along!" Natasha said, extending one elbow to her and the other to Orlene.

They took the elbows. The region darkened, then turned gray. They were traveling into the vagueness of the Void.

Then Natasha called to someone beyond. His voice made the ether ripple magically; the pattern of it could be seen all around them, curling in strange wave patterns into diminishing spirals and out to infinity. The effect was weird and beautiful and hypnotic, both auditory and visual.

It's an aspect of the Llano, Jolie explained. *The Llano is one of the only things that penetrates the Void. Gaea uses it to control the forces of nature, but she's not adept with chaos.*

There came an answering call. The waves and spirals changed, assuming a new configuration. The restless tapestry of their convolutions became the walls of an austere chamber.

They faced a kindly, bearded man. "Thank You for answering, JHVH," Natasha said. "This is Gaea, the Incarnation of Nature."

"I have admired your work," JHVH said politely.

"And this is Orlene, her daughter, My stepdaughter, in the mortal host of another person."

"And Jolie too," JHVH remarked, glancing at them.

"Jolie too," Natasha agreed. "I asked Jolie to watch over Orlene in life, and when Orlene died, she felt responsible, and is helping her accomplish a task set by the Incarnation of Night."

"Ah, I have known Nox of old."

«Have I been named?» It was Nox, coalescing beside them. Her vague outline solidified, until she had the form of a stunningly beautiful woman. But she was in black and white, while the others were in full color.

That's weird! Vita thought.

"Nox has my baby," Orlene said. "He has a malady of the soul, which can be cured only by special things provided by each of the major Incarnations. I have obtained the agreements of six, and now must gain the last from God."

"I shall be happy to guide you to Heaven," JHVH said. "But I am curious about the involvement of the Incarnation of Night, who is not of your pantheon, any more than I am. I am not conversant with the politics of such interactions, but suspect this is rare."

«It is the first time in the current millennium I have done so,» Nox said.

"I should think you would have a more important concern than the welfare of a single baby," JHVH said. "Such as the approaching termination of most mortal existence."

«I have no power over that. I do have power over the baby.» As she spoke, the baby appeared in her arms. Nox opened her robe to expose one breast, and nursed him.

The three sharing the host reacted in different ways. Orlene felt an exquisite pang to see another woman nursing her baby, yet noted that the baby was being well cared for. Nox held him closely, with evident concern and even love, and Gaw-Two seemed quite comfortable with her. Orlene remembered how her own mother, here right now, had given her up; was this the way it felt? She wanted so much to go and take her baby back! She made an effort and buried her mixed emotions, lest she embarrass herself by breaking down in tears. Her thoughts, hitherto unguarded, abruptly became opaque to Jolie.

How can she nurse when she hasn't given birth? Vita thought, amazed. She had no awareness of the pang of separation Orlene felt, but was simply curious about the technical aspect.

She isn't human, Jolie replied. *She can adapt herself to any form and function she chooses.* But Jolie herself was amazed that Nox, the most aloof of Incarnations, should have chosen to do this, and indeed to be so open about it. There was no need for the baby to feed in the Afterlife; this was only to give him comfort. Why should Nox *care*? Or was Nox deliberately torturing Orlene? Was she trying to make Orlene do something foolish, and so forfeit the recovery of her baby which she had labored so hard to achieve?

Gaea looked at the Incarnation of Night. "Dreams may seem to the uninformed to be the stuff of chaos, but it is only ignorance that makes it seem so. Your realm mirrors ours, Nox; what is it you see that we do not?"

Nox merely smiled and faded out, still nursing Gaw.

"She is up to something," JHVH remarked. "But let us attend to the business at hand. I will guide you to Heaven, Orlene, though I will not enter it with you. Take My hand."

Orlene took his hand. Suddenly chaos was rushing past them. It was formless, yet seemed to suggest form; efforts to perceive it were frustrating, yet it was hard to ignore.

Ahead loomed a star. It expanded to a sun, and then to a globe of light which filled their vision. They came right up to the fringe, and the brilliance diminished with proximity. Beyond it lay a shining terrain.

"This is your Heaven," JHVH said. "Pass through the veil of light, and return to this point when you are finished. I will await you here."

"Thank you." Orlene floated through the veil.

Who is that guy? Vita asked. *How come he knows his way here when the Incarnations don't?*

He is the God of the Hebrews, Jolie replied. *Once the God of all, but his power has declined with the ascent of newer religions, such as Christianity.*

But I thought it was the same God!

In theory, perhaps—but in practice, no. The Christians have become a different and more aggressive tribe.

Then why does he help us?

He has become tolerant in his age, and I understand that Satan once did him a favor.

Vita made a thought of laughter. *I wonder if Satan was trying to corrupt JHVH, the same as he does everyone else! I don't think it worked.*

Orlene stood at the edge of Heaven, uncertain where to proceed. She stood on a white cloudbank, which merged with others, the landscape resembling a giant mattress. The inhabitants of Heaven stood around, faintly glowing. They looked bored.

Orlene approached the nearest. This was an old woman who looked much the way she must have in life before she died. "Excuse me—how do I find God?"

"Live better than you did," the woman replied, uninterested.

"Oh, I'm not dead, exactly. I mean, I'm just visiting, in a mortal host. I have to see God."

"Well, God isn't here in Limbo! We are the imperfect souls, just barely good enough to qualify. We have evil in us and cannot proceed to the more pleasant aspects of Heaven until we expunge it."

"How do you do that?"

"I'm not sure, and not very curious."

"Can you tell me some path to follow that perhaps leads to God?"

The woman shrugged. "Why should I bother?"

I don't think this biddy's going to make fast progress! Vita thought.

Perhaps you should use your magic, Jolie suggested.

Orlene brightened. The moment she oriented, the glows of the souls in Heaven changed. Now some were brighter than others. But none seemed bright enough.

Why not just yell? Vita thought.

Orlene considered, then tried it. "Please, anybody!" she called. "I am a visitor here, and I need guidance. Will anyone help me to go in the direction of God?"

There was no reaction. The souls in Limbo just weren't interested.

Then a new one appeared. This was a young woman who looked somewhat worn, but she glowed brightly. "Hello. I am Rita."

I like that name! Vita thought. *And she's young, like me!*

"I am Orlene. Are you coming in answer to—"

"Did you save a baby?" she asked.

"I lost my baby," Orlene said. "I am trying to recover him."

"No—a baby in a Dumpster. Newborn."

309

Orlene gazed at her more closely. "Why, yes! The Incarnation of Death told me to—but I couldn't—"

"I am his mother."

"Oh! You mean you died, Rita? That's why—"

"Not exactly. I had to work—I had taken all my vacation time, and I had used a slim-spell to hide my pregnancy—but I would have lost my job at the restaurant if they knew. So I brought the baby with me and hid him in the Dumpster, where nobody would suspect, so I could run out and tend to him. I knew the collection schedule, see, so I could move him before they came. But I pushed it too hard, being back on my feet all day so soon after, and I hemorrhaged, and they didn't know and I didn't tell, so as not to lose my job—and, well, I lost my life instead. I was in Heaven before I knew, and couldn't get back—and what could I have done as a ghost, anyway? I knew my baby would die, and oh, how that hurt—"

"Oh, I know, don't I know!" Orlene said, putting her arms around the young woman as she choked up.

"All I could do was watch. But then you came, and you took him, and brought him to the hospital, so he lived, after all, and now he's been adopted by a nice couple, and he's much better off than I could ever—I mean, even if I had lived—"

"Yes. I was adopted too. I never knew my natural parents until after I died."

"So I owe you a debt of thanks I thought I could never repay! I can't go to the highest levels, because of the sin of having the baby out of wedlock, but I can take you most of the way."

"You didn't marry?" Orlene asked.

"Well, we were going to, you know, but he had to get through college first—and then when I learned I was—"

"He disappeared," Orlene finished, and Rita nodded tearfully. "And for that you have sin on your soul."

"Yes. I never had much sin before, but I loved him so much, I really thought—"

"I think we need new definitions," Orlene muttered. "I'm glad I saved your baby. I didn't realize that I would ever meet you."

Rita brightened. "Come, I must show you the way! I'm so glad to be able to do this!"

They followed the young woman. There were stairs at some places where the cloud banks intersected, spiraling up to the higher levels, and they climbed these. Halfway up was a guardian angel, a forbidding figure with solid, birdlike wings furled behind. "What is this?" he demanded gruffly.

"This is Orlene," Rita said. "She has come to see God."

"Get out of here!" the angel snapped, barring the way.

"But she has important business!"

"I don't care what she claims! She has no clearance for this ascent. Now vacate, before I lay an Atonement on you both!" He raised his fist.

Orlene lifted her hand, intercepting his. Her glow brightened. The angel froze in place.

She's doing it again! Vita thought. *I bet she really could have used that magic in life, instead of just seeing whether anyone's right for anyone else.*

Jolie did not respond. She wasn't sure whether this was a newly discovered talent or a newly developed one. Certainly there had been no hint of it before that moment in Hell. She didn't understand it, so was disquieted by it. Could Nox have done something else to Orlene, without her knowledge? If so, to what would it lead? Jolie had no confidence at all in the motives of the Incarnation of Night; she remembered too well that episode of Orlene's maleness.

They passed the still angel and went on up to the next level—where they were similarly challenged by an angel who seemed more like a bureaucratic thug than any spirit of goodness. Orlene touched him as she had the first, and he was similarly nullified. In this manner they ascended several levels. "This is as high as I can go," Rita said. "We've passed Limbo, and the Moon, and Venus, and the Sphere of the Sun. This is the Fifth Heaven, which is the Sphere of Mars, with the idle warrior spirits. I'm not a warrior, of course; I'm in a different part of the level, for those who tried to fight discrimination. There are five more Heavens, and in the Tenth Heaven you'll find God."

"Perhaps you can show me farther," Orlene said. "Let's see."

They ascended to the Sixth Heaven, where the Righteous Rulers dwelt. The guardian angel on duty tried to bar them, as the others had, but with no better success. Orlene's new power triumphed.

In the Ninth Heaven they encountered resistance of another nature. "Greetings, girls. I am the Angel Gabriel. I will deal with you."

They gazed at Gabriel. He looked exactly like a man, in contrast to the guardian angels, who had sported anything from two to six wings each. That argued for his legitimacy: he felt no need for affectation.

"I am Orlene, visiting in mortal host. I have come to talk with God."

"So I understand. You have generated some disruption here. We do not encourage mortal visits, and we admit to a certain prejudice against brides of Satan."

"Please let me pass," Orlene said. "I will depart with my friends as soon as my business with God is done."

"God is distracted at the moment. Perhaps I can settle your business instead."

Orlene, growing impatient, sought to brush past him, but Gabriel gently barred her. She tried to use the glow to immobilize him, but it had no effect.

"Such magic can not affect Seraphim or above," Gabriel said. "Now that you have made proof of it, perhaps you will reconsider my offer."

He's legitimate, Jolie thought. *Better talk with him.*

"All right," Orlene said, disgruntled.

Gabriel made a gesture as of drawing a curtain around them. The stairs faded out, and they were in a compact office. Gabriel sat behind a square desk, checking a scroll.

"I see you have been to six major Incarnations and obtained commitments from them all," Gabriel remarked.

"Yes. I need only a blessing from God and I can recover my baby from the Incarnation of Night. Then I can relax, my mission accomplished."

Gabriel gazed at her with what seemed like more than

ordinary interest. "You expect to retire thereafter to Heaven, taking no further interest in worldly things?"

Orlene had to smile. "More likely Hell, because of the disruption I have caused to Incarnations during my quest."

"You do not, then, regard yourself as perfect."

She laughed. "Hardly! I knew when I committed suicide that I placed my soul in peril, and I have not improved my balance since."

"Yet I have the impression that you seek to criticize God, who is by definition perfect."

"Even that!" she agreed ruefully. "In my mind I have indeed criticized God, and I know that is sinful. But in my heart I know that I must do what I must do, without heeding the cost to my own poor soul. I have encountered errors of application which only God can correct, and I do mean to bring them to His attention. I have just learned—" She broke off, fearing that she had no right to continue.

"That the other Incarnations seek to replace God," Gabriel finished for her. "Set your mind at ease about that; this is not your doing. Satan has from time immemorial coveted the power and glory of the highest office, and once again sees what he takes to be an opportunity to forward his suit. I negotiated with him some centuries back, and we agreed to a challenge involving your grandmother, Niobe, now an Aspect of the Incarnation of Fate."

"My grandmother!" Orlene exclaimed.

"The challenge was of this nature: I designated the individual, whose influence could be critical to world events. If he could not corrupt that person, or her child or grandchild, in such a way as to enable him to take power, then he would forever abate his effort. I would say that he has not succeeded in corrupting Niobe, or her daughter Orb, who now holds the Office of the Incarnation of Nature. One generation remains, in which there are two representatives: Luna and yourself. When you died, your onus abated. Now only Luna remains. Satan's effort to corrupt her or neutralize her has been ceaseless, for she is his last chance. The final showdown is now close, and much attention focuses on it."

Orlene nodded. "I had not known that this was the result

of a deal between you and Satan! He tried to Tempt me to influence Luna, so that she would sit out the big vote."

"Of course. The fact that you are here now indicates that you turned him down."

"Yes. I want my baby more than anything—but not at the expense of the world! So I must talk to God and obtain His blessing, and then I can recover my baby without wronging others."

"I am afraid you will be disappointed."

"I have not come this far only to be balked!" she flared. "Only let me talk to Him, and I will not bother you again!"

"There is something you must understand about God. He no longer talks to supplicants."

"I can't accept that. Just let me see Him!" she pleaded.

"I really think you would be better off to let this go. Your baby seems to be in competent hands."

"I have no idea why Nox got into this!" Orlene said. "But I can't just let her take my baby with impunity!"

"I agree that it is a curious matter. Ordinarily she has no interest in the affairs of mortals or Incarnations, other than their dreams. It seems that she selected your baby by no coincidence. She evidently has some interest in you."

"I don't care what her interest is! If she thought I wouldn't do everything I could to recover my baby, she was mistaken! Now let me talk to God!"

"It is with regret I do this. He is the Tenth Heaven. Do what you must do." He gestured, and the office disappeared.

She faced an enormous pattern of light, roughly globular in outline. She stared, trying to fathom that grand radiance. Slowly she discerned a great halo. Framed within it was a second, brighter halo. Framed within that was a third, blindingly brilliant halo. Within that was an infinitely detailed and beautiful face, whose effulgence transcended all mortal understanding. This was the Face of God.

Orlene fell to her knees and raised her hands in the position of prayer. "Oh, my Lord God!" she cried. "I have worshipped You since childhood! I have tried always to do right by Your definition! Now I come to You, a supplicant, to beg only for Your blessing for my child. Please, God, grant me that!"

She waited, but there was no answer. The phenomenal face of God showed no reaction.

Somewhat out of sorts, she repeated her request. God still ignored her. It was as if He hadn't heard.

Orlene began to understand what others had hinted. It was hard to get God's attention.

But she had not come all this way just to be ignored. "Listen to me, my Lord!" she cried. "Your enemies are gathering. Satan seeks to displace You. The Incarnations are making ready to replace You! You must act to stop that! You must take an interest in the affairs of the world!"

The huge face stared straight ahead. Now she was able to make out the spherical curves of the three halos. God's face was reflected there, triply, each surface showing a different aspect. God was contemplating Himself!

"And the world is going to Hell!" she cried, getting desperate. "Satan hopes to assume Your power, in the face of Your inaction. You must stop him, for the sake of all!"

God's narcissistic contemplation continued without interruption.

"And World War Three is coming! In five years all mortality will be in peril. Only You can act to prevent this, or someone wielding the power that should be Yours. Don't leave it to Gabriel, for he will only be displaced by the Incarnation of Evil! I beg of you, God, give me a sign. I will give up my baby, if only You will take some interest in the world before it is too late! Give me a sign that You understand!"

She waited, her tears flowing. There was no sign.

"I would have preferred to conceal this from you," Gabriel said. "You cannot obtain God's blessing, for He does not respond to any outside input. He is contemplating His own greatness, to the exclusion of all else."

"How long has this been the case?" Orlene asked, numbed by the discovery.

"It is hard to say. It came on Him gradually. Perhaps a thousand years, for this end-stage. I have covered for Him as well as I could, but it has become increasingly difficult."

"All my prayers—all the prayers of every mortal—He has heard none of them?"

"If He hears, He doesn't care. No prayer has been directly granted in the past five hundred years, that I know of."

"But I know that some have been answered!"

"My own powers are quite limited, but sometimes I have been able to effect cures or other beneficial occurrences."

"You? In lieu of God?"

"Inadequate as that may be," he agreed. "But more often I have been unable to act, and so the prayers of most mortals have been unanswered, even the most worthy ones. I note this with extreme regret. Yet, short of blowing my Horn, I am helpless. I am the most powerful of angels, but can never approach the power of the least of Incarnations. Only God can do what must be done—yet He will not."

"But the world may end, without His intercession!"

"No, I suspect it will merely be damned, as Satan assumes greater power. This is why it is so important for Luna to cast her vote. This will prevent Satan from achieving power by default. Then the Incarnations can choose another Officeholder, and we shall have an activist God."

"But you support this God!"

"I have supported Him to the best of my ability through-out," Gabriel agreed. "But I find I have a greater loyalty: to the Office itself, rather than to the Officeholder. I can now serve God best by letting the Office change hands. That will save the world. This God will never notice." He made a wan smile. "So, instead of your baby, you have found truth. But perhaps the next God will grant your request."

Orlene stared at him, appalled by the realization. It was now to her interest to facilitate the replacement of God! Satan had tried to persuade her to support the existing Officeholder, but she could prevail by doing the opposite. Never in all her life and death had she dreamed of such a thing, yet it made sense.

Jolie and Vita were similarly awed by the thought.

"What will happen to you?" Orlene asked, trying to bring her churning emotions into a semblance of order.

"I will serve whoever holds the Office, if He wishes my services. Otherwise, I do have another offer."

"Another offer? You mean, some other Incarnation?"

"Satan."

"How can you serve him after serving God?" she demanded, appalled.

"I am not a mortal, or a spirit," he explained. "I am an angel. It is my nature to serve one power or another, loyally until dismissed. My present position is not my first—or, I think, my last. I will, of course, be sorry to see this tour end, but few things are eternal."

"But Satan!"

"He is not truly evil. He is the Incarnation of Evil, which is another matter. He supervises the disposition of souls on which evil remains, but he himself is good. Did you know that he saved JHVH's people from a persecution so severe that virtually none remained in Europe?"

"But there are millions of Jews in Europe!"

"Precisely. But without his intercession, there would have been almost none—and no Romani, either."

"Gypsies!" Orlene exclaimed. "It was a Gypsy girl who took care of me when my mother had to leave me, and who arranged for my adoption by tourists! Now that girl's father is an aspect of Fate! Do you mean to say that Satan—"

"It is not generally known today, or even among Incarnations, but it is true. Satan owed JHVH a favor, and when the occasion came to repay it, he did so in singular fashion. In fact, I would deem the current Incarnation of Evil to be the most effective Officeholder of that line, because he has not been corrupted by his power."

Orlene glanced in the direction of the Tenth Heaven. "As the Incarnation of Good has been corrupted by His power?"

"So it would seem. The power of an Incarnation is great indeed, but it is there to be used, not enjoyed. God came to the Office of Good with excellent credentials. I think perhaps they were too apt; as it turned out, He had little concept of mortal frailty. He simply did not understand

317

human weakness, and in time lost what little interest He had had in it."

"He tuned out," Orlene said.

"He tuned out. It seems that He lacked sufficient evil in His being to relate to the evil in others, so could not properly address it. As a result, the mortal world was left increasingly to fend for itself, and is now in an unfortunate state. It grieves me to see this, but I cannot deny it."

"It grieves me too," Orlene said. "I thank you for explaining things to me. I see that my concern is trivial compared to yours, and I will leave now."

"We each must follow our own paths," Gabriel said. "You have been forthright in yours, and I in mine. I do not regret that they have crossed." He extended his hand.

Surprised, she took it. Then she walked to the stairs.

What a surprise! Vita thought as they descended. *God zonked out on His own Image, and the world going to Hell!*

And God to be replaced, Jolie thought. *We exist in truly momentous times!*

At the Fifth Heaven, Rita was waiting for them. "Did you talk to God?" she asked eagerly.

"I talked to God," Orlene agreed. "But He did not respond."

"Oh. They say that He hasn't taken much of an interest in recent events. Maybe He's ill."

"Maybe," Orlene agreed.

Mentally ill! Vita thought.

They proceeded on down to First Heaven, and to the fringe. Now it was clear why the folk here in Limbo—and in the other Heavens—weren't much interested in anything. The benign neglect extended from the top to the bottom.

Orlene turned to Rita. "Good-bye," she said. "I am glad I was able to help your baby, even if I couldn't help mine. Thank you for putting me on the right track to find God."

"Oh, you are most welcome! When I saw my baby safe after all—"

"I understand," Orlene said, concealing the sudden surge of grief she felt for her own baby. She hugged Rita, then turned and stepped through the glowing veil

JHVH was there. "Oh—were you waiting the whole time?" Orlene asked, surprised. "I thought you would be back with Gaea and Sa—Natasha!"

"I thought they might prefer to be alone for a time."

In chaos, where none can know, Jolie agreed wistfully. Always before, she had been along, so that technically Satan's second marriage had never been consummated, only his first. But she really could not resent their joy; it did not exclude her.

Orlene took JHVH's hand and they moved through chaos. Again the fascinating pseudoimages manifested, understandably inchoate. This was the raw stuff of the universe, which was being systematically refined and separated. Eventually there would be no more chaos; all would be in order. That almost seemed sad.

Not if World War Three blows everything to smithereens! Vita thought. *Then it'll be right back to the start!*

"Let us hope it does not come to that, Vita," JHVH said. "I confess to some alarm at the prospect of all My work, and that of all other Gods and Incarnations, being so summarily abolished."

"The Angel Gabriel mentioned you," Orlene said cautiously.

"Yes, he once was in My employ," JHVH agreed. "He does good work."

"Is it true that Satan saved the Jews and the Gypsies?"

"It is true, in this framework. But he never speaks of it, because he has an image to maintain."

"I see." Indeed, she was coming to see much that she had never suspected. No wonder JHVH was glad to do Satan a favor! She herself owed Satan far more than she had dreamed.

Did Gaea know? Then no wonder she loved Satan! Her best friend in her pre-Incarnation days had been a Gypsy— who would never have existed without Satan's action.

I hadn't known! Jolie thought. *But it's the kind of thing Parry would do.*

You mean Satan? Vita asked.

I mean the man I love, by whatever name.

319

They arrived back at the chamber JHVH had fashioned in chaos. Gaea and Natasha were within, looking satisfied. No one commented.

"I suspect I do not need to inquire as to the success of your mission," Natasha said.

"It was a failure," Orlene replied bluntly. "God would not respond."

Gaea nodded. "We wanted you to understand why we feel it necessary to replace Him. All through the cosmos, pleas as significant as yours are being denied, because God does not respond. We other Incarnations have done our best to make up the difference, but we are near our limit now. We must have a functioning Deity."

"But who could replace Him?" Orlene asked. "Unless..." She looked at JHVH.

"No, My turn is past," JHVH said. "A Christian will have to be appointed. I am sure a number of candidates have been considered."

We know of one, Jolie thought, remembering Roque.

"But few candidates would be acceptable to all," Natasha said. "It may be that it would be best to allow the default—"

"Forget it!" Gaea snapped, elbowing him.

They all laughed. But beneath the banter was a serious core. When the crisis came, they would be on opposite sides—with the world at stake.

CHAPTER FOURTEEN

Decision

THEY RETURNED TO THE MORTAL REALM AND TO Luna's house. Two more years had passed, and now the crisis of the vote was upon the world.

Roque explained it, after Vita had had her passionate fling with him. "All over the world, wherever those who follow the Christian God hold sway, the vote has been taken: whether to declare the Office vacant, so that the remaining Incarnations can name a new Incarnation of Good. Those who follow other Gods have not participated, but are watching with interest, because it is the warlike Christian forces that are generating the pressures leading toward World War Three. That war would destroy the non-Christians, too, you see. So the fate of the world does hang on this decision. It is widely believed that only the establishment of a new Deity can enable the Incarnations to alleviate the pressing problems that have arisen in the past few centuries."

"Then why is there any fuss about it?" Vita asked, for of

course she was in control of her body now. "Why not just put in a new God and save the world?"

Roque smiled indulgently. "This is reminiscent of the problem of the Constitutional Convention in America. On occasion an effort has been made to convene one, but it has failed because too many are afraid that the Convention would not necessarily limit itself to the issue for which it was convened. Once the genie is out of the bottle—"

"Nobody can put it back! Gotcha! But you know, if I had to choose between the genie and World War Three, I'd sure take my chances with the genie!"

He stroked her hair, a gesture so natural and loving that Jolie felt a wash of love for him herself. "Surely you would, my straight-speaking delight! But there are those who doubt the inevitability of war, and those who hope to make some significant profit from it, and, of course, the forces of Satan are active. An ad hoc coalition has formed in opposition to this move. Its elements are remarkable: many leaders of Christian denominations, and those who support Satan. They prefer the existing order and distrust any change—and I cannot say that their concern is unjustified."

"Hey, which side are you on?" she demanded.

"The side of sanity, my earthly angel. Consider the consequence if a nominee of Satan's were to achieve the Office of the Incarnation of Good. Satan is the Lord of Lies; he might arrange for a seemingly good person to be chosen— and thereafter Satan's will would govern."

"But Satan is fighting the change!"

"So he claims. But how can we know what is in his mind?"

Satan did say something about a deal with Nox, Jolie thought. *Still, he seems to have more to gain by maintaining the status quo.*

Vita relayed that thought, and Roque agreed. "Satan is almost certain to gain if the vote is against the declaration. He will naturally go for the certainty, rather than take a chance. But he surely has a strategy to implement in the event he loses this vote. I merely point out that a case can be made: stick with the known situation, make no change, and let Satan assume greater power. He has no more desire for World War Three than the others do."

"But you don't really believe that!" Vita said. "Do you?"

He smiled. "No. I prefer to take my chances with a new God, arduous though the change may be at first. I am sure the Incarnations will not allow Satan to deceive them about any nominee. Still, it is certain to be a very difficult decision."

"Because Satan won't let any good man in, and the others won't let any bad man in," Vita said. "But they've got to agree sometime!"

"Sometime," he agreed.

Luna returned in the evening, looking worn. "It is indeed going to be close," she said. "The other bodies have come to a tie; tomorrow the Senate takes its vote, according to the terms worked out by arduous compromise. It is very nearly even there too."

"As it was fated to be," Roque said.

"As it was fated to be," she agreed grimly. "All my research and action has succeeded only in preserving parity; my vote will be critical. We have known it would come to this for twenty years, but it is not easier now that it is at hand."

"At least it will be done."

"My part, perhaps. But I will not be able to rest until I know there is an activist Deity in Office."

"Your endeavor has been selfless, for twenty years," Roque said. "There could not have been a better person to see it through."

Luna shrugged that off. "You will stay for supper?"

"Why, I was about to leave—" But he saw how tired she was. "Of course, my old friend. My support is always yours."

"Thank you." Luna lifted a bright garnet from the mantel, set it on the table and tapped it. The stone expanded, becoming irregular. It spread across the table.

It became a banquet for three, the sundry dishes steaming. "Gee," Vita remarked.

"My father was a Magician," Luna explained with a smile. "He left me a number of unusual stones. I use them only for special occasions, as ones of this nature are good for only a single invocation." She glanced at Roque. "If you will serve the wine . . ."

"With pleasure," he said, lifting a bottle from its cold support.

"But I'm underage!" Vita protested. "I'd better put Orlene on!"

"I believe you are now nineteen," Roque said. "In this region, eighteen is sufficient. The legal age of consent brings the rights to drive car or carpet, to vote, to serve in the military or social services, to eschew further schooling, to live apart from family, participate in such liaisons of whatever nature one chooses, and to indulge in the popular vices. There is no need to attempt them all at once, however."

"Oh. Sure. I forgot. But you know, I've only lived fifteen years."

He turned to Luna. "Does the calendar lie, Senator?"

Luna smiled. "We would not wish to accuse it of that. There is already enough deception elsewhere to concern us."

Roque poured Vita a small glass. She took it gingerly. She had had experience with the worst of drugs, Spelled H, but treated this glass as if it were her first flirtation with adult privilege—as perhaps it was.

It was a fine meal. When Vita's manners faltered, Orlene prompted her, so that she behaved like a perfect little lady. She reveled in it. Her appetite was excellent, after the two days in Purgatory.

"And what will the three of you be doing, after the decision?" Luna asked Vita. She seemed satisfied to relax with minor concerns, after her efforts to stave off world disaster.

"Gee—I guess Orlene and Jolie won't want to stay, once it's done," Vita said. "They only came to get me off the H and out of trouble." She clouded up. "But I don't know if I can make it alone."

"You need not be alone," Roque said. "You are now of age to marry."

"Yeah, I guess. But—" She did a double-take. "Hey, did you mean—I mean—" She gazed at him with round eyes.

"I suspect I do. I have been busy, the past four years, but the hope of a union with you sustained me."

"Oh, Roque! Of course I—" Then she sobered. "But you

don't know me alone! I mean, from when I first met you I've had Orlene with me, and Jolie, too, mostly. Without them I'd be just an underage snot. I couldn't stand to turn you off like that!"

"Such is the sin on my soul, the very qualities that you feel are turnoffs are in fact turn-ons, to use your language. I do not think there would be a problem."

"I do! I'd get the shakes, trying to be a lady! It sure doesn't come naturally! But with them—oh, Orlene, Jolie, will you stay?"

Luna took another stone. "This will enable spirits to manifest tangibly within its ambience. Perhaps they should speak for themselves." The stone glowed.

Jolie moved out of the host and manifested in her own form. "Thank you, Luna."

Orlene followed, becoming as she had been after her recovery from the ravages of her death.

"I came to help Orlene," Jolie said. "I think she is now well established in the Afterlife, and no longer needs my support. I will return to Gaea, who needs me in another way." But as she spoke, a sadness came on her. She had enjoyed the company of both ghost and mortal, and felt alive. She had always known it was temporary, but it would be painful to leave.

"And you, Orlene?" Luna asked.

Orlene considered for some time before answering. "I fought to remain a ghost, uncommitted to Heaven, Hell or Purgatory, so that I could try to rescue my baby. Now I know I cannot recover Gaw-Two, and somehow that is not the disaster I expected, for I have seen that he is in competent and perhaps loving hands. The Incarnation of Night evidently wanted him for herself, and I think I must accede to that in my heart as well as in practice. So I am without reason to remain among the mortals. But after what I have seen of Heaven and Hell, I think I do not care for either region. I think I would prefer to remain with Vita—if she truly wishes my company."

"Oh, yes, Orlene, yes!" Vita cried, standing to embrace her. The girl's hands and arms passed through Orlene's image without contact, but the gesture was sincere. "You—I need you so much, your maturity, your perspective, and if I have a baby—"

"Oh," Orlene said, awed by the thought. "You would share your baby with me?"

"Sure! What do I know about babies? I'd drop it for sure, or something."

They all had to smile at that. *No* woman dropped a baby! "But what we propose is not only our business," Orlene said. "Roque—"

"I have a confession to make," Roque said. "I have always liked and respected you, Orlene. As a matter of propriety, such as it was in the circumstance, I never expressed this to you. But what Vita says is true: your relative maturity and experience contributed to her appeal from the outset, and though I would be prepared to deal with her alone, I am also prepared to deal with the two of you. I have no objection to your continued presence."

"But I was being supported by Jolie!" Orlene protested.

"The same is true of her. While I have been delighted by Vita's uncritical enthusiasm, I have been reassured by the presence of maturity. For brief liaisons the enthusiasm is sufficient, but for an extended relationship, the maturity is necessary. The combination represents the complete woman." He shrugged. "But Jolie has another commitment. If you do not—"

"It seems I do not," Orlene said.

"I am pleased that some good has come of this ordeal," Luna said. "I asked Jolie to help with Vita because I was in desperate need of the services of Vita's mother, my researcher Vera. There was also a need for a temporary mortal host for Orlene. I had no idea that that liaison of temporary convenience would prove to be so significant. When Judge Scott got involved, there was another surprise." She smiled. "I had not realized that you were lonely, Roque."

"Neither had I," he confessed. "My career had taken up all of my attention, until Vita's first outburst made me aware that a buried dream might achieve reality."

"So it seems that despite the mischief of the Incarnation

of Night, things have turned out satisfactorily on the personal level."

Roque frowned. "I am not certain that Nox's involvement was mere mischief. I happened to be along on one of her enterprises, and it seemed more like a course of education. She made clear that there has been a long history of magical and scientific interaction, with truth in both the Creationist and Evolutionary perspectives, and of course in the mergence that includes the interaction of the several Incarnations of Immortality. Why she should go to such trouble to impress this on a small selection of mortals and ghosts is a mystery to me. I would like to know her reason."

"I think I was the one she was after," Orlene said. "She took my baby, and put me through extreme unpleasantness when I sought to recover him, but she did tell me the way to succeed. Perhaps she thought I was neglecting my pursuit."

"What do you mean by unpleasantness?" Luna asked.

Orlene grimaced. "She turned me into a man. I—I let myself be overcome by the masculine impulse, and—" She shuddered. "One thing that taught me was the nature of the engine that is within men. It has caused me to be considerably more tolerant. One of the things that impressed me about Roque was his control of that same impulse; I saw that when tamed, it could be a good thing, just as fire when tamed is a most useful tool. But even where it ran wild, at least I understood how it could happen, and that enabled me to have some compassion even for rapists."

"Yeah, she really helped Kane!" Vita said. "He was going to rape us and kill us, and he went to Hell, but she helped him, and I thought she was crazy, but I guess she knew better than I did."

"Why should Nox care about the compassion of a ghost?" Luna asked.

"Maybe so I would better understand my son, when I got him back," Orlene said. "To know why the procedure for saving him was so complicated. Now I do understand, and I see also that she is equipped to handle him as he is, so it makes it possible for me to let him go."

"Which still does not explain why she should review

Evolution with you," Roque said. "Or clarify the nature of the Incarnations, as also occurred when I was present."

"Yes, until that time I had not properly appreciated that God was an Incarnation like the rest," Orlene said. "Now I have much less trouble accepting the notion of His replacement. Otherwise I think I would have had to join the forces of Satan, in their support of the status quo."

"She was the one who sent you on a tour that introduced you to all the major Incarnations including God!" Luna said. "This grows more interesting."

"Well, of course, Jolie was alone," Orlene said.

Luna looked at Jolie. "Satan's bride—and Gaea's handmaid," she said. "And Nox has had an interest in Satan. Could it be that all this was a device to distract Jolie for an extended period?"

Jolie was startled. "But to what point? I have no power—I'm a ghost!"

"Suppose something had happened to you?" Luna asked. "Such as getting lost in chaos, where even Incarnations could not find you?"

"Both Satan and Gaea would have been distracted, of course, in much the manner Vita's mother was distracted by Vita's absence, but—"

"Between them, those two Incarnations hold the balance of immortal power," Roque said. "With God not functioning, that would leave the entire Incarnations framework in peril. Could it be that Nox essayed a devious ploy to wrest power from the Incarnations of Day?"

They gazed at each other, mutually horrified. Suddenly the great mystery of the actions of the Incarnation of Night was being resolved. Orlene had been used as a decoy to distract Jolie, and meanwhile Nox had been active, sometimes openly, sometimes covertly—who knew to what extent? Satan had mentioned a deal he had made with her, to do something Nox's way. To do what, what way?

"I don't think this is over," Jolie said.

"I think the Incarnations of Day had better get their act in order in a hurry," Roque said.

"I think you, Orlene, had better remain with me for the

next few days," Luna said. "And Vita and Roque too. You, Jolie, should return immediately to Gaea, where you will be safe until the current issues are settled."

"Yes." Jolie turned to Orlene. "I must bid you adieu, for the time being. It has been wonderful being with you—and with you, Vita!"

"But come back when it's over!" Vita cried as Jolie faded out.

"When it's over!" Jolie agreed. Then she was racing through the ether, home to her drop of blood on Gaea's wrist.

She arrived safely. It had never before occurred to her that she could be in danger; ghosts were proof against molestation by mortals, and not of much interest to immortals. But Nox had all the powers of the night, and it was evident that she could touch ghosts when she chose.

That business of making Orlene into a man, for example: they had assumed that this was intended to discourage Orlene from her quest for her baby. But suppose she had intended to get Jolie raped? How would that have affected Satan, or Gaea? Had Nox believed that Jolie, shamed, would have vacated the drop of blood that tied her to the mortal realm and gone to Heaven as a spirit, so that Gaea could no longer arrange private liaisons with Satan? Or, later, in the debate between Creationism and Evolution—had this been intended as a wedge between Jolie and Orlene, to break up their association?

It was impossible to know—but certainly a case could be made for it. Nox might have sought first to put Jolie and Orlene together, and then to foment stress between them, whether sexual or intellectual. All this could have been a mere bypath on the Incarnation of Night's larger play for mischief. Now that Nox had made a deal with Satan—using Orlene!—did it mean that she expected to win? What *was* that deal?

Jolie decided that she had better find out. *Gaea!* she called.

Gaea, at the moment attending to an obscure element of weather, heard her, for Jolie was now with her. "Yes, Jolie; I had not realized that you were back. What is it?"

I fear a ploy by Nox.

Gaea paused in her work. "Of what nature?"

It involves Orlene. Nox involved herself with Orlene's activities three times, and the third time may be critical. She made a deal with Satan, to try something his way, then to try it her way. He Tempted Orlene by saying he could get her baby back for her, with Nox's acquiescence, but she declined. That means that Satan will now do it Nox's way. I fear that Orlene is just a tool for some more devious ploy that may involve me. Orlene is close to both of you, as am I; if one or both of us were put into serious trouble, what implications for the coming crisis would this have?

Gaea considered. "Nox is the only female I fear, as far as Satan is concerned. She can take any man she wishes, at any time. But she has no need to bargain; she can do it at her whim. I don't think her interest in him is of that nature."

I agree. He would tell you—and me—if she made him unfaithful to us. But Orlene is your daughter. A threat to her could make him react. Do you think Nox did that?

"We had better find out," Gaea said grimly. "Take the body."

Jolie moved into control and shaped the body to her living image. Then she turned a page and stood in Hell.

Ozymandias looked up. "Satan is busy on Earth at the moment," he said. "Shall I notify Him?"

"Yes."

Ozymandias picked up the telephone on his desk. "Priority call to the Master," he said. Then: "Your wife is here, and I think she is not in quest of love."

Satan appeared beside them in a puff of smoke. "Jolie! What brings you here out of turn?"

"A private concern."

He extended his hand. She took it. Ozymandias' office faded, and Satan's suite appeared.

"What is the nature of your deal with Nox?" Jolie asked.

"Oh, that. I am not free to tell you."

"You are keeping secrets from me—and her whose body I borrow?" Jolie asked angrily.

"I am the Lord of Lies, and Nox is the Mistress of Secrets.

There is a deal between us, and it must not be shared with any other at this time."

Jolie felt Gaea's own anger rising, and knew that storms were forming all over the mortal globe. "I must insist on information. How can you have a loyalty to Nox you do not have to me?" She meant herself and Gaea, as he knew.

Satan frowned. "I have never reneged on a deal. I made one with Nox, and must honor it. Exposure could spoil it. I think you know I would not make a deal that would harm you."

"That depends on your definition of harm!"

He sighed. "The inquisitivity of women! Let me compromise only to this extent: I will answer three peripheral questions about it. With those you must be satisfied, until the deal is complete. That may not be long."

He is a man of honor, Gaea thought. *We had better settle for what he offers.*

"Agreed," Jolie said tightly. "Does your deal involve sex with her?"

"No."

"Does it threaten Orlene, or any other person close to us?"

"No."

Jolie checked with Gaea, then asked the third: "Does it affect the welfare of the mortal realm?"

"Yes."

That was it. Nox *was* interfering with the affairs of the Incarnations, and was now using Satan himself as her agent. Yet without using Nox's power of sex, or threatening anyone close to them, how could she do it?

"Thank you," she said shortly, and turned a page back to Gaea's Treehouse. There she returned the body to the Incarnation.

"I think we wasted a question," Gaea said. "We already knew that no ploy is needed for Nox to take him sexually. But it may have been futile anyway; no one can make Satan give information he doesn't choose to give. At least now we have confirmation of Nox's interest in the present crisis and know that no one close to us is to be hurt. That will have to suffice."

Damn the man! Jolie thought. *I can't stand such a mystery!*

"Well, we shall play it through one stage at a time. If we prevail on the Declaration of Vacancy, and manage to install an active God, his deal with Nox should not matter. We must watch our moves most carefully."

One hour before the scheduled vote, the news flashed across the holo nets: a senator had died abruptly from a stroke. There was no foul play; Gaea would have known about that. His thread had ended legitimately. Unfortunately, he happened to be a staunch supporter of the Declaration. The vote, indicated to be 51 to 49 in favor, was now 50 to 49. If even one senator changed his vote, the case would be lost.

Jolie and Gaea watched the key mortal vote through their window. It was oriented on the Senate, and there had evidently been some commotion, for armed guards were stationed at the periphery. There had been a great deal of controversy in the mortal press, and the partisans of either side ranged from committed to fanatic.

Jolie, in tangible ghost form, sat beside Gaea. "But where is Luna?" she asked, peering at the Senate floor.

"I don't know. She's supposed to be there for the vote."

She was not there. The vote proceeded, headed for a likely tie, 49 to 49, in Luna's absence. Gaea turned a page to check on Luna's house, but it was empty, without sign of disturbance. She oriented on Thanatos—and there he was, riding through the worst traffic jam of the year, cars in gridlock on the road and carpets jammed above. There was no free avenue for progress.

"Satan's ploy!" Gaea muttered with rueful respect. "The oldest trick in the business—and we never prepared for it! To make her arrive too late for the vote."

But Thanatos simply rode his horse, Mortis, over the cars and under the carpets until he came to the carpet with Luna, Vita and Judge Scott. He lifted Luna onto the horse, who then galloped through the carpets and buildings, ghostlike, to the Senate building. As the roll-call vote came to its conclusion, Luna appeared in her place. "Mr. Chairman!" she called.

Thanatos went back for Roque and Vita, but already the jam was unsnarling. It had indeed been magically induced: a nominally harmless, but potentially devastating device. By the time they reached the building, the vote had been concluded. By a margin of one, the mortal vote to declare the Office of the Incarnation of Good vacant had been con-firmed.

"The first hurdle is over!" Jolie exclaimed. "The one for which Luna prepared for twenty years! But I think the second will be worse."

"It will be," Gaea agreed.

There was furor all across the mortal realm as the decision was spread. Churches held special services wherein the vacancy was denounced. Mock Hell was closed in dis-honor of the occasion. Messages of outrage were pouring in. There were riots in all the major western cities. Martial law was declared in several regions. But it was done. The next step was up to the Incarnations.

The mortals would not be privy to the deliberations of the six remaining Incarnations, but their decision would be pub-licized. The mortal identity of the one who became the next God would be announced, but there would be no interviews, for that person would be gone from the mortal scene.

The decision was to be announced one hour from the time of the Senate's declaration. During that hour the normal functions of the Incarnations were suspended. No one was to die, or be born, or marry, or suffer any significant change. All wars were put on hold. The weather assumed a state of perfect blandness. All exercises of great good and evil were suspended. The world waited; there was little else for it to do.

The Incarnations would meet at the Mansion of Time, where for this occasion time, too, was suspended. They could debate the matter for a hundred years, but at the end only a single hour would have passed. Chronos himself declined to participate, because for him it was a conflict of interest. If he acted in any way to affect the decision, it could change the outcome and thus his own past, generating a paradox from which even he was not immune. So he remained apart, and allowed his successor of two years down the line to return for this occasion. His successor was the Chronos they had all known for most of their tenures, who had been replaced, by mortal definition, two years before this event. He was able to come here/now by orienting on the grain of sand from the Hourglass which Orlene had given up. He would participate only this hour, then return to his own time. In this manner Nox's participation had had perhaps the opposite effect intended, because instead of interfering with the vote, it facilitated it. Had Orlene not gone to Chronos for that grain of sand, this substitution of the Incarnation of Time would not have been possible.

"But how will it actually be done?" Jolie asked. "I mean, it's such a big step, deciding on God!"

"The process is simple," Gaea said. "The Incarnations will take turns nominating mortals for the office. Any Incarnation can nominate, and any can speak for the nominee, and any can veto. Only a unanimous decision, all six votes, will be decisive. Now merge with me; you will get to see it directly."

They went. Deck chairs had been set in Chronos' garden, and the six settled into them. They looked like ordinary people, four men and two women, gathering for a social occasion. Gaea went to say hello to Chronos, whom she had not seen in two years. She had known him much longer, but he had known her only for two, because of the point in his tenure from which he had come here. The grain of sand aligned exactly with its point of separation from the Hourglass.

They settled down for business, knowing that it could be grueling. It might be hours before they got down to the necessary business of serious compromise.

"I have a nomination to make for the Office of the Incarnation of Good," Thanatos said. "This mortal is a good man, experienced in law and government. In fact, he is one of the senators who supported the Declaration of Vacancy." He named the man.

The others checked their notes. Satan looked up. "Veto," he said. "This man is too good to suit Me."

They had expected this. It was the main reason they had spent years researching for good men. They might have to nominate hundreds before one was accepted.

Chronos nominated a man he had known in life, a model of fairness and perspective. Satan checked his notes, and vetoed.

Fate nominated a man who not only was good, but who had made a study of the interactions of the threads of fate. Satan vetoed him.

Mars nominated a top martial artist who had in his senior years gone far to define a workable philosophy of peace through force. Satan vetoed.

Gaea nominated Judge Roque Scott.

They looked to Satan, expecting his veto.

"Now, this one is interesting," Satan said. "According to My notes, this man has had an illicit affair with an underage girl put in his charge. There is a fair amount of sin associated with that."

"Since you will not accept any nominee without sin, we are constrained to nominate one with sin we can accept," Gaea said evenly.

"Then let's take a look at him. Let the object of his sinning speak for him, if she cares to."

Fate, in her middle guise of Lachesis, pursed her lips. This was an interesting gambit. Surely Satan would not accept as good a man as Roque. What was he up to? "Rather than bring her here, let us go to her," she said. "Chronos can suspend outside time as readily from the field as from his residence."

"Indeed," Chronos agreed.

They stood, came together, and linked hands. Then Gaea turned a page to Luna's house. Abruptly the six of them were standing in Luna's living room.

The moon moth, Muir, gave a start. He was visible through the eyes of the Incarnation. But he did not protest; he blinked out of sight, summoning Luna.

Luna entered. "All six?" she asked, taken aback.

"We have business with Judge Scott," Gaea said. "He is here at the moment, and this is a suitably private place, so we shall settle the matter here. Please have him and Vita come in."

Luna turned away, and returned a moment later with Roque and Vita. Both were wearing little kitchen aprons; it seemed they had been helping with the chores the old-fashioned way. Luna, with much magic available, had a rather sedate lifestyle.

"It's the Incarnations!" Vita exclaimed, round-eyed.

"Why, hello, all," Roque said. "What can we do for you?"

"I have nominated you to assume the Office of the Incarnation of Good," Gaea said formally. "We are asking Vita to speak on your behalf."

Roque, ordinarily composed, was caught completely off guard. "But that's impossible!" he protested.

"You may not speak for yourself," Gaea said. "Vita, if you will, please."

Vita had known that Roque was a potential nominee, but she seemed as aghast as he by the event. "Oh, I can't!" she protested. "I love him!"

"It has been suggested that his relationship with you is sinful," Gaea said. "This makes it possible for Satan to accept him, as Satan will not accept any candidate without sufficient sin. Compromise is necessary. Speak."

But Vita, realizing the significance of the matter, yet knowing also that she would lose Roque if he were confirmed, could not. Her awe and conflict were too great. "Maybe— Maybe Orlene can do it," she said, her eyes brimming over.

Satan made a negligent gesture. "Very well, so that we can get on with this. Let Orlene make the case."

The figure of Vita straightened. She brought out a handkerchief and wiped her face. Jolie was interested; she had not seen this change as it looked from outside, before. The entire bearing was different.

"I am Orlene," Orlene said. "I can speak from experience of this man's credentials to assume the Office for which he has been nominated. He is a good man, the best of men; indeed, he was recognized as such years ago, when Jolie was

336

allowed to observe him as a prospect for Immortality. But there is no need to dwell on this. The question is whether Satan can accept him, knowing his goodness. I will address his evil."

There was a master stroke, Jolie realized. Satan was the problem; Satan's objection had to be met. Orlene had caught on to this immediately. The woman had grown steadily in competence and poise since her early setbacks, and now might do as great a service for mankind as Luna had. Orlene was, after all, of that fateful third generation, Niobe's grandchild.

She paused, collecting her thoughts. "I went to see God, and God would not respond to me. He was absorbed in His contemplation of His own greatness. He had no faults, no flaws, no sin. He could not relate to these things. But the mortal realm is rife with faults and flaws and sin. I think that only a person who knows something of evil can relate to the mortal human condition well enough to lead mortals to goodness.

"Judge Scott has sinned. He had an affair with a girl he knew to be underage. This was in violation of his principles as an administrator of the law, and a betrayal of his personal trust. He knew it was wrong. But he yielded to his masculine impulse and did it. The girl was willing, even eager, and not inexperienced, but the law and conscience were clear. Judge Scott did wrong. At one time he thought to resign his position, but he did not, and so he retained his status and power because of that guilty secret.

"I cannot see Judge Scott being deaf to the pleas of those who have sinned or are otherwise imperfect. He knows what it is to be tempted, to be weak, to succumb. He knows himself to be imperfect, so will not hasten to dismiss others of this way. I think he can serve the Office better *because* of his sin than he could have without it. God is the Incarnation of Good; that does not mean that He himself must be absolutely good, any more than the Incarnation of Evil must be absolutely evil, or the Incarnation of Death must be dead. It means only that he must strive to forward the cause of good to the best of his ability, always.

"Perhaps Satan does not want an effective Incarnation of Good. But the world faces a crisis that will bring down us all, mortal and immortal alike, unless an effective Deity is named. I can recommend Judge Scott as a choice who will do more good for all of us, even for Satan, than any other likely compromise. I believe he should be confirmed to this Office."

There was a silence. Jolie wanted to applaud; Orlene had done a superlative job! Even Satan must have felt the force of her argument. Was he to reject the logic of the one he had cared for so much that he had sent Jolie herself to watch her?

Then Satan spoke. "I think this woman is in love with this man."

"I think I am," Orlene replied, undismayed. "But I think what I have said of him is correct. My emotion has no relevance. I am a ghost, with no body of my own. The loss is to the mortal who loves him, and will lose him, and for her I suffer, but the need of the world is greater than the joy of any one person. I will return the body to her now, so she can speak for herself, if you feel this is relevant."

"No, wait," Roque said. "It is not relevant. I must with all due respect decline the honor of this nomination."

Gaea stared at him. "You *decline?*"

"I do. It is not that I feel unworthy, though I do. It is not that I am indifferent to the cares of the world, for I am not. It is that I am weak. I cannot bring myself to desert the woman I love. Such sin as I have had I can now ameliorate, and I wish only to complete my mortal tenure with an open realization of what was secret. I cannot leave Vita, and do not wish to leave that component of her present existence which is Orlene, who has defended me so ably. My place is here among the mortals."

Gaea nodded. "Then we must let you go, good man." She extended her hands, ready for the return to Purgatory.

"Let's hold a moment more," Satan said. "You hypocrites are missing the obvious. There is another right here who would do."

Thanatos' skull lifted. "Hypocrites?"

Fate angled her head at Satan. "What are you talking about? There is no other mortal man here."

"Indeed there is not," Satan agreed. "But there is a prospect. You have excluded from consideration half of the mortals! Every one of your nominees has been a man!"

The others stared at him. *He's right!* Jolie thought. *Fate took a man as an Aspect; why can't God be a woman?*

Slowly Gaea turned to face Luna. "Then shall we nominate Luna Kaftan?"

Thanatos jumped.

"No!" Luna exclaimed. "I decline also! My business is here!"

"Then let Me take My turn," Satan said. "I nominate the bastard."

They looked at him, baffled.

"Oh, come now!" Satan said. "We all know that a bastard is born with a significant charge of sin, by current definition. We all know that this is unjustified, for the one person who is blameless in that matter is the bastard himself. Such a person, in the Office of Good, would be sure to update the definitions of such sins, and make My job easier. I am swamped with souls who really don't belong in Hell, because they are good folk who only by definition are evil. I say it is time for a bastard! Do you disagree, Gaea? Would you veto such a nominee?"

Gaea stood frozen, her mouth open. She had caught his meaning and was awed. She did not reply.

Jolie tried to read what Gaea had seen, but could not. All she could discover was that Satan had completely floored her. Whom was he nominating?

"And you, Thanatos!" Satan said, turning on the figure of Death. "You are just as big a hypocrite! You fought Me from the first, to prevent your paramour from being taken—but did you nominate any from your domain? *I nominate the dead!*"

"The dead are not eligible," Thanatos replied, shaken. "Once they reach Heaven, Hell or Purgatory, they are gone. Only those who remain of the mortal realm—"

"Such as the ghosts," Satan said. "The rules do not say the dead are ineligible, only that the choice must be from among those who remain in the mortal realm. Can you deny the ghosts?"

Now it was the fleshless jaw of Thanatos that dropped. The eye sockets stared at Satan.

"And you, Chronos," Satan continued, turning on the Incarnation of Time. "You nominated one of your period of tenure. What of those who pass beyond your tenure? What of an adulteress?" The Incarnation of Time stared, amazed.

He turned to Fate. "And what of one whose thread you have cut?"

And to Mars. "What of one who never fought a war or competed for power?"

All of them stood amazed, understanding Satan's references. But Jolie didn't! About whom was he talking?

Satan's gaze swung back to cover Gaea. "Jolie!" he said. *What?!*

"Speak for My nominee," he said. "You know her best."

Then, in a blaze of revelation, Jolie understood. She found herself in charge of Gaea's body, facing Orlene.

"Indeed I know her," Jolie said. "I came to her when she was a child, a love child, adopted into a worthy family. She always knew she was a bastard, denied by her own parents. She sought in consequence to right the wrong of her origin, and to become the finest mother a woman could be. She resolved never to abandon her own child in the way she herself had been abandoned. Her baby was conceived by a man other than her husband, bringing more evil on her soul, but she loved him perfectly and intended never to give him up. When he died, through no fault of hers, she was unable to survive this denial of her motherhood, and killed herself, thereby bringing yet more evil on her soul. But all of this evil was by definition; none of it related to her true nature, which was as good and kind and compassionate as it was possible for a mortal to be."

Now Orlene, in Vita's body, was staring.

"I came again to her after she died, and helped her pursue her baby," Jolie continued. "Even in death she remained true to her ideal. Despite the sin charged to her soul, she was so completely good in other respects that her balance was positive, and she was bound for Heaven. But she fought to remain among the mortals, as a ghost, so that she could take her baby with her. She put her own soul in peril for the sake of the one she loved. I know no greater love than this: to turn down Heaven itself for the sake of her baby. I know of no person more deserving of Heaven than that one."

Orlene found her voice. "No . . ."

"Yet when offered the chance to save her baby at the expense of others," Jolie continued, "she did not. When she learned that the girl she was helping, Vita, would suffer if the course of time were changed to spare the baby, she refused. She wanted her baby safe and well more than anything else—except at the price of harming another person. Yet even this was not the limit. In Hell she was offered the recovery of her baby without harm to any other, in return for a simple action which might well have had no effect. She felt that action was wrong, so again she gave up her baby. Yet even there in Hell she risked her soul to help one she knew to be evil, because of the unfairness of his punishment."

Orlene looked at the assembled Incarnations. "I could go on, but I think I don't need to. Satan has made a nomination none of you can oppose, for it is in keeping with the deal Satan made long ago with the Angel Gabriel. This woman, Orlene, is the third generation, the grandchild of Niobe, whom Satan had to corrupt within three generations. Satan could not corrupt her, and indeed I think did not wish to, for she is the daughter of the woman he loves, and his step-daughter. Satan made a deal with the Incarnation of Night, who agreed to give up Orlene's baby if Satan could use him to corrupt Orlene. If he failed, Nox would keep the baby, and Satan would nominate her candidate—the one she had been grooming all along for this Office—to be God. Now he has done so, and it is good. She is a bastard, an adulteress, a rapist, and a suicide—surely a creature destined for Hell by current definitions. She is also marvelously competent, compassionate, and good—and the very items she labored so hard to obtain to save her baby can now be used to facilitate her admission as an Incarnation."

Jolie turned on Thanatos. "Can you veto a ghost, whom you know to be good despite the record on her soul, so closely related to the woman you love? Give her the blank soul you promised, that her slate may be clean." She turned to Chronos. "Can you veto the woman you loved in life, who died in the pursuit of your baby? Let your grain of sand facilitate her transfer to that clean soul." And to Fate, in the form of Lachesis: "Your granddaughter? Use your thread to realign her life after death." To Mars: "Your daughter? Give her your seed!"

The Incarnation of War smiled grimly. "I gave it at her conception."

"And I gave My curse, when I damned the hypocrites and nominated her," Satan said.

Then Jolie addressed Gaea, whose body she was using: "And your daughter, whom you could not keep? Give her your tear, to animate her in her new soul!" She discovered that the host was weeping, and not for grief; the tears were streaming down her face.

Jolie turned around, addressing them all. "Satan has nominated the bastard; which among you can deny him his choice?"

None of them spoke. Their astonishment was giving way to understanding—and acceptance. Indeed, they could not deny this one, for either ethical or personal reasons.

Jolie turned again to Orlene. Now, behind her, two glowing figures appeared, one male, one female. The Angel Gabriel and the Incarnation of Night, holding the baby. A glow was playing about Orlene, too, as the gifts of the Incarnations came to her. "And can you decline this most deserved of all nominations, Orlene?" Jolie demanded. "You, most of all, know what is needed in Heaven! You know what has to be done, and you have the training and education and compassion to do it. All that has been wrong in the cosmos, you may now address—with the cooperation of those who cannot deny you. Yea, not even Satan, who loved you from the start, as did I. All of us love you, and you love us, and you cannot deny us or the cosmos. You can do no other than accept. You must be the new Incarnation of Good—for now, and Eternity!"

"And Eternity," Roque echoed.

Orlene struggled to speak but could not. Tears stood on her face. The glow about her intensified. Now Jolie understood what had happened when Orlene helped the soul in Hell: her glow of suitability had been but the hint of her larger potential. As with the musical magic of Orb, which had become the ability to use the phenomenal power of the Llano and equip her to be the Incarnation of Nature, Orlene's ability to see the glow had become the ability to *use* the glow to make things right—and, ultimately, to make the world right, as God. When she had withstood Satan's Temptation, she had sealed her fate, unknowingly, for that had led directly to this nomination. She had not known, but Satan had known, and perhaps Gabriel—and certainly Nox. Her power had begun to manifest. Now she was assuming the aspect of the Office, becoming immortal.

Orlene bowed Her head, nodding in acquiescence. She had given up Her baby, but now She would be Mother to the cosmos itself. She walked slowly across to Satan, who stood watching Her. "All that you hoped for shall be, for the love of Evil, and for the love of Good, for now—and Eternity," She said. She put Her arms around him, drew his head down, and kissed him.

Chronos, who had loved Her as a woman, applauded. Then the others joined in, and Jolie too. *When God Kisses Satan, and the Incarnations applaud,* she remembered. Orlene herself had prompted that answer to the hijackers of the saucer: the Captain's declaration when he would capitulate. Now it had come to pass! It was indeed the beginning of a new era.

She turned to Jolie. "I think you must help Vita, for I have assumed other duties."

Go to her, Jolie, Gaea thought. *You will always be welcome with me, too, but I think you are not yet done with the mortal realm.*

Jolie embraced Orlene. She felt the awesome Presence, in that moment of their contact, not distant and aloof as it had been in the Tenth Heaven, but immediate and generous and loving. Then she transferred to the other

343

host, and Orlene rose out of it. Vita would not be left to fend for herself.

Orlene, a ghost again, but imbued by the substance of the Incarnation of Good, turned to the Incarnation of Night. "I give My baby to you—and My blessing. My Office will always be open to you." Nox nodded, and faded out.

God turned to the Angel Gabriel. "Will you serve and advise the Office, as before?" she asked.

"Always, Lord Goddess."

"Then guide Me now to Heaven, for there is much to do. I shall depend on your advice." She took his hand. "I will be seeing all of you again, soon."

The glow became blinding. Then it was gone, and She with it, and the Angel Gabriel. But Her Presence lingered.

"We have business too," Gaea said. "Luna, make the announcement: we have chosen God, and She is Ghost and Goddess."

Luna nodded, and left the room. In just a moment, it seemed, there was a sound from all around: the sound of the mortals of the world, cheering.

The Incarnations linked hands and disappeared. Jolie was left with Roque. "I will remain with Vita as long as she needs me," she told him. "I hope you can settle for that."

"I can settle for that," he said.

"We thought Nox was plotting something sinister, but instead she plotted to save the cosmos. Why do you think she did that?"

"I suspect she feared the game would end if she did not, and she wanted the game to continue. Even Nox must get bored with just dreams. Also, it may be that she really does like the baby, with his ornery malady. She well understands the undisciplined passions of the male. So, in effect, she traded for Gaw-Two, giving good value in return."

"I suppose so," Jolie agreed, awed now by the audacity of it. "Certainly she made our lives more interesting."

Jolie returned the body to Vita. "Orlene's a Holy Ghost!" the girl said, and giggled. Then she sobered. "Gee, Roque, you gave up being an Incarnation, to be with me!"

"It was selfish of me, I know," he agreed.

"You are still God to me."

"You are still a nymphet to me."

"Yeah? And what are you going to do about it?" But she gave him no time to decide. She leaped into his arms.

Jolie shook her head, in her thoughts. These were interesting times!

Author's Note

DURING THE COURSE OF MY WORK ON THIS novel, we moved. Did it affect my writing? Perhaps you can judge by the change in the text at what point the move occurred. I will tell you later in this Note, so you don't have to write me any letters. Leave the letters to those who are properly outraged by the novel's theme and conclusion.

This is the final novel of this series; I have no plan to write another. Readers have suggested that I follow up with the Lesser Incarnations, but I am disinclined; after God, all else . is anticlimactic. Originally I planned on just five novels, because I thought that readers would not care for the inclusion of Satan and God, but I became satisfied as I read my voluminous fan mail that the readers did indeed want those Incarnations covered. So I extended the series, and thereby hangs a tale.

It happened that at about the point I made the decision to extend the series, I also decided to change publishers. I do not change wives or publishers lightly, but the latter is more

likely than the former. I was having serious editorial problems, and felt that the integrity of my work could be
guaranteed only by making the change. When push came to
shove, that counted more than either money or convenience.

The change of publishers was complicated. Options had
to be voided and new understandings worked out. My
literary agent—the man who handled my American sales—
labored heroically to work things out with the old and new
publishers. By the time it was done, some 45 of my novels
had been affected to some degree, and more than half a
million dollars was allocated. My first 17 fantasy novels
remained with Del Rey, while the new Adept trilogy went to
Putnam/Ace and the final two novels of the Incarnations
series to Morrow/Avon. A new Xanth trilogy also went to
Avon. I had resolved, you see, to split my fantasy between
publishers, so as not to have too many eggs in one basket.

This was an amicable change, complicated by the shock of
the death of Judy-Lynn del Rey. Del Rey was the publisher
who put me on the best-seller lists and made me one of the
most successful writers of the genre. I did not want to leave,
and they did not want me to leave; it was just one of those
things. I still receive enormous royalties from my titles with
them, and great piles of fan mail, and expect to do new
business with them in the future. Certainly we wish each
other no evil.

But in the complicated process of transition, there was a
minor glitch. Del Rey did not get the word about my two new
Incarnations novels, and on the cover of the hardcover
edition of *Being a Green Mother,* printed, "A Brilliant Conclusion to an Extraordinary Series." I notified them of the error
when I saw the cover proofs, but it was evidently too late;
those words remained.

Several readers wrote in to inquire about that, when the
hardcover edition was published, because I had told them
that there were more Incarnations coming. I had to explain
about the glitch, with some irritation. One reader hit the
ceiling. He decided to make a public campaign against the
publisher because of the lie. I demurred, explaining that
though the matter annoyed me, I could not claim it was

malice; it was a foul-up, of the kind that occurs not infrequently in Parnassus. Certainly I would not allow my name to be used in an attack on this publisher, who had treated me very well over the years. I hoped to get it straightened out privately. This reader then attacked *me,* claiming that I had to be lying, and demanding, in abusive language, a clarification of my lie.

Well, now. Few folk have the temerity to address the Ogre in such fashion, and those who do, generally regret it. I have too much mail as it is, and it is enough of a chore to keep up with the positive letters without having to take on such negative missives too. My response to him began: "Listen, Blivet-Brain, I have little patience with fools or knaves." Thereafter it became less polite. For those who are not up on the vernacular of a prior generation, I should explain that a blivet is a five-pound container with ten pounds of excrement. I understand it is a useful weapon when arguments get ugly.

So now you know why I changed publishers, and some of the consequences thereof. You may consider this an update on my autobiography, *Bio of an Ogre,* which was published in hardcover in Mayhem (naturally!) while I was writing this novel. I admit to running second to Harlan Ellison when it comes to perpetual trouble, but believe me, I am trying to close the gap. An ogre's reach should exceed his grasp, else what's Hell for?

But I was trying to tell you about my move. In 1977 we moved to the forest, preferring it to the city. We still prefer it, but three things have changed. First, our financial resources have improved, as my writing income progressed from five figures to six figures, thanks to the support of readers like you. About ten percent of each book of mine you buy comes eventually to me in royalties, and that adds up when sales are good. So we can now afford a six-figure house instead of a five-figure house. Second, our daughters grew up. Penny is now in college, and Cheryl, having made the highest SAT score in the history of her school, is about to go to college too. It is an irony that after I struggled to reach a level of income that would enable us to afford college for our daughters, Cheryl is getting Merit Scholarships that make it relatively cheap. My fault, as I should have seen it coming. I married the smartest woman I could catch, because I wanted smart children. I didn't want my children following my example and taking three years to get out of first grade. But do you know what college kids do? They came back home for surprise visits, with six of their classmates in tow. Three of each sex. They think it is like a convention, where they can pile up eight deep in one room, sharing two and a half sleeping bags and a submarine sandwich. I won't try to explain why this disturbs parents, who are, of course, hopelessly out of touch with current mores. I'll just say that we now need more room than we did a decade ago. Third, we were already so crowded that we had to thread mazes to get from one part of a room to another. I am a writer, you know; I have books, and they keep multiplying, and no, I can't part with a single solitary one without suffering a seizure of one or two valves of the heart. When folk visit, we have to move books out of chairs so they can sit down. Actually, piles of books can make decent temporary chairs, but visitors don't seem to understand very well about this, particularly when the piles fall over.

So we moved, as I said. It was my wife's project; she took about six months without much sleep drawing up the house plans, and our friendly neighborhood building contractor, a man named Lou Dolbow, undertook the construction.

According to the contract, the house was to be complete in Jamboree 1988, but I hoped that it would move along well so that we would be able to move before then: say OctOgre. The Ogre hates to travel, but when he does, that's the month. That would save me from having to saw and haul and split wood for the winter's heat. I like working with wood, and since we burn only trees that have died and fallen naturally, nothing suffers. It is good exercise, and our wood stove not only heats our house, it heats our water, too, so that our bills are small. I have not counted the hours I spend per winter chopping wood, but I think it would be somewhere over 20. Florida is warm, and our house is insulated, so our needs are relatively small, but still it takes a cord or so. The problem with this is that I now earn much more than it would cost me to pay for an automatic heating system; my time spent on free wood is no bargain. So the prospect of recovering those 20+ hours for my paying work appealed.

Well, the house wasn't finished early. We had to go and struggle with the cutting up of a huge fallen tree whose main trunk arched over the forest floor: a real challenge. Yes, I succeeded in binding the saw several times, but finally got the job done, and we loaded wood into our car and hauled it to the house. Why didn't I use the wheelbarrow? Because the tree was about 3/16 of a mile distant—naturally, it had fallen on our farthest piece of property—and downhill from our house. A couple of wheelbarrow loads convinced me that there had to be a better way. So we had wood for the winter, and the time was lost; my writing slowed accordingly.

The house was not complete in Jamboree. When would it be done? In FeBlueberry, Lou assured us. But it wasn't done then either. The completion date receded like the horizon, always about two weeks distant. Marsh, Apull, Mayhem, while I worked on this novel, expecting to break off momentarily for the move and never quite doing so. What was the problem? Well, a contractor does not do it all himself; he subcontracts the various parts of the job, and coordinates the whole. Again and again one crew or another would be scheduled for a job, and wouldn't show—and so other crews were delayed, because they could not do their jobs until the first was done. Or something would be done wrong, so that corrections entailed more delay. The choice seemed to be between quality and speed, and Lou opted for quality. There seems to be a failure in the work ethic; many people just do not seem to be much interested in working, or in doing their jobs promptly and correctly. I wonder to what extent this represents the effects of the so-called drug culture. The availability of increasingly potent drugs like cocaine (but not Spelled H, yet) has cost me more than one associate and made direct and indirect mischief of more than incidental nature. I stay clear of such things, avoiding even nicotine and caffeine; I resist taking aspirin or the equivalent unless I have a rare bad headache. I want no baffle between me and

reality, so I am usually in possession of my natural faculties.
I suspect that many others are not.

You know, I am not the greatest writer in the world, but
I am one of the most successful. Perhaps this offers a hint
why: I always do my job, promptly and well. I am amazed at
the number of others who don't. I have pride in my work,
which will cause me to leave a good publisher, at great
inconvenience, rather than allow a novel to be unduly
compromised. I will speak out in protest when I see wrong
done. Not only does this attitude seem to be atypical, it has
brought me the reputation of a troublemaker—in fact, of an
Ogre. As I watched my new house being built, I couldn't help
wishing that there were more ogres on the crews. I'll go into
more positive detail about the house further along, but first
let me change subjects.

There is another huge tax on my working time: the mail.
It takes me about half an hour to answer the average letter,
so the hours lost can be calculated by dividing the number of
letters by two. I decided to get a secretary, so that I could still
answer personally but not lose as much time. But we had no
room for such a person. Our new house, twice the size of our
old one, would have room; I could put her in a corner with
my backup computer system and let her do the letters. (I say
her, but a male secretary would do as well, or a very smart
robot.) I figured on hiring maybe a retired teacher, so that I
wouldn't have to teach her basic English, and educating her
in the type of response I normally did, so that I wouldn't
have to dictate each letter verbatim. I receive quite a number
of "Dear Mr. Anthony, I am eleven years old and this is my
first fan letter. Here are ten puns for Xanth. When is the
next Xanth novel coming out, and what's it about?" missives,
and a fairly standard answer would do for these, with
whatever individual touches were appropriate. So, once we
moved, I could look for such a secretary.

And then we kept not moving. Had we moved in Oct-
Ogre, and set up secretarily then—well, I answered 99 letters
that month, which was about standard. If a secretary cut my
average answering time in half, that would be about 25 hours
saved. Right—one winter's worth of wood! In NoRemember

the pace increased, to 132 letters. This was because I had several novels published in the fall season, and the mail follows the sales figures. Readers keep asking why I don't have my address published in my novels, so that more folk could write to me. I hope I don't need to answer that. In DisMember there were 166 letters, bringing the total for the year to 1393. Understand, that's just the ones I answered; I don't answer them all, though I do the best I can. But when I could move in Jamboree . . .

By this time Fate had discovered that I had no ready way to handle letters, because I couldn't get a secretary because I couldn't move. I was tied down. So the Jamboree total was 221, a record. That meant that my approximate 180-hour working month (actually, I'm working all the time, but I don't count meals, chores, reading [unless it is direct research], exercise, family demands and such, so it nets 40 to 45 hours a week) lost about 110 hours to the mail. Between that and wood chopping, guess how fast my paying work was moving then! I had to do something. I had already resolved to avoid conventions and similar distractions for the year, to recover time, but it was draining away as fast as I could save it.

FeBlueberry is a short month. I answered only 163 letters. That meant that just over half my working time was available for my writing. But somehow I wasn't satisfied; I wanted more. I was working on Xanth #12, *Man from Mundania,* and it was moving well yet taking an extra month because I put so little time in on it. Xanth is relatively easy and fun to do. What would happen when I came to Incarnations #7, a more significant challenge? *When the #$%&*!! would that house get finished?*

Then in mid-Marsh we saw an article about a local lady who was setting up a business called "My Private Secretary." She would supply secretarial skills for small businesses of the area for $15 an hour. Since she had her own office and was self-employed, no special paperwork was needed. So I called her, and next day my wife and I went to see her. We decided to try it. I scribbled notes for my answers on the backs of the envelopes, and she typed them up into coherent letters. Then I reviewed the letters, signed them, and mailed them.

It worked. She handled most of my fan mail, while I continued to handle my business mail and those fan letters requiring special handling—suicidal teenagers, for example. I timed some batches, and concluded that it was now taking me just under fifteen minutes per secretarial letter, average. Half my letter time was being saved! As a result, this novel, started at the same time as the secretary, moved better than the last one had, despite being more difficult. I was devoting more time to it. It was a wonderful feeling, putting about three quarters of my working time into my novel instead of only half my time. And we hadn't even moved yet! The secretary was not conversant with my work and had to check with her husband, who knew the genre. He assured her that I was a legitimate writer. I gave her a box of my books, and paid her the going rate per hour for reading them, because she has a better idea how to answer a letter when she knows what the fan is talking about. Thus when I scribble "Not end; Evil out 11–88," she can type "No, *Being a Green Mother* is not the conclusion of the series, despite what it says on the cover. The next one, *For Love of Evil*, concerning Satan, will be published in hardcover in NoRemember 1988. I hope you like it as much as you did the prior novels in the series." Sometimes she adds: "My secretary likes this series best."

Still, a lot of my time still goes to the mail. About half of it is new letters, and the rest is repeat letters. Some fans just keep writing back. I try to answer all the first-timers, but don't feel obliged to keep up perpetually with the repeaters. But it isn't necessarily easy to cut off a correspondence. Let me make an example of an extreme case: this was a boy who had written to me a dozen times, and had a dozen responses, and asked how often it was all right to keep writing. I explained gently that it was difficult for me to keep up, so less was better. Hurt, he signed off with one last letter. Then he continued to write, about once a month. Finally, when the total was about 18 letters, which had used up more than a thousand dollars worth of my writing time, I got more pointed. I told him that I hoped he would understand when I didn't answer his next.

In due course he responded with his "last and final"

letter. In it he informed me that he had arranged to go to Florida, where he had traced down my address and taken one drive past my house. He expressed extreme disappointment. "You had made yourself seem so important and so wonderful. . . . such a humanitarian, such a busy man, with no time to do everything you want to . . . but I saw the dead ugly trees in your yard, and the waist-high weeds, and the dismal house you call home. . . . I really don't mind if you write about this letter in your future author's notes. Maybe the others will know the real Piers Anthony. It is my hope that they do." He added that he took pictures to show to his friends, who couldn't believe it, and that I should remember that it was my fans who put food on my table and let me get my books even PUBLISHED. He thanked me for his rude but wonderful awakening; at last his eyes were open to the reality behind the facade. He signed his name with the subtitle "ex-Anthony fan."

As I said, this was an extreme case, but it illustrates the type. None of this revelation came to him until I cut him off after he refused to take a hint. Most others have taken the hint, but are nevertheless hurt, and I do get some hate mail. It is apparent that there is no way short of this to protect my time from those who are determined to take it. This letter arrived in FeBlueberry, but isn't one of the 163 because I didn't answer it. I have left a small trail of disillusioned ex-Anthony fans, and I don't like doing it, but the alternative is to allow my working time to become monopolized by just such folk. One of my reasons for getting a secretary was to make my answers less personal, so that those who craved a large collection of personal Anthony notes would be dissuaded without coming to emotional violence. In this sense, ironically, I can sympathize with God: how do I get on with my business when those who idolize me insist on my complete attention? How could God function, with billions of personal demands being made on Him?

But, having taken this ex-fan up on his challenge to publish his exposé, let me address the points he raises. I make no money from fans like him; I answer them at a financial loss, and would very soon be broke if every one of my readers were like this. It is my business to write novels; I answer correspondence only as a courtesy, sometimes receiving little in return. The ones who put food on my table are the great majority who buy, read, and enjoy my novels, and who do not seek to correspond with me. I also do not attempt to make myself out as "important and wonderful"; in fact these same Author's Notes strike reviewers as "boring and offensive." I simply display my thoughts and activities, positive and negative, for the period during which I write one of these novels. I would call them feisty rather than either wonderful or offensive, but each reader is free to interpret as he chooses. Most seem to consider the Notes to be personal letters to my readers, and that seems close enough.

This fan thought he could make a judgment on my competence as a writer and my character—by driving by my house. This illustrates the problem with critics in general, who make what amount to similar judgments. Nevertheless, there are indications. A person's residence can tell a lot about him, if the one who looks at it has the wit to understand. You see, this fan did give an accurate description of my house. The roof is dull metal, the siding weathered, the yard overgrown, and there are half-a-dozen dead trees standing in it. (Make that four; two blew down later.) There is little evidence that any of it has been touched in years. But this is not neglect. The roof is terne-coated stainless steel, which a builder will tell you is the finest it is possible to make; it will last without repair just a shade short of eternity. The siding is red cedar shakes which are supposed to weather to their own shade, never needing paint. They look old after a year in the sun, but they are great no-maintenance protection. The "weeds" are dog fennel, this region's natural ground cover. We don't mow them down because they are harmless— and because it is our philosophy to do as little damage to the natural forest and field as possible. Others move to the country and promptly extinguish the natural flora and fauna, rendering their lots into manicured suburbia. We left our forest as we found it, deliberately. No mower has touched our yard, other than horses; no tree has been cut unless it threatened the house. We sought not to drive out the creatures of the forest, but to share with them. We love to see the big burrowing box turtles locally called "gophers" and the occasional armadillo. There are mounds of dirt left by the tunneling pocket gopher—the "vole" of Xanth—and by the dung beetles, who sanitize the pasture by burying clods of dung. Wrens and squirrels nest in our eves, to our delight; we have come to know families of them. Wild rabbits play hide and seek with our dogs. (Yes, on occasion a dog does catch a bunny. We hate that, and try to warn the bunnies before letting the dogs out.) Those "dead ugly trees" are what is called standing deadwood, and it, too, contributes to the way of the forest. Woodpeckers peck in it, and nest in it. We have a family of the rare, spectacular, crow-sized Pileated woodpeckers which call on our deadwood; we can watch them right from the house. The national forest service once took out deadwood, but discovered that this despoiled the habitat for woodpeckers, and now lets it stand. Nature does know best. Only after it falls by itself do I saw it up for the stove.

So this disaffected fan did see my house—but how little he understood it or me! It does represent the real Piers Anthony, whose values are not for appearances, and I shall be glad if my readers know it. We did, as I said, move—but our philosophy is unchanged, and the new house is even deeper in the forest than the old. I don't give much of a curse about the opinion of strangers, so my house may look as dull as I do—but it is sound. The same goes for my philosophy. I do what I feel is right, and if a fan can idolize me yet have no idea of my values, then I think the fault is not where he supposes. I really do care about my work, and would much prefer to stay with it than to put effort into a conventional yard or into attendance at conventions.

But for all that, we have made some compromises with the new house. It does have a grassy yard, which we expect our horses to mow. But the property also has a fox, owl, rabbits, fireflies, dragonflies, and a big box turtle who insists on sharing the dog's yard. We tried to fence that turtle out, fearing what the dogs might do to it, but it plowed back in and the dogs couldn't hurt it. Great; I love having it. There are blue, black and huckle berries aplenty, and passion fruit with its lovely purple flowers. Also some big rat snakes and rattlers, which we leave alone. Our mailbox is half a mile away; we have a drive lined with pines, laurel oaks, hickory and magnolia trees, because we gave orders to curve it around them instead of 'dozing them out. We are deep in our private jungle, and fifty feet out from the house nature is undisturbed. Ye who would judge me by my residence, judge me by that.

I read an article in *Boardroom Reports,* a periodical devoted to business management. It was titled, "Beware the Mind Blowers," and described the way some others react to highly successful people. Envy verging on malevolence, it suggests, is common, and there is a desire to diminish the successful one. "Many professional critics, for instance, are in this category," it says. That seems to explain a lot, and not just about reviewers. The article warns that flatterers, too, are dangerous. I agree. Some who have greeted me with fulsome praise have not understood why it turned me off. I don't want flattery or condemnation, I want the truth, whatever it may be. Readers who call errors in my novels to my attention receive my thanks, and sometimes mentions in Author's Notes.

Meanwhile, as I wrote this novel, events continued. Robert A. Heinlein, perhaps the leading figure in our genre, died. A reader, pained by this news as I was, suggested that I mention this here, and I agreed. Heinlein was a giant, and with him passes an age. Clifford Simak, less well-known but the author of *City,* one of my favorite genre novels, also died. And, in the adjacent Western genre, Louis L'Amour. It hurts to see such figures pass, yet time is inexorable.

Then I received a query from another reader, who noted that some of my recent novels didn't have Author's Notes: had I died? she inquired worriedly. I tried to reassure her; I remain reasonably healthy for my age.

Ah, yes: health. A study was published which showed that vitamin C does halt a cold. For decades the medical profession has disparaged this notion, claiming that there is no way to stop a cold, when actually this is one of several. I am glad to see that the experts are finally trying it, instead of condemning it untried. Another way to stop a cold is heat. I wonder whether this attitude of condemning things untried is like prayer: you have to have faith. The doctors had faith in what wouldn't work, so never had to try it. But those of us with open minds suffer fewer colds.

Meanwhile, how is my career doing? Two lady editors came to see me at this time about a seven-figure offer—which I did not feel free to accept, because it threatened to commit me too far ahead. It's like signing a contract with Satan: once you take the money, you had better be prepared to deliver. I wasn't quite sure I was ready. I want to get some less commercial projects done before returning to the solidly paying ones. But never fear; I do not sneer at commercial writing. I just don't want to be totally governed by it.

At this time my Xanth Pin-Up Calendar was also progressing: luscious half-ladies of many kinds, painted by a number of top genre artists. But we discovered that the publishers had already locked in their calendars for 1989; we had to postpone ours until the calendar year 1990. Sigh.

I received two letters that put me into a dilemma: both were requests that I agree to complete the novels of hopeful writers who had died. One had been killed at the age of sixteen in an auto accident; the other had been murdered at age twenty-two. Now, I hate untimely death, and hate to have the hopes of aspiring writers cut off. But death is no guarantee that the manuscripts are good ones. So I demurred, but did look at one—and it will be the next novel I do, as a collaboration with a dead teenager: *Through the Ice*.

Let's see: I promised to get into our new house. Those who hate such detail should now tune out; it's a long story. We got books of designs and pored over them, getting notions for this feature and that. One that appealed was based on George Washington's house, with curving wings for a garage on one side and a guest house on the other. Well, now—there was my separate study, in that two-story wing, with a covered walkway to the main house. We liked the symmetry of it, but my wife had other notions for the main house. So we merged notions, and pulled in the wings, and finally perfected a two-story house with garage and storage room on one side and my study complex on the other, and everything she wanted in the center. At last count it was somewhere over 4000 square feet.

Actually, after she designed it we saw an article in *Popular Science* about dome houses made of special insulated cement blocks. The notion intrigued us, and we worked out a dome-house complex that did all the same things: a main dome for the house, an attached study dome, a garage dome, a daughters-bedroom dome, a pool dome, I forget what. But when we talked to the contractor, he said, "What about resale value?" We did a double-take and pulled out the old plans. A house is not just a place to live, it's an investment. Ours, to be built on a tree farm, would represent a nice estate that should hold its value for our grandchildren, when.

I think the contractor, Lou Dolbow, enjoyed the project. We took him in our four-wheel drive Toyota deep into the wilderness and said, "Build it here." We put colored bands around trees to mark where the access road should be. He had to arrange to build a half-mile road to that spot, and then build the house, deep in the jungle adjacent to the young slash pines. "Don't hurt the rattlesnakes," I warned. The power company wanted to cut a 25-foot-wide swath through the center of the tree farm; Lou hassled until they agreed to bury the line beside the new road. The bulldozer man got lost, and I showed him the route. Right in front of him was a little magnolia. "Curve the road around that tree," I said. Even so, some of its roots got chopped; we're nursing that tree along, and I think it will survive. We have a beautiful lane, to be called Ogre Drive, because we care about what nature offers. No, don't write to me begging for the address; this property is intended to be private. There will be a thorough description of it in my mainstream novel *Firefly*, but it won't be where the novel says it is.

Alcoa Aluminum is expanding. It now makes roofing and siding. We used both, and it is our understanding that we used more Alcoa than they sold for any other project in Florida up to this time. They sent a party to photograph it for their records. The roof is aluminum made to resemble weathered wood shakes, and the siding is vinyl made to resemble aluminum. Inside we have teak parquet flooring that we bought over a decade ago for our present house, and couldn't install because of the crowding when our contractor never finished the house. We sued him and put him out of business, and used the bare concrete slab for the floor. Lou did improvements on that house, before building the new one from scratch. And so on—I won't bore you further with details. Take my word that it is a nice house, in a nice setting, though at this writing books and boxes are piled on the floor, as we continue to ferry our things across.

Yes, of course the dogs and horses went with us. We had a little barn built, just like the one on the old property, so the horses would feel at home. Penny's mare Blue is thirty years old, gray-headed but still spry, and her companion Snowflake is twenty. We had to have somewhere over a mile of fencing done for their pasture.

I mentioned computers. This novel was done using my Dec Rainbow computer system, with MS-DOS and her garden directories, and FinalWord. No, I don't promise to stay with either indefinitely; computer technology is moving too rapidly. I'm looking toward a so-called 386 machine. You will no doubt learn all about it in some future Note in some future series. Having been satisfied for thirty years with penciled drafts and manual typewriters, I went reluctantly to the computer, but now I am hopelessly spoiled by it and constantly want more.

One evening a car stopped by our mailbox, at the old address. Oh, no, surely more fans! I went out, and my fear was confirmed: they were college students who had made it a game to locate me. I really don't appreciate such games; I was trying to eat supper at the time, and there was a dull drizzle outside. But then they gave me a plaque commemorating the Incarnations series. It was beautiful. There's a skull for Death, an hourglass for Time, a web and spider for Fate, a red sword for War, and a circling rose vine for Nature, all made of a claylike plastic that didn't exist in my day. It was made by Elisa Velásquez, and will hang on the wall of my new study. Another reader, J. P. Morris, made

PIERS ANTHONY

and sent a string-art portrait of Neysa Unicorn, another beautiful item. I really don't seek gifts from my readers, and don't wish to encourage this sort of thing, but have to admit I like these ones very well.

At this time I was reading Samuel (Chip) Delany's autobiography, *The Motion of Light in Water.* His autobio and mine were published two months apart, so the two invite comparison. I knew Chip briefly, and liked some of his work. He is an award-winning science fiction writer. On the surface the two of us are quite different. He is a black, dyslexic, homosexual literary writer, while I am a white, heterosexual commercial writer. But these differences may be superficial. Underneath there are parallels. Both of us differ from others to more than average degree. I may have been dyslexic myself; in my day there were no learning-disabled children, only stupid or perverse ones, so I had no excuse for struggling to get through first grade. But I made sure that my dyslexic daughter Penny did not have to endure what I did. It may be said that when I finally got fed up with taking it, I started dishing it out, and the evidences of that militancy are all around me and in this Note. Chip seems to have been nicer, and so he may have suffered more and had a less dramatic career. I wonder whether he read my book with as much interest as I read his?

I finished that book, and started on the next: *Chaos,* by James Gleick. We had bought a copy through the Book-of-the-Month Club, but I had not yet looked at it. Then a fan, the artist Kurt Cagle, sent me a copy, and I looked at it and saw the illustrations of the Mandelbrot Set. I had seen such pictures before, but this time they registered, because I had a need of a simple way to structure a complex new universe for a new series of novels. The Set offered such a way. Thus the footing of my future work occurred in the late stages of my present work. The Mandelbrot Set is too complicated a matter to get into here, but those who are interested in art and mathematics should find it fascinating. It held me for hours at a time, when I had a novel to finish.

In Incarnations #4 I discussed "Ligeia," the suicidal teenage girl I tried to help. Mail continues to come in about that, and there have been several other Ligeias. I am pondering whether to write a book on them, titled *Ligeia: The Early Part of Dying*. I am no expert on suicide, but I find myself drawn into their lives, and I must either respond or refuse to respond. They aren't just girls, and not limited to teenage, and suicide is not the only symptom of depression. Once a runaway came to my house; I wanted to be fair with him, but as a parent myself I insisted that he let his mother know where he was. The relief in her voice was almost tangible when I called her, and he did decide to return home. Another phoned me from the hospital where she had landed after they found her in time, before the pills had full effect; I was able to give her news that improved her outlook. But it isn't always positive, and it's generally chancy. When I hear from one, and then, without explanation, I don't hear, I get nervous. Once a reader told me how a relative had recommended *On a Pale Horse* to him as the finest novel— and then killed himself.

I think in most cases the depression is physiological in origin. That is, something in the body causes it. For example, there is SAD: Seasonal Affective Disorder. People suffer from it in the darker winter months, and recover in the brighter summer months. It can sometimes be treated by bright lights. There may also be hormonal imbalance. I feel that a competent physical exam should be the first step in checking out a Ligeia. A person should not be left to suffer in darkness, when relief might be as simple as a bright light. I can't forget how I myself was considered mentally ill because of my depression and fatigue—until a blood test showed that I am diabetic. It *isn't* necessarily all in the mind. In fact, I suspect that it seldom is. But again this reminder: I am no expert, only a fantasy writer who got involved more or less coincidentally, when the first Ligeia wrote me.

Let me talk to the other Ligeias out there directly: if you are suffering, and no one seems to care, and you don't know where to turn or whom to trust, and you really would rather be dead but you're afraid to kill yourself, and you cannot talk to your parents—well, I tried to find out what number you could call for help. If your local phone book is like mine, there won't be anything under SUICIDE. But check the index at the beginning and see if it lists "Human Services Guide." Turn to that part, and look for "Counseling." Under that section look for "Suicide Prevention." Call that number. They should help you. If you are worried about getting in trouble, don't give your name, just your problem.

If you are abused, or need some advice about your situation—it can be hard to tell what constitutes abuse, sometimes—a similar approach should get you a number: look under "Abuse" in the Counseling section. If you are a runaway, call the National Runaway Switchboard: 1–800–621–4000 (but it was always busy when I tried) or the Covenant House hotline, 1–800–999–9999, which can also handle abuse or suicide. They will keep your confidence and try to put you in touch with someone local who can help you.

The thing to remember is that, whatever your problem, you aren't the only one with it, by a long shot. There is help and comfort for you, if you can reach it. It seems worth a try. This series is ending, but the organizations remain, and it may be that you won't have to depend on God alone for help.

I pondered for months whether to end these Notes with the conclusion of this series, and finally asked an editor, who I think also sweated the matter somewhat. We concluded that there will be Notes in a different series, though perhaps not as autobiographical as the present ones. So this may be the last of the intensely personal, militant essays, at least for a while. If you are a Notes freak, though, keep your eyes open, and sometime, somewhere, when you least expect it, there'll be another.

Which brings me to the matter of the effect of my move on my writing. Well, the delays continued so long that I completed the novel and this Note in first draft before moving. Only the editing—that is, going over it to correct spelling and syntax, add in omitted bits, and set the format for printing out the copy for the publisher—took place after the move. My spot research for Ligeia helplines was the last thing I did; that was at the new house. Now you know.

We have had a total of three hard-disk crashes since computerizing, and each has been a colossal headache, costing me everything I had saved for the prior year or so. Of course, I had my novels backed up on floppy disks, but still it was a pain. The last one wiped out three months of daily records I hadn't gotten around to printing out. I agonized, and decided to drop the records. I had kept them for 21 years, recording each day's production and events, and that should be enough for posterity to examine. Now I just type my ongoing thoughts in a separate file as I go along, and print and erase that file each day. So the computer has changed my life in a way, whether for good or ill I can't say. I worked out a little song about it. Do you remember the popular song "Winchester Cathedral"? Well, the hard disk is called a Winchester. So my variant goes: "Winchester Computer,/ you're breaking down,/ You stood and you watched as/ My data left town." That's from the heart.

In each of these Incarnations novels, I have noted the manner that the subject seems to affect my life. Death, Time, Fate, War, Nature, Evil—did it continue for Good? It seemed it hadn't, for though many interesting things happened, including our move to the new house, none of it seemed supernatural. It is true that our move represents achievement of a residence that is larger and nicer and more private than what we have known before, and probably this is our final mortal home, so there is a certain symmetry in its occurrence at the time I wrap up this series, but that's about the extent of it. So it seemed that this time the magic did not operate, except perhaps in little ways. For example, two Jehovah's Witnesses appeared at our door in this period, seeking to alert me to the approaching termination of the world we know. I try to address all such visitors politely, though the chances of my being converted to such belief are minimal. They left their book, *Life—How Did It Get Here? By Evolution or by Creation?* and promised to return in two weeks to discuss the matter further. I looked at the book, but though it makes superficial sense, I feel that its points have been effectively answered by Richard Dawkins' *The Blind Watchmaker*. In short, for me, Evolution has carried the day. I looked forward to discussing this, but the Jehovah's Witnesses did not return, and then we moved. So I put the discussion in

Chapter 9, using Nox's vision to clarify the base of the Incarnations series. Actually, I think the Bible speaks more realistically than many of its apologists think, and makes more real-world sense than they credit. But it speaks in language the common man of two millennia ago understood: "day" rather than "eon." Whereupon modern man misunderstood it.

I completed the first draft of Novel and Note on my daughter Cheryl's eighteenth birthday in late Mayhem. (My daughter Penny's birthday is in OctOgre, of course. I believe I mentioned that the Ogre does things in such months, with maybe a bit of help from my wife, who is another Mayhem.) All that remained was the editing, which I did after we moved—on my wife's birthday. My birthday gift to Cheryl was enough of my time to get her through her driving license. Penny was pushing to drive at fifteen, but Cheryl wasn't as eager, so still wasn't licensed. She also had a problem with coordination of the clutch and gearshift. We pondered, and decided that it would be best to teach her with automatic shift. We also wanted four-wheel drive, because our tree farm has some back roads and sugar sand that can be treacherous. We had each feature, but not in the right cars. We wound up trading in both car and van, to get auto-shift in the first and 4W drive in the second. Two trade-ins and about $25,000 took care of it. Ouch! But at this writing, Cheryl is learning. Oh yes, my time is precious—but so is my daughter.

It happened that the school year was wrapping up, and the Citrus High School Senior Awards Ceremony was held on Cheryl's birthday. Now Cheryl, despite her record SAT score, was not the top student in her class, or the second; in fact she wasn't in the top five. Grades can be a chancy thing, depending on a student's luck in the draw of classes and teachers, absence owing to illness, conformity to the system's expectations, and the vagaries of the grading curve. The most intelligent or motivated or honest students are not necessarily those with the highest grades. But what Cheryl lacked in height she made up in breadth. I counted the number of times she was called to the stage, and it became apparent to all present that this was indeed her day. She had a total of 18 awards, scholarships and recognitions, from the National Merit Scholarship on down, nicely matching her birthday age, far outstripping those of any other student. Among other things, she had assumed the editorship of the moribund school newspaper, the *Whirlwind* (a minor echo of the name of the school's football team, the Hurricanes) and brought it up to second in its class in the state. Not only had I not been doing any of this for her, or even helping her, I had hardly been aware of her school activities. It is not that I am a neglectful parent; I will help if asked. Rather, I am busy with my own work, and Cheryl is an independent cuss. I wonder where she inherits that from?

About this time I began to get a glimmer of something. Just as the revelation of the identity of the new Incarnation of Good came only at the very end, and by surprise, so did the revelation of the good that was associated with this novel come to me. The final impetus was not for me, but for my daughter. Perhaps I should have seen it coming, as it seems obvious in retrospect, but I was somehow blind to it beforehand. Parents typically seek to vindicate themselves through their children. I wasn't even in the top half of my graduating high school class, 36 years ago; I was a complete nonentity. My wife did better, but married me instead of completing college. We had five babies, the first three of which died at birth, and the fourth was learning-disabled. Cheryl was the last. So the scholastic proof of our family lay in her success— and what a success it turned out to be! Often when I attend public functions, I am the center of attention; this time I was glad to be known as Cheryl's father.

When we moved to the forest in 1977, not only did we try to preserve the trees there, we planted five hundred more. These were red cedars, which we bought from the state forestry department as seedlings and planted around our border. About three quarters of them died in the first year, but we still have a generous hundred surviving, some of them now fifteen feet tall, some still under a foot tall. I discovered one that was growing well, but it was being crowded out by a laurel oak sapling that intercepted most of its light. Now the laurel oak is a nice tree, and we like it, but this one was in the wrong place. If I left it, my cedar would in due course die. So I got my axe and chopped down the laurel oak.

I felt horribly guilty doing that. Here was a nice tree, minding its own business, cut down in the prime of its youth. I had taken a life, for a reason that neither that tree nor the one I had saved would understand. I had played God, deciding which one was to be saved and which one was to perish. It was true that there were thousands of laurel oaks and only a few cedars. Still, was it right for me to condemn to death one in favor of the other?

This bothered me for several days—indeed, it bothers me now, a year and a half after the event. I take life seriously wherever I encounter it. Yet such decisions are necessary all the time. Every time I eat, something is perishing. I don't eat meat, because I prefer not to take a life unnecessarily—but what of the plants I eat? This has been a lifelong concern of mine, and the guilt never quite fades. In order to live, I must kill other living things. I don't like it, and I suspect I shall never truly come to terms with it.

Now take the concept of God. Mine differs from that of most of my readers, but for the sake of this discussion, let's assume that there is a God, and His (Her) nature is somewhere in the ballpark of that described in this novel. Every day, every hour, every minute, He must make decisions, choosing between lives, because of an overall picture that we mortals can hardly understand. How much pain must there be in every one of those decisions! He must not have it all His own way, any more than I as a novelist have my fiction all my own way. I joy and suffer as I deal with fictional characters, trying to put together a significant whole. How much worse it would be if they truly lived and the fates I decreed for them were real! Yet God must handle real lives.

I think I can understand how He, after centuries of such effort, reaping the praise of those whose only interest is to get ahead of their neighbors, and the condemnation of those whose selfish interest He declines to endorse—while the world slowly deteriorates because of their ignorance and rapacity—might finally just tune out. What is the average prayer, other than an appeal for some unwarranted advantage? The engines quit on an airplane, and the passengers pray for deliverance, not because they are benefiting the cosmos, but simply because they don't want to die. They seldom express much genuine interest in doing His will, just their own. They continually put their own words in His mouth: God wants you to contribute to this church, God considers you a sinner if you don't do what I say. He might not want to destroy the world He had labored so imperfectly to perfect, but neither would He want to continue with a futile effort. I can see how He could get disgusted and conclude that it was best to simply let the world wend its way to Hell in its own fashion. I really couldn't blame Him. Could you?

But I see no salvation in tuning out the world. So, in the end, I do feel that reform is necessary, and this novel represents a suggestion of the kind of action required. I believe it bears consideration.

JeJune 17, 1988